FLAME OF RUIN

SPARK OF CHAOS
BOOK TWO

SABRINA FLYNN

FLAME OF RUIN

SPARK OF CHAOS

BOOK TWO

SABRINA FLYNN

Published by Ink & Sea Publishing
www.sabrinaflynn.com

ISBN 978-1-955207-22-5
ebook ISBN 978-1-955207-23-2

Book 2 of Spark of Chaos
Book cover by Miblart

ALSO BY SABRINA FLYNN

Ravenwood Mysteries

From the Ashes

A Bitter Draught

Record of Blood

Conspiracy of Silence

The Devil's Teeth

Uncharted Waters

Where Cowards Tread

Beyond the Pale

A Grim Telling

Spark of Chaos

Flame of Ruin

God of Ash

Untold Tales: Prequel

Bedlam

Windwalker

www.sabrinaflynn.com

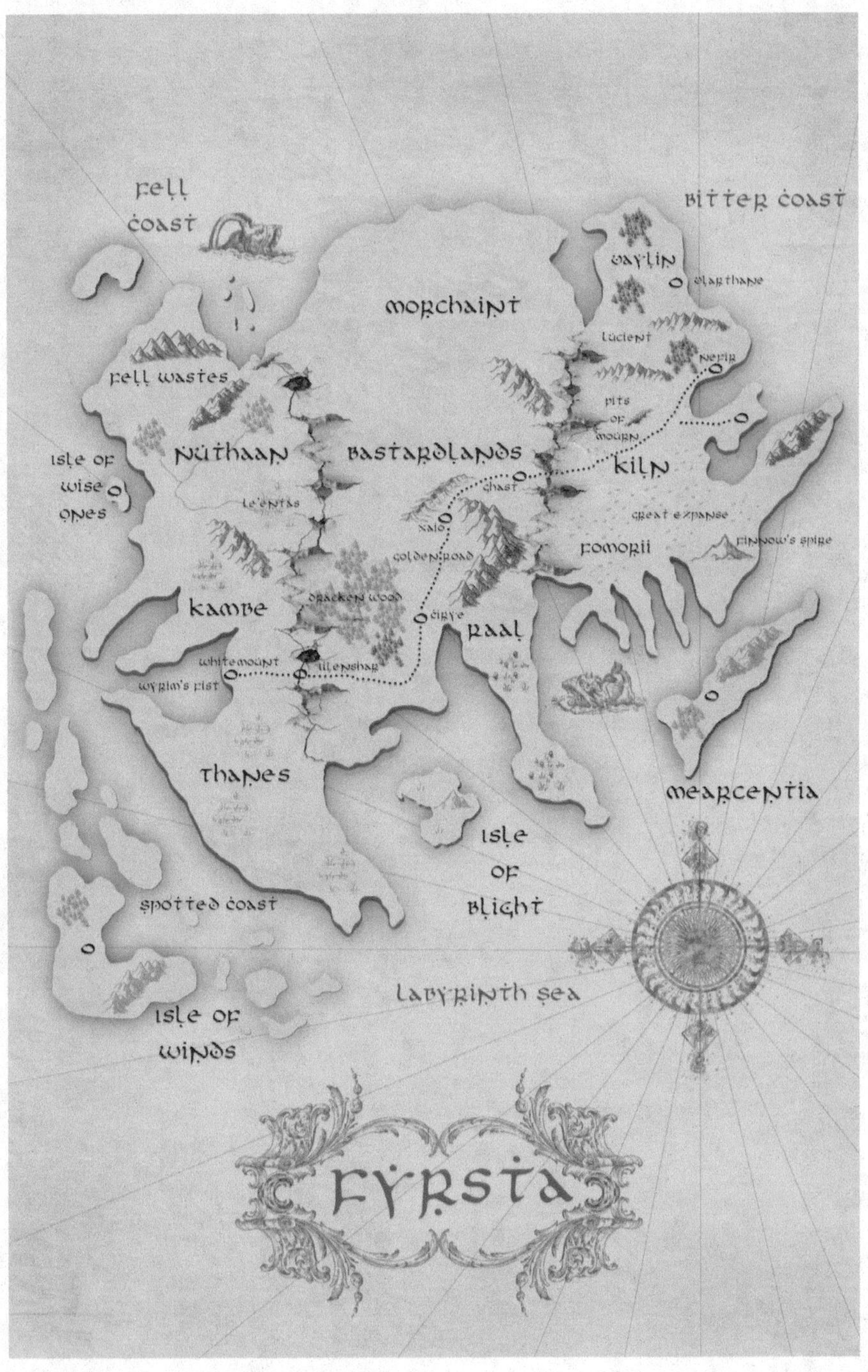

fell coast
bitter coast
morchaint
waylin
olagthane
lucient
nefir
fell wastes
pits of mourn
isle of wise ones
nūthaan
bastardlands
kiln
le'entas
chast
great expanse
xalo
finnow's spire
golden road
fomorii
kambe
dracken wood
eirye
raal
whitemount
lilenshag
wyrim's fist
mearcentia
thanes
spotted coast
isle of blight
isle of winds
labyrinth sea
FYRSTA

"One must start at the end to find a beginning."
—*Galvier Longstride*

CHAPTER I

Fire sang in her blood. It was a song of rage that licked her skin, but she felt cold and hollow. She blinked in confusion.

Where was she?

Isiilde Jaal'Yasine dangled over an armored shoulder, staring at a kilt, moving boots, and the ground. Not stone, but moss-covered earth.

For a moment, she was back on Isek's shoulder beneath the Wise One's stronghold, trapped with a group of traitors. She felt the click of shackles around her limbs, the rough wood at her back, the bite of teeth on her neck.

Isiilde panicked.

"It's all right, Sprite," a deep voice rumbled.

Oenghus.

Relief washed over her as confusion cleared, making way for memory: a battle in the bowels of the Spine, a dead end, and a desperate escape through a portal.

Marsais.

Oenghus had shoved Marsais through the portal. Where was he? She didn't even know where *she* was.

Isiilde slid off Oenghus' shoulder. The moss under foot was comforting, but the night was chilly and the oversized shirt she wore offered little in the way of warmth. She'd burned away her clothing in a firestorm—one of her making.

Isiilde shied away from that memory.

She turned to study the runic portal, but the light seared her eyes and all she glimpsed was a swirl of chaotic runes between two stone pillars.

The portal deactivated, plunging them into darkness. With the blinding blue light gone, the softer moonlight illuminated a forest. The trees were as large as towers, and stone ruins crumbled around the Gateway.

This place *felt* ancient. Not the ruins, but the trees. The forest was pleased with their intrusion at all.

A nearby fern rustled, and a shadow shifted with a groan. "Marsais," she breathed, rushing to his side. His hands were shattered, his fingers a bloodied, torn mess of bone. They were bandaged and useless, but then that had been the point—to ravage his hands so he couldn't weave.

She could feel his pain, lurking beyond the veil of their Bond—a bond of intertwined spirits.

Oenghus stood on a fallen pillar, with war hammer and shield in hand as he searched the darkness for threat.

"Oen, you must heal him."

"Not yet," he growled. "It's not safe."

Something stirred in the shadows between trees. Despite her own exhaustion, she put a shoulder under Marsais and helped him stand.

Staggering under his weight, she retreated to Oenghus' side, and then heard a soft scrape and a click that held a rhythm of movement.

They weren't alone in the forest.

The air between pillars rippled, runes flared to life, and a winged-imp shot out of the portal, flapping away with a squeal of delight.

Luccub was free.

Deep in the ruins, a flash of icy light blinked and disappeared.

"What was that?" Isiilde whispered.

"Void," Oenghus growled. "You're bleeding all over the place, Scarecrow."

"It's not like he can help it," Isiilde shot back. She could smell the blood on Marsais, seeping from the spear wound on his side. His duel with the Hound seemed a lifetime ago.

As the portal's blue glow faded, Oenghus wove a rune around his shield. It erupted with light, pushing back the darkness of the surrounding forest. A tangle of shadows moved unnaturally to the sides.

The air between the standing stones distorted again, and Knight Captain Acacia Mael stepped out of the portal. She took in the forest, the ruins, and the night, and moved to guard Isiilde and Marsais, shield and sword held at the ready.

The two paladins, Rivan and Lucas, followed on their captain's heels: one young and smooth, the other seasoned and scarred.

The shadows beyond the light writhed like a pit of snakes. Clicks and scrapes and a sibilant chorus whispered between trees.

"What is that?" Isiilde whispered.

Lucas spat. "Reapers."

THAT SINGLE WORD clutched her throat. Creatures of nightmare that feasted on blood. Voidspawn.

Isiilde wanted to bolt back through the portal, but Marsais' arm circled her neck, pulling her protectively against his body.

Another flare of runic power spit out a confused enemy soldier, who hesitated a fraction of a second too long. In that second, Oenghus swung his war hammer, catching him off guard. Bone and brain misted the night.

The scent of blood sparked a feeding frenzy. Shadows came alive, and a hundred glowing eyes snapped open, burning with hunger.

"Shields on the nymph!" Acacia ordered.

The paladins surrounded Isiilde and Marsais with a barrier of steel. Oenghus roared, picked up the soldier's body with one hand, and chucked the corpse towards a cluster of icy eyes. Reapers converged on the dead soldier with a chorus of gnashing teeth and ripping flesh.

It was gruesome and mesmerizing, and Isiilde could not look away, until a humanoid shadow leapt from a branch—all fang and claw and sleek scale. It lashed at her with a swipe of claws, but Marsais was quicker. Before she'd even registered the attack, Marsais stepped forward and kicked the Reaper in the head. The blow dropped the creature to the ground, and Acacia spun, felling it with a sweep of her blade.

Acacia chanted in a clear, ringing voice, then her shield burst with light, cutting through the murk and slamming into a knot of reapers. A path opened through the tangle.

"Get out of the ruins!" Acacia ordered.

As one, the fighting unit moved forward in a tight formation, all save Oenghus. He waded into the fray, crushing, charring, and flinging reapers against trees.

The portal activated again, and a cloaked figure stepped from the shimmering Gateway. Above the clamor of scraping claw and steel, Isiilde heard the guttural chant of the Lore and glimpsed the quick movements of a man tracing runes.

Marsais broke through the circle of paladins with a shout of alarm, racing through the ruin, back the way they had come, towards the traitorous Wise One at the Gateway.

Before Isiilde could follow, Acacia shoved her back and bolted after him. A few seconds later, Marsais slammed into the man with a bone jarring force that sent both men to the ground. The enemy came out on top. He straddled Marsais, raising a wicked dagger, his eyes to the sky.

Isiilde screamed.

The Wise One brought the dagger down, but instead of plunging it into Marsais' chest, he sank it into his own heart. The Wise One's fingers spasmed. He twitched and fell to the side.

"No," Marsais rasped.

What in all the realms? Why had the man killed himself? It didn't make sense. There was no time to wonder.

Acacia kicked the Wise One off Marsais, and the reapers fell on the corpse, fangs sinking into flesh. But something was gathering in the air over the dead man. Both power and perversion. The Wise One's body began to harden and warp.

Whatever the Wise One had done, it was no weave Isiilde recognized. It was more like a... ritual. Bloodmagic.

Acacia dragged Marsais to his feet, pulling him away from the transforming remains, but Isiilde's view was blocked when a wave of reapers converged, crashing against the paladins' shields.

Before Isiilde could dash into the fray, a single word of power split the night. Energy crackled around Oenghus' hammer. A chain of lightning lashed towards the standing stones, slicing a path through the horde. Marsais and Acacia raced through the opening.

Behind them, in the clear path, a stone-like corpse cracked and eerie light seeped from its hardened flesh, burning brighter with every heartbeat. As the searing light consumed the corpse, the reapers scattered like rats and an inky spot appeared in the brightness, devouring the dead man's spirit. It grew and slithered until there was nothing left save an eternity of torment.

An inhuman screech sliced through the forest.

Isiilde could not tear her eyes from the abomination as she was dragged away. Finally, her feet remembered they were attached to legs, and she ran.

A frigid wind infused the scream, beating at her back, sucking the air from her lungs. She pressed her hands against her ears, but the sound rattled inside her skull, until she forgot to think, forgot to move. She stopped along with the paladin at her side.

Terror rooted her and Rivan in place.

Frost climbed the trees, foliage wilted, and a great flapping form rose in the wind—of tatters and bleakness and hungry death.

Hardened warriors to the bone, Oenghus and Lucas turned to face the monstrosity. Tendrils of inky rot spread, snaking through the forest, striving towards life. She could feel its touch like a cold tongue, flicking beneath her skin to lick her bones.

Oenghus roared, sending a bolt of jagged lightning into the center of the Forsaken spirit. It twisted and wavered, then snapped back into focus with renewed strength.

A shadowy tentacle lashed at Oenghus. He threw himself to the side, bringing his hammer down on the limb. But his blow passed harmlessly through. Oenghus bellowed the Lore, awakening the earth. The ground answered his call, rising over the Forsaken blot. Trees groaned, and dirt and vines surged like a wave, drowning the writhing form.

The earth shook Isiilde off her feet. She hit the ground, and in the settling aftermath, Lucas Cutter ran towards the center of misery. His blade burned white and pure, pulsing with a prayer. Inky tendrils whipped at the charging paladin, groping for his soul.

The warrior leapt from crumbled stone to fallen tree, and off, plunging his blade into the Forsaken's heart.

Rage filled the forest, pounding at her eardrums. The tendrils folded in on themselves, retracting into a shapeless mass. The Forsaken was pinned to the ground, twisting beneath the searing blade, and with a snap of air, the ink-like spirit broke free, flying towards the tree tops until it disappeared.

Isiilde could not breathe. Her heart spasmed, forgetting its rhythm. Marsais was in front of her, cupping her face with bandaged hands. His lips moved, eyes urgent, but so very far away.

One word cut through her terror. "Move!"

She moved.

CHAPTER 2

"THEY'RE SWARMING!" Acacia shouted.

Stone bit into Isiilde's bare feet as she ran. A jangle of armor, haggard breathing, and hurried boots joined her flight. The group raced towards a ruined tower, its top shorn but its foundations strong.

Oenghus roared. And lightning answered. It charged the air, slammed to the earth, and seared holes through the reapers. They dropped like flies. But there were so many of them—an endless horde of shadow and claw.

Isiilde flew through a stone archway and was headed for the next when Marsais dragged her to a stop. They stood in the ruin of a toppled tower, its stone walls crumbling but intact.

The paladins planted themselves at the exits while Oenghus turned to face the swarming pack of reapers nipping at their heels. Over seven feet of fury, of death and carnage, made for a formidable gatekeeper.

Isiilde was lost in the chaos, detached from her body as battle raged around her. Time moved sluggishly, and she watched as a reaper crawled across the ceiling like a spider on its web.

There was no flame nearby. No knife in her belt. She was helpless. Somewhere, in a distant corner of her shocked mind, a voice urged her to scream. She obeyed.

The reaper sprang at her. Quick as a whipcord, Marsais slammed into the reaper, catching it in midair and knocking Isiilde to the ground. He drove a shoulder into the creature, ramming it against the tower wall. But his hands were useless; he couldn't hope to defend himself.

Rivan rushed forward to help, pinning the reaper with his shield and running it through. It went still.

Oenghus roared, shaking loose dust and stone, as he sent another charge of lightning into a knot of reapers. They fell dead, piling up at the archway, but more surged to fill the gap.

Dust swirled in the air. Isiilde sneezed, sending three fiery bursts puffing from her ears.

Marsais raked his eyes over the debris. Decay in all its morbid stages surrounded them: rotting flesh and dried bone; brittle timber and climbing vines.

"Rivan," he ordered. "Gather timber, dead vines, anything that will burn." Marsais kicked a branch against a thigh bone that was still attached to a brittle trouser leg.

Rivan blinked in confusion. Blood and sweat streaked the young paladin's face, but Isiilde was used to confusing orders from Marsais, so she rushed to obey without question. She picked up a rotted sack and tossed it in the pile. Rivan caught on, adding more kindling as he found it.

It felt like she was moving in a fog. Fear was distant. The sounds of battle muted. She could only hear the rush of blood in her ears.

And then Marsais was standing in front of her. "Forgive me, my dear." He shook out a filthy cloth in front of her face.

A puff of dust tickled her nose, and she sneezed, fire bursting from her ears. The cloth ignited. He dropped the burning fragment onto the pile of debris, and it caught on fire.

Isiilde stared at the growing flames, transfixed. It filled her vision and consumed her mind. The raging fire in the dungeon seared her memories. Sweet release and power, as she had never known. It terrified her.

"More," Marsais urged. "Reapers fear fire."

Isiilde watched the fire grow into a bonfire, captivated by its hiss and seductive dance. It whispered to her and drew her away from the carnage to a place of tempting beauty.

An explosion of sparks made her blink. She came back to herself with a start, her toes buried in the fiery ashes of the bonfire. How long had she been standing here?

Everyone was moving, fighting, and Rivan was picking up a burning brand from the fire.

"Light it!" Acacia shouted.

Rivan rushed to the archway, touching his torch to a makeshift barrier. Acacia and Lucas held the opening until the fire caught, then backed away to pile on more wood. As the fire grew, the frenzied reapers retreated a fraction.

Rivan darted back across the chamber, snatched another brand, and touched it to a third pile of tinder behind Oenghus.

"Back up," Marsais yelled. But Oenghus ignored the order, along with the flames licking at his kilt. "Oen, you bull-headed idiot, retreat!"

No response, no retreat, only another bellow that knocked loose a shower of stone on their heads.

Marsais clenched his jaw, backing well away from the berserker's reach. He glanced at Acacia, cocked his head, and shouted, "Captain Mael is naked!"

Acacia narrowed her eyes, Lucas blinked, and Rivan stopped to gape. Oenghus slammed his targe against a reaper, then glanced around. Surprise quenched his blood lust. He cursed at his smoking kilt and hopped out of the fire.

Rivan braced his shield against a flaming barrier and pushed it forward, blocking the archway, chasing the reapers back. But Isiilde could sense them, just beyond the roaring flame, pacing restlessly in the dark.

"Needs must, Captain," Marsais said by way of apology.

Oenghus glanced from Acacia to Marsais. "You lied."

Acacia snorted, surveying the carnage. She wiped blood from her eyes and pressed a hand to a gash on her forehead. "There isn't enough timber to last the hour."

Isiilde could sing to her flame, make it dance and grow until it licked the heavens, but she felt utterly burnt out like a pile of cold ash. Besides, she was more likely to burn the forest down and everyone in it. So no one asked her to feed the flames.

"Don't reapers fear sunlight?" Rivan asked.

"We don't even know if the sun will rise in this Void-cursed land," Lucas said. "Where are we, Seer?" The scarred paladin was coal-black, and his eyes were as hard as flint, just like his voice.

"Not a thousand feet up, and I'd wager it's not the Nine Halls," Oenghus grunted. He was covered in gashes, and blood ran down his legs, matting the hair. Yet, despite his wounds, he stood tall and straight, eyes focused on the forest in thought.

"Are you hurt?" Marsais asked.

His voice came from far away, and it took a moment to sort through their meaning. Isiilde looked into his eyes, but he felt distant. She could not even feel her own body.

"You're doing fine, Isiilde," he said, checking her over for wounds. "Stay close to me. They're just reapers."

Just reapers.

"What was that thing... The man who came through the portal? Why did he stab himself with his own dagger instead of Marsais?" Rivan asked.

Lucas shivered with memory. "A Forsaken."

"And something more," Acacia added. "How long do we have before the portal closes?"

"A Runic Gateway is unstable without someone to control it," Marsais replied. "I doubt it's still pointed here."

"One less thing to worry about then. Injuries?" Acacia asked, looking at Rivan.

He touched his face. "Cuts, I think."

"Are you injured or not, soldier?"

"No, sir."

"We're not out of this yet, Rivan. Stay focused. What about you, Lucas?"

"I'll live," her lieutenant grunted.

"You always say that," Acacia said. "Is the nymph injured?"

"She is," Marsais said. "But it's nothing a healer can mend."

"We can't stay here all bloody night," Oenghus said. "The forest is as thick as can be. Even in daylight, there will be shadows under trees. We walked right into a reaper nest." Oenghus eyed Marsais' wounds. "Can you manage?"

"When have I not?"

Oenghus smirked. "Good. I refuse to carry your bony arse." He stomped over to Isiilde. "But I will carry you. Up on my back."

Oenghus knelt, and she obeyed, wrapping her arms around his thick neck. He adjusted his kilt, freeing the long ends of cloth, bringing them up and over his back and head, and wearing the kilt in winter fashion. "Captain, I'll need you as rear guard."

"Only a fool follows a berserker into battle," Acacia said.

Oenghus bared his teeth at the woman. "I don't take you for a fool."

"You don't know me." She hoisted her shield. "Do we have a plan?"

He shrugged. "Fire, steel, and swift feet."

"As usual," Marsais sighed.

"There'll be nothing usual about this fight." Oenghus removed his sacred flask. "I've been practicing since you bested me, ye ol' Bastard."

"I'll wager ten gold crowns that you singe your beard again."

CHAPTER 3

Oenghus Saevaldr brought his flask to his lips. Brimgrog, the sacred drink few dared taste, burned down his throat. Fire filled his veins, and he roared. The berserker's battle cry shook the night, rippling through the forest.

Oenghus charged out of the archway, a burning brand clutched in his shield hand. Acacia followed, with Rivan on her heels, helping Marsais while Lucas brought up the rear.

The mass of reapers hissed in sibilant song as the group plunged into the forest. When the shadows converged, Oenghus was ready. He held up the torch and blew Brimgrog at its flickering top. Flames surged towards the enemy, sparking on scales and catching trees. The reapers shrank back, and the group raced onwards, leaving a trail of fire in their wake.

Thunder rolled across the sky, then a flash of lightning illuminated an endless stream of reapers. The first drop of rain hit Acacia's helm, and the paladin bit back a curse.

Luck wasn't on their side tonight.

Breathing fire into the reapers, Oenghus chose a direction and stuck to it. But another rolling boom of thunder knocked rain from the heavens, and it fell in a torrent, smothering their torches.

Oenghus hurled his useless torch at a reaper's head with a curse. Unfortunately, the resulting crunch did little to ease his fury—he had singed his beard and was ten crowns poorer for the wager.

THE BARRAGE of reapers thinned when they broke free from the forest and climbed a mountain slope. It was a grueling trek. Lightning slashed across the sky, rain beat on their backs, and the wind threw it in their faces. But the storm washed away the scent of blood, and the reapers eventually fell back to their ruins.

Halfway up the mountain, Marsais gave out, buckling to the ground.

"Oen, stop!" Isiilde tugged on his beard. He turned, eyes wild with battle, hammer raised to strike.

She untangled herself from his kilt, slid off her guardian's back, and stumbled over to Marsais, who was seized by a coughing fit. Rivan shielded Marsais from the storm while Isiilde knelt by his side, trying to keep his face out of the mud.

"We need shelter," Acacia called over the wind.

"Stay here. I'll scout ahead!" Oenghus bellowed. "Guard her, Captain."

"Upon my honor," Acacia swore.

Oenghus locked eyes with her before trotting into the night.

Acacia drew Isiilde under the canopy of a tree, its wide trunk offering protection from the wind, while Lucas and Rivan hoisted Marsais upright to help him under the shelter.

"Isiilde," Marsais wheezed.

She knelt at his side, feeling helpless.

The last time Oenghus tried teaching her to heal with the Gift, she burnt every pigeon in the coop to ash. But even if she could heal him, Marsais would sink into a deep sleep afterward, and they'd be forced to carry him, which was why Oenghus hadn't healed him yet.

Marsais reached for her, and she went, burying her face against his neck, reassured by the rise and fall of his chest. And while she took refuge in his arms, the three paladins waited, swords at the ready, squinting through sheets of rain for threat.

"What did you mean the man was something more than a Forsaken?" Rivan asked his captain.

"We'll discuss it later."

Some of the shock wore off in Marsais' arms, leaving her body shaky in the aftermath of adrenaline but her mind clear. She wondered which Wise One had stepped through the portal to sacrifice himself for Tharios. In the chaos of battle and shadows, she had not seen the traitor's face.

Had it been Isek?

When Isek Beirnuckle betrayed them all to Tharios, there had been ten other Wise Ones with N'Jalss, Eiji, and Tharios. Two had revealed themselves: Shimei Al'eeth, the haughty Kilnish lord who had gleefully crushed Marsais' hands with a mace, and Zander, whom she burnt to a crisp. But what of the others who'd stayed behind to guard intersections in the maze beneath the Spine? How many Wise Ones and Isle Guards were loyal to Tharios?

And how did someone turn themselves into a Forsaken?

"Something's wrong," Lucas growled. "He shouldn't have gone alone."

"Steady, Lucas," Acacia warned. "Oenghus is a berserker. It'd take more than a handful of reapers to bring him down."

"And *if* it's more?"

"Then we'd best ready ourselves."

"To run," Marsais added, letting his head fall against the bark. Then, he closed his eyes and did not move.

Isiilde touched his cheek. "Marsais?"

"I'm fine," he murmured.

He was not *fine*. Marsais had a spear wound in his side and his hands were crushed. But Isiilde didn't argue the point.

Movement in the trees and a crack of branches alerted the paladins. They braced themselves as a large shadow emerged from the trees.

Oenghus bared his teeth. "Come on."

Rivan and Lucas hoisted Marsais to his feet, dragging him along as the group followed Oenghus. He took them to a massive slab of stone that jutted out from the slope, creating a natural overhang. Water poured over the ledge, but the ground was dry and sheltered from the wind beneath the rock.

Acacia whispered a prayer, and her shield began to glow, illuminating the space. "We'll need a fire, lieutenant."

Lucas slapped Rivan on the shoulder and the two men left to gather wood.

CHAPTER 4

Isiilde helped Marsais to the back of the cave, where he collapsed against a rock.

"Hold on, Sprite," Oenghus said.

The back of the cave was low, and he had to duck his head to reach them. He eased Marsais off the rock, then stared at it. After a minute, he began to chant in a low, murmuring whisper, more prayer than Lore.

"Is that wise?" Marsais asked.

Oenghus ignored his former master, tracing an intricate pattern on the stone. When the weave was complete, he opened his eyes and stepped back, holding his breath. Slowly, the rock began to glow, pulsing with increasing warmth.

Marsais stared warily at the enchantment.

The rock glowed as if molten and the nearby water turned to steam. "Bollocks." Oenghus quickly retreated, grabbing his daughter and pulling her away.

"What?" Acacia asked, backing up, too.

Then the pulsing subsided, and the rock glowed evenly, throwing heat into the cavern.

Marsais blew out a relieved breath. "It only took you eight hundred years."

"Shut it, Scarecrow," Oenghus grunted.

Isiilde tentatively touched the rock. It felt like a heating stone.

"What usually happens?" Acacia asked, helping Marsais over.

"Very ill occurrences," Marsais wheezed.

Oenghus knelt. "Let me heal you, Sprite."

"Marsais needs healing. I'm fine."

He eyed her, but didn't argue.

Acacia was unwrapping Marsais' hands. "What was the traitor weaving?" she asked.

"A message to Tharios," Marsais said.

"Were you able to stop it?"

"Not precisely."

"A Blood Oath?" Oenghus guessed.

"Of course." Acacia frowned at Marsais' mangled hands.

"What's that?" Isiilde asked.

"Oaths bind a Forsaken," Acacia explained. "His spirit will return to the Oath Taker. In this case, likely Tharios. But to enter that state willingly is madness."

"Fanaticism," Marsais corrected, then bit back a cry as Acacia slid the rings off his broken fingers.

Isiilde couldn't look at his hands, so she loosened his collar and pressed a hand over the scar on his chest. He rested his head against hers.

"In the dungeon, when you were trying to distract Zander, were you serious about Karbonek?" Acacia asked.

"Unfortunately. Only an Unspoken would be so devout. Tharios will know we're alive. And if a Blood Oath was involved, then he'll see through the spirit's eyes."

"Save your breath," Oenghus said. "You'll need all the strength you have left."

Acacia moved to the side, and Isiilde helped Oenghus unlace the long sleeves of Marsais' robe. Working slowly, they peeled the fabric from his skin, then tugged the robe over his head. The rain had washed away the grit and sand from the duel, leaving a clear view of the damage. Burns covered his body. A reaper's bite had savaged his right shoulder, and fresh blood soaked the bandage around his torso.

"Water," Oenghus grunted.

Acacia grabbed her helm and filled it with rainwater. After helping Marsais drink from the helm, Oenghus uncorked his flask of Brimgrog and added a single drop.

Acacia looked at him in question.

"If I heal him with debris in the wound—sand or cloth, what have you—it'll rot. Brimgrog burns the water clean."

"You've been guzzling that since you were poisoned. Won't you run out at this rate?" she asked.

"I haven't refilled it since my Rite—six hundred years ago, give or take." While Acacia grappled with his claim, Oenghus poured water over his patient's wounds.

Marsais spasmed with pain.

"Keep flushing that wound, Captain. The Hound nearly gutted him." Oenghus had the bedside manner of a bear, but his touch was gentle as he picked up Marsais' right wrist. He rested the mangled mess in his own massive hand. "Am I right in thinking you want these back the way they were?"

"You know how vain I am." His tone was light but forced, and the words that followed were a whispered plea. "They're the only weapons I have, Oen."

"I know, old friend," Oenghus whispered before giving Isiilde a firm look. "Keep him from moving."

"He's stronger than me, Oen."

"Just make sure he doesn't crack his head on the rock," Acacia said.

Isiilde cradled Marsais' head against her breast, and began stroking one of his pointed ears. He relaxed against her.

"By the way," Oenghus said. "I'm up a hundred crowns."

"A hundred?"

"I was exiled from Kambe. That puts me one kingdom above you."

"No," Marsais argued. "We would be tied if you hadn't burnt your beard."

"The Void we are," Oenghus glared, stuffing a piece of leather between Marsais' teeth. "I have Gwaith, the Isle of Winds." He directed a pointed glare at the captain. "Kambe and that little kingdom along the coast—Carpinvale. That's four kingdoms I've been exiled from."

Before Marsais could argue the tally, Oenghus invoked the Lore, and one by one, he began pulling each finger straight, mending the delicate bones an inch at a time.

Marsais spat the leather out. "I have Gwaith, Kiln—" He forced each word past clenched teeth, fighting to stay conscious. "—and the *entire* bloody Ocean. That counts as two." Sweat beaded on his forehead.

"The ocean counts as one," Oenghus growled when he was done. "Bandage that hand, Captain, and wrap it snug. The bones need to settle and mend for a few days, or he'll end up with crooked fingers."

"That's absurd." Marsais' voice cracked with pain as Oenghus started on the left hand. Bone shifted, grated and straightened, and when Marsais' back arched with a cry, Isiilde tightened her hold.

The veins on his neck strained as he fought for breath, forcing out his words in defiance. "I had a blasted god banish me from his domain. Carpinvale is ruled by a self-proclaimed king who was a fisherman."

"Isn't that what you were?" Oenghus grinned, surveying his work. After a moment, he huffed in satisfaction. "I think these will stand up to your scrutiny, ol'bastard."

"We're tied," Marsais insisted, slumping against Isiilde.

"Not if you want me to heal the rest of you."

"You can go to the Pits. I'm the one who taught you how to use the Gift."

Oenghus snorted at the remark. "Aye, like my father taught me to swim. Tossed me in a river and hoped I'd float while he watched and laughed." He placed his hands on Marsais' stomach and forehead. "Shut your trap, and don't you dare dream about Isiilde."

Oenghus focused his inner sight on Marsais, and surged into his body to repair wounds and close flesh. Marsais was never easy to heal. His spirit was blinding. And confusing. There was not just one of him, but a multitude that stretched into eternity.

Oenghus focused fully on the task, avoiding the fractured spirit of the immortal. To dwell on its ever-shifting shape, to study it, to comprehend, would drive him to insanity. As soon as flesh was mended, he withdrew, shaking the chaotic spirit from his mind.

It left him exhausted.

"Thank you, Oen," Isiilde said.

Healing always demanded a price from the body, and Marsais now slept, his head resting in her lap.

"Your wrists and ankles need healing."

"I'm fine."

"No, you aren't."

Oenghus left no room for argument. At his direction, she stretched between the heated rock and Marsais, and soon enough, Isiilde spiraled into a deep, dreamless sleep.

Lucas and Rivan returned with firewood, and both men paused inside the cave, puzzling over the temperature. The heated rock quickly cleared their confusion.

"All quiet?" Acacia asked.

"All quiet, sir."

"Still want a fire?"

Acacia looked at Oenghus in question.

"I'd rather not try that weave again."

"A fire will do then. Take first watch, Rivan." The young paladin set down his armful of wood, and trudged outside into the storm to find a sheltered tree.

Oenghus refilled the helm, and took a long drink. When he turned, Acacia was eyeing his leg. He glanced down and discovered a reaper had gnawed on his calf.

"I can heal that," she said, cinching the last of Marsais' bandages. "Along with your other wounds. Although my skill is nothing compared to yours. You have a gifted touch."

"You sound surprised."

"The words healer and berserker don't exactly go together."

"I'm a man of many talents." He offered her his most charming smile.

"I'm sure you think so." She nodded towards his calf. "Are you talented enough to heal yourself?"

"I'm fine," he said, sitting beside Marsais.

"I've seen a corpse look brighter."

"Aye, well, the stone adder venom almost sent me there. It's all the worthless drinking I do. Not much will kill you when your veins are full of brew."

Acacia snorted. "You don't trust me."

"I don't trust the other two," he corrected.

"They're good men. I chose them for a reason."

"So was Isek Beirnuckle."

"So you're going to stand guard until you pass out? Typical Nuthaanian," Acacia muttered, running a hand over her short hair.

"Don't you dare call me stubborn. I only permit that from my Oathbounds."

"You'll be no good to the nymph until that poison is gone."

His beard twitched.

"Would it help to know that I was ordered to assist the Archlord?"

"By who?"

"The night before the duel, a Whisperer from Iilenshar sent me a message, asking me to assist the Archlord without question. If I'd known you'd be involved, I wouldn't have accepted."

"Who gave the order?"

Acacia glanced at the sleeping pair. "A Cleric of Chaim," she said, simply.

"I'm honored you would've defied a holy man to avoid me," Oenghus said. "I don't care about my hairy hide, but no one touches my Sprite."

"Except the seer." She smirked at his scowl, then turned serious, standing to meet his eye. "With the Sylph as my witness, I'll watch over her like she was one of my daughters, Oenghus."

"You have children? Must be an uptight lot."

"There is nothing wrong with a little discipline."

Oenghus loosened his leather breastplate, slid his forearm through his shield's straps, folded it close, then sat against the heated rock with his right hand resting over his rune-etched hammer.

It was far from a comfortable sleeping position, but Acacia knew the warrior wouldn't rest easy otherwise.

Acacia slipped a hand beneath his armor, resting it over the rock-hard muscles beneath.

"Never could resist a woman with calloused hands."

Acacia narrowed her eyes. "I'm surprised you can feel a thing under that layer of fur."

"You'd never go cold."

"Does comparing yourself to a dead animal pelt usually work with the whores?"

"I like a sharp tongue, too."

"Remind me to introduce you to my commander. He has a sharp tongue *and* calloused hands."

Before Oenghus could comment, she bowed her head in prayer. A warm glow surrounded her hand, and the Gift seeped into his body. She drew out poison and mended flesh, leaving the berserker sitting upright, ready for battle, and snoring.

CHAPTER 5

Teeth pierced her neck. Isiilde cried out, but no sound emerged. She was gagged and struggling against her bonds as fire seared her wrists and ankles. It had betrayed her.

Isiilde wanted to leave her skin and never return.

Her eyes snapped open. She was cradled between a warm rock and a reassuring presence. Marsais. She turned to him for comfort, burying her face in the curve of his neck.

His scent soothed her—he smelled of the sun, of salt and sea, and he stirred at her breath, shifting his arm to place a bandaged hand over her ear.

Memory crashed over her. It had not been a nightmare. She touched her neck, searching for N'Jalss' bite, but the skin was smooth. It'd been healed.

Isiilde lifted the robe that covered their bodies. Marsais slept deeply. Angry bruises marred his flesh, but there were no other wounds save an ever-present scar slashing across his chest. She placed a hand over it and the tension left his face.

A shift of wood and a spark of flame drew her attention. A fire blazed in the shallow cave and the stench of roasting meat made her gag.

Oenghus sat by the fire, poking at its embers, while Lucas turned a makeshift spit. Acacia slept nearby, and Rivan was perched on a fallen log beneath the overhanging rock, watching the misty forest.

Isiilde shivered against Marsais. Her shirt was damp and caked with dried mud. The campfire called to her, but she didn't want to face the paladins alone.

She lay beside Marsais for a time, willing him to wake. He did not. So she brushed her lips against his shoulder and moved to the fire to sit beside Oenghus.

The scarred paladin, Lucas Cutter, gazed at her across the firepit, and even though Oenghus' shirt came past her knees, she felt exposed beneath his scrutiny.

"Afternoon, Sprite." Oenghus wrapped an arm around her. He was always as warm as a furnace. "You'll never guess what I found."

"Clothes?"

"Even better." He handed her a handkerchief full of strawberries, pine nuts, and a motley assortment of vegetation.

Isiilde's stomach growled its gratitude, and she occupied herself with eating. Lucas removed four roasting rabbits from the spit and set them aside to cool. The carcasses sparked a memory, and she stiffened, feeling the terror and press of stone again. In her mind's eye, Zander's charred corpse flashed around and around like a child's gruesome top.

Isiilde gazed into the fire. With a single frantic call, the flames in the dungeon had leapt to her defense, burning everything in their path. She rested her head on Oenghus. What if she had accidentally set Marsais on fire? She'd nearly killed everyone in that dungeon. She had no control —only rage and fear. And when those beasts lay quiet, there was emptiness.

Isiilde stared until her eyes burned. When a figure approached, she blinked, heart jumping in her throat.

Rivan stopped short. "I didn't see you there."

Oenghus glared, and the blood drained from the younger man's face. Rivan turned, reached for a pair of leggings drying on a nearby root, and thrust them at Oenghus.

"I thought she could use these, sir. I'm from Mearcentia. I'm not used to the cold, so I always wear layers. I tried to clean them as best I could."

"Thank you," Isiilde whispered.

Oenghus took the offering. Rivan bowed, and Lucas handed him a stick with an impaled rabbit before he retreated to his post.

Isiilde sniffed at the leggings. They were, she supposed, better than nothing. With a sigh, she untangled herself from Oenghus' side.

"Wake the ol' Bastard up while you're at it."

"He's not old." She snatched her strawberries, and moved to the back of the cave.

"He's still a bastard," Oenghus called.

The leggings were coarse, scratchy, and smelled like Oenghus after he'd been chopping wood all day, but they were warm and dry though far too long. She retrieved Marsais' knife and sat down to trim the legs. There was enough fabric left over to fashion a belt.

A movement drew her eye to Marsais, shifting restlessly in his sleep. He jerked his head, murmured something, then his body twitched. His eyes snapped open; they were as white as snow.

Isiilde had seen those sightless eyes before. At the time, she hadn't understood what was happening, but now she knew. Marsais was in the clutch of a vision. And there was nothing she could do as his mouth opened in a soundless scream.

Isiilde moved to shield him from the paladins' eyes and placed a hand over his heart. When she touched his scar, the tension bled from his body. Slowly, his muscles released their hold and grey eyes blinked in confusion and fear.

"Marsais?"

"Isiilde," he whispered. "A moment, my dear."

She lay her head on his chest and listened to his pounding heart as he regained his senses. Finally, when his breathing evened, he rested a bandaged hand on her head, but whether it was to comfort himself or her, she did not know.

"A vision," he explained.

"I know."

"Do you?"

She raised her head. "What else could frighten you?"

"A great many things."

"I won't ask what you saw."

"It's best not to know."

"Is it?"

"Oh, yes," he breathed. "By the gods, yes."

"But our eyes change when we know."

Marsais looked into hers. "That they do." There was sorrow in his voice. He pulled her close through their bond and his blazing spirit chased away the darkness within her.

"Is it bad?" she asked.

"When is it not?"

"Presently."

He chuckled and she returned to her pillow, listening to the rhythm of his heart. After a time, when thought had turned to decision, he stirred, turning his lips towards her ear.

"My dear," he whispered. "If you forget everything else, I beg of you, never forget that day on the beach."

"I don't understand."

"No one ever understands a prophecy until the time is upon them."

"You could tell me."

"One day, I will explain why I can't."

"Until that day, there is food on the fire, and I saved some berries for you."

"I'm honored," he said, kissing her palm. The touch left her skin tingling, and she smiled, pressing her lips to his with a soft moan.

"I said to wake him, not kiss the bastard," Oenghus growled from the firepit.

Isiilde ignored him. "Thank you for saving me," she whispered to Marsais.

"I didn't save you—you rescued us."

"But not before you ordered Luccub to remove my gag." She shivered at the memory, fingers straying to her neck, but Marsais caught her hand and held it gently between his.

"Thedus brought the tooth," he said, tracing her knuckles. "Without that seemingly inconsequential act, Luccub wouldn't have come. And you, my dear, released our fiendish ally in the first place."

"And if you had remembered what was in the flagon to begin with, I would have never opened it. So it was still you and your absentminded-ness," she said with an air of triumph.

He grunted in defeat.

"Regardless, I'm glad you remembered what Tharios wanted."

Marsais cleared his throat and sat up. "I must confess, I never forgot. I had hoped he was bluffing, or that Isek would redeem himself in the end. I'm sorry."

"What you told Tharios about the tomb... It's not good, is it?"

"No, it's not. If it had been anyone else—" A shudder stopped his tongue. He sighed wearily, running a hand over his face. "Not you."

"Why me?"

Warmth and wonder softened his features. "Because I'm a love-struck fool."

"You love me?" she asked in surprise.

"With all that is left of me, yes."

To hide her blush, she helped him put on his robe and began lacing up his sleeves. When she had cinched the last tie, she said, "I love what is left of you, but will miss this." She tugged on his scruffy goatee.

Marsais grinned. "Hmm, that reminds me. Would you get the coins from my trouser pocket and weave them in as they were?"

She did as he asked, but not before studying the odd trinkets. The little round coins, each with a hole in its center, appeared ancient, their etchings obscured by time. They were cool as ice, and yet familiar.

She quickly wove what was left of his goatee into three short braids, and threaded a coin onto each end. When the coins were attached, they warmed and chimed a single note.

Marsais looked like a proper scoundrel.

Isiilde tilted her head. "One of these days, you will tell me what these do."

"Far faster to tell you what they don't do."

"What don't they do this time?"

"They don't stop lunatics from butchering my goatee."

Isiilde rolled her eyes.

CHAPTER 6

"WE'VE SCOUTED the immediate area. Plenty of wildlife, which is always a good sign," Oenghus said, handing Marsais a rabbit on a stick, who held it awkwardly between his bandaged hands. "I figured we'd rest up a bit until the sky clears. No use climbing to the top in this weather."

Isiilde squeezed between the two men, laying her head on Marsais' shoulder as he ate. Words passed over her, but she did not hear. She sat and stared numbly at the flames, drifting in a haze. Eventually, she blinked. Sometime during her sightless stare, the paladins, Acacia and Lucas, had joined them at the fire.

"Any idea where we are?" Acacia was asking.

"Somewhere north." Oenghus shrugged.

Acacia looked to Marsais, but he was busy staring at a rock. "There's enough for you, Nymph," she said, offering her a rabbit leg.

Isiilde recoiled from the carcass. "I don't like meat."

"You can't be picky out here, or you'll starve."

Isiilde already felt like she was starving.

"She's not being fussy," Oenghus said. "The flesh of a living thing is like poison to her. I gave her a piece of bacon when she was young and it nearly killed her."

Lucas and Rivan looked shocked by the declaration. Isiilde's meat intolerance was apparently a greater offense than shooting fire out of her ears when she sneezed.

"Archlord, I'd like a few answers," Acacia said.

"I sincerely doubt I still hold that title. Marsais will do."

"I have orders from Iilenshar to follow you without question," Acacia confided.

Her men nearly choked on their food. After their initial shock, Lucas settled into a scowl, and Rivan listened with interest.

"You said the man who came through the portal was an Unspoken, a Disciple of Karbonek. I assume Tharios is as well?"

Marsais gave a nod.

"Tharios spoke of a tomb, of something unknown beneath the Isle. I'd like to know what's at stake."

"It's a delicate matter, Captain. One that puts the entire realm in danger."

"I want details, not vagueness," Acacia said.

Marsais pressed his lips together.

"I have Iilenshar's full confidence," she continued. "Lucas has my trust, and Rivan is too terrified of me to utter a word. We're neck-deep in this already. And only the gods know where we've ended up."

Isiilde studied the woman. Why would Iilenshar order the captain of a Chapterhouse to aid Marsais rather than the High Inquisitor himself? And how would the Guardians have known what was happening, or about to happen?

The tales of Iilenshar fascinated her. Legend claimed that the Keeper erected the Gates to stem the tide of war and trap the Guardians of Morchaint in the Bastardlands.

She had seen the white cliffs, the long tunnel, the endless chasm, and the floating Isle of Iilenshar in Marsais' gift—the memory orb—but it wasn't the same as seeing it in person.

The memory of their day on the beach was distant—a warm little bubble that was drifting ever farther from her reach. And that girl in the memory was a stranger and an utter fool.

'*Never forget that day on the beach.*' Marsais' odd request rang in her mind. She remembered it, but the memory belonged to another person.

"I'd like to bloody know what Tharios is after, too." Oenghus' voice shook her back to the present. She caught Rivan staring at her, and he quickly looked to the forest while keeping an ear cocked towards the conversation.

"You don't know, Oen?" Marsais asked.

"Why the Void should I?"

Marsais gave him a pointed look.

Oenghus grunted, tugged on his beard, and promptly changed the subject. "I knew Tharios was trouble, but I didn't think he'd have the bollocks to do something like that."

"I underestimated him as well. And Isek, too. I thought Tharios would wait until after the Nine had cast their vote and ousted me. In fact, I was counting on it."

"You *knew* Tharios was after something? And yet you didn't stop him sooner?" Acacia regarded Marsais as if he were a raw recruit.

"I knew he was after *something*, yes. I did not know precisely what until the day Isiilde was attacked." There was pain and regret in his voice. "I intended to act at the proper time, but they outmaneuvered me."

Isiilde felt queasy with guilt. She had distracted him and left him open to betrayal. She felt his gaze on her, and a bandaged hand covered her own, but the gesture of comfort only caused her more distress—bandaged as they were, he could not even squeeze her hands.

"Before I answer your question, Captain, we need to go back some three thousand years to the founding of the Order of Wise Ones."

"I know the stories," Acacia said.

"They are lies."

This statement earned everyone's attention.

"THE FOUNDING LEGEND says that Hengist Heartfang, one of nine scholars, took refuge on an uninhabited island. The group wanted to guard their secret of rune magic. Supposedly, Hengist, in his infinite and near divine wisdom," his voice dripped with sarcasm, "raised the Spine from the bedrock, becoming the first Archlord of the Isle."

Isiilde had heard the story before. She was no longer surprised the tale was false. It seemed everything was more complicated than history claimed. There was no black and white in the realms, only grey, full of blunder and shameful deeds.

"As with most things, there is some truth in the lie," Marsais muttered. He paused to suck the marrow from a bone before chucking it into the fire.

His sharp features were imperious, calm, and slightly sardonic, as if life were some grand joke. But Isiilde now shared a bond with his spirit. She could *feel* his hesitation and sense the turmoil of emotions in his heart.

Marsais was stalling—long enough for the paladins to grow impatient as he grappled with a decision: to trust the paladins or not? She felt the moment he made a choice.

"The greatest lie in that story is that the island was uninhabited," Marsais continued. "The truth has been carefully and deliberately erased from history. Have you all heard the name Pyrderi Har'Feydd?"

Acacia and Lucas sucked in a sharp breath. Oenghus shut his eyes and winced, pressing a hand to his forehead. Isiilde looked at her guardian with concern, but the pain seemed fleeting. He leaned against a rock, crossing his massive arms.

"For the sake of Isiilde and Rivan, let me explain," Marsais said. "Pyrderi Har'Feydd was a faerie. Mind you, not as they are now, but as they were before the Shattering—he was an elf, one of the Lindale, of the highest order.

"The Lindale bore a connection with all life. They only killed when needed, even for food, and took no pleasure in war. But Pyrderi was not content with the way things were. He began wondering about things better left unthought, dabbling in darkness and slaughter, and eventually opened his spirit to the Void.

"Deeds of torture and cruelty twisted his spirit. In short, he changed his very nature. Eventually, a fiend from the Nine Halls began whispering to him in dreams, slicing through the veil between realms. Pyrderi welcomed every shadowed touch, and he became the first Fey— a lifeless heart beating in his cold body."

Isiilde shivered. Every child was threatened with tales of the Fey—

that they came in the night to snatch naughty children away. As a nymphling, Isiilde had been told that a lot.

"Pyrderi liked to experiment and torture. He created the Fomorri—a race of every nightmare ever dreamt."

The Fomorri lived in the east, to the south of Kiln, bordering the Great Expanse. Legend said they had been formed by the maggots of the slain and cast no shadow.

Isiilde had come across a sketch of one in a forbidden library. It was a disjointed mutation, twisted and haphazard, with a maw that split its face from ear to ear, bristling with three rows of teeth.

"With that explained—" Marsais paused, stroking his goatee, gazing at some unseen thing on the rocks. "Hmm, try the red one. That ought to do the trick."

The paladins glanced over their shoulders, but nothing was there. Instead of gazing at what wasn't there, Isiilde focused on the bond she shared with Marsais. Something inside of him had shifted, and she had an impression of a beam of light hitting a fractured glass to reveal a new angle. Whoever Marsais had addressed, he believed they were there.

Sensing her confusion, he shared a secretive smile with her before continuing. "The Sylph was heartbroken. One of her treasured creations had embraced her enemy. It was the beginning of the end of her favored realm."

Across the fire, Lucas' dark eyes blazed. "Are you privy to the Sylph's moods, Seer?"

"I'm telling the story, so for the rest of my narration, yes, I am privy to her moods. Feel free to haul my arse to an inquiry."

Lucas seethed from across the fire, but Marsais ignored the man.

The paladin unnerved her. Scars covered his bald head, and presumably, the rest of his body. There were pale, discolored patches on his ebony skin. Though the injuries were healed, the man had been burned horribly at some point. Twin scars curved upwards from his lips, twisting his cheeks into a gruesome smile. Only a purposeful blade could have made those cuts.

"Chaos spread as Pyrderi gathered followers, and a new threat whispered in the lands: Pyrderi's fiendish mentor, Karbonek, wanted to visit Fyrsta. His growing number of followers searched and found a way. On a certain island off the coast of the Fell Wastes, the veil between realms is thin, as thin as it is on the Isle of Blight."

"I don't like where this is going," Acacia said slowly. Her words sounded like a curse.

"At the Sylph's urging, Ulfhidhin recruited a group of warriors known as the Nine. Hengist Heartfang was their leader. Together, with the god's elite fighters, they stormed the island."

"That's ridiculous," Lucas spat.

"It is the truth."

"The wild god, Ulfhidhin, once abducted the Sylph. They are sworn enemies."

"Are they?" Marsais glanced at Oenghus in question, who grumbled in reply.

"By the Sacred Texts, yes."

"Well," Marsais said with a shrug, "it seems you have your answers already."

"Let him finish," Acacia warned. "No more interruptions. If you would be so kind?"

Marsais inclined his head. "Unfortunately, Ulfhidhin and his warriors were too late. Pyrderi had already completed the ritual. However, the crossing between veils had weakened the greater fiend, along with Pyrderi. Although the Fey outnumbered them, and Karbonek, even weakened, was formidable, the Nine knew they would never get another opportunity. So they attacked.

"Ulfhidhin fought the greater fiend, and pushed him back, blow by blow, but the fiend was too powerful. Karbonek impaled the god. With the last of his strength, Ulfhidhin wrapped a chain around the fiend's neck and dragged him back through the Gateway.

"In that moment, Hengist killed Pyrderi. The Fey's spirit was tied to the ritual that summoned his god and the Gateway closed, but the chain remained, trapping Karbonek between veils. The Gateway's abrupt closure resulted in an ill occurrence—when Karbonek began to claw and tear his way back, the earth stirred.

"The tunnels that his followers had hewn from the bedrock were raised, and Hengist, in his desperation, bound himself to the rock, sacrificing himself for eternity. In essence, he warded the Spine with his spirit, entombing Karbonek and trapping the Fey. Only one of the Nine survived.

"You see, the Spine is not a stronghold. It is not a monument to knowledge, nor a testament to greatness—it is a prison."

SILENCE ANSWERED THE REVELATION. Gentle rain drummed against the earth and flames crackled in the firepit.

Oenghus shook off the silence. "That gods' forsaken room that has no name... Let me guess: Pyrderi and his followers are trapped there?"

"Very insightful for a barbarian." The jab earned Marsais a baleful glare.

Acacia cut to the point. "You handed a madman a map to a trapped fiend who was powerful enough to kill Ulfhidhin?"

"I told him where he could find the map, yes."

"Can Tharios free Karbonek?"

"Ordinarily, no." Marsais cleared his throat. "However, I've learned that Tharios has recently acquired Soisskeli's Stave."

"*The* Soisskeli?" Acacia nearly choked. "The Chaos Lord who bound the dragons and used them to fight Iilenshar? The same Chaos Lord who was defeated by the Serene One in battle?"

"I believe there is only one Soisskeli."

Acacia sat back, stunned. The implications were daunting. "Legend claims that the Stave has infinite binding capabilities. Is that true?"

"Anything not of this realm, yes."

"Can Tharios reopen the Gateway?" Acacia asked, slowly.

"Not without aid."

Isiilde held her breath. She could feel Marsais' unease through their bond. Whatever his internal conflict, when he said the next, it felt like plunging over a cliff. "Not only can Soisskeli's Stave bind, but it can also activate a Runic Gateway—a portal between realms."

Oenghus cursed.

"The Sylph preserve us," Acacia breathed, touching her lips in supplication.

Lucas surged to his feet. "You knew this, yet you spilled your cowardly guts to save a nymph some discomfort?" Rage rolled off the paladin as he clenched his sword hilt.

"There is far more at stake than you know, Sir Lucas," Marsais said evenly.

"What could be worse than freeing the Fomorrian god from his prison? It will be the Isle of Blight all over again!" Lucas took a threatening step forward.

"Lieutenant," Acacia warned.

Lucas stiffened and took a step back, but the smoldering glare he directed at Marsais made Isiilde shrink.

"I have to agree with my lieutenant," Acacia said. "Any of us would have suffered to keep the map a secret without question. You've traded this realm for a single life. How many innocents will find a far worse fate than the one that awaited us in that dungeon?"

All eyes were on Marsais. Even Rivan turned from his post to stare with disappointment. Isiilde could hardly breathe. Marsais' words rang in her mind: *'If it had been anyone else.'* Guilt, she discovered, was a stifling burden.

"The choice was mine. Their blood will stain my hands."

"Then you will bathe in it," Lucas spat. "All for a *nymph*!"

CHAPTER 7

The man had needed help finding a house. He paid well, too much to pass up. The work would have been enough to feed Zoshi's brothers, sisters, and mum for a week.

The three boys never stood a chance. A sharp crack on the back of the skull had knocked them out, and maybe a bit more. Pip stirred behind him, but Tuck hadn't moved since he'd fallen in the mud.

Zoshi couldn't make a sound. Something raw and burning seized his throat. It was worse than eating sand. Every breath was a hard-won fight in the stifling confinement—never mind the pounding against the back of his head.

The cage rattled and dipped. The three boys were stuffed in a rolling wagon, hidden under a tarp like fish in a barrel. There were others. Children, women, and men, snatched from the docks as the three of them had been, packed so tightly no one could twitch without someone knowing.

There were criminals in Drivel called Runners. They knocked drunks over the head and dragged them to ships in the harbor. Zoshi always thought it a good business, if dangerous. A Runner earned ten gold a head. But Runners didn't take street rats as young as Zoshi and his brothers.

Zoshi wormed his way around until his head was closer to Tuck. If there had been more room, he could have slipped his tied hands around his feet and had them in front. But for now, wiggling was the best he could do. His shoulder cramped with the movement as he grit his teeth, focusing on his brother, nudging Tuck as best he could with his forehead. Nothing. Not even a stir.

Zoshi didn't cry. *Cryin' never did nothin' for no one.* That's what his mum always told him.

The wagon stopped. A rough voice gave orders and something heavy opened—gates from the sound of it. Zoshi tried to think of all the places he knew with gates in Drivel. There was a lot. All of them belonged to rich lords and Wise Ones who strutted around doing only the Guardians knew what.

Zoshi had met a few Wise Ones with common sense in his short lifetime, like the Giant, but most stone dwellers didn't have a copper's worth of decency.

Maybe the Wise Ones needed slaves, he thought. That wouldn't be so bad. Slaves ate pretty well.

The wagon lurched, then rolled along for a while before stopping again. Wherever they were, it was somewhere big. The wagon swayed as the driver hopped down, and voices called out.

"No trouble, I take it?" Definitely not a sailor. The voice had a high and mighty sound.

"None. This should be the last batch."

"Bring them in."

The tarp was thrown back, and sunlight shone through the mist. Seagulls circled overhead and pine trees rose all around. They had stopped somewhere by the coast with trees. That narrowed the location down. Zoshi knew of ten gated manors that fit that description.

Rough hands hauled Zoshi out, and tossed him to the ground with the rest of the captives. There wasn't much to see. They were in a courtyard surrounded by high walls and pleasant fountains. Armed men in steel helms stood guard, watching the motley assortment with indifference.

The soldiers weren't wearing uniforms, but they didn't look like local militia either. These men were focused and didn't slouch at their posts. They were too disciplined to be militia.

Zoshi tried to stand—he always liked to have his feet under him. At eight years, he could outrun the best of them. But the blunt end of a spear knocked him back down.

One by one, the captives were dragged into what looked like a simple shed. Inside, a gaping stairwell plunged into the ground. When Zoshi saw the stairs disappearing into the pit, his predicament settled like a stone in his gut.

Something about the darkness in the center of the shed terrified the boy. It was wide, the stairs too big to be some simple pit for slaves. Zoshi's heartbeat filled his ears, and the older folks panicked, but it was useless. The guards were too eager with their spears.

Zoshi tried to bolt, but a large guard scooped him up. The boy kicked and thrashed, but he was no match for a grown man. Eventually, Zoshi gave up, letting his feet drag over the stone. He craned his neck, and caught sight of his brother Tuck dangling from the soldier's left hand. There was a sickly stain on the back of his head.

Tuck was only four.

Tears came then, streaming down Zoshi's cheeks. He couldn't stop them, no matter what his mother said.

At the bottom of the dark stairwell, the guards sliced off the prisoners' clothes with long knives. Those who struggled were quickly stilled with a cudgel.

The sight of discarded rags and shoes made him sick. It reminded him of how fishermen dumped the entrails of their catch. The guts were of no worth to anyone but the birds and rats.

A guard dragged Zoshi forward and tossed him into something more like a corral than a cage.

"This one's dead," his guard said.

There wasn't anything worse than hearing those three words.

THE DOOR SLAMMED SHUT, and the bolt was thrown. Most of the prisoners lay where they'd landed, staring blankly forward. Men, women, and children—there was no rhyme or reason.

Despite the tangle of limbs, Zoshi squirmed and twisted. With a child's flexibility, he worked his shoulders, slipping his hands under his feet so they were in front. The ropes were tight. His wrists bled, but he struggled with them anyway as he searched the tangle of bodies for Pip.

Some prisoners had found their feet. They looked at one another with the same helpless plea. In his experience, it wasn't good when the old folks started looking like that. He didn't like those looks.

Zoshi pushed his way through the press towards what he figured would be the front of the corral.

He wished he hadn't moved.

The underground chamber was large, the stone shaped by skilled hands, smoothed to a polish. It smelled of death. Other corrals opened up across the way and a walkway traveled around a circle of sand that was white and grainy and pure. A silk-robed man with black hair stood in the center, tracing a maze of strange markings into the sand. He held a foul-looking stave capped with a twisted sun.

Obsidian stone slabs were spaced evenly around the sandpit. They sloped downwards like a slide, with deep grooves running the length of smooth stone. A carved, open-mouthed face decorated the front of each. The wide, lolling tongues and gaping mouths reminded Zoshi of the adornments that served as gutters on manors.

The forced silence imposed on the prisoners made the chamber eerily quiet except for the careful work of the man. A copper-skinned Rahuatl walked into view. Ritual scars decorated his face, along with the ivory studs common to his kind. Despite his tribal markings, he wore a robe, and looked like he knew everything better than everyone else— like one of those Wise Ones.

Anyone who calls themselves wise, isn't wise at all, Zoshi's mum would say.

"The exit point is ready," the Rahuatl hissed.

Zoshi couldn't hear them, but he could see their lips move. He had always prided himself on his ability to read lips.

"I want them dead, N'Jalss," said the black-haired man. "I want their heads."

"It shall be done."

The black-haired man nodded, as if his orders had already been carried out, and then he paused in thought, surveying his work. "We'll need ten from the herd for each. Get them in position."

The Rahuatl turned towards the shadows. "Bring the Devout!"

Zoshi scrambled backwards, pushing himself between legs. With a sense of growing panic, he searched for Pip.

Whatever entered the chamber startled the prisoners. The captives retreated at once, fighting to push their way to the back of the corral, heedless of those being crushed underfoot.

Zoshi nearly fell, but kept his feet, moving with the tide. The gate at the front swung open, and the panic reached a crescendo. Through gaps in frantic limbs, Zoshi saw the guards. They grabbed people at random, snapping collars around the necks of the unlucky.

A mud-covered child was on the ground. It was Pip. His hands were free, and he was squashed against the side of the corral, digging like a dog in the dirt. There was a hole between the steel and the earth, where the slats had rusted away.

Zoshi fell in beside his younger brother. They exchanged silent glances and while battling crushing feet, dug their fingers raw.

Pip was only five, and he was little, even for his age. Just a bit more, and the smaller boy could squeeze through. Hope entered his heart; one of his brothers would escape.

But even if Pip wiggled out of this cage, the guards would spot him running back up the stairs.

A desperate plan struck Zoshi. He gestured with his hands until understanding shone in Pip's wide eyes. The younger boy shook his head violently, but was stopped by his older brother's hands. Zoshi grabbed the small face awkwardly and nodded again, firmer: *Do as I say*.

Their corral was being emptied. There wasn't time to argue. Zoshi rose to his feet, giving Pip little choice in the matter. If the little boy refused, then his brother's sacrifice would be for nothing.

Zoshi thought about all the stories he had ever heard about brave knights and warriors. Sacrifice was supposed to be a grand, heroic thing full of glory. He wanted to save his brother's life, but he didn't feel heroic—he was terrified and piss ran down his leg.

A gap opened in the press of bodies. His muscles tensed, and before he lost his nerve, he scrambled between legs and sprang up, charging the guards. His bare feet slapped on the iron walkway.

The boy skidded under the first guard's legs, and a collared captive with some fight in him drove his shoulder into the second guard.

Zoshi skidded right off the walkway, grabbed the lip with his tied hands and swung down and under with agile ease. Boots pounded overhead as guards rushed forward to subdue the chained line of captives. Heavy cudgels pounded flesh, quelling the fight within moments.

The distraction had been enough.

Hidden in the shadows, Zoshi turned in time to glimpse Pip's fleeing form dart down a passage.

Guards rushed after the boy.

Zoshi tried screaming to draw their attention, but his throat was stopped by the unseen enchantment. He braced to charge from his concealment, but the sudden, dreadful twang of a bowstring drew him up short. In his mind, he screamed.

"We got the quick little brat," a guard announced, coming into view. The man casually dragged Pip by the hair. An arrow protruded from his neck.

The guards thought Pip was the boy who ran out of the corral.

Zoshi crouched beneath the walkway, frozen with grief. This wasn't at all how the grand stories went. Zoshi was supposed to have an arrow through his skin, not Pip.

"He's still fresh," the guard said.

"Get him up on the slab, and we'll begin."

A cart sat nearby, waiting on the other side of the raised walkway. Zoshi scrambled from his cover to hide behind a wheel.

The Rahuatl's eyes gleamed in the shadow as he walked from the center of the pit, stepping over the careful tracings. The slick, dark-haired man remained in his maze.

A dull chopping sound drew Zoshi's attention. Across the sandpit, other prisoners in identical corrals stared in shock. He followed their gazes to the space between the walkway and pit, where the tip of a statue's tongue lolled.

Bright blood leaked from the spigot, staining the pristine sand. The next chop made Zoshi flinch. The blood pooled in the deep grooves and seeped through the maze of tracings.

"Bleed the rest," the Rahuatl hissed.

At his calm command, the guards yanked more prisoners from the corrals, slamming a captive on each stone slab. There was no ceremony, no elaborate ritual, or showy chanting from black-hooded priests. Instead, the guards were quick, efficient and heedless of their victims' flopping. Men, women, and children were gutted and chopped like fish for the market.

The cart shuddered overhead as something fell into its bed. With a sickening twist, Zoshi realized that similar carts were waiting by each slab.

Knives flashed and the bound captives thrashed as they were bled dry. Neck, wrists, thighs. The butchers didn't bother killing them first. Just let them bleed while their lives faded and their bodies were dumped in the waiting cart. Not all the sacrifices were dead when they were tossed away.

It was fortunate that Zoshi couldn't feel his throat—he would have been screaming. All he could do was cower beneath the cart and brace himself for every thud that rocked his hiding place.

Zoshi squeezed his eyes shut. He could not remember what the clerics said over the dead, but he did his best, praying to the Guardian of Life to see the spirits of the slaughtered safely to the ol'River.

At least Pip and Tuck would be together.

The grooves in the sand ran red with streams of converging sacrifice. Strange powers stirred over the pit while the silk-robed man stood in the center of the storm. His smooth chant rose on invisible wings, beating at Zoshi's mind.

When the blood pathways converged, crimson threads of light

stirred around the man. With a final incantation, he gripped the stave with both hands and plunged it into the sand. The air was torn from Zoshi's lungs as an inky Portal snapped into focus.

A mirage rippled through the dark lens. It was like gazing at a pebble in a pool. Only a cavern swam murkily at the bottom and people were waiting on the other side.

The sleek man was frozen in place, gripping the stave. His fine features were strained with pain and sweat beaded on his forehead— no, it was blood. Crimson droplets rolled down his face.

The Rahuatl gave a sharp order. Four massive litters were shoved into the Portal, the shapes beneath hidden by heavy black tarps.

Four lines of collared prisoners, ten in each, were driven through the Portal against their will. When the last had disappeared, the Rahuatl stepped through, and the silk-robed man uttered a word.

The Portal snapped shut, and the man dropped to his knees.

An eerie stillness settled over the chamber. It smelled of slaughter, and a woman's voice broke it. "Get the bodies into the pit," she ordered before hurrying across the sand to kneel at her master's side. She was tall and graceful, and Zoshi had never been so revolted by beauty.

As boots hurried towards his cart, he tore his eyes from the grim tableau. All around the walkways, guards hoisted the carts and hauled them away. His own hiding place joined the procession.

Zoshi's nostrils flared as he fought the urge to bolt, concentrating instead on keeping pace with the cart. And yet, all his instincts told him not to go any deeper into this Void-cursed place.

There was one cart behind him and one guard pulling it. Seizing the opportunity, Zoshi snatched up a rock as they circled the chamber. When a side passage came into view, Zoshi jammed the rock between wheel and cart and it lurched to a stop.

The guard dragging it stumbled forward.

The fellow behind abandoned his own cart to help steady the load, and Zoshi slipped from underneath, darting up the nearest passage. Luck was with him, or as much as he would get. It was the tunnel leading to the shed.

As he ran past the discarded piles of clothing, he snatched a pair of breeches, and darted up the stairwell, praying that no one waited at the top.

Part of his prayer was answered. There was no guard inside the shed, but the heavy iron door was shut. He felt his way through the dark until he came to a corner. With his back against the wall, he twisted and worked his wrists against the rope until they were slick with his own blood.

Ignoring the pain, he freed his hands. He slipped the oversized breeches on and rolled up the cuffs, cinching the rope around his waist to hold them up.

Zoshi probed the dark corner with trembling hands. His whole body shook, but fear wouldn't do. He sucked air through his snotty nose, trying to steady his nerves. Bracing himself against each wall, he inched his way up the corner. Calloused feet and hands barely felt the rough stone as he clambered towards the ceiling. He caught a rafter and hauled himself up.

The shed didn't have windows, but the gap between the roof and stone was enough for the boy. After a tense minute and careful maneuvering, he slipped beneath the eaves into the chill night air and dropped to the soil. The soft scuffle of his landing rang loudly in his ears and he quickly pressed himself against the shed's wall.

Zoshi did not move. He only listened.

Guards patrolled the night but kept to the large manor house, moving silently beneath the glow of everlights.

If there was a guard nearby, he'd likely be in front of the shed. Zoshi wasn't about to risk a peek. Instead, he spied a grouping of bushes that offered cover next to the outer wall. Keeping low, he darted to the bushes like a frightened rabbit and slithered under their protection.

The wall was high, but he was desperate. Some inner voice of survival screamed at him to keep going. Zoshi didn't stop to think. He didn't know what was on the other side of the wall; he only knew he couldn't linger.

A section of wall caught his attention, and before he lost his nerve, he crawled swiftly towards the spot in the courtyard. He tested the corner. It wouldn't be the trickiest thing he had climbed.

Placing one hand on either wall, he braced himself as before and scuttled up the corner. Iron spikes decorated the top, which made for convenient handholds. Zoshi pulled himself up, squeezing between the rods to dangle on the other side.

The outer wall was completely smooth, and there was no convenient corner. The drop would surely break a leg if not his neck. Farther down, a shadow rose from the darkness of the ground. He hoped it was a tree.

Swallowing his fear, he worked sideways, using the spikes until the shadow was directly behind him. It was a tree, but the branches were five feet away from his perch.

Zoshi braced his feet on the stone, bent his knees, and sprang with all his power. He twisted midair, trying to turn all around, but hit the tree with his side instead. Branches snapped as he whipped past raking needles.

He was falling.

His leg caught something hard and he was slapped to the side, slamming against a branch. The wind was knocked from his body, and he dangled, draped over the bough like a limp rag over blackness.

There wasn't any time to recover. Before his breath had returned, he let himself slide off the branch, hoping the earth would catch him. It did.

Shouts erupted from the courtyard as he hit the ground and rolled. Dazed and reeling with pain, instinct urged his legs to move. Zoshi staggered to his feet, and stumbled to undergrowth as torches bobbed between trees.

Nostrils flaring, vision blurred, the boy's feet kept moving of their own accord—one in front of the other. He ran blindly, away from Tuck's limp body, away from an arrow's twang and Pip's bloody flesh.

Anywhere but where he had been. The mist embraced the boy, and eventually his legs failed.

CHAPTER 8

TWO WARRIORS STOOD toe to toe. Lucas and Oenghus locked eyes, on the verge of striking, their aggression crackling in the air.

"Don't you *dare* put this on her head," Oenghus growled. "We'll take care of it."

"Take care of it?" Lucas parroted. "How are we going to do that? We have no idea where we are."

"Aye, we'll bloody take care of it." Oenghus bared his teeth. "We'll go kill the bastard. Then I'll gut the traitorous little weasel."

"Brilliant plan. Direct and simple," Acacia said dryly.

Oenghus shrugged. "I'm sure the Scarecrow has a plan. He always does."

All eyes focused on Marsais, and a sudden flutter of panic seized Isiilde. The cave narrowed, and the rock pressed on her head, squeezing the air from her lungs.

Marsais quickly stood. "I need to stretch my legs. Walk with me, my dear?"

Isiilde took his offered hand.

With no memory of the path they traveled, Isiilde soon found herself leaning against a redwood tree. The bark was soft against her forehead and the mossy earth was warm beneath her feet.

Marsais rested a calming hand on her back. Silence filled her ears. "Is it safe here?" she asked.

"Is anywhere truly safe?"

Numbly, she followed him as he walked, watching as he picked mushrooms and plants, passing them over to eat. The strange mushrooms were gold, and smelled like apricots but tasted like pepper. She'd eaten her fill when they came across a gurgling stream.

Fifty paces downstream, the flow plunged over a boulder, forming a crystal curtain of water. The pool was stained by the fibrous bark of redwood. It reminded her of blood.

Isiilde stood on the bank, gazing at her reflection. Her hair was matted and tangled, her face smudged with mud and blood, and her clothing tattered. She no longer recognized herself.

An immediate urgency proved impossible to ignore, and she left Marsais to relieve herself behind a tree. When she emerged, he was perched on a boulder, legs crossed. A flat rock sat in the palm of his bandaged hand and his face was creased with concentration as he tried, and failed, to trace a single rune onto its surface.

A mournful howl rose in the forest, and Isiilde hurried over to him.

"Just a wolf, my dear." He looked at her with knowing eyes. "If I'm not mistaken, you desire a bath. I can feel—" his voice caught. "Zander's hands on you."

"I think I'll freeze in that water."

"The seer has a plan," he said, then frowned at the rock. "Hopefully."

He threw it aside and reached for another stone, attempting the fire rune again, but his fingers were stiff and clumsy and the weave complex. A wave of frustration traveled through their bond.

Isiilde stood patiently by his side, watching him with concern. Rage churned in her stomach. She wanted to burn Tharios to a crisp for what he'd done. She wanted to burn all the traitors.

Marsais' hands were his life—his only link to the Gift. They were thin and elegant, like the rest of him. And ever so gentle. He traced runes with the same passion he had caressed her body. Without his hands, he could not practice his art.

He tossed another rock aside, but she touched his arm before he could snatch a third. "It's all right, Marsais. You need to let the bones heal. The cold water will help."

Her suggestion nudged him off the rock. Slowly, she unwrapped his bandages. The flesh beneath was bruised and swollen and his fingers trembled with pain.

Isiilde set aside the loose bandages, and helped Marsais roll up his sleeves. When he placed his hands in the water, he sucked in a breath, but slowly relaxed as it numbed his pain.

Isiilde dipped a toe in, and winced. She could try to heat the water herself, but a heating stone was a complex weave, requiring a deft touch. It could easily end in disaster.

Resigned, Isiilde shed her clothes and moved to the gentle waterfall to scrub off unwanted hands. Their bond sharpened, and she glanced over to find Marsais watching her. The touch of his eyes warmed her, and she smiled in return. Only the heat cooled when she stepped into the mountain stream.

The water washed away the feel of hands and blood, leaving her feeling restored but shivering.

"What will we do?" she chattered.

"Take one day at a time."

"But we have to stop Tharios."

Marsais gently shook the water from his hands as he walked over to a flat boulder. "We should probably warm you up first."

"You're not supposed to use your hands."

Marsais arched an imperious brow at her. "Are you going to tell on me?"

Before she could answer, Marsais traced a crude rune on the rock. It began to glow with heat until the moss smoked and curled to a blackened crisp.

Isiilde snatched her clothes and hurried over to curl on the heated rock. "I suppose Oen doesn't need to know. Why didn't you tell the others where we are?"

"Hmm?"

"You know where we are."

"Do I?" He sounded amused.

"I doubt you'd pick mushrooms for me without knowing if they're poisonous."

Marsais chuckled. "Have I ever told you what an amazing mind you have?" A surge of desire traveled through their bond. "Among other things."

"*That* would definitely warm me up."

"Yes, and burn down the forest," Marsais quipped.

"I think you're trying to distract me."

"Oh, it's quite involuntary. This is hardly the place, though."

"The place being?" The rock was cooling, so she pulled on her makeshift clothing, wishing she had her cloak and boots.

"Vaylin. Although I'm not precisely sure where. We could be in the far north, or more towards the border of Kiln. The entire region is mountainous. Some of the deeper valleys stay warm, even through winter. These little mushrooms are native to the forests. Regardless of where, we have a long way to travel to stop Tharios."

Isiilde loved studying maps—all the connecting roads of civilization and the unknown in between. Vaylin was on the opposite side of Fyrsta, as far east as one could go without falling into the ocean.

"Well, that's good."

At her optimistic remark, Marsais arched a brow in question.

"It gives you time to think of a plan."

CHAPTER 9

THEY HIKED ALONG A RIDGE. Far below, ruins poked through the distant canopy, marking the start of their journey; or was it another valley with another ruined kingdom? She did not know. She'd fallen asleep on Oenghus' back.

With a yawn, she slipped to the ground.

"Will your feet be all right, Sprite?"

"You spent the first half of my life trying to put boots on me." She frowned at the brooding sky. "I'll be fine as long as it doesn't snow."

Marsais fell in beside her with an offering of berries, mushrooms, and a twisted root that he peeled pale slivers from with a knife.

"How are you feeling?" he asked.

"Hungry," she said between mouthfuls. "You walked through the night?"

"We thought it wise."

"Nothing followed us, I hope?"

"One can certainly hope." Marsais stopped and pointed north. "That is where we began. You can see the top of a ruin poking through the trees. We're heading south towards those smoke trails."

To the south, a river snaked through the valley, and thin trails of smoke reached beyond the treetops. It looked like a long way to walk.

Isiilde's body ached; the air was cold and the wind bitter, but Marsais was alive. That was all that mattered.

A sudden thought sprang to mind. "Did you tell them yet?"

"Tell who what?"

"The paladins," she whispered. "Did you tell them where we are?"

Marsais blinked. "I'm not precisely sure. We could be in the far north or south—"

"Yes, you said that already. Why don't you want to tell them we're in Vaylin?"

"Because they'll get angry."

"They're already angry, Marsais."

"Yes, but it's a vague sort of anger."

Isiilde raised a brow at him.

"More or less," he muttered.

While Marsais scratched at the rough stubble on his cheek, Isiilde chewed on a sliver of root. She was discovering that their bond worked both ways. If she concentrated, she could sense his mood and emotions. At the moment, he was weighing options.

It was, she mused, much like considering a strategy in her favorite game of runes: King's Folly. She studied his sharp profile in the sunlight. To all outward appearance, he was as aloof and confident as a bird of prey surveying his domain. However, she now knew better. The glimpse their bond offered was enlightening, and disturbing: Marsais was not as confident as he appeared.

"Captain."

Acacia stopped at Marsais' call, her pale gaze flickering from shivering nymph to seer.

"Vaylin. We're in Vaylin, somewhere north, I think."

"I know."

Surprise rippled through their bond. "You do?"

"The mushrooms," Acacia explained. "I had them in Nefir. I wanted to see how long you would wait before telling us."

Marsais tapped his head. "My mind is not what it was."

"I think your mind is in perfect order."

Oenghus barked a laugh.

Acacia stepped up to Marsais and met his gaze. "I don't like games. It sows distrust."

"Did you tell your men where we are, Captain?" he asked, for her ears alone.

"I am here to aid you, not take orders from you. Do not play games with me."

"I don't play games. I do what I must for this realm."

Acacia searched his eyes, long enough for the others to take note. At last, when the captain spoke, her voice was low and calm. "Your judgment thus far does not inspire confidence."

Marsais inclined his head. "It rarely does."

The edge of Acacia's lip twitched upwards. Then, to everyone's surprise, she removed her golden tunic and handed it to Isiilde. "You need this more than I do, Nymph."

OENGHUS CALLED for a halt at a grouping of boulders. Rainwater from the night before had gathered in crevices and dripped down the rock. Save for Lucas' tobacco pouch, weapons, armor, and a piece of flint, they had walked through the Gateway without supplies—not even a waterskin.

Isiilde started to drink the rainwater, but Acacia stopped her with a hand. "Let Rivan purify it first."

"I'm sure it's fine," Oenghus said.

"He needs the practice." Acacia nodded to the young man, who stepped forward and knelt beside a shallow basin.

The Wise Ones' Lore was simply a path, one among many, that tapped into the Sylph's Gift. The Blessed Order, barbarian shamans, and Mystics all had their own unique disciplines, but Runes were the most efficient way to channel the Gift, or so the Wise Ones claimed.

Marsais had once told her (never to be repeated) that Bloodmagi used a mixture of energies, including the Sylph's Gift. Life was like a powerful river from which good, evil, and everything in between drank. Anyone could dip his hand into Life's current, but what a being used the water for was an entirely different matter.

There was one exception to the rule: the Void. It was everything opposite to the River of Life.

Rivan withdrew a slender stone from his belt pouch and bowed his head, whispering unfamiliar words in an undertone. When his prayer to the divine was complete, he placed the stone in the water and it floated to the top, glowing with a pure light.

The light filled the pool for a brilliant second, then it dimmed, leaving the stone covered in filth. Rivan plucked it out of the water, cupped it in the palm of his hands, and bowed his head again. A searing light illuminated his features. When he raised his head a second time, the stone was clean. He slipped it into his pouch, and looked over at her with surprise.

Isiilde smiled. "That was beautiful."

Rivan rubbed his neck in embarrassment. "It's only a simple ritual, but the water is safe to drink now."

A sharp burst of emotion passed through her bond with Marsais. She glanced at him in confusion, not quite knowing what to make of it. His steely gaze flickered between her and Rivan and then away. She recognized anger, which left her puzzled, but Lucas interrupted before she could question Marsais.

"How long do we have until Tharios releases Karbonek, Seer?" The scarred paladin was sitting on a rock, sharpening the edge of his longsword with a stone.

"The Shadowed Dawn," Marsais replied, staring down at the valley.

"And how do you know this?"

"You asked." He waved a vague hand.

"That's only two months away," Acacia pointed out. "Not near enough time to make the return journey."

"We'll have to inform the High Inquisitor. Can you send a message, Seer?"

"I could, but are you entirely sure you can trust the High Inquisitor?"

"Blasphemy!"

Marsais ignored the fuming paladin, looking to Acacia instead. She said nothing, confirming what Marsais had long suspected: High Inquisitor Multist was as corrupt as they came. She had replaced the former Knight Captain for a reason.

Marsais returned to his survey, clasping hands behind his back in silent thought.

Lucas started to rise, but Oenghus grabbed his arm. "Leave it. Trust me, you don't want to mess with the Scarecrow when he's like that."

For a moment, Isiilde thought the ill-tempered paladin would strike Oenghus, but he glanced at Marsais, perhaps recalling his duel with the Hound, and sat back down.

"A message from a Whisperer can be caught and even changed," Oenghus said. "Tharios and his followers will be waiting for a message. We don't know who we can trust on the Isle."

"Can Tharios open a Gateway to Vaylin using the Stave?" Acacia asked.

Oenghus shrugged. "I only know the Stave by legend—didn't know it could open one at all."

"We better get moving," Marsais said suddenly.

He struck off without waiting for the others, long legs carrying him rapidly away. The paladins blinked at the seer. And Isiilde, accustomed to his sudden mood swings, hastened to catch up, flitting over the terrain with ease.

"Marsais."

"Hmm?"

"Are you angry with me?"

The question knocked him out of his brooding. "I can't imagine ever being angry with you. Why do you ask?"

"After Rivan purified the water, you looked at me and I sensed... something. Was it because I urged you to tell the paladins we're in Vaylin?"

"That wasn't it at all," he said, taking her hand. "I was angry with myself." She waited for him to explain. "I'm ashamed to admit that your attentiveness to Rivan sparked an unexpected reaction in me, one I believed was impossible—jealousy."

She was oddly touched by his confession.

"We've barely been bonded for two days and I'm already acting a fool. I'm not sure how the druids did it."

"Did what?"

"Let go of their nymphs. A druid is their first, but never their last."

Isiilde stepped aside to avoid a jagged rock, pulling his arm across the distance, unwilling to relinquish his hand. When they returned, side by side, she smiled, reminding him of everything wonderful. "But I don't want you to let go of me, Marsais."

Warmth entered his eyes, chasing away his disquiet. "Perhaps," he mused, "it's as simple as that. After all, a nymph never does anything until she's ready."

"Why is Oenghus angry with you? Was it so surprising—you and me?"

"Hmm, that's a delicate subject. You're better off asking him, but don't worry, it's not the first bone he's had to pick with me. I'm more afraid of your wrath."

"Like in the King's Walk?" Heat rose to the tips of her ears.

"I feared a goddess was about to smite me."

"I'm sorry I said those things."

"I deserved it," he said. "As I told you in the King's Walk, I see every possibility—every pathway in Time. I wanted nothing more than to keep you from harm, but that path ended badly, and yet, I was sorely tempted."

"You saw what would happen in the kitchens," she said in a thready whisper. "That's why you asked me to stay away."

"Your attack in the kitchens was one of many possibilities, but—" he sighed, gazing into the trees. "I tried to steer you from that fate, and I failed. Even then, it did not end this way—with you and me as we are now. You're unpredictable, my dear."

Minutes passed in silence, with only his bandaged palm against hers and an easy gait.

"I'm not really unpredictable, Marsais," she said at last. "You just didn't see it—how much I wanted you. How much I needed you." Her words were as soft and beautiful as a breeze. "I would endure it all again to be with you, so don't worry about Rivan because there's no comparison to you. And despite what I once said in anger, you are a gentleman."

Marsais pressed his lips together. Though it must have pained him, he squeezed her hand, and when he found his voice, he was forced to clear the emotion from his throat.

"I don't know... I thought Rivan was rather handsome."

"Are you trying to make me jealous now?" Isiilde smiled up at him, but her amusement was short-lived, as memory gripped her. She glanced back at the chiseled warrior and shivered. "I don't want to be alone with any man but you, Marsais. Even before... Stievin. Humans are cruel and they frighten me."

"I wish I could tell you otherwise. But as I said in the King's Walk, the realms, for you especially, are a cruel place. But one day, you will meet a good man worthy of you."

"I already have."

"I'm far from worthy—trust me."

"But I do, completely."

Marsais raised her hand to his lips, briefly closing his eyes. He did not utter another word for some time.

CHAPTER 10

"I was walking along the Mearcentian coast when I stumbled upon a woman who'd washed ashore." Marsais' grey eyes sparkled in memory.

"You'd think the scales would have warned him away," Oenghus grunted.

"She was covered in seaweed, but when I went to help, I noticed she wasn't human. Pearlescent scales covered her body from head to toe. Her eyes were large and black and she had webbed fingers and toes."

"Eyes like a Grawl?" Rivan asked.

"No, nothing of the sort. Voidspawn, like Grawl, are—" Marsais frowned, searching for words. "Their eyes are nonexistent, a hollow pit of nothingness that feeds on your life force. This woman had eyes like black pearls.

"She was injured, so I carried her back to my cottage to treat her wounds. She was clumsy in her movements, grabbing things faster than needed, as if they were an inch away." He demonstrated the odd movements. "She wasn't used to being on land."

"Again. You'd think he would have gotten the hint."

Marsais ignored Oenghus. "She stayed with me for a few days, eating only fish and clams. She never said a word, but seemed to understand me." Marsais cleared his throat. "I swear I was a perfect gentleman, but for whatever reason, she climbed into my bed one night."

Rivan gawked and Lucas edged closer to listen.

"You probably got her drunk," Oenghus said.

"Oh, you're just smarting because it wasn't your bed. She would have mistaken you for a walrus," Marsais shot back.

"I know why she climbed into his bed, Oen."

Isiilde raised her brows suggestively, and Oenghus looked on the verge of hitting Marsais for it.

"Why, thank you." Marsais moved away from the scowling giant. "You had your one shot," he warned before continuing. "About a week later, I woke up one morning to find her gone. Thinking something had happened to her, I searched for days—"

"Hold up, what's that?" Acacia pointed towards the snow-capped mountains.

Two large, bird-like shapes flapped after a smaller one on the horizon. It was Luccub, the imp. But unfortunately, the two larger shapes were not birds.

"Off the ridge!" Oenghus hissed.

The group plunged over the side, down the steep slope. In a rush to take cover, Isiilde glanced over her shoulder and skidded to a stop. Marsais had not moved. He stood in the open, utterly exposed, and altogether lost.

"Oen," she shouted, scrambling back up the slope. The winged monsters were getting larger.

Isiilde reached Marsais first. She grabbed his wrist and tugged, hissing his name, but he was all muscle and bone and, therefore, heavier than he appeared. She could not budge him as the flying trio neared.

Desperate, Isiilde summoned the Lore, fingers flashing. In quick succession, she wove a feather rune around his ankles, and a layer of air and spirit overtop. When he drifted an inch off the ground, she pushed him towards a boulder, shoving him over. As he hit the ground, his coins chimed in warning.

Luccub zipped from the sky towards Oenghus, who smacked him out of the way and turned to face the flying horrors. His gaze flickered to

Isiilde on the ridge. He hesitated, then ducked, dropping to the ground and motioning for the paladins to follow suit.

Two monstrous, leather-winged reptiles landed on the ridge with a roar. Isiilde clamped a hand over her mouth and pressed against the rock as a tail lashed overhead.

When Marsais blinked in confusion, she caught his eye, silently warning him to be still. The beasts were on the other side of the boulder, pounding and huffing—something cracked, and a clawed foot stomped on the dirt beside her.

Marsais scrambled forward, pressing against the rock and nudging her to the side. As the beasts battled like bulls over the ridge, Marsais and Isiilde skirted the boulder. A stinger thundered from the sky, impaling the earth. The tail was as thick as a tree trunk.

Isiilde tensed to run, but Marsais grabbed her arm, anchoring her in place. A shadow blotted out the sun, the air turned noxious, and a presence hovered above.

Marsais' eyes rolled upwards, and Isiilde's gaze was pulled in the same direction. A head the size of a boulder sniffed the air, nostrils flaring, tongue tasting. The scales along its throat were like armor, thick and scarred.

Something moved off to the side, drawing the monster's attention. Its head snapped towards the edge of the ridge where Luccub rolled through the air, end over end. The beast bellowed in triumph, lunging towards the imp, catching him in its maw, crunching and gnawing in satisfaction.

The beast's jaws worked, then it stiffened and gagged, choking on its meal. A moment later, the dragon-like monster spat out a slimy imp. Luccub flapped into the air with a cackle and a prize. He clutched a dagger-sized fang in his feet.

Both monsters roared, stirring up a whirlwind. Marsais shielded her from the wind as the monsters took flight. No one dared move for a time. When the monsters had finally vanished beyond the horizon, Marsais blew out a breath.

"I'm going to chop that imp into a thousand pieces and send them to the four corners of the realm!" Oenghus growled, stomping into view. "Right after I kick your bony arse down this mountain, Scarecrow."

"I'll let the imp have its turn first," Marsais nobly offered, climbing to his feet. "Besides, you'd need to send the pieces to a thousand corners —not four."

"Were those dragons?" Isiilde's voice trembled. She found she could not move.

Oenghus hoisted her to her feet. "Wyverns. One's bad enough; two will give you trouble."

Anything that gave Oenghus trouble was best avoided.

"Can we get off this ridge?" Acacia hissed from the slope.

"A grand idea."

"Next time, move your feet sooner, Scarecrow."

"He was lost, Oen."

"He'd also be dead if it wasn't for you." Oenghus grabbed Marsais' arm and propelled him towards the waiting paladins.

Isiilde followed. "Did Luccub save us again?"

"No." Oenghus bared his teeth. "The bastard was trying to hide behind us. Lucas pinned the imp under his shield. I grabbed it, and hit it towards the Wyverns with my hammer."

"Can the imp be killed?" Acacia asked Marsais, but he was lost again, staring but seeing nothing. Isiilde took his hand.

Acacia frowned. "Does he do this often?"

"Aye," Oenghus grunted. "At the most Void-cursed times."

Acacia accepted Marsais' limitations with a nod. "I was hoping to avoid the forest, but I don't think we can with those two fighting over their territory."

"At least there are signs of civilization," Rivan said.

Far away, over an evergreen sea, smoke trails slithered into the sky.

"And who knows what's in between," Acacia added.

"Civilization," Lucas spat. "Valyinish barbarians are Void-worshiping heathens. They offer their women to Grawl."

"Not all of them, Sir Lucas," Marsais said suddenly.

All eyes looked at him in surprise.

"There are many tribes in Vaylin. Not all of them revere the Dark One. It could be a Medwin or a Da'len village—both are reasonable. Some of the Lome and Suevi tribes have been known to provide help for a price."

"It's the Ardmoor we don't want," Oenghus said.

"And heathen is such a narrow term." Marsais scratched at the scar beneath his robe. "Before the Shattering, the Guardians themselves revered the Eldar gods—the same gods the Medwin and Da'len currently worship. So we are not in a heathen land, but an ancient one."

Lucas did not respond.

"How can we tell the tribes apart?" Rivan asked.

"Oh, we'll know," Marsais said.

"Hopefully, it'll be from a safe distance when we find out," Acacia added.

CHAPTER II

THE GROUP MADE camp beside a stream and the toppled statue of a forgotten king. His moss-covered head was half-buried, and one eye watched the group as they ate a light meal. Marsais volunteered for the first watch, and others put their backs to the king and slept.

Isiilde joined Marsais, where he sat on a rock by the stream, away from the firelight, unwinding his bandages. Although his face was impassive, she could feel his pain like a dim thought at the back of her mind.

"Are my hands bothering you?"

"The only bother is that you're in pain," she said softly.

"Only a little now. I don't want to cause you any discomfort."

"You're not. I don't want you to leave me—when you do, I feel so empty."

The moon shone through gaps in the distant canopy. She focused on the tiny windows of light, trying to ignore the darkness.

Marsais flexed his hands. They were bruised and clumsy and he thrust them into the icy water.

"I think I chose the wrong Gateway, Marsais."

"You chose what was familiar."

Isiilde tilted her head. "I've never been here."

"No, but *I* have." He smiled. "These trees remember me."

"I hope you didn't anger them."

Marsais chuckled. "Let us hope not."

Isiilde hugged her knees and watched the moonlight seeping through the shadows as he soaked his hands. Slowly, her eyes adjusted to the deepening night. Insects danced over the water, bats swooped to feast, and an owl asked an eternal question.

Marsais paused, listening, and then relaxed. "Still," he muttered, "precautions are needed." He gently shook the water from his hands and held them in front of her. "Would you be so kind?"

She patted them dry, then deftly wrapped the bandages in a way that would give him more mobility. "I can't believe they did this to you."

"A wise precaution for what Tharios intended."

"It's terrible."

"So it is. But my hands are mending."

"I don't know how you kept going—after your injuries from the duel, and then Tharios..."

"The mind is a powerful thing. Sheer willpower kept Oenghus breathing. We do what we must because the alternative is failure."

"Oen is too stubborn for that, and you..." She looked into his eyes. "You've dealt with all the trouble I've brought you over the years without complaint." Her gaze fell as she cinched the bandage. "I think Tulipin was right. Nymphs are only good for one thing."

Marsais flexed his hands. "Good for tying bandages?"

She snorted.

"I think I can manage a crude weave or two with these." He stood and beckoned her over to a jutting rock that might have been the statue's fallen ear. "But I'd like you to weave instead."

"Weave what?"

"A ward."

Isiilde stiffened in alarm. "Are you sure?"

"No." Marsais cleared his throat. "But we'll start simple—with a ward at each corner and a thread connecting them. This will be our cornerstone. First, weave a copper rune on the rock and a water rune in the air above. But *don't* let them touch. Then bind them together with a very, *very* thin strand of earth. Don't tie off the weave, though."

"What shall I do with it?"

"You are going to pull the earth rune to that rock over there—the statue's thumb, I believe—and repeat the process."

"All the way around?"

"Yes."

Isiilde chewed on her lip. "Lightning?"

"Exactly."

It was a complicated weave. "But Marsais, anyone could trigger the ward, even us."

"And how might you fix that problem?"

Isiilde had only ever *untangled* wards. She had never paid attention to how they were constructed. She simply enjoyed bringing chaos to order—the more complex the weave, the more delicious the mess.

"Tell them not to pass the rocks?"

Marsais grinned. "Simple, yet effective."

"But not ideal."

"No," he agreed.

"I could bind an earth rune to their boots."

"Aah, excellent, my dear." His eyes twinkled.

"Isn't that dangerous?"

"Yes—it could crush their feet if done improperly."

Isiilde's mouth went dry, and she paled in the darkness. "I can't, Marsais."

"I think you can. You've never botched up a weave."

She raised her brows.

"Rarely."

"I've always watched you first."

"True," he admitted. "Not to worry, with these bandages, I can manage. Will you watch? Yes? All right."

Marsais made exaggerated, but adequate runes on each rock, binding the ward together, and creating a perimeter of charged death. He paused at the earth bind. After flexing his fingers for a painful minute, he clenched his jaw and wove a more complicated earth rune over his boots.

Marsais stood, waiting. Isiilde fidgeted. And then he moved on to her feet, repeating the weave for her and over each of their companions.

Satisfied, he sat away from the fire, leaning against a boulder and keeping his eyes on the night. Isiilde settled herself under his arm.

"Will you try the ward tomorrow night?"

"I will."

"Good."

"I feel useless," she said after a time.

"Cautious is not useless. It's a step to wisdom. Everyone has different gifts and talents."

"I'm terrified of my fire," she confessed. "Everything I touch is destroyed—everything I attempt to do turns to ruin."

"Not everything. You do more for me than you realize."

Isiilde looked up at him in question.

"You saved my life on the ridge today."

"It was only a quick weave."

"Not just today, but before as well."

"I nearly killed everyone in the dungeon, even you."

Marsais sidestepped her observation. "Last year, I left the Isle because the Keening took hold."

"You told me."

"But I didn't tell you all."

"Imagine that," she said dryly.

Marsais' chest spasmed with a laugh.

"What didn't you tell me?" she asked.

"The farther I traveled, the deeper the Keening burrowed until it gripped my heart. It was only after that day on the beach with you that it released its hold."

His words touched her deeply. She did not immediately reply, but gazed at the moonlight shimmering over the stream.

"I understand now," she murmured.

"Hmm?"

"The Keening." She shifted so she could study his face. "Death is a mercy, isn't it, Marsais?"

The light in his eyes dimmed with sorrow. "Yes," he admitted. "But do you see that star?" He pointed towards the sky.

"Which one?"

In answer, Marsais reached out to pluck a star from the heavens.

Isiilde gasped as he pressed its light into her palm. She cupped the little star gently, gazing at its light in awe.

He had not muttered a word of the Lore.

"Death is kind and merciful, my dear," he whispered in her ear, "but never marvelous and never warm. There is no wonder in death, only rest."

Isiilde leaned against him, listening to the breath of his lungs while the little star glowed brightly in her hands.

CHAPTER 12

A FURIOUS STORM rolled in before sunset. Ice would have turned to snow if the air had been warmer. Instead, needles sliced from the sky, burning the lungs.

Brinehilde pinched a small nose and upended a draught of cold ward into her stubborn charge. The girl gagged, but one stern look from the priestess, and the child swallowed.

It was cold enough to freeze to death, like every winter on the island. The pot belly stoves smoldered in the sleeping areas, but coal and wood were precious, and she couldn't spare the coin to heat the rest of the orphanage.

She bade the children a warm night and shut their door. The chill in the hallway slipped under her collar and nipped her skin as she hurried toward her room.

Her heart was heavy. The allegations leveled against Marsais and Oenghus were on everyone's lips. All of it rubbish. Well, maybe not all of it. Oenghus was no saint.

Brinehilde paused at her bedroom door. Tiny needles prickled the back of her neck—born of threat rather than chill. She opened the door, grabbed her steel-capped quarterstaff, and marched down the hallway, alert and ready. Something drew her down the steps, towards the front door.

The priestess had learned long ago to listen to that prickle.

She shoved a metal slat aside, squinting into the storm. The wind howled, shooting ice through the narrow opening and into her eyes.

"Void," she muttered, slapping the slat back in place. Bracing against the cold, she hefted the heavy bar and opened the door.

A small boy lay on her doorstep with his hand thrust towards the threshold. Tiny winged faeries fluttered frantically around his body, trying to keep the boy warm.

Brinehilde scooped him up, and slammed the door with a curse. The Wisps scattered, then converged on the boy with renewed efforts. He was as cold as ice, covered in bloody grime, and wearing only a pair of oversized trousers. She felt for a pulse. It was thready and weak, but he was alive.

"Thank the Sylph." The Wisps buzzed in her ear, and she added, "And for your efforts, wee ones."

Brinehilde rushed the boy to her room, forced a draught of cold ward potion past his blue lips, stripped the wet breeches from his filthy body and tucked him against her own flesh, planting herself in front of the burning stove.

Sometime later, Brinehilde stood over the bundled-up boy, frowning down at his feverish face. The stripes on his wrists were telling. After a lifetime spent rescuing children from the worst of humanity, she knew rope burns when she saw them.

The boy had been bound, and rubbed his wrists raw while trying to escape. Abduction and slavery were illegal, but a dark underbelly flourished on the island. This boy was different, though. Something had been done to his tongue and throat.

While the rest of his body returned to a normal shade of brown, his tongue remained blue, and he wasn't swallowing well. Brinehilde was no Wise One, but she recognized a weave when she saw one.

Enchantments were beyond her skill.

Since Oenghus was off being charged with treason and foul deeds, there was only one person left she could trust—another Nuthaanian.

She needed Morigan, but the boy was too sick to travel and pigeons couldn't fly in this weather.

The priestess grabbed her cloak, roused one of the older girls to watch the boy, and charged into the storm to threaten a messenger.

CHAPTER 13

A CHILL ARRIVED during the night. It lingered on the leaves, and clung to the bark, seeping through layers and skin.

Isiilde took the excess cloth from Rivan's trousers and wrapped the length around her feet. Marsais watched wordlessly. There was nothing to be done about her lack of boots.

But at least there was food.

"More strawberries?" Acacia asked as Isiilde stuffed another one into her mouth. "Winter is nearly here—far too late for strawberries to grow."

Isiilde edged away from the woman, who was suspiciously eyeing the strawberries.

"Never look a gift horse in the eye," Marsais recited.

"It's a mouth, sir," Rivan corrected. "Never look a gift horse in the mouth."

"Yes, but I always prefer to look a creature in the eye when speaking to it."

"Then why not with a horse?" Isiilde asked.

"Because they bite, which would make looking a horse in the mouth even more foolish. Mules, my dear," he said, handing her a mushroom, "are far more reasonable."

"I think that's only true for you, Marsais."

"Why do you say that?"

"Because you sing like one."

Marsais placed a hand over his heart in mock injury. "Whatever wins your favor."

"But horse meat tastes better," said Oenghus. "In Nuthaan, the saying goes, never argue over a free pint."

The edge of Lucas' lip raised. "Now that I can agree on."

Isiilde decided it was the closest the scarred paladin could come to a grin.

"You don't find it strange that we're coming across untouched patches of strawberries?" Acacia interrupted.

"Never question a free pint."

"I thought it was 'never argue'?" Acacia asked.

"Same difference," he grunted.

Acacia shook her head. "If the pint is sitting in the middle of a forest, I would advise questioning it."

"I've never had a pint answer, have you, Oenghus?"

"Once or twice," he admitted to Marsais.

"I'm sure, of the two, the pint had more sense," Acacia noted dryly.

"Your concern for Isiilde is admirable," Marsais said. "But in this case, I think it's a blessing. And I, for one, would never question a gift from the Sylph."

"You're claiming the Sylph is growing strawberries in a forest for us?" Lucas asked.

"Not for us, no. But for Isiilde, yes."

Acacia and Lucas shared a look. The Blessed Order was generally lenient with those whose sanity was in question. And Marsais' lack of sanity was never in question to begin with.

"May I have one?"

Isiilde started in surprise. Rivan was walking alongside her. She eyed the man warily, suspicious of his friendliness, of his easy smile, and his strength.

"No," she said.

The hours melted away, but the frost remained. A cool mist ghosted between primordial trees. Something had changed in the forest. She gazed down the slope, ears alert, watching the mist writhe through the leaves.

It seemed the forest was waiting.

"I don't like this forest, Marsais."

"How so?"

"It feels wrong." She hesitated, eyeing the shadows. "It's restless, I think."

Beams of sunlight sliced through the canopy, giving birth to deeper shadows. The ferns and leaves quivered like an animal with its hackles raised.

"Always trust your instincts—it's not your imagination," Marsais said.

"I was hoping you would tell me I'm imagining things."

"Unlikely," he muttered. "Any thoughts?"

"I don't feel a breeze, but the leaves are moving."

Marsais raised his brows. "Do you feel like singing?"

Her shoulders slumped. "No, but I will if you wish it."

"It's all right, my dear. It's no use if your heart isn't in it," he said, then called the others over. "Isiilde doesn't like the forest. I think it wise to stay close and alert and tell your men to be wary of what they touch."

"And tell them to take off that bloody armor," Oenghus said. "A party of Fell giants could ambush us with the noise they're making."

"All the more reason to keep our armor on," Lucas defended. "We've already tied it down to dampen noise."

"Those coins of his aren't much quieter," Rivan pointed out.

Oenghus thrust a finger at Marsais' scruffy goatee. "Those coins are likely keeping us safe."

"They are?" Rivan squinted at the coins. "What do they do?"

Since Marsais was staring at a tree, Isiilde answered with an air of mystery. "What *don't* they do?"

"Well, what are they doing now?" Rivan asked.

Grey eyes shifted back to the present, focusing fully on the young man. The weight of the elf's gaze froze Rivan in his tracks.

"We're in Vaylin," Isiilde supplied, sensing his confusion.

Marsais looked around in surprise. "Are we? Hmm."

"Rivan was wondering why your coins are making so much noise."

Marsais' touched the coins under his chin. "They're a warning."

Isiilde frowned. "Do they chime when something is coming?"

"Yes." He smiled down at her. "I am."

No one laughed, not even Oenghus.

CHAPTER 14

Oenghus gripped a sturdy branch and edged forward until the toes of his boots hung over a chasm. Vines clung to the sides, climbing from the black pit. He could not see the bottom.

"We'll have to go around," Acacia said at his shoulder.

"That looks like a perfect nest for reapers," Lucas said.

"You're bloody right."

"We could levitate across," Marsais offered.

The paladins paled as one while Oenghus glared. "Isiilde's been leading you around like a mule when you go… wherever the bloody place you go. Do you really think that's a good idea, Scarecrow?"

A levitation weave took sustained concentration and Marsais had already lost focus again, absently scratching his chest.

"If we can't find a place to cross, then we'll risk it," Acacia said.

Isiilde edged forward, peering into the void. Blackbirds swam in its currents. On the far side, the forest continued, thick with trees and ferns.

"Careful, Nymph," a voice said at her side, followed by a hand wrapping protectively around her arm. She glanced at the captain. "These chasms are all over the realm."

"You've seen this before?" Isiilde asked.

"Many times. They're like scars over the land."

"An apt description, Captain," Marsais said, stepping up to the edge. "When the Orb shattered, a devastating power rippled from the core like a wave." His voice lowered to a hoarse whisper. "Entire kingdoms fell, swallowed in one gulp. A hand might have rested in your own one moment, and in the next it was gone. The earth screamed and the sky was filled with ash."

An ache of memory rippled through their bond, and Isiilde seized his hand, reminding him of the present.

"Come on, Scarecrow," Oenghus said, gripping his shoulder. "I don't want to fish your bony arse out of this pit."

Oenghus picked up the pace, searching for a crossing before nightfall, but Marsais' haunting words followed them along the chasm.

Eventually, Lucas breached the silence. "You talk as if you were there during the Shattering, Seer."

Marsais did not answer.

"He was," Acacia said. "So rumor claims."

"But that would make him..." Rivan faltered. "Really old."

"He's not old," Isiilde said. "He's just lived a long time."

Her voice nudged Marsais from his grim memories. "I wouldn't call all of those years living, my dear, but yes—I was born in the spring of 800, in the age now known as the Era of Blight."

Rivan furtively moved his fingers, mentally counting.

"2211 years ago," Isiilde said for the paladin's benefit.

"Some eighty years after Ramashan's reign was finally stopped," he murmured. "When the Druidic Orders still existed. And when Zahra and Dagenir were just two of many guardians who watched over the Orb."

"My Lord?"

"Hmm?" Marsais focused on Rivan, and the paladin faltered, looking as though he regretted speaking.

"That fellow on the Isle—the Kilnish Wise One," Rivan stuttered. "He called you Marsais zar'Vaylin. Wasn't zar'Vaylin the name of the first King of Vaylin?"

"Aha! The Blessed Order teaches history." Marsais was pleasantly surprised.

Rivan fidgeted nervously with his armor. And Isiilde recognized the signs of fear. She'd often seen it in Marsais' company—something about him made people afraid. She couldn't fathom their reaction. But then humans were strange.

"Of our enemies, mostly," Rivan said. "Vaylin being what it is and all."

"You mean what it is *now*. Vaylin didn't always serve the dark gods."

"Right, well, it always had the druids. Are you related to the first king?"

"You could say that."

"Wasn't the first king of Vaylin a seer, too? But he went mad?"

"Hmm, yes, I think you're right."

Oenghus chuckled. "Captain, your greenie is as curious as Isiilde. He must have some faerie blood in him."

"No, he's just nosey. He'll make an excellent Inquisitor."

"How old are you, lad?" Oenghus asked, eyeing Rivan.

"Nearly twenty, sir." That surprised Isiilde. He was only two years older than she was. "I wanted to join the Isle, but they said I was too young."

"So you joined the Blessed Order?" Oenghus didn't bother hiding his distaste.

"They're the only family I have, sir. Captain Mael found—" Rivan cleared his throat. "She recruited me. No one says no to the captain." The light remark sounded forced.

"You definitely don't have a drop of Nuthaanian in you," Oenghus said. "I say no to her all the time."

"And here I was going to ask you to be my bed warmer."

Oenghus looked sharply at Acacia, who appeared utterly serious. Marsais and Lucas laughed, but Rivan kept on with his questions.

"Archlord... er, sir, what did you do to the Hound's spear?"

"I bound his weapon to his armor. But first, I had to whittle away his defenses."

"But how'd you survive the Sylph's wrath?" Rivan pressed. "The Hound was a Silverknight. He stood against Indrazor, a god." There was awe in his voice.

"Guthre had the Sylph's blessing when he fought Indrazor," Marsais explained. "And 'god' is such a relative word, really."

"Be careful where you tread," Lucas warned. "To claim the Guardians of Morchaint aren't gods is to suggest the Guardians of Iilenshar aren't either."

"Ah, but when did they become gods, Sir Lucas?"

The paladin did not answer. Marsais' recounting of the Shattering was too fresh in their minds. What did one say to a man as old as their gods?

"WELL, HERE'S OUR CROSSING," Acacia said without enthusiasm.

Isiilde frowned at the fallen redwood that stretched across the chasm. Its twisted roots served as an anchor against gravity, but the tangle reminded Isiilde of the Forsaken with its grasping tentacles. She shivered in the tree's shadow.

"Are we crossing now?" Rivan asked.

Lucas eyed the ruins on the other side. "I don't like this. It feels like an ambush."

Oenghus grunted in agreement. "Any dire warnings of doom, Scarecrow?"

Marsais shrugged. "Do harvesters ever heed the jaws of a Rraalish finger trap when stealing its succulent nectar?"

Acacia and Oenghus glanced at each other, nodded, and both turned—heading away from the bridge to find a suitable place to camp.

They'd cross the chasm in the morning.

The group made camp by a stream, fashioning a crude shelter and risking a small fire, while Marsais and Isiilde set wards.

With Marsais watching like a hawk, she wove copper and water and a thin strand of earth, gently tugging it towards the next rock. But the strand broke, and the weave collapsed, snapping towards its origin. Water touched copper, and a backlash of energy lashed towards the weaver.

One moment, Marsais was at her side, and the next, he stepped in front of her. The surge of power slammed into his chest instead of hers with a chaotic chime of coins. It blew him off his feet.

"Are you all right, Marsais?" she gasped, scrambling over to him.

"A small setback, nothing more," he said, lifting his head. He groaned and put his head back on the ground.

"What the Void?" Oenghus demanded, stomping over to the pair.

"My weave collapsed," Isiilde said. "Marsais shielded me."

Oenghus grunted. "About bloody time he did something useful."

"I'm sorry," she said.

Oenghus snorted and hauled Marsais upright by the arm. "Don't worry. The ol'Bastard usually does it to himself."

When he was on his feet, Isiilde stepped into his arms, and buried her face against his chest. He smelled like the sky after a storm.

Marsais caught Oenghus' eye over her head. Isiilde had never botched a weave in her life. Her guardian briefly rested a hand on her shoulder before stomping towards the stream.

"No harm done," Marsais said. A smile touched his eyes, and she reached up to smooth his hair. It crackled and shifted with her touch.

"That was a very ill occurrence."

"Only a slight mishap," he corrected.

"Something is wrong with me," she whispered.

"You are cold, hungry, and exhausted—like the rest of us. I'll finish the wards."

As she turned towards camp, a sense of failure pressed on her shoulders, clouding her mind. She sat by the fire without feeling its heat.

Acacia was crouched by the fire, laying a row of gutted fish on a hot stone. "That was quick thinking earlier today on the ridge."

Isiilde rested her chin on her knees and raised a shoulder. "It was a simple weave."

"Most nymphs don't even speak, let alone use the Gift."

"My name is Isiilde."

"Acacia Mael."

Isiilde stared at the woman's offered hand, then raised her eyes to an expectant gaze. No one had ever tried to shake her hand before.

"Usually, you shake it."

Isiilde warily shook hands, fearing the woman was about to play some cruel trick, as Zianna often had. But Acacia merely shook it.

"I'm usually reduced to a title, too."

Isiilde narrowed her eyes. "Captain is said with respect. Nymph is not."

"You'd be surprised," Acacia said dryly. "But it's true. Most nymphs are not so well-spoken. The nymphs I've met barely uttered two words."

Isiilde scooted closer to the fire. "You've met other nymphs?"

"I've overseen several disputes regarding nymphs. The Blessed Order prefers to send women to handle the trials—for obvious reasons. Do you eat fish?"

"Hmm?"

"Fish." Acacia gestured to the baking trout, and Isiilde pulled her thoughts back to the present.

"Anything that doesn't breathe air is fine."

"Interesting."

"Are there a lot of nymphs? I've never met anyone else like me."

Acacia's eyes turned soft as she regarded the slight creature huddled by the fire. "They're rare, but King Syre of Mearcentia has four."

"Has?" Isiilde did not like that word.

"In his palace."

"Are they happy with him?"

Acacia looked surprised by the question. No one ever asked whether a nymph was happy. "I suppose they are. They have everything they could ever want. King Syre indulges their every whim. They live like queens."

Isiilde's ears twitched. "Are they free to leave?"

"Of course not. It would be dangerous for them."

"Do you have an owner, Captain?"

Acacia hesitated. "I see what you're saying, but King Syre protects his nymphs."

"Where is their mark?"

"Where every mark is... except yours. Around their necks."

Isiilde surged to her feet. "Then it's nothing but a *slave's collar*."

The fire roared in response to her fury, and Acacia rolled backward, dodging the explosion of flame.

The fish turned to ash. Coins chimed, chanting filled the forest, and the heat was sucked into a vortex of air. Marsais gathered the flame, hurling the fireball into the stream. The water popped and sizzled, boiling fish alive.

Isiilde bolted.

STRICKEN WITH FEAR, light of foot and in her element, Isiilde flew over the earth. Branches scraped together, ferns quivered, and the moon watched her flight.

Marsais ran on her heels. He reached out to her through their bond, but fear and pain consumed her. He could not see her, but he could *feel* her. So Marsais let their bond pull him in her wake.

He ducked beneath branches, leapt over fallen logs, and stretched his long legs, striving after a dream. Branches lashed his face and needles grabbed at his clothes.

He pressed on, catching glimpses of her. With hair as bright as fire, and skin as pale as moonlight, she glistened in the darkness. He did not have breath to spare for her name.

Marsais caught up to her by a stream. She was in the water, scrubbing ruthlessly at her skin. Her clothing littered the bank. The trees groaned overhead, and he slowed, approaching with caution. His fingers flew, and his breath stirred, sending a Whisper to Oenghus to return to camp.

"Isiilde." He stopped at the water's edge. "It's freezing. Come out of the stream."

"I'm filthy!" she growled.

The surrounding water sizzled.

"Look at me, Isiilde." She did, but her eyes were unfocused, living in another moment—another memory. He took a step forward.

"Stay back," she warned. A fiery dragon, the nymph's mark, swam beneath her skin like a pacing predator.

"Why, Isiilde?"

Rage rippled through their bond, cooled by emptiness, and stoked with shame. She balled up her fist and drove it ruthlessly into her stomach.

"I can't." She punched her gut again, as if something festered within. "I feel—" Her knuckles slapped against flesh, unable to put words to her agony.

Broken, he finished silently.

When her fist rose again, Marsais stepped into the stream, seizing her wrists. But instead of fight, instead of fire, or resistance, Isiilde's fury propelled her into his arms. In a moment, her hands clutched his neck, her legs wrapped around his waist, and she brought her lips down on his own with vicious need.

Their bond churned with confusion, lust, and anger. Her nails bit into his flesh, and he met her aggression with rough hands. For frantic seconds and breathless moments, passion consumed the pair.

Marsais fought his way through the mental chaos to regain his senses. "Not like this." His voice was harsh and breathless, and she answered with hungry lips.

Marsais gripped her shoulders. "*Stop.*"

Isiilde froze, then let go, taking a step back. A drop of blood slipped from her lips.

Marsais cupped her face in his hands. "Don't fill your emptiness with rage. Not like this—not between you and me."

Isiilde stared quietly into his eyes. He could feel her trembling, deep in her bones, and finally a sob tore from her throat as she collapsed into his arms.

Marsais sat on the bank, buried his face in her hair, and held her as she wept.

CHAPTER 15

MARSAIS STROKED a cascade of silken tresses. The campfire warmed Isiilde's back while he warmed the rest of her. Dried of tears, she'd finally passed out from exhaustion.

But sleep eluded Marsais. And as he stared into the night, he turned a single question around in his mind: How does one control chaos? He knew now that Isiilde was pure chaos. The essence of it ran through her veins as surely as time ran through his.

With a sigh, he eased himself away from the sleeping nymph, and covered her with the captain's tunic. Frost had gathered on the ground, covering two slumbering forms by the fire. Oenghus and Rivan slept while Acacia and Lucas took first watch.

Marsais crouched by the stream and unwrapped his bandages. Gritting his teeth, he thrust his hands into icy water, and watched the byways of time swirl in the moonlight. His coins chimed, nudging him into the present. Lucas stood behind him, or more accurately, where the man would soon be standing.

Visions of the immediate future were usually accurate. Marsais waited for time to catch up to itself. Sure enough, Lucas and Acacia soon stopped at his side. They wanted answers.

But Acacia's question surprised him—a rare thing. "How is Isiilde? I didn't mean to upset her."

"Hmm, words are rarely wrong, Captain, but rather the memories they invoke. A soft bed, a quiet cottage, and warm food would do her good."

Lucas scowled down at him. "Wishes are useless. You said you knew about Tharios and his schemes. Did you know about your friend Isek Beirnuckle, too?"

"The answer should be obvious," Marsais replied with measured words. His tone gave the paladins pause. "And yes, I completely agree with your next words: where a nymph is involved, there is always trouble. But remember, Sir Lucas, men who make the trouble, not the nymph."

The scarred paladin adjusted his helm, as if the metal would keep the seer out of his mind.

"What are your plans?" Acacia asked.

"Currently, I'm soaking my hands while I watch a sea monster gnaw off my fingers."

Acacia narrowed her eyes at the stream.

"Answer the question," Lucas growled. "Enough with your games. What of Tharios and his schemes?"

"Ah, well, what do you plan on doing about him?"

"I'm not the one who handed him a map to a dark god," Lucas pointed out.

"No, but you know about it, and it's in your district—is it not? So really, I should ask what the Blessed Order will do about Tharios."

"It's your problem, Seer."

"It is a legitimate question. I wonder, what would you do if I wasn't here?"

Acacia placed a hand on her lieutenant. "Depending on where we are in Vaylin, I would make for a large city, Vlarthane, or if we're in the south, I would head to Nefir and pay for a message to be delivered."

"To whom?"

"High Inquisitor Multist may accept bribes, but he is no Void worshipper."

"That you know of." Marsais arched a brow, and silence answered.

"For the moment, let's assume he's not. If we send a Whisper, and if by some chance Tharios is not intercepting messages, what would our good Inquisitor do, hmm? March up to the Storm Gate in his pretty armor, knock, and arrest Tharios and his cabal of Unspoken?"

Lucas grunted. The High Inquisitor loved his comfort and was utterly useless.

"Can you contact Iilenshar?" Acacia asked.

"Why would *he* be able to speak to Iilenshar—only the Blessed Order can." Lucas looked from Acacia to the elf, but his captain was quite serious.

"We're discussing what *you* would do," Marsais reminded.

"As I said, I'd send a message."

"And how long might the journey to Vlarthane or Nefir take?"

"Depending on where we are in Vaylin, it could take far more time than you say we have."

"Oh, my good Captain, there is always time and always will be. Past, present, and future are an indefinite weave. So let me watch and listen for a time. I ask only for your patience—for your own plans are little better than my caution."

CHAPTER 16

Morigan Freyr stood in the repulsive throne room of the Order of Wise Ones. She hated the place. Its dizzyingly high columns and mutilated carvings had one purpose: to intimidate.

She missed the great halls of Nuthaan, with their bonfires and feasting, with the press of roaring voices and raucous singing.

Morigan missed her home.

Her hands curled into fists as she gazed at the newly appointed Archlord. He was everything the Order was looking for: focused, poised, and powerful. But Tharios made her skin crawl.

A ripple of shock had traveled through the Isle after the duel. Dead guards. Slain Wise Ones. And Marsais charged with Bloodmagic.

It wasn't hard to spot Oenghus' work: crushed skulls and broken bodies. But then there were those guards who'd been sliced and stabbed instead.

There was the fire, too. Only Isiilde could have gutted a dungeon. The bodies were impossible to identify, save for chunks of melted armor. Investigators claimed it was the remains of the three missing paladins.

Morigan kept her mouth shut.

In a matter of hours, members of the Blessed Order swarmed the castle to investigate, and one witness after another gave evidence against Marsais and Oenghus. But even more damning was the solid proof in Marsais' private research chambers.

Everything fit neatly together. And in less than four days, the Order had turned its back on the man who'd served it for nearly one hundred years.

The Circle of Nine cast their vote for Tharios. It was the fastest turnover of Archlords the Isle had ever seen.

Morigan kept her anger in check as the final words were spoken by a circle of Wise Ones surrounding the new Archlord. Tharios was dressed in well-cut robes of crimson silk, and stared forward with determination, hands held up, palms facing outward.

Thira and a Mearcentian Wise One by the name of Sidonie filled the two vacant seats left by Marsais and Oenghus. One by one the eight traced the Weave of Confirmation until Tharios stood illuminated by a column of swirling blue.

The enchantment hung in the air, but only for a moment. A wind swept through the throne room, and the columns flared in acceptance, bathing Tharios in bluish light. When the light faded, a cheer rose in the hall as Tharios displayed the Archlord's Runic Eye on the palm of his hand.

It was done.

Tharios sat on the obsidian throne, and the audience fell silent. "These are dark times," he said, his voice carrying to all ears via the Voiceless. "The shock of betrayal is still fresh in our hearts, but the blight of our former Archlord has been cleansed. We will remain stagnant no longer. I will lead this Order into the light of a new era."

By the gods, Morigan thought, resisting the urge to roll her eyes. She'd heard that one before.

The audience applauded with genuine enthusiasm, and when the crowd dispersed, she forced herself to mingle, eavesdropping on conversations.

In the Order of Wise Ones, Morigan was renowned as a healer. Most did not know her history. She preferred it that way.

Rumors and idle speculation filled her ears. Some expressed sadness, but most claimed to have suspected Marsais and Oenghus all along. A few braggarts boasted they would round up the fugitives themselves.

Morigan would like to see anyone try to 'round up' Oenghus. She spotted Isek and Thira with their heads bent together in conversation.

Isek had been Marsais' trusted advisor. And yet he'd testified against Marsais—reluctantly, of course. And in a state of shock.

"But I can't deny what I saw," Isek told the paladins. "Marsais commanded a fiend, he spoke Abyssal, and what he ordered Isiilde to do to those paladins... I'm afraid Marsais was a disturbed man. His madness finally consumed him."

Morigan wished she could get close enough to hear their conversation, but considering her relationship with Oenghus and Isiilde, she was already under suspicion.

Caution was the wisest course until she could figure out who to trust and what the Void she would do about Tharios now that Marsais was gone. She'd warned him not to get cocky. And now she was left to clean up the mess—whatever that might be.

CHAPTER 17

Isiilde stood in a frozen wasteland. She was naked and freezing, but not from the frost beneath her feet or the sky stretching into eternity.

A ring of shadowy forms surrounded her, their eyes burning with hunger. Tearing her gaze from the wraiths, she glanced down. Each of her delicate feet rested on a body as white as the ice below: Oenghus and Marsais.

Searching for escape, she turned her eyes skyward. The sun and moon sped in dizzying circles—a day's cycle in the flutter of an eyelash. Storm clouds rolled overhead, blocking out the chaotic heavens. And a dark, brooding thing stirred in the storm.

The clouds parted, revealing a barbed chain as thick as the Spine. It dropped to the earth, slick with blood.

Isiilde could not move. Ice climbed up her legs, rooting her to the backs of the dead. She tried to scream, but no sound emerged, only a raw, familiar burn.

She clawed at her throat as a chain slithered around her neck like an iron snake with digging barbs. The shadows converged, and the chain snapped tight, yanking her higher and higher towards the blackened sky.

Inch by dreadful inch, the unseen horror dragged the squirming nymph towards oblivion.

"Isiilde!" A familiar voice shattered her nightmare, and she jerked awake with a strangled scream. "You're dreaming," Marsais whispered in her ear.

She was safe in his arms.

"Am I still dreaming?" Every bone in her body ached.

"I'm afraid not." There was a hint of amusement in his soft reply.

"I think I'm frozen." A campfire burned at her back but offered little relief.

"You need to get moving," he said, rubbing her vigorously to ease her discomfort.

When he touched her hip, she flinched with pain. Marsais' hands stilled. He propped himself on an elbow and discreetly shifted her clothing. His breath caught. The skin was bruised where he'd gripped her hip in the stream.

"I do apologize, Isiilde."

"I was the one who..." Heat rose to her ears and she trailed off. Grey eyes sought hers, but she looked away, conscious of the others moving around the little camp.

"How are your feet?"

"Everything hurts," she admitted, shivering with cold.

"All the more reason to get you moving."

The forest was covered with frost, and tiny icicles hung from needles. Oenghus and Rivan crouched by a nearby bank, washing away grime, while Acacia and Lucas slept beneath a layer of frost.

Isiilde limped stiffly beside Marsais, puffing air into her numb hands, trying to restore feeling.

When they approached, Rivan hastily donned his shirt, covering his muscled back. He stood, then froze, his eyes widening at the pair. "Good morning," he blurted out. "Well, it's not good, exactly. It'd be nicer if it was warmer, I mean, and not so..." He trailed off, gesturing at the forest.

"Quite," Marsais agreed. "Why don't you wake the others, Rivan."

"Yes, m'lord, of course."

Rivan bowed, and walked away, but his eyes remained fixed on them until he tripped over a root.

"Blasted faerie," Oenghus snorted.

Isiilde crouched beside the bank, scrubbing the night from her eyes. The water felt like ice, but then so did everything else. "What about them?" she demanded of her guardian.

"The rest of us look like unwashed heathens..."

"You *are* one," Marsais pointed out.

"...and the pair of you look like..." Oenghus gestured at them in disgust.

Isiilde glanced at Marsais. His long white hair practically shimmered in the early morning sun. His movements were graceful, his face serene. He looked like he *belonged* beneath the trees.

What did she look like?

"Restored?" Marsais suggested.

Oenghus grunted. "Bloody dandy."

"Well, I don't *feel* restored," Isiilde said.

"Let me look you over." Oenghus unwrapped and examined her feet. "They're fine today, but the temperature is dropping."

"The ground is warmer than the air."

"For now. If it snows, you'll have to ride on my back. How's the rest of you?"

"Just bruised. It's nothing."

Oenghus frowned at her. "Make sure you watch your toes." His lips brushed her forehead. "Did that bag o' bones keep you warm last night?"

The bag o' bones was crouched at the bank. The top half of his robe hung around his waist as he splashed water on his face, letting rivulets roll down his muscled chest. Marsais had removed the bandages on his hands during the night. The swelling had gone down, but his fingers were stiff and the flesh was mottled with black and yellow.

"Well enough," she replied.

"Make sure you stay close to one of us with those two paladins around. You understand?"

She did, unfortunately. "I was planning on it."

Oenghus nodded. "I'll see if I can find you something to eat."

"If only we had my rucksack," Marsais mused when they were alone. "I'm sure there'd be a pair of boots in there for you. I'd offer my own, but I think they might be more hindrance than help considering the size of my feet."

"Is that an innuendo?"

Marsais started in surprise. Then splashed her.

"Bastard," she said with a glare. "At least I can climb on Oen's back. I doubt he'd let you if I take your boots."

"We do what we must."

She snorted. But her reaction took her by surprise. It felt like an echo of some long ago time—a shadow of someone else.

Marsais sensed her sudden disquiet and looked at her with understanding in his eyes.

"I'm sorry, Marsais. I don't know why—" She looked away. "I acted a fool."

"Isiilde." He pulled her gaze back with a word. "After what you've been through, there is no right or wrong way to act. You cannot help what you feel."

"But not right."

"Isn't it?" The scars on his flesh rippled and stretched with his movements as he tied back his hair with a strip of cloth. "At being betrayed and attacked? I'm certainly angry for you. And with Isek for betraying us."

"But you don't take it out on me," she whispered.

"No..." he hesitated. "Rage is understandable, but don't let it consume you."

"Easier said than done," she muttered. "Nothing makes sense at the moment. I don't even understand myself. But I wasn't angry at you."

"I know." His eyes shone with wisdom, and his words held kindness.

"I only—" She blinked away tears. "I want to *feel* something, anything other than this." Her hand curled into a fist and she pressed it against her stomach.

"You will when things have settled. Then you can ravish me all you like."

A small smile tugged at the corner of her lips.

"WHAT ARE YOUR VISIONS LIKE?" Isiilde asked as they unraveled the protective wards around the camp.

Marsais frowned at her question. She'd never dared ask before. Or perhaps she'd never thought to ask.

After a time, he sighed. "I stopped telling people what I see long ago. I find it easier that way. In rare cases, I may divulge the destination, but minor details are best left in the darkness where they belong."

"No, that's not what I meant." She searched for words, and Marsais waited, his eyes warm and patient. "How do you know if they're visions or just dreams?"

"Can I ask you a question without sparking your ire?"

Isiilde blushed, recalling their fight in the King's Walk. "I was angry when I said you annoyed me."

"In that case, how do you know the difference between fire and water?"

"That's simple."

"Humor me, and explain it."

"Fire is hot and water is... wet."

"Can't water be hot?"

She narrowed her eyes. "Yes, but fire can't be wet."

"What is wet?"

"Liquid."

"Hmm, you know, I once watched a volcano erupt in the Bastard-lands. Liquid fire burst from its crown, rolling along the ground in glowing rivers. It nearly killed me."

Isiilde's heart began to gallop, but not out of concern for Marsais. He smiled at her knowingly.

When she found her breath, she argued, "But it's obvious what the difference is."

"Precisely my point. The difference between my visions, reality, and dreams is obvious, but it's near impossible to explain how and why."

"You just know?" she asked, stopping in front of a shimmering web stretched from one frosty tree to the next. "What if you didn't know you knew?"

Marsais scratched at the stubble on his cheek. "My dear, does this line of questioning have anything to do with your nightmare?"

Isiilde shivered in answer.

"That wasn't a vision," he said.

"How do you know?"

Marsais raised his hand, brandishing the mark of their bond: a fiery dragon's head nestled in his palm. "I woke up when I heard you whimpering, and I saw what you saw."

"Were you scared, too?"

"It was only a dream—if a disturbing one. My visions are not so obscure and full of symbolism."

"But you and Oen were dead."

He turned to face her. "Do you know how often I've watched my own death and all the horrid ways I can arrive there?"

Isiilde's breath caught. "That's why you always cover your mirrors with a veil." She paled with shock and her vision blurred. "That's horrible, Marsais."

"By the gods, your tears are even worse to bear now that we're bonded." His fingertips brushed the curve of her ear. "Let me explain. The future is not etched in stone; although even if it were—stone can be manipulated by the elements. The future is a thing of interconnecting Pathways. Take this splendid spiderweb."

Marsais tapped a strand ever so gently, and a large, palm-sized spider crept out of its nest towards his hand. Its body was black, save for a single teardrop of vibrant orange.

Isiilde took a step back.

"Ah, the Weeping Mark. Extremely venomous. If you see one, leave it alone."

"Why are you teasing it, then?" she squeaked, taking another hasty step backward.

The spider bent its eight hairy legs, looking like it intended to spring. Despite its aggressive stance, Marsais continued tapping the strand.

"This is the problem with visions. We both see the web in its entirety, but what path will the spider take? What choice will it make? Will it go right or left? Will the spider follow the vibration or spring for you?" Marsais looked at her in question, and she gulped. She did not know.

"We both see the same web, the same spider, the same catalyst. That's what sets seers apart. You see, my dear, knowing the past is the key to unraveling the future. I know this spider's habits, and therefore it's easier for me to predict its actions in the same way you and I can predict each other's moves in King's Folly. The Weeping Mark is cautious and intelligent: it didn't get this big by charging every vibration. So it will go back to its nest."

As if by command, the spider retreated, folding itself back into a cocoon.

"And there you have it."

Isiilde chewed on her lip in thought, following the maze of spun crystal. The web's layout reminded her of King's Folly, and its complicated pattern of cycles and rune pieces. The implications hurt her head. Small wonder Marsais was so distracted. It was like he was playing a never-ending game where the pieces constantly shifted after every move.

"That's why you didn't know what Isek would do," she realized aloud. "His betrayal didn't fit with his past—all those years you called him a friend."

"And Isek made his choice too quickly." His quiet words were heavy with regret. "Time does not account for chaos."

"I'm beginning to see why nymphs are treated as they are," she admitted softly. "Perhaps we *should* be cloistered away from the rest of the lands."

Her mere presence had sparked betrayal, ruined a family, caused death and heartache, and she had been used as a pawn in a plot that threatened the realm.

"It's no excuse for Isek's actions, or anyone else's, for that matter." Marsais placed a finger under her chin, tilting her head so she might meet his gaze. "Do not blame yourself for the weaknesses of others, Isiilde."

She shrugged. "How can I not? I'm a nymph."

"You are, true," he admitted. "But nymphs aren't supposed to ponder such matters. Really, my dear, if you blame yourself, then I'll be forced to blame myself too, and we'd be a rather pathetic pair, don't you agree?"

"Why are you to blame? You don't intoxicate men with your mere presence," she said dryly.

"Are you implying that I'm not handsome enough?"

Isiilde rolled her eyes. "That *must* be what happened last night. Your intoxicating scent consumed me."

"Obviously," he said, flashing a charming smile. "You know, Isiilde, I'm beginning to suspect you're not a nymph after all. They don't usually worry."

"If I'm not a nymph, then what am I?"

"You could be an Assumer in disguise." His eyes twinkled with mirth.

"Well, if I am, I don't know it."

"That could be part of your disguise. You are talented."

"Wouldn't talent like that practically make me a nymph?"

"Ah, but there's a way to spot an Assumer."

"There is?" Her ears perked up with interest.

Marsais gave a slight nod, and drew her close, kissing her tenderly. In response, Isiilde wrapped her arms around his neck, savoring the taste of him. Worry and fear fluttered out of her mind, and when he finally pulled away, she couldn't help but smile into his eyes.

"I was wrong," he breathed. "You are definitely a nymph."

"I believe you're right," she agreed. Their single night together filled her thoughts, leaving her body aching with desire. "I'm also much warmer."

"I can tell."

"But I'm still hungry."

Marsais gestured to the ward. "One more to unravel, and we'll see what Oenghus has for you."

Considerably cheered, Isiilde turned to the ward, and eagerly laid her hands on the weave, bringing chaos to order.

CHAPTER 18

Two cowled guards escorted Isek Beirnuckle towards the newly appointed Archlord's study. All traces of its former occupant were being removed, including Isek's access to the pinnacle.

The Spine had seen more activity in the past week than it had in the past hundred years. Tharios was driven; Isek would give him that.

As a guard dragged a charred body down the hall, his escort pulled him to a stop. The corpse was missing both hands.

How many unwilling Wise Ones had died trying to unravel one of Marsais' complex wards? He could be absolutely fiendish at times.

"How difficult can one ward be?" Tharios demanded, staring at the vault. And yet, Isek noted, the new Archlord hadn't made an attempt.

Eiji stood off to the side, studying the rune-etched door. In theory, it was impossible to trace wards onto witchwood, which is precisely why the Storm Gate had proved such a puzzle to the Wise Ones. So how had Marsais managed it with his vault?

"There isn't any pattern to it," Eiji marveled. She looked up as Isek approached and a slow smile spread across her all too innocent-looking face.

"Much like Marsais' mind," Tharios said, turning to the traitor.

Isek bowed deeply. "Archlord."

"I need this vault opened, Isek."

It was a death sentence. Isek was no match for Marsais' wards.

"I'm sure you're intelligent enough to realize that as it stands right now, you are expendable."

"And a liability," Isek added, weaving a crown across his knuckles.

"I'm glad we can be honest with one another." Tharios stepped aside, gesturing towards a knot of runes comparable to the Storm Gate. "Fail, and I won't mourn you. But succeed, and your usefulness to me will have increased considerably."

"I've already been plenty useful. I fulfilled my part of the bargain. You, on the other hand, never delivered yours. I still want my nymph."

"Plans have already been set into motion. My Hunters will bring her back. But meanwhile, I need this vault opened more than your loyalty."

"You gave me your word."

Tharios spread his hands. "And you said you could control the nymph. You didn't uphold your end of the bargain."

Isek wove his gold coin over his hand twice in consideration. There was no use arguing over details; Tharios had the upper hand.

"I've never had a knack for Wards," Isek admitted. "But I can be of use to you in other ways. Not everyone is convinced of Marsais' guilt."

"I don't need the obvious stated."

"Yes, but I have the means to spy on the disbelieving."

"You don't think I do? Stop trying to delay, Isek. The one thing I don't have is time."

"It's your choice, Archlord. I'm not in any position to resist, but my death will certainly raise suspicion."

"I don't care about suspicion."

"In that case, I know someone who can open this vault."

Eiji cocked her head, and Tharios narrowed his eyes, his lips forming a single question. "Who?"

"Witman the Wondrous."

"The legendary enchanter is on the island?" Eiji asked in shock.

"Where?" Tharios demanded.

"Do you really think I'll tell you when that knowledge is the only thing keeping me alive?"

Tharios gave a slow sort of laugh. "Of course not. But will the enchanter help us?"

"For a price," Isek answered. "Witman the Wondrous always has a price."

CHAPTER 19

Isiilde stood at the edge of the chasm, studying the far side. Streams of sunlight pierced the high canopy, but few touched the earth.

"I don't like those ruins," she said with a shiver, leaning closer to Marsais. She never wanted to meet another Reaper as long as she lived.

"There's plenty of daylight."

"And shadows."

"Reapers prefer the night, not shadows."

"Maybe so, but the other side feels... angry."

"It is."

"That's not reassuring."

"I'll lie next time. Stay close."

Oenghus was tugging on his braided beard by the fallen tree. Isiilde knew that gesture well—he was uneasy, and his mood was not helping her nerves.

"Are we going to stand here staring all day?" Lucas asked.

Oenghus frowned at the paladins. "It might be better if everyone else went across first. I'm not the lightest of men."

Acacia nodded to Lucas, who climbed on top of the log and began to edge across. The log was sturdy, but the wind currents in the gorge battered it from below, making it sway over the chasm. When the knight touched the ground on the other side, Acacia followed, moving confidently across without pause.

Isiilde understood Oenghus' hesitation. He *was* a large man, over seven feet tall, with solid muscle, weighing five times more than most men.

"Oen is afraid of heights," Marsais confided, sensing her thoughts.

Isiilde eyed her guardian in a new light. "I had no idea."

Marsais gestured towards the blackness. "There's nothing to fight."

"Except fear," she murmured. A ripple of surprise traveled through their bond.

"Yes," he agreed. "Fear of falling, fear of succumbing."

"Fear of surrendering."

Grey eyes sharpened on her—searching.

The edge of her lip twitched upwards. "Don't worry, Marsais. You taught me to levitate, remember?"

Marsais opened his mouth, but before he could reply, she hopped on the log and hurried across, quickly stepping around branches and obstacles. Only she paused in the middle to stare into the abyss. Birds spiraled in its embrace. Curiosity consumed her, and before thought could catch up, she summoned the Lore, weaving a neat ball of light.

"Isiilde," Oenghus growled.

She dropped her light into the chasm and watched it fall until the darkness swallowed it whole.

"Like a pebble in an ocean," Marsais mused beside her shoulder.

Isiilde jerked in surprise. He was floating in midair, legs crossed as comfortably as if sitting on a cushion. "Does it ever end?" she asked.

"Some scars run deeper than others. They cut to the very heart of this realm."

Isiilde did not think he was talking about the chasm. "Could you turn me into a bird?"

"I could," he said slowly.

"But you won't?"

"You would likely forget who you are and never return. There's a certain amount of self-control involved with transmutation. It's easy to lose yourself. And I'd miss you too much to risk it."

She smiled at his confession before continuing across the bridge.

The waiting forest, the rising ruins, and the shadows gave her pause. A murder of crows sat on the branches overhead, mocking her fear with screeching calls.

Marsais unfolded his legs, unraveled the weave, and let his boots touch the ground. "Your soldier is pale as a worm, Captain."

Rivan was halfway across. The log shook with his legs as he grabbed for every branch before taking a step. He might as well crawl.

"So is your berserker."

"Hmm," Marsais agreed, offering a hand to Isiilde. She took it, more for courage than support, and hopped down.

The ground made her shiver. Something was wrong on this side of the gorge.

"There's Blight here." Lucas pointed his longsword at some sickly vines.

The trees overhead creaked in answer.

"They're moving," Acacia hissed, readying her shield and sword. They weren't just moving; they were slithering like snakes and gathering around the group. "We should find another way."

"We don't have time," Marsais said. His fingers flashed. When the weave was complete, he plucked Rivan from the log and whisked him through the air with a levitation weave. The paladin landed hard, falling to his knees.

"Don't you dare, Scarecrow."

"We need you here now, Oen." Words turned to power, plucking the giant off his feet with a gesture. Then the forest erupted. Black vines lashed from the gorge, detached themselves from ruin, and snaked towards the intruders.

"Back across!" Acacia ordered.

Marsais hurled Oenghus at the attackers like a stone. He hit the ground, rolled, and came up fighting. "You bloody, flea-bitten, cock sucking, dandy son of a lord!" Every word was emphasized with a pounding swing.

As the others fought, Marsais switched focus. An ethereal hand materialized above the bridge, and he brought it down on the bridge before anyone could stop him. Their only link to the other side split and fell into the chasm.

There was nowhere to go but forward.

Crows descended, beaks and claws scratching at their heads, as brambles of bristling spikes broke from trees, writhing with spores of sickly mold.

Isiilde coughed, her eyes watering as she staggered in the middle of the fighting warriors. A vine snaked around her legs, and then another, slamming her to the ground.

The barbed vines tightened around her waist and pulled her back towards the chasm. She screamed, clawing at the dirt, but the warriors were fighting off their own vines and bramble men.

Two spiky attackers charged Oenghus, exploding on impact with a spray of thorns. He grunted, absorbing the impact as the vines tried to pull him towards the edge. Finally, a vine snapped under strain, and he freed his arm, swinging at the next knot of swarming bramble men.

Frantically, Isiilde wove a lightning weave. A bolt exploded from her clumsy fingertips, crackling along her legs. Pain shot through her bones and set her teeth aching, but the vines around her legs loosened, oozing a sickly black rot.

Marsais cursed. His coins chimed in the chaos, and he tapped her head with a single finger. A warm, tingling sensation spread over her body, and the vines recoiled from his weave, slithering away.

A bramble leapt from a high branch, falling like a stone into the middle of the group. Isiilde curled into a defensive ball, and Marsais stepped over her, shielding her from impact. Thorns slammed into his back, piercing skin and dropping him to his knees with an explosion of twigs.

Acacia caught the second suicidal hedge on her shield, then sliced through tugging vines. With a chanting shout, her shield flared to life. Searing light ripped through the wave of vegetation, illuminating horror in all its twisted glory.

The forest pulsed with malevolence—lashing trees, thorns, clawing carrion, and snake-like vines pushed them towards doom.

Marsais flung his arms wide with a shout, sending a cracking force rippling from his fingertips. The first wave of bramble and thorn exploded, but another wave rose to take its place.

"Shields!" Marsais shouted.

The bramble unleashed a hail of needle-sized thorns, but Oenghus' shield appeared in front of Isiilde's eyes, and another at her back. Pain slashed up her arm.

Marsais thrust out his hand. A searing light erupted from his palm, opening a pathway. He darted through, past clutching thorn and vine, then ran into a tree. And disappeared.

Isiilde stared in shock. She lay in the center of a knot of warriors, all with their backs to her as they hewed the wood, fighting for their lives. Roots reached from the earth, locked around her wrists, and yanked her down into the soil before she could scream.

Isiilde was being buried alive. She fought to free herself, clawing at the dirt and slowly suffocating. Abruptly, the earth spat her out, and she fell to the ground.

She cleaned the dirt from her nose and mouth, then gulped in a breath, only to choke on stagnant air. All was dark. The ground had swallowed her whole.

And now I'm in its stomach.

Isiilde climbed to her feet, and summoned the Lore with a coughing breath. A blue orb flared to life. She stood in a long tunnel. Roots twisted and writhed like worms along its walls.

The tunnel ended at her back. She did not want to pass the slithering black roots, but standing in the dead-end was little better. Surely Marsais would come for her?

She could feel him through their bond, calm and centered in the eye of a storm—his focus absolute.

The tunnel was narrow, barely tall enough for her to stand. The blue light pushed at the blackness, but only seemed to deepen the unknown.

The earth above her head was crushing. Her heartbeat filled her ears, and whispers followed in the dark. She was alone, and trapped.

White teeth flashed behind her eyes, and she felt rough hands and a crushing weight on her. *I've missed you.* The memory of Stievin filled her bones.

The light blurred, and Isiilde ran. Roots lashed her arms, grasping, but she charged heedlessly forward, beyond the present and past horrors.

One tunnel twisted into another, and still she ran, until right and left and up and down held little meaning. One dead end hurled her back to another intersection, through tangles of roots and darkness, until she bounced off the next.

Out of breath, lungs aching from strain and suffocation, she stumbled to a stop, doubling over in agony.

Air brushed her cheek.

Isiilde's ears straightened. She lifted her eyes to a wall of blackness. With a gesture, she sent the orb drifting forward. The dirt walls widened, opening into a greater space. Her ball of blue light brushed stone.

She edged forward. Jagged rocks rose from the earth, from walls, and a feeling of vastness filled her heart. Somewhere in the expanse, water trickled and shadows moved. She pressed herself against a wall, realizing too late that her light was like a beacon, alerting everyone and everything to her presence.

A sound chilled her blood. A rattle, like a child's toy, shook in the unknown. Isiilde murmured the Lore, weaving threads with clumsy fingers. The orb of light expanded, but her movements were heavy with fear and the weave unraveled, plunging her into a lightless nightmare.

Isiilde screamed for Marsais through their bond.

The rattling moved like a breeze, shifting from one side to the next, and a great slithering mass followed in its wake. She edged back into the tunnel, weaving another orb, but this time, as soon as the light snapped to life, she hurled it into the expanse.

The orb flashed, illuminating a vast cavern of ruin. Monolithic pillars lay on their sides, toppled and broken, claimed by gnarled growth and lost to time. A sheet of dark water covered the cavern's basin, ripples stirring its surface.

Isiilde blew a slow breath from her lips, taking a step back, and retreating into the narrow tunnel. A hiss brought her up short—sibilant and gleeful, topped with a tasting tongue. She knew that sound.

Chilling eyes blinked to life in the dark. Reapers. The predators slunk towards her, crawling on the walls, and ceiling, blocking the tunnel. Their bodies were quivering with anticipation.

The Lore trembled from her lips as she backed into the larger cavern, towards the rattling noise. Isiilde wanted to disappear, but before she could put her mind to the task, the closest Reaper sprang with a flash of a claw. Lightning crackled from her fingertips. The weave hit the Reaper square, flinging him aside, where he jerked and howled on the floor.

Isiilde darted into the cavern. She flew over rubble, fallen pillars, and shot up vines, scrambling over the underground ruins. The Reapers charged on her heels like a pack of dogs sensing fear—and flesh.

Abruptly, the ground stopped, dropping into the cavern's basin. She leapt off the edge in desperate terror. Her fingers flashed midair and a levitation weave took hold.

The Reapers sprang, and Isiilde shot up, towards a maw of waiting stalactites.

The Reapers' claws raked air, and their bodies went down. One after another slammed into the ruin below, rolling to the edge of the black pool. A great ripple stirred the glassy surface and dark water rose like a wave, crashing over the closest Reaper. But the tide did not ebb. It separated into a writhing mass of eel-like creatures.

Isiilde's concentration faltered. She clutched at the weave, threads slipping through her mind and fingers. A tenuous thread slowed her descent, but it wasn't enough. She crashed to the ground alongside the Reapers.

The orb of light zipped down with her, illuminating the pool and a knot of reaching eels: slippery, slithering, and headless. She scrambled back and squeezed beneath a fallen stone, dodging a funnel-like mouth ringed with jagged teeth.

A Reaper lunged and she sent a bolt of energy barreling into its head. The blast sent it hurling backward into a thirsty mass of eels. Sickening sounds filled the cavern, amplified a hundredfold as the inky mass sucked and slurped their way to the Reaper's bones.

Isiilde pressed her back to a rock, and covered her ears. But there was another Reaper close by—and a presence. Dread pulled her gaze upwards. A giant hag opened her mouth and screeched, thrusting out a flapping, rattling tongue.

CHAPTER 20

Acacia Mael blinked away the seer's blinding light. Black spots danced at the edge of her vision as she fought, but it cleared in time to watch Marsais run into a tree. He vanished.

"Blood and ashes!" Oenghus cursed at her back.

Despair cracked his oath. Acacia shifted her attention from the trees to the center of their protective ring. The nymph was gone.

"Where is she?" Acacia shouted over the rush of battle.

"Isiilde!" There was no answering call. Fear rolled off Oenghus in tangible waves. His muscles quivered, transforming to rage as he fought with wild abandon.

Berserkers were the shock troops of an army and the bane of battle formations—as likely to decimate their own ranks as their enemies. The paladins scrambled out of his reach.

"Captain, to me!"

Acacia whirled, searching for Marsais as Oenghus hurled a crackling bolt at their enemies. A path opened through the brambles.

Acacia charged down the path, thorns snagging at her armor and ripping her cheeks. She broke through the maze a moment later.

Marsais stood on a flat boulder; burnt and withered vegetation surrounded his tall form. His hands were a blur, weaving hypnotically, keeping time with the haunting chime of his coins.

A long-limbed creature hung like a spider on a redwood tree. It had been a woman once, but tainted powers had twisted her into something contrary to nature: branch-like claws, disjointed movements, and oozing sores—a Blight hag.

The hag unhinged her jaws, and a swarm of locusts surged from her throat. Acacia called to her gods. Her shield flared with light, and she aimed it at the locusts. It cut a path through the swarm and hit the hag. The creature dove into a tree and disappeared.

A heartbeat later, the witch emerged from another tree. But Marsais was waiting with a weave. He clenched his fist, and an ethereal hand rushed towards the hag with a swirl of runes. It caught her around the neck, pinning her in place.

Acacia rushed forward, shining her shield at the creature. It writhed on the ground like a legless spider.

The locusts swarmed over Marsais. His rune hand slipped, his hold loosened, and the witch sprang. Acacia lunged, the tip of her blade piercing the creature's heart. Black blood oozed from the wound. The hag thrashed, raking talon-like fingers across Acacia's calf, cutting boots like parchment as a thousand insects battered and gnawed, crawling beneath her armor.

Acacia gritted her teeth, and bore down on the hilt, wrenching the blade. With a final rattling breath, the hag stilled.

Marsais chanted in the swarm. Fire surged, igniting the insects, and their charred corpses fell to the ground. He calmly strode forward, fire dancing in his palm. With a soft murmur, he thrust his hand towards the hag, and blew. The body caught like dried pine needles. A quick gesture snatched the fire back, and he dispersed it with a clap.

The forest stilled.

"Thank you, Captain. She was slippery."

"Your nymph is gone."

Marsais' gaze turned inward, searching.

"Where is she?" Oenghus demanded.

Without a word, Marsais turned and ran deeper into the ruin with Oenghus close on his heels.

Acacia glanced at her men—their armor was streaked with blood, and Rivan swayed on his feet, looking on the verge of collapse. "After them," she ordered.

"By the gods," Rivan breathed.

Lucas shoved the younger man into a run, and Acacia paused long enough to hack the hag's head off. At this rate, she doubted any of them would survive the company of a madman, a berserker, and a nymph.

"Underneath?" Oenghus asked.

Marsais was standing on an overgrown expanse of stone. "She's in danger, and moving fast."

Oenghus climbed up the stone, shoved Marsais aside, and swung his hammer at the rock. It split with a crack, revealing the pinnacle of a massive dome. He hooked his hammer on his belt and focused on the gap. With an earthshaking roar, Oenghus thrust his hands towards the stone and it answered his call—inch by strenuous inch, the gap widened. Then the earth stilled.

Silence rang in her ears. Acacia coughed, squinting through the settling debris. Marsais was clearing away rubble from a dark opening. She moved to help, and as soon as the opening was wide enough, Marsais folded his long body through the crack. Acacia squeezed in after.

Given the size of the dome's top, the underlying structure must have been massive. How far had the building fallen?

Acacia summoned light to her shield and followed Marsais through a maze of stone and roots. The space abruptly opened up, and the stone floor dropped with a waterfall of dangling vines.

Marsais skidded to a stop at the edge.

The temple was tilted. It had sunk into a great cavern millennia ago, and was held aloft by its domed top and broad shoulders. The lower sections lay strewn on the distant ground. Stalactites hung from the cavern's ceiling, and stalagmites rose from its floor. A black pool sat in the middle of a monolithic ruin, and far below on its shore, something was being consumed by a mass of writhing, snake-like creatures.

From the way Marsais calmly watched, she did not think his nymph was part of the feast.

The light from her shield hit something long, pale, and massive that slithered between stones. Its head rose, its body coiled, and a rattling filled the cavern. Not from a tail, but from the head—a human-like head, topped with a mass of writhing snakes. A naga: a creature of Blight and vileness.

"Here lies the rot," Marsais said as he traced a complicated weave. Searing energy crackled from his fingertips, blasting the creature's head.

The naga's massive head whipped around. Her eyes burned as her mouth opened, rattling a barbed tongue at Marsais and Acacia. The great body coiled and lashed, whipping its tail at the base of their perch.

The ruin quaked and rocks clattered off the edge. The hag returned to a pile of fallen stone, clawing at the rubble with distended arms. A weak bolt of energy zapped from the darkness.

Isiilde.

Acacia stepped back, secured her shield, turned her sword around, and caught Marsais' eye. "Catch me, Seer."

Without waiting for confirmation, she took two steps towards the edge, and leapt. Acacia fell.

For a split second, she feared the madman had forgotten how to weave. But the descent slowed, and she drifted like a feather, until the naga's tail swept underneath her and Marsais withdrew his hand.

Acacia landed on the naga, plunging her blade into thick scales. The naga jerked in pain, flinging her off like a rag doll. She hit stone, rolled, and came up, chopping at the serpent's body.

The grotesque head was topped with Stone Lickers, reaching, seeking, and sniffing for blood with their fanged mouths. Acacia dodged the naga's attack, swung her shield from her shoulder in time to block the Stone Lickers, and hacked off one.

The naga's tail slammed into her from the side. She hit a pillar and slid to the ground, stunned.

Marsais shot a beam of energy at the naga's head, but the creature ignored the blow, focusing on a quick kill.

Acacia abandoned her shield and threw herself to the side, reaching for the Stone Lickers that served as hair. Eel-like creatures coiled around her hands and forearms as the naga lifted its head and jerked her off the ground.

Teeth bit into her armor, searching for exposed flesh. As momentum carried her up and over the naga's head, she slammed down against rotting scales attached by blood-sucking carrion. The naga swung Acacia like a child's rag doll, knocking her against stone and battering her against its diseased body.

Momentum again lifted her upwards, and she brought her blade to bear on her downward spiral. The tip pierced the base of the naga's head. Its body arched and quivered with a rattle that shook the cavern. And with one final, rasping exhale, everything collapsed.

Monster and paladin crashed to the cavern floor.

Acacia hit the body, bounced, and was ripped free from the sucking carrion. She rolled to a stop near the pool. The black water rippled as inky forms surged, but a force slammed into her, pushing her out of reach.

High overhead, Marsais tipped an imaginary hat, and Acacia raised her sword in an answering salute. A whimper brought her back to her senses. Acacia reached for her shield and winced as pain sliced up her shoulder. Gritting her teeth, she grabbed the shield with her sword hand and brought it to bear.

The nymph was huddled in a hole. She stared from the darkness with wide, emerald eyes. Even petrified with terror, the creature looked ethereal, possessing a beauty reserved for dreams.

"Are you all right, Isiilde?"

"Are you?" Her voice trembled.

"Not really."

"Is it dead?"

"I hope so," Acacia sighed, ripping a Stone Licker from her cheek.

MARSAIS DRIFTED TO THE GROUND, trotting quickly to his nymph. When he crouched in front of the hole, Isiilde scrambled out to take refuge in his arms.

Acacia gave them their privacy, holding her injured arm close as she struggled to her feet. The abomination appeared good and dead—for now.

"Do you realize how difficult it is to weave a levitation enchantment around a falling person in armor?"

His sharp tone made her turn back around. "As difficult as destroying our only means of retreat during a skirmish? Why did you cut off our escape, Marsais?"

"The tree was old and tired. It needed liberating."

The odd comment caught her off guard. She narrowed her eyes at the immortal, but he was difficult to read. He was neither young nor old; but tall and lean, a charmer and wanderer with high cheekbones and pointed ears. An elf. And not just any elf.

With his snowy hair, agile body and elegant hands, Marsais reminded her of the Guardians. But there was something more—something vast. His eyes were like a myriad of stars, and she felt exposed beneath his gaze.

Still, she was never one to back down. "Next time a tree wants liberating, kindly free it after we've crossed."

"We need to move forward, not backward."

"Last night, you told Lucas and me that there is always time, and there always will be. What changed?"

"Never listen to a madman, Captain. And in the future, some warning would be appreciated before you throw yourself off a cliff."

"You're the seer."

Marsais snorted. "Foresight doesn't account for insanity."

Before she could question him further, he wove a complex rune in the air. A flame formed in his palm. Marsais hurled the ball of fire at the naga's body and it went up in flames.

"What was that?" Isiilde asked, covering her nose with a hand.

The stench of burning rot was appalling.

"A powerful Blight Witch. The afflicted take many forms, especially those who do so willingly."

"Willingly?"

"The thirst for power leaves no room for reason. It consumes and twists, and ultimately corrupts."

"Did you run off during the battle, Isiilde?" Acacia asked.

The nymph's ears flicked with irritation. "Of course not. The roots pulled me through the ground."

"Did they?"

"Yes," Isiilde snapped.

"I'm not accusing you of anything, only thinking. This naga seemed to want you. I suspect your separation from us was deliberate."

"A wise assessment, Captain. Nymphs are not just coveted by human males, but by all manner of creatures for various... reasons."

Acacia studied the faerie with sympathy. It was true. Nymphs often sat at the heart of violence, betrayal, and wars. They were delicate creatures, useless really, and yet... Acacia was reminded of the dainty blossoms that sprouted on corpse-strewn battlefields. The flowers grew in defiance of everything else, contrary to the madness of men. And even now, covered in dirt and blood, the nymph stood on her own two feet, ethereal and beautiful in the flame's flickering light.

The others had climbed down the cave wall, and now Oenghus charged across the cavern floor and swept the blossom in a crushing embrace.

"I'm fine, Oen." Aside from the thorns embedded in her arms. The nymph grimaced as her guardian plucked them out, but to her credit, she stood her ground. She was heartier than she appeared.

Acacia had never met another nymph like her, and she had encountered far more of the faerie than most people.

"We shouldn't linger."

"Agreed, Captain," Marsais said. "There are always plenty of Reapers in the deep, but I think the burning Blighted will keep them at bay for now."

Oenghus nodded to Acacia with respect. "You made quick work of that thing, Captain."

"Killing should always be quick. Did those Reapers attack you, Isiilde?"

She turned away from the half-eaten corpses. "Yes."

"You killed them?" Oenghus asked in surprise.

"I used a bolt to knock them back."

Oenghus beamed down at the redhead with, Acacia noted, what could only be fatherly pride. No man was immune to a nymph's allure, save her kin. But if Oenghus were indeed Isiilde's father, as she suspected, the implications were serious—both from the Blessed Order's viewpoint and that of Kambe.

Acacia pushed the matter aside, and turned her back on the pair to search for an exit. A nymph's illegitimate bloodline was the least of her worries.

When Lucas and Rivan arrived, Acacia moved farther into the ruins, shining her shield over the ancient stone. Considering her throbbing shoulder, she did not much like the idea of climbing back up the way they'd come.

"That's ugly," Rivan panted. He was out of breath, and doubled over, resting his hands on his knees.

"So are those," Oenghus jerked his chin towards the stagnant pool. "I bloody hate Stone Lickers. You fall in that pit, Sprite, and there's no warrior alive who could survive."

"Can we leave?" The nymph's voice drifted eerily in the empty expanse.

Marsais reached up to stroke his goatee, but found it shorter than before and scowled at the empty air between chin and chest. The strange coins chimed in response. "Without exploring? Where has your curiosity gone, my dear?"

"I left it above ground."

"That's not a bad thing, especially here," Acacia pointed out.

Marsais sighed. "One can always count on the Blessed Order to smother the thrill of adventure."

"I'd prefer a more comfortable adventure," Isiilde admitted.

"But who knows what we'll find," Marsais mused. "There might be a feather bed buried down here."

"Good," Oenghus grunted, "you can use it to float us all topside."

CHAPTER 21

CURIOSITY WON OUT. After they'd patched their wounds with Brimgrog and bandages, they picked their way through the ruins.

Marsais wove a light that illuminated every facet of the cavern. It was remarkable. His light rune shone like the moon, hanging bright and blue overhead.

Underneath the fallen remains of the temple lay another ruin—layers upon layers of rock, all toppled during the Shattering. Something caught Isiilde's eye. She bent to retrieve a small stone, and dusted it off. It was a piece of marble, etched with whorls. She showed it to Marsais.

"Ah," he said, plucking it from her fingertips to study. "Elven artwork."

"I thought they favored the forests. Why would they build underground?"

"The Lindale revered the Sylph and cherished her realm, including what lay underneath." Marsais gestured at their surroundings. "In other words, everything beautiful."

"There are Gnomish markings on some of these pillars, too," Acacia noted.

"What are we looking for, exactly?"

"There was a city here once, Sir Lucas," Marsais replied. "We might be able to salvage something."

"It's a two-thousand-year-old ruin. What are you expecting to find aside from a Reaper's lair?"

"I'll know when I find it."

A quick laugh escaped Rivan's throat. Lucas glared at the young solider, who quickly swallowed his amusement.

The group wandered inside a ring of standing stones. The dome top had shattered, and was strewn across the cracked floor. Veins of gold and silver shot through the rock, and a shallow basin sat in its center—a fountain, dry and crumbling.

Isiilde looked up, and a sky of glowing lichen greeted her, shining like greenish stars. Given the underground lake in the center—the fountains, precious metals, and intricate carvings—the cavern must have been beautiful once.

"Look at this." Acacia crouched in front of a crumbling wall, pulling away vines to reveal a relatively intact bas-relief. Three rings intertwined with three wolves. Each wolf held the other's tail in its mouth to form a continuous, never-ending cycle.

"What is it?" Rivan and Isiilde asked as one.

Rivan peered over her shoulder, and when she glared at him, he took a step back.

"I think this was a temple to the ol'Father." Acacia pointed at each of the circles.

"I've never heard of him," Rivan said.

"I doubt you would," Acacia said. "He was an Eldar god who was worshipped long before the Shattering. There are only a few surviving texts that mention the god, and those that exist are forbidden by the Blessed Order."

"Hah!" Oenghus barked from the far edge of the pillars. "I knew you weren't as straight-laced as you give off."

"I'm a Knight Captain. At my rank, the Order assumes one is immune to heretical teachings."

"And are you immune, Captain?" Marsais asked.

"If a mere myth turned me towards the Void, then I wouldn't be much of a Knight Captain, now would I?"

"Did the ol'Father serve the Void?" Isiilde asked, tracing the carving with her fingertips.

"No."

Rivan and Isiilde waited for more. And Acacia pressed her lips together, weighing the mandates of her Order versus knowledge.

The latter won out.

"These three rings represent the moons: the Silver Crescent of the Sylph, the Red Moon of the Keeper, and the Dark One's moon."

"The moons have had many names," Marsais mused.

"The ol'Father was the Weaver of Fates and Time. The wolves in the symbol represent endless time and his control of it. Myth claims that Time holds no sway over the Eldar god—that he alone knows the Fate of the Sylph and Void. He's a god who stands apart from all others."

"Oh, Fate is just a word made up by those afraid of the future," Marsais grumbled, scratching his chest. "May I make one correction, Captain?"

"Of course."

"I believe your Order may have changed the meaning of this symbol from truly blasphemous to only slightly blasphemous. So brace yourselves, my good paladins." Marsais ensured he had their attention before continuing, except for Oenghus, who was rooting around the ruins like a disgruntled badger. "Those rings do not represent the moons; they represent the Sylphs."

"There is only one Sylph," Lucas objected.

"Those who worshipped the ol'Father believed there were originally three Sylphs—three sisters."

"You're right; that is blasphemous," Acacia said.

"Not to the people who built this temple. There is an old legend, long-buried, regarding the birth of Life and the Void."

"It's best left lost, then."

"Ignorance is viler than knowledge," Marsais said.

Lucas bristled, but his captain cut him short. "It's only a story, Lucas."

"Ah, eons condensed into a few words," Marsais whispered hoarsely. "How quaint."

"What did the old ones say about the Sylphs?" asked Rivan.

"This first circle is the Sylph that you worship, the Goddess of All—she holds the essence of Life itself. And here, the second is her sister Chaos." Marsais traced the last circle with care: a brush and caress, and a faraway stare.

A wave of disorientation swept through their bond. He closed his eyes and swayed, but no one noticed except for Isiilde. As quickly as it happened, he recovered and met her worried eyes with a shadow of sadness. "The third sister is Death."

Abruptly, Marsais rose, dusting off his knees and turning to the cavern.

"What happened to the Sylphs, sir?" Rivan pressed. "Why aren't all three still worshipped?" The young man glanced at Lucas, and cleared his throat. "I mean if they lived at all. How does the story go?"

"It's a story for the fireside, not down here. But you bring up an interesting question—one for you to ponder. When people stop worshipping a god, is he still a god?"

Rivan opened his mouth with an answer, but quickly shut it, frowning in thought instead.

"Scarecrow." They all turned at Oenghus' call. "I think there might be a door here." The group climbed over fallen stone and earth to where he stood—in front of a rock face.

Marsais traced a runic eye over a spirit rune and nudged it towards the cavern wall. Green runes flared to life on the rock, intertwined as tightly as a knot. It was a ward—an ancient one.

"I would've never spotted that," Acacia said.

Oenghus flashed her a grin.

"What do you think is in there?" Rivan leaned towards the ward, squinting at the swirling runes.

Marsais quickly pulled him back with an irritated glare. "The last thing you want to do is activate it."

"Can I unravel it, Marsais?" Isiilde's ears quivered with anticipation.

He shrugged. "I don't see why not."

"No, she can't bloody unravel it," Oenghus growled. "What if *she* sets it off?"

"Oh, come now, Isiilde can unravel my best ward with barely a strain on her brilliant mind. It's her right. She led us into the cavern."

"But I found the door," Oenghus argued.

"Did you want to unravel it, Oen?"

Oenghus crossed his massive arms, and Isiilde stared up at him, waiting for his reply. Her guardian would have better luck using his head than using the Lore. Wards were not his strong point.

On the other hand, Isiilde loved wards. The enchanted traps were a lot like unraveling a puzzle knot; only she was dangling from the same rope she was unraveling. And if she pulled the wrong strand, the rope would unravel completely, setting off the trap.

"Absolutely not, Sprite."

Before the words had completely formed on his tongue, she had shot forward, pressing hands to rock and summoning the Lore. Her mind surged into the complicated weave, leaving her body with careless abandon, following a pulsing web of deadly triggers. She tugged and snipped and teased the runes free, until the entire knot unwound, revealing its secrets.

Isiilde opened her eyes. She muttered the Lore of Opening, then swept a hand over the rock. Stone grated on stone, and a crack appeared, poisonous gas seeping from the dark opening.

Marsais quickly wove a breeze to disperse the air.

"But I didn't set it off," she coughed.

"Bad air," Oenghus grunted. "I don't think this will lead us to the surface."

Acacia's shield flared with light as she thrust it into the darkness. "The stairs lead down."

"We might as well take a look." Oenghus hoisted his hammer and ducked, moving into the narrow staircase.

"We're going down there?" asked Rivan.

"You can stay," Oenghus bellowed.

Rivan glanced at Isiilde and Marsais, straightened his shoulders, and drew his sword before plunging into the dark.

Lucas looked at his captain. "He's eager to impress."

"Aren't all men?" Acacia asked.

"Until he accidentally stabs someone," Lucas grumbled.

"I doubt Oenghus would notice," Marsais quipped. "After you, Captain."

Acacia ducked inside, and Isiilde made to follow, but Marsais brought her up short. "Doors do not always remain open, my dear."

She shuddered at the thought. "Being buried alive is not one of my preferred ways of dying."

"I thought as much."

"I'll stand guard," Lucas offered.

"Appreciated."

THE PASSAGE WAS LONG, scattered with intersections and alcoves storing the dead and their brittle bones in all their untouched splendor—until now. Oenghus tugged at a skeleton in a chamber of alcoves, stripping it of a jeweled necklace.

"You can't take that!" Rivan gasped. "Don't you have any honor?"

"He doesn't bloody need it, now does he?"

Every frazzled nerve in Isiilde's body screamed at her to leave. She tugged on Marsais' sleeve as he examined a cobweb-covered sword.

When Isiilde found her voice, a frigid wind swept through the room, stirring her hair and sending needles of ice through her bones. The room erupted with a piercing wail as a hazy form shot from an alcove.

A tattered funeral robe swirled around the swift apparition. It came at her, its eyes seething with hate. Oenghus threw his hammer, but it passed through the howling spirit. Marsais stepped in front of Isiilde, coins chiming as he brought the sword's point to bear.

"I think not," he said simply.

The fluttering rags drew up short, opening a shapeless mouth and unleashing fury. The wail was pure torture.

Acacia chanted a prayer, and Rivan swung his sword at the creature as it retreated. But his blade passed through the Forsaken. He screamed in pain as his sword clattered to the ground.

Oenghus threw himself to the side, narrowly dodging an attack. An instant later, Acacia raised her sword. "Leave us!" Her blade flared and caught the Forsaken in a whirlwind of searing light. Rags dissipated, the form shimmered and churned, and a tremendous shrieking rent the air.

Anguish beat at Isiilde's heart—hunger, rage, and madness. The sound tore at her sanity.

"Silence!" Marsais' voice cut through the shriek.

Acacia's blade ripped through the spirit, turning it to ash. And suddenly, all was quiet, and all was still.

"Stubborn bugger," Oenghus spat, retrieving his hammer with a long string of inventive oaths.

"A Forsaken," Marsais explained, wrapping an arm around her trembling shoulders. She turned to him, willing the world away. "It was just a Forsaken—an ancient and faded spirit."

"Aye, Sprite, they're a miserable bunch." A heavy hand patted her back, knocking the air from her lungs before moving on.

"That's an understatement," Acacia muttered, inspecting Rivan's arm. It was limp and his fingers refused to bend.

"It feels like ice, Captain," Rivan said with grimace.

"It will pass."

Isiilde pressed against Marsais, shaking with terror. "I can't do this," she whispered.

He tightened his grip. "But you already are."

"Is everything so terrible in this realm?"

She felt him shrug. "It could always be worse."

Isiilde arched her neck, seeking his calm, grey eyes. "That's not very reassuring."

"Have I ever lied to you?"

"You seem a talented liar, Marsais. I doubt I'd know."

"You wouldn't," he agreed. "All the same, upon my honor, I swear there is joy to be had."

"We didn't find a feather bed."

"Not yet." Marsais' eyes glittered. "But we do have a tomb to loot, and grave robbing has always been one of my guilty pleasures."

Isiilde nearly laughed because she knew, beyond a doubt, he was telling the truth.

"You approve of this, Marsais?" Acacia asked, gesturing at Oenghus.

"The dead have little need for such things in the Spirit River. Just think, one of these slumbering mounds of dust could have held Rivan's spirit in a past life."

Rivan took a hasty step back.

"That sounds like a thief's reasoning," Acacia said.

"I have been many things in my lifetime, Captain. And I freely admit to being a rogue at heart." Marsais held up his pillaged sword, inspecting the blade with a critical eye. Its cross-guard was short, the blade was double-edged.

"This sword would have connected with the Forsaken. I'm surprised the Blessed Order doesn't issue better weapons for their soldiers."

Marsais presented the hilt to Acacia. Without hesitation, she accepted the offering, inspected it, and blew on the blade. An intricate pattern materialized on the metal.

Isiilde edged forward, as did Rivan, and her guardian peered over their heads at the sword. A row of wolves chased each other along the blade. Acacia handed it to Rivan, and Marsais plucked a smooth stone from the crypt.

"This is the blade's Heartstone," Marsais said, pressing the plunder into Rivan's hand. "Do not lose it."

"What does it do?"

"Smites the good-hearted," Oenghus rumbled. "What do you think it does, lad?"

Rivan studied the design on the sword. "It's the ol'Father's symbol, isn't it?"

"Aye, and he's been fighting the Void longer than your blasted Order."

"Have a care, Oenghus." Acacia said.

"Never been my strong point."

Acacia turned her back on the berserker as he swept aside a pile of bones, and tapped the stone in Rivan's hand. "Use this to sharpen the blade. The stones are usually attached to the scabbard, though I'm sure it's long rotted."

Isiilde found Marsais standing in front of an alcove, gently shifting the brittle occupant. It had once been a woman. The long strands of hair were whisper thin and brittle as ash, but they were still clinging to her skull.

He tugged a garment free and shook it out. A cloud of grave dust flew into the air, and Isiilde sneezed, a burst of flame puffing from her ears. Rivan gaped at her.

She shot him an irritated glare, but the effect was ruined when Marsais gave the garment another shake. It was a cloak. When he handed it to her, she protested.

"That was on a dead person."

"Better dead than half dead. I'd wager this smells better than Rivan's leggings."

Isiilde glanced at Rivan, who quickly began fiddling with his plundered sword. "It probably does," she agreed. Despite its age and dust, it was lightweight and warm, and she said as much.

"It's a traveler's cloak. The Lindale were excellent tailors, which is why it has survived all these years. Unfortunately, I don't see any boots for you."

"Do tombs usually have more of a clothing selection?"

"You'd be surprised."

"Here, Sprite," Oenghus said.

Isiilde accepted the offered knife without thinking and the feel of the hilt in her palm triggered a rush of sensations: pain, leering eyes and stone digging into her skin. She was back in the washroom, trapped with Stievin. She could smell blood, muck, and lust. Panic surged through her veins.

"Oenghus," Marsais hissed. He snatched the knife from her fingers and the weapon disappeared behind his back. "I'll keep it until you're ready."

Oenghus frowned at his daughter. He wished he could kill the bastard who'd attacked her all over again, but no amount of killing could change the past. "Let's find you some sunlight," he said.

Isiilde wrapped the cloak tightly around herself as she stared at its previous owner. The Dead, she decided, looked very peaceful.

CHAPTER 22

"I SEE why you don't stay in one place for long."

After emerging from the underground ruin, smells of ripe earth and a lush forest filled Isiilde's senses.

"Hmm, and this is just *one* realm."

"Don't get her curious, Scarecrow," Oenghus grumbled. "There's plenty to see in this one."

"And plenty of danger," Marsais said.

They walked through a city in ruin. Yet, despite the shadows beneath the towering canopy, Isiilde felt at peace amid the trees. They'd cleansed the forest of a festering plague and the trees were happier for it.

"Aye, well, I'm still looking for the best ale in the realm."

"One pleasure house at a time," Marsais quipped.

Lucas snorted. "I'm surprised you can't turn water into ale."

"Don't think I haven't tried."

From the looks of the group, Isiilde thought that enchantment would be most welcome. They were a ragged-looking bunch.

"The river is that way," Oenghus said.

Acacia raised her brows. "How do you know?"

Isiilde was curious to know, too. They'd spotted a river from the ridgeline, but one direction looked the same as the next in the thick forest.

He shrugged. "I've never been lost."

"I've always thought it had to do with his stature," Marsais mused. "He's so large that heading south feels like walking downhill."

"By that reasoning, I could just walk on stilts," Isiilde pointed out.

"Have you tried it?"

"No, but you're tall and get lost all the time."

Marsais frowned in thought. "Perhaps it's his girth, then?"

"Like a marble rolling downhill?"

Marsais snapped his fingers and pointed at her. "There's the answer."

Oenghus glanced back at the pair, tugged on his beard, and pressed on with a muttered oath.

The river was wide and fierce, and the afternoon sun shone brightly on the water. They followed the river as the terrain allowed until it split. One fork flowed sluggishly. Reeds grew along the red banks and large, flat boulders caught the sunlight, reflecting heat into the cool mountain water.

"Stay here," Oenghus ordered.

While he stomped off to scout, Isiilde wandered to the bank. Ancient stone steps clung to the edge. A fallen pillar marked the ruin. She thought it might have supported a bridge at one time. Something caught her eye, and she wandered farther, conscious of Marsais on her heels, and another—Rivan.

A ring of redwoods gathered in a cluster. One was burnt and hollow, but still alive and thriving. She peered into its shadows.

A snorting huff was the only warning as a boar charged from the hollow. Isiilde threw herself to the side. The tusked keg slid and turned, madly scraping dirt to gain traction. And then it came back for her.

Marsais stepped in front, fingers flashing, but Rivan was quicker. He thrust his sword into the beast's ribs. The boar ripped the hilt from his grasp, turning towards its attacker. Rivan tripped over a root, and threw up his shield as the boar pounded into him.

Unwilling to risk hitting the paladin, Marsais dropped his weave, grunted in annoyance, stepped forward, and drove the heel of his boot into the pommel of the protruding sword. The blow forced the blade deeper. The boar thrashed and twitched, until it stilled, falling on top of Rivan and his shield.

The others ran into the grove to find Rivan on his back, struggling under three hundred pounds of dead boar.

"Didn't I bloody tell you lot to stay still?" Oenghus growled, dragging the boar off Rivan.

"We got bored." Marsais shrugged. "Besides, Isiilde found us dinner, and Rivan killed it. Huzzah."

"No, I didn't—" Rivan began, but Marsais stepped into the hollow, weaving a light rune. Isiilde followed.

The tree's hollow was empty, save for a few creeping spiders and salamanders. The interior was spacious and tall and the earth was soft and yielding.

Marsais ran his fingers over the charred bark. "These trees are resistant to fire, and can thrive long after their core is hollowed. We ancients are a hardy bunch, aren't we?"

The question was more for the tree than for her. If it answered, she couldn't hear.

"And look," Marsais pointed, "someone used this as a campsite before."

A small hole in the side appeared too perfect a vent to have been caused by coincidence. "Who made it?"

"Someone very tall," he quipped.

Isiilde grinned.

Oenghus poked his head inside. "Can you come and look at what I found, Scarecrow, or do you already know?"

"I do."

"Well, I don't," she said. "Do I want to?"

"It's not near as pleasant as this."

"All the same," Acacia said from the entrance. "I'd like to see. And by the way, another untouched patch of strawberries is nearby."

"Luck follows a faerie," Marsais said.

Isiilde wasn't sure about that, but her stomach reminded her that she was starving.

Rivan and Lucas dragged the boar away from camp to skin and gut it, and Isiilde picked a handful of strawberries before hurrying after the others. She caught up to them in front of a crude totem carved into a pillar.

A mass of grotesque images and a spidery filigree of foreign runes twisted the totem's surface. Leering eyes watched from the stone. Something dark and filthy had been rubbed onto the fangs and beaks of the carved faces.

"A border marker," Acacia said. "Is it the Ardmoor?"

"No, see this..." Marsais traced an image of a foul-looking bird. "It's the Suevi—we'll stop here for the night."

Isiilde lay drying on a rock in the river. Sunlight caressed her limp body and her tired feet drifted in the water. A pile of strawberries, mushrooms, and nuts lay beside her, and she ate as she watched Marsais bathe and fish.

"Do you want to try fishing?"

She sat up. "Do you think it hurts the fish?"

"Death?"

"The getting there."

Marsais considered her question as he scrubbed the grime from his forearms. Cuts and bruises marred his body, but none were severe enough to warrant healing. "You hit me with the same bolt the other day."

Isiilde frowned at the spidery bruise on his chest. "Did that hurt?"

"Only because I lived."

"And that's a good thing." She started weaving, but Marsais pulled himself up beside her, and she forgot her weave. His lack of clothing was distracting.

"It must be cold," she said with a grin. "Aren't you worried the captain will look over here?" But the only one eyeing their fishing spot was Rivan.

"As you so delicately put it, there isn't much to look at. Now concentrate, or I'll send you to retrieve the fish."

Isiilde's fingers flashed, holding the weave until a fish zipped into view.

"Wait!"

Marsais' warning came too late. A jolt of electricity slammed into the water, and a surge of tingling energy traveled up her legs.

"Blood and ashes," she cursed, pulling her feet out of the river. Her toes were numb.

"And that's why I didn't teach you a more powerful weave."

Marsais slipped back into the water to retrieve two fish that had floated to the top. She glared, and hurled a lesser bolt at his back. His coins chimed, and her bolt careened to the side, brushing a nearby boulder.

"Hmm, and that's the other reason, although you handled yourself well with the Reapers."

She did not like being reminded of the Reapers, or anything in the past, for that matter. Isiilde bunched her oversized shirt up to her thighs, and eased her legs back into the water.

"Is it true what Rivan suspected?" she asked. "Were you the first king of Vaylin?"

"There were men before me. But I'm the one who united the warring clans, so history remembers my name. How many fish do you want?"

The fish weren't large. This time, before sending a bolt into the water, she tucked her feet safely on the rock and waited for Marsais to do the same.

"My history in Vaylin isn't something I want to be known."

"Because of how others view Vaylin?"

Marsais hopped back into the river to retrieve more fish. "Vaylin didn't become what it is until after the Shattering. Though we were at perpetual war with Kiln—a lot like Nuthaan is with the Fell Wastes."

"Only Nuthaan has good reason."

Marsais paused in front of her. Sitting on the rock as she was, they were eye level. "If Nuthaan were not warring with the Fell Wastes, they would fight with someone else."

"Have they ever not been at war with the Fell Wastes?"

"They were once united."

Isiilde blinked.

"Time has a way of twisting everything."

"Is it true that the first king went insane?" she asked softly, pressing her hand against the scar on his chest.

Marsais closed his eyes with a sigh. "Yes, he did," he whispered. "The first king was plagued with visions. And he failed his kingdom and family when they needed him most."

"You have children?" She felt a stab of pain in his heart—of grief and loss.

"Not anymore. I had three daughters." He smiled sadly in memory. "And an infant son. My Oathbound, son, and two daughters perished during the Shattering. I—" His voice caught, and his eyes flickered. "I failed my remaining daughter in the months that followed. She died."

There was depth to those two words: horror, revulsion, and utter despair.

Isiilde wrapped her arms around his neck and drew him near. "Even the gods fail, Marsais," she whispered. He buried his face in the curve of her neck.

When his breath evened and his heart calmed, his lips moved against her skin. "I fear you could make a man forget anything."

"Even that he's standing in frigid water?"

"Hmm, that, but apparently not the seven-foot berserker currently glaring at me from shore."

"I don't care," she said, and proved it with a kiss.

IsiiLDE STOPPED AT SEVEN FISH. Marsais carried them off to clean, leaving her lounging on the rock to braid her hair.

"Are you finished zapping fish?" Acacia asked from the bank.

"I am."

Acacia stripped off her armor and clothing. The reeds along the bank offered some cover, but Isiilde could still see the men as they moved inside the circle of redwoods.

The woman's shoulder was badly bruised, and deep scars crisscrossed her lean body. She slipped beneath the water without a wince from the cold.

"I'm a soldier," Acacia said, noting Isiilde's surprise when she surfaced. "Modesty is a luxury in an army."

"I can vouch for Marsais as a gentleman, but Oenghus has his own definition—he's staring," Isiilde said, loudly.

Oenghus quickly found something else to do.

"I'm not surprised."

"It doesn't bother you?"

"Wouldn't you look if Rivan stripped on shore?"

Isiilde clicked her mouth shut. She *would* look. "It's more curiosity."

"Exactly."

"I think Oenghus likes you."

"I think Oenghus likes anything with breasts."

Isiilde grinned.

"Can I ask you something, lass?"

"You already have."

Acacia was not amused by her cheeky reply. "Why were you angry with me the other night?"

"I'm sorry—I didn't mean to make the fire do that. It just does."

Acacia inclined her head. "Apology accepted. But why the reaction?"

Isiilde reached for Marsais through their bond, taking comfort in his presence. He looked up from the bank, and met her eyes. The brief touch fortified her.

"I wasn't angry with you, Captain." Isiilde turned slightly, brushed aside her braids, and let her shirt slide off her shoulders, revealing the top half of the fiery dragon that curled around her spine.

"This is the bond I share with Marsais," she explained. "I can feel him—his thoughts, his desires. He's *inside* of me. And he feels like a blazing sun. But the thought of being bonded to someone I don't love is terrifying... My mind would not be my own."

The usually cool, unaffected paladin paled. "I had no idea," Acacia whispered. "Other nymphs I've met appear content—happy even."

"Am I so different from the others?"

"None of them write or read, and they definitely don't use the Gift. If you ever meet another nymph—you'll see what I mean. To be sure, nymphs are beautiful, but they're so oblivious that it's easy to view them as less than human."

Isiilde frowned. She felt more awkward and out of place than ever before. Through the years, she'd imagined being with her kind, as if there were an untouched grove somewhere with a group of lounging nymphs, waiting for her to join them. But now it seemed a foolish fantasy.

"Do any of them play King's Folly?"

Acacia arched a brow. "I can barely play it. Can you?"

"It's my favorite game." Isiilde couldn't contain her curiosity any longer. "Where did you get all those scars?"

Acacia laughed as she turned to show off a jagged splotch of white skin. "This one is from a Reaper's bite. And this other one is from a Formorrian axe. If I hadn't been wearing my armor, I wouldn't be bathing in this freezing water. And this," she pointed to a circular scar on her rib, "is from a Wedamen arrow."

"You've been all over the realms, then?"

"Nearly."

"What about the ones on your forearm?"

Acacia grinned. "A fierce kitten my youngest daughter brought home."

Isiilde's musical laugh drifted into the air, melting with the stirring breeze and dancing with the leaves. All eyes fell on the shimmering dream. The men stopped to stare at the creature on the rock. The forest sighed, and the wood spirits calmed—all was at peace.

CHAPTER 23

"I took you for a picky eater. Where do you put it all?" Rivan asked as Isiilde tossed the bones of another fish into the fire.

"I was hungry."

Rivan cleared his throat and returned to his polishing duties. Five fish was a lot to eat.

"I've always wondered that, too," Oenghus said. "I've had sons who ate less than you, Sprite."

"Maybe I'm not done growing," she said hopefully.

"I think you have an enchanted bag for a stomach."

Isiilde glared at her guardian as she dipped a toe in the flames, and kicked a lump of red-hot coal towards him. Oenghus batted at the flames with a curse, and she felt Marsais chuckling behind her.

Night had descended, bringing a chilling wind, and the outcast group huddled around the campfire. She lounged against Marsais, savoring his warmth and the security his arms offered.

"Do you have children, Oenghus?" Acacia asked.

"Oen's fathered a small army," Marsais said.

"Don't scare her off, Scarecrow. I've been trying to impress her."

"Is that what you call it?"

Oenghus ignored the comment. "I have sixteen children still

breathing—as far as I know. With the realms being as they are, likely less now." He frowned down at the branch he was whittling into a pipe. "I've had one hundred and eight, and I'm on my eighth generation of grandchildren—don't ask me to count that brood."

Rivan gave a low whistle. "Did you live through the Shattering, too?"

"Nah, I'm not near as ancient as the ol' Bastard here. I was born in the winter of 1013 A.S."

"That makes you nearly a thousand," Rivan said.

"Oh, the Order teaches arithmetic too." Marsais sounded pleased.

"Actually, it's 997 years," Isiilde corrected.

Marsais cocked his head. "You told me you were born in 1014."

"Well, it was winter."

"We have a wager. You can't change the date of your unfortunate birth."

"It's only a bloody year."

"A year later."

Acacia sighed. "A wager... Do I want to know?"

"I do," Rivan said.

"I have a thousand crowns that say I'll live longer than the ol' Bastard."

Acacia opened her mouth to comment, tilted her head, but decided to remain silent. Reason was often lost on the two men.

"And I thought the captain was old," Rivan said.

Acacia looked sharply at her soldier. He shifted under her pale gaze, quickly changing the subject. "What are the legends about the ol' Father?"

Isiilde shared Rivan's curiosity. He glanced over at her, and seemed relieved to find that he wasn't the only one interested. Even the captain looked attentive.

"Your Order condemned the legends as blasphemous."

"It's only a myth," Acacia stated.

"Hmm." Marsais rubbed his chin, the coins chiming softly in response. "Yet, out of all the creation myths, one must be true."

Isiilde could feel his heart beating against his back. And the certainty of his next words. This was no myth.

"Light and Dark warred eternally," Marsais began. "And from their fevered clashes sprang Time, who watched and counted the millennia alone. But even Time grew weary, so he dipped his hand into the light and drew out Life. But she was so brilliant that he could not stare at her for long, so Time dipped his hand into darkness and drew out a shadow. Chaos was born.

"Life created, but Chaos surprised—sometimes delightfully, sometimes dreadfully. Time was content. But Chaos became jealous of her sister, for she could not shape, only hope. And in her spite, she twisted her sister's creations, shaping them into her own. Life and Chaos warred.

"Time despaired. He dipped one hand into the light and the other into the dark and brought the two together. The two opposites joined, and Death was born, restoring balance. Of the three sisters, Time loved Death most of all, for she was easy on the eyes, patient as he never could be, and merciful to all—even to him.

"Death was Time's companion, everlasting and faithful. But Life and Chaos did not share Time's love. Their sister, Death, had the power to snuff out their children at will. So Life called to the Light and poured it into a River, binding the end to the beginning, an endless cycle of rebirth that Death could not touch. Meanwhile, Chaos flung her children into the darkness so Death could not find them, but her children reached out to drag her in. Darkness swallowed Chaos, and the Void was born.

"The Void devoured the Darkness, then turned to the Light. Life cowered, but Death stood firm, standing before the Void in defiance. In an act of love, she shoved her sister into the arms of Time and attacked the Void with fury.

"Balance was lost, and Time grieved. And while Life survived, even thrived, the Void continues to devour, seeking to destroy her down to this day."

Marsais fell silent.

Oenghus continued to whittle, and the fire popped and shifted, sending sparks drifting towards the trees.

"That's an interesting tale," Acacia finally said.

"So, Life, Chaos, and Death were the three Sylphs?" Rivan asked.

Isiilde felt Marsais incline his head in answer.

"And the ol'Father is Time?"

"Hmm, yes, and that reminds me," Marsais said, untangling himself from Isiilde. "The moon is out and shining perfectly on that boulder. It's time I sent a message. I won't be long, my dear." She craned her neck, and he kissed her lips, eliciting a growl from the giant beside her.

Marsais strode through the ring of trees, and hopped from shore onto the flat rock. He stood poised on the boulder, head raised towards the stars, his white hair gleaming in the moonlight. He looked magnificent.

Isiilde knew that stance. He took it whenever he was about to perform a complex weave.

The wind whipped his hair, and snatched at his robe, and somewhere far off, a wolf's mournful cry rose into the night. Marsais surged into motion—his long fingers were a blur, his arms elegant, and every step was grace as he wove luminescent runes that swirled around his snaking form. It was more dance than Lore, and the runes flared to life, one after another, moving with his steps as he navigated the powerful currents of the Gift.

The amount of energy Isiilde felt him channeling left her awestruck. The Gift filled him. It rushed through his veins, and seeped into his bones, until she thought he would be swept away in the surging tides. And then realization dawned. Marsais didn't wade into the torrent of power; he threw himself into it and let its currents carry him away.

Stranger still, Isiilde had never felt him enter the current. He was always connected to the Gift. Impossible, she thought, and yet she had seen the proof with her own eyes.

How many times had he completed a quick weave without uttering the Lore? She had always thought he whispered it, or that she simply missed the words, but now that they were bonded, she could feel the great river coursing through his bones.

"What's he weaving, Oen? I can't follow him at all."

Oenghus gave a shrug and returned to his whittling. "I never know what the bastard is doing. Maybe he's summoning a keg."

Marsais stopped so suddenly that wisps of trailing energy continued to flutter as he stilled. He spread his arms and peered at the swirling column of runes. His eyes glowed silver. He withdrew his spirit from her, and stepped inside the complex weave.

Darkness crashed over Isiilde: pain, despair, and numbing ache. Shadows clutched at her heart and coldness gripped her bones.

Her sun was gone.

"What's wrong, Sprite?" Oenghus was at her side, his hand on her shoulder, his eyes searching her face.

"Marsais left." She shivered and blinked, finding herself lying on the ground, curled in a tight ball. Acacia was beside her as well, but she could not remember anyone moving.

"He's standing right there."

"No. Inside." Moisture trailed down her cheeks, but she could not connect the sensation to her own flesh.

A calloused hand brushed the hair from her cheek. "A man can't be without his nymph for long. He'll be back soon as he can."

Another wolf howled, and something fluttered in the dark. Oenghus frowned. "Although I best stand guard. With his luck, a clutch of harpies will snatch him up. Just stay here, Sprite, you'll be fine."

Isiilde nodded numbly and pushed herself up, trying to remember falling. She wrapped her cloak tightly around herself, and Acacia sat down beside her as Oenghus trotted off to stand guard.

"What did you mean when you said he left you?" Acacia asked.

"His spirit inside of me is as bright as a sun."

Acacia's gaze flickered towards the elf standing frozen on the rock, arms by his side, head raised, as if he intended to take flight and speed towards the moon at any moment.

Isiilde ran her hand through a wave of flame. With Marsais gone, she craved its protection, its light and power. As unpredictable as her fire was, it was always eager to defend. And just as eager to consume.

"Don't you ever get burned?" Rivan asked.

Isiilde flinched at the deep voice. The fire crackled and popped, and leapt towards the paladin across the pit. He edged backwards.

"It likes me."

"I'm glad it does." Rivan hesitated. "Back on the Isle—well, I didn't fancy being tortured to death. You saved us all, you know?"

"I nearly killed everyone."

"And yet we're all here," Acacia pointed out. "A soldier doesn't question luck."

"Don't bother arguing with the captain," Rivan advised. "Trust me, I gave up years ago."

A smile tugged at Isiilde's lips.

"Did you grow up on the Isle?" Rivan pressed.

Isiilde met the deep brown eyes across the fire's light. He appeared interested, as curious as she was about most things. She searched for any deceit or ill intent in his eyes, but only sensed sincerity.

He reminded her of Coyle. Open, earnest, and honest. But if he asked her for a vial of her piss, she would brain him with his own helmet.

Rivan filled in her answering silence with another question. "Did the Archlord teach you how to use the Gift? What you did with the bolt and the levitation was amazing."

"I was his apprentice on the Isle."

"Wait—they let you join? You can't tell me you're a hundred." Rivan's shock was so sincere that she laughed.

"No," she said, grinning. "I'm eighteen."

Rivan gaped in surprise.

"Marsais made an exception. I guess he knew I'd be bored otherwise."

"Probably helps that you're a nymph," Rivan mumbled.

"No, it didn't." At her sharp reply, hissing flames gathered around the logs, burning dangerously low.

"I didn't mean anything by it," he stammered. "You're not going to explode again, are you?" He scooted away from the fire.

Isiilde took a deep breath, closing her eyes, and blocked out the flames. "I can't really control it."

"I'm sorry," Rivan said.

No one ever apologized to her, save for Marsais.

"It's just a sore spot," he continued. "I tried to join the Isle, but they wouldn't take me. What the Wise Ones do with the Gift—it's amazing, especially the Archlord."

"You should be honored to serve the Blessed Order," Lucas growled from the edge of camp.

"I am," Rivan defended. "But I'd be lying if I said I didn't want to learn more."

"Honesty is an admirable trait, Lucas," Acacia pointed out.

"Should have left him where you found him."

"Then there'd be no one to annoy you," Acacia shot back.

Lucas grumbled in reply, and Rivan grinned so openly that something began to unwind inside of her. In response to her changing mood, the campfire resumed its cheerful dance.

"Maybe Marsais could teach you," she offered.

"I don't know," Rivan said, poking at his bandages. "I think I annoy him, too."

"If you annoy him too much, he'll turn you into a toad."

Rivan laughed, but Isiilde was quite serious.

"Speaking of learning," Acacia interrupted. "We might be halfway across the realm, but you still need to keep up your drills."

"We've been marching all day," he protested.

Acacia arched a brow.

"Yes, sir."

"Aren't you going to let Oen heal your shoulder?" Isiilde asked as Acacia climbed to her feet.

"I will later. In battle, a soldier must make do, whether with one hand or two."

As Isiilde soon learned, Knight Captain Mael was just as adept with one hand as she was with two. The nymph watched with a great deal of interest as Rivan got his arse kicked.

There was, she realized, a strategy to sword fighting, every bit as complicated as King's Folly. Attacks and counter-attacks, only instead of runes, one used the body.

Acacia noticed her interest while Rivan was picking himself off the ground. "Do you want to learn?"

"Me?"

"There's no one else here."

The world wavered, shifted, and rough leather lay in her palm, as real as the moment it had happened, followed by the plunge of steel into flesh. "I don't like weapons," she said, trying to shake the past from her mind.

"It's not a weapon, it's a stick." Acacia waved the branch in the air.

Put like that, Isiilde could not say no.

Acacia handed her the branch. It was heavy, and it felt awkward in her hands, nothing like the knife had. She instantly relaxed.

"Now, follow my lead."

Isiilde slowly worked through sword drills with the captain, but she was nowhere near as graceful. After a half an hour, her arms shook with fatigue. One foot tangled with the other when she tried to pivot. She stumbled, caught herself, and dropped her practice sword.

"Not bad for a first time," Rivan said.

"You're supposed to hold on to the bloody thing!" Oenghus called from the river bank.

Marsais' spirit flared to life inside of her, and he drew her close through their bond. A moment later, the two men entered the camp.

"The captain is giving lessons. Do you want to try, Marsais?" she asked.

"I find the sword an unwieldy weapon."

"In other words, he might get callouses on his pretty hands."

Marsais ignored the verbal jab. His mind was elsewhere, and she could sense his worry. Isiilde caught his eye in question, but he looked away.

"Any news?" Acacia asked.

"Apparently I'm a Bloodmagi who conspires with fiends, and Oenghus and I murdered you three."

Isiilde narrowed her eyes. Surely the Wise Ones wouldn't believe that? She tilted her head, looking at the situation sideways, and amended her first reaction. They probably would believe it. "What about me?"

"I did what any good Bloodmagi would do—I ravished you and carried you off for sinister purposes."

"To your evil lair?"

"Why, yes, my dear, it's in there." He pointed to the hollow tree.

"It looks dreadful," she said to his twinkling eyes.

"Who did you speak with?" Acacia asked.

"A cleric of Chaim. He'll pass my message on to the Guardians."

"A cleric on Iilenshar?"

"It's the same cleric who instructed you to look after me, Captain."

Acacia pressed her lips together and inclined her head, satisfied with his answer. Isiilde wondered who this cleric was.

"Now, if you'll excuse me, I'm rather tired." Marsais turned away and ducked into the hollowed tree before anyone could press him for more information.

Isiilde followed. Inside the hollow, Marsais crouched in front of a ring of stones, coaxing a fire to life. Someone had prepared a firepit and a soft bed of ferns.

"Did you arrange this, Marsais?" she asked.

"Oen thought you'd be warmer in here," he said, tossing two logs into the blaze.

"I'll be warm as long as you stay."

"I had planned to," he said with a smile.

It wasn't a feather bed, but the ferns were soft, and Marsais' arms made up for the rest. It was easy to imagine they were back in the Spine. Isiilde sighed, relishing the heat, but she sensed an uneasiness through their bond. Marsais was deeply troubled.

"I like your evil lair," she said, twisting in his arms to search his eyes. "Are you all right?"

"Don't worry about me."

"How can I not, Marsais?" She reached up to trace the stark line of his jaw. "It has to do with your conversation, doesn't it?"

"Among other things."

"Why didn't you tell the paladins everything?"

"How do you know I didn't tell them everything?"

"Really, Marsais, you should know me by now." She tugged on his scruffy goatee. "The cleric of Chaim knows about the Isle now, and he knows we're not really Bloodmagi. That's good news, and yet you're still troubled."

"I can't hide much from you, can I?"

"Why do you try?"

Marsais caressed the curve of her ear. "To save you the worry—the burden. Let it fall on my shoulders, Isiilde."

"We're bonded," she whispered. "You forget that what you feel, I feel too." She unlaced the front of his robe, and slipped a hand beneath, placing it over his scarred chest.

The wound, whatever it was, constantly ached, but when he was fatigued, it burned and throbbed as if it were fresh. Yet when she touched it, the pain melted away.

Marsais shuddered at her touch. The strain at the corners of his eyes and mouth smoothed, and he gave a soft sigh.

"You live with so much pain. I don't know how you bear it."

"This," he placed his hand over hers, "never lets me lower my guard. It keeps me alive."

"How did you get it? Why won't it heal?"

"When the Orb shattered, I was ripped open along with this realm. I should have perished, but... I lived."

His gaze turned inward in thought, and unconsciously, his hand slipped beneath her shirt to trace her spine. It felt like being caressed by the sun.

"But why would the Orb's Shattering wound you?"

"Why do you think, my dear?" His fingertips slid up her spine before brushing her neck.

"I think you're trying to distract me," she breathed.

"I can stop trying."

In answer, she pressed her lips against his. Passion ignited, and she buried her fingers in his hair. Desire echoed through their bond, building in intensity. His pleasure was hers, and hers was his, shuddering through their bodies as one.

"Marsais," she pulled away, breathless and aching, and vaguely aware of voices. "Please tell me you have something to drape over the entrance."

"What entrance?" he murmured against the hollow of her throat.

Isiilde swallowed, fighting for thought. "The one Oen and the paladins are sitting outside of."

That got his attention. Marsais cleared his throat, adjusted his trousers, and rose to a crouch, looking dazed. It seemed to take a fair amount of thought, but eventually, his eyes focused with something resembling intelligence.

"Ah, the seer has a plan." Marsais' fingers flashed, creating a veil of gossamer runes in the air before he swept his hand over the entrance. The air shimmered, rippled, then snapped into focus. The entrance vanished, leaving them encased in a cocoon of redwood.

"A mirror rune. But you can still walk out."

"I don't want to leave. And I won't let you."

Marsais backed against the tree wall, his eyes widening by the second. "Wait." Another weave flashed through the air: an Orb of Silence. Marsais was ever thoughtful.

Isiilde deftly unlaced the rest of his robe, and slid it from his shoulders. Her fingers trailed down his chest, over his taut stomach, to the twin muscles dipping beneath his trousers.

"Give me a moment," he gulped.

"For what?" she purred, tugging his belt free.

"I'm trying to think."

"I'm not stopping you." His laces certainly were not stopping her deft fingers.

"You're making it very—" He cut off with a moan and leaned against the tree as she found another use for her lips. It was a full minute before he found his voice again. "Difficult."

Isiilde reached up, grabbed the remnants of his goatee, and pulled him down to her level. "You are always thinking," she whispered.

Another long, passionate kiss and Marsais found himself on his back beside the fire with a nymph straddling his hips. Hot breath and an eager tongue sent fire racing through his veins, but still he struggled, trying to recall something important.

Isiilde sat up, arching her back with a rock of her hips, and then she paused, tilting her head. "Why do you look scared, Marsais?"

"I don't have any—" She moved her hips again, and his body betrayed his mind, robbing him of the ability to speak.

Marsais forgot he had been speaking altogether as he caressed the nymph, running hands over firm breasts and silken skin, hips thrusting with her hypnotic undulations and quickening with her breaths.

"What were you saying?" she moaned.

The fire beside his head flared and popped, and the threat knocked his mind back in order.

"Fire potions," he murmured. "I don't have any protection."

Isiilde growled in frustration.

"I have an idea."

"Good." Her lips returned to his hot skin, trailing downwards with her touch.

"You won't like it."

"That doesn't sound promising."

"I think—" Marsais lost his train of thought and Isiilde grinned against his chest.

"Yes?"

"Hmm?"

"You were saying?"

"Was I saying something?"

"Shall I stop?"

"Gods, no," he said, hoarsely.

"I want to hear your idea." She sat up, and his mind finally traveled in the same direction.

"Fire," he gasped, and cleared his throat, gathering his thoughts. "I believe your fire resides in your voice. I can silence you. Although I'd rather not..."

It took a moment for her mind to catch up with his words because his hands were rather distracting. When his idea took root, she stiffened, and fear filled her eyes.

"You mean like what Thira did to me?" Her throat went dreadfully dry.

"My dear," he soothed, gripping her hips, and with gentle persuasion, switched positions, pressing her against the soft earth. "I would never weave something so crude."

A feather's touch slid down her hip and thigh, eliciting a moan. It was the last of the night, but her silence was well worth the pleasure.

CHAPTER 24

Isiilde awoke to a looming presence. Marsais stirred beneath her, mumbling to the intruder. "Is it my watch?"

Oenghus scowled down at the pair. "I took your bloody watch. It's an hour past sunrise. We need to get moving."

"It's too early, Oen," she moaned, returning her face to the curve of a warm neck. Marsais smelled delicious.

"Next time you weave a bloody Orb of Silence, take it down before you go to sleep. A legion of razor beasts could have attacked the camp and you two would have slept through the entire battle."

"Sounds like a good thing," Isiilde mused. "There'd be more beasts for you to squash."

"Excellent point, my dear," Marsais agreed, propping himself up on his elbows despite the nymph still draped over his body.

"Since the ward is still up, you best tell me what has you so worried."

"We're traveling with three devout paladins who can't even hold a simple conversation without crying blasphemy. And while the Suevi and Ardmoor are bitter enemies, the Suevi include the Dark One among their worshipped deities."

"What did you see on the marker?" Oenghus pressed.

"Eaters of the Dead—or the living. The skull and crow are their symbols."

Isiilde's stomach lurched. "Can't we just go around?"

"The winter wind is stirring, and we aren't equipped for the approaching storm."

Oenghus tugged on his beard in thought. "We don't even know how far their territory stretches."

"You could summon a griffin again and we could fly over them."

"That was an illusion," Marsais explained. "But even if I were to summon one—summoning is just that. It doesn't grant control over the beast."

Oenghus shrugged. "So we'll scout it out and if the tribe doesn't look that bad, I'll tell the metal heads to shut their traps."

"Nicely put."

An hour into their trek towards the hoped-for village, Isiilde felt as if she had walked all day. Every muscle in her body was sore and her feet dragged with exhaustion.

"I don't think nymphs are supposed to get up so early," she said to the man at her side.

"I would have to agree." Grey eyes twinkled down at her. "They're definitely nocturnal."

She glared at the bounce in his step.

"How are your feet?" he asked.

They were currently filthy and the ground was cold. She said as much.

"I could levitate you, if you wish."

"That would be wonderful."

He traced a quick weave, and his deft touch caught her, wrapping around her body with tingling warmth. A moment later, she drifted off the ground, and crossed her legs, sitting comfortably on a cushion of air.

As they passed the border marker, Lucas spat at its base. And Isiilde realized there was merit to Marsais' concerns. Even if the Suevi were not flesh eaters, the paladins, especially Lucas, would take offense to anything contrary to the Blessed Order.

Would the Knight Captain put aside her fervent devotion long enough to barter for supplies, and possibly aid?

Isiilde's thoughts scattered when the levitation weave unraveled, and gravity slammed her onto the earth.

Rivan rushed forward to help, but she scrambled away from the paladin. He froze, as startled as she.

"Are you all right?"

"I'm fine." Isiilde ignored his offered hand and stood, searching for Marsais. He was staring at the ground.

"And that's why I didn't want him floating us across the chasm," Oenghus grunted.

"What has he found?" Rivan asked.

Isiilde bent to examine the spot that held him in thrall. "A stick," she announced.

"Oh."

"Marsais?"

His grey eyes were wide and unseeing, or perhaps seeing too much.

"We don't have time for this. Just slap his bloody back, Sprite."

"I don't want to disturb him."

"That bastard has stared at a leaf for an entire day before."

"And you stood staring at him?" Acacia asked.

Oenghus narrowed his eyes. "I was young and dumb."

Isiilde tilted her head at the stick. A sudden urge gripped her, and before common sense could halt her curiosity, she nudged the stick with her toe.

Marsais sucked in a sharp breath. He blinked at her, muttered under his breath, then turned to walk away.

"Grab him," Oenghus ordered.

Isiilde grabbed his arm.

"Oh, hello, my dear."

"Welcome back."

"Was I gone long?"

"Long enough to drop me."

Marsais glanced from Oenghus to the paladins, to the tops of the trees, and then down at his palm where the head of a fiery dragon rested. "Ah."

"We're bonded, and somewhere in Vaylin. Oen is about to toss you off a cliff."

"I like the first part. Not the rest of it." He gave her a roguish grin. "We're wasting valuable daylight. We really must hurry."

Without waiting for the others, he took off at a near gallop.

"Does he know where he's going?" Lucas asked.

"As long as he doesn't keep making left turns." Before Marsais disappeared, Oenghus caught up and grabbed his shoulder. "Back with the women, Scarecrow."

"As long as you hurry."

Oenghus swore under his breath. "Watch him, Sprite."

She kept a firm hold on his hand as they walked.

The sun peaked, then began to fall, and still they walked with a sense of urgency at their backs. Whatever the others thought of Marsais, his behavior had put them on edge.

After a time, Marsais' ebbing sanity faltered, and reversed direction. Isiilde felt his calmness return and his heart began beating in a relaxed rhythm that echoed his gait. Soon, Marsais and Isiilde were falling behind.

"Marsais?"

"Isiilde."

"When the hag attacked us, why did the vines leave after you tapped my head?"

"Aha! A lesson for today." Marsais called the party to a halt.

"Why are we stopping?"

"An opportunity, my dear Captain."

Isiilde sat on a moss covered rock, and Oenghus sighed, removing his knife and a crude pipe that was a work in progress.

"Because I shielded you." Marsais traced three runes at her feet: stone, air, and a bind.

Lucas glared. "We've been marching double time for hours, and now you stop to conduct a class?"

"Sir Lucas, when my apprentice—"

"Former," she corrected.

"—shows an interest in the Gift, I'd probably stop in the middle of a pitched battle to train her. Consider this a brief halt. Soldiers still do that, don't they?"

"It's a waste of daylight."

"At ease, Lieutenant." There was an edge to the captain's voice as she walked to the river. Lucas followed without comment, and the two bent their heads together in quiet conversation.

Rivan tucked his helmet beneath his arm, and crouched, trying to copy Marsais' runes, crudely tracing them in the dirt.

"Don't start weaving, Isiilde," Marsais warned. "You can't bind stone and iron to your flesh. That would result in ill occurrences—far worse than binding earth to your skin."

"Is there anything worse than an ill occurrence?"

"Yes, a devastating occurrence. Now, weave stone around iron, and an air rune *into* the stone rune like so—into the cracks." He traced three bold strokes before interlacing the flowing air rune between columns. "And a bind to tether them all."

A gossamer thread stretched from the bluish runes hovering in midair to his fingers, like strings of a puppet. Quick as a snake, he took a step to the side, and tapped Rivan on the head. The paladin blinked.

Isiilde waited for something noticeable to happen, but nothing changed.

Oenghus snatched a rock from the ground and threw it at Rivan. It hit him square in the forehead, but there wasn't a mark on his skin.

"Hey," Rivan said, rubbing the spot.

Isiilde invoked the Lore without hesitation, wading into the coursing streams of energy to weave the complicated pattern. Wispy blue strands stirred in the air, waiting. She beckoned the weave closer and it flew at her like a net, encasing her body.

The weave was suffocating.

Isiilde made a strangled sound. It was crushing her. Suffocating. She couldn't breathe.

Marsais grabbed her wrists. "Relax, it's normal. You did everything perfectly."

"Get it off!" she gasped.

With a brush of his fingers, he pulled the weave from her body, letting it dissipate on the wind. She sucked in a breath, walked to the nearest tree, and turned her back on the group. All eyes followed the trembling nymph.

"It's not that bad once you get used to it," Rivan said.

Her ears twitched with irritation.

"It's better than an arrow in your back, Sprite."

Fury burned in her blood. "I felt trapped."

Oenghus gave a bark of laughter. "You'd make a fine berserker."

"Hmm, I doubt Brimgrog would affect her."

Oenghus jabbed a finger at him. "Don't dare give her any."

"I would never gamble with her life."

Before the pair started arguing, Isiilde cut in. "What did I do wrong, Marsais?"

"You wove the shield perfectly, but I must confess—I always add a feather rune to anything I weave for you. It distracts you."

"Is that why your weaves always tickle?"

Oenghus grunted. "You mean you take the extra time to add a feather rune in the middle of a fight?"

"A small matter when compared to Isiilde's comfort."

"I hate it when I agree with you, Scarecrow."

"Precisely why I said it."

"Can I add a feather rune to my own shield?" she asked.

"Hmm, it might backfire. It'd be like trying to tickle yourself. At best, it wouldn't work, but at worst, it might be painfully itchy. Don't let me stop you from trying, though. As long as I'm nearby to unravel the weave, you should be fine."

"The shield really isn't that bad. You should try wearing this plate and mail sometime," Rivan said.

Perhaps not for him. But Isiilde's skin crawled with memory, and any sensation of being trapped sent her heart racing.

"Will the shield weave really stop an arrow?" he asked.

"His weaves are as good as full plate armor," Oenghus boasted. "I couldn't stop a stone with one of mine."

"But even my shields don't last, not like armor. The weave fades over time—highly inconvenient during a drawn-out battle."

"Could you teach me?" Rivan asked.

He reminded Isiilde of an eager puppy.

"Teach you what?"

"The Gift, sir."

"I'm afraid not."

The disappointment in Rivan's eyes twisted her heart. "But why not, Marsais? You don't have an apprentice anymore."

Marsais raised his brows. "Neither do you, Isiilde."

"I'm not a Wise One."

"Neither am I. We've all been cast out."

"Good riddance," Oenghus spat.

"You were?"

"Void-worshipping murderers usually are. The Order has standards, low as they may be."

"I can't teach Rivan," she protested.

Marsais looked at the paladin. "Do you play King's Folly, young man?"

"The lord's game? No, I'm not of noble blood, sir."

"Hmm, well then, Isiilde can teach you."

Isiilde glared. Marsais smiled.

"We don't have the pieces." She crossed her arms, attempting to work out of the corner she'd just maneuvered herself into.

"Then I suggest, while we walk, that you gather two hundred flat stones from the shore. You can trace the runes on them tonight."

Her ears flicked with irritation. Although she loved the game, teaching a novice how to play would be sheer torture. She'd never needed teaching—the game had come naturally to her. As a nymphling, she intuitively knew which runes interacted and which repelled the others.

Still, she'd talked herself into the corner, so she turned to Rivan and told him to gather the stones. Amusement rippled along their bond, adding fuel to her anger. She stomped ahead to walk beside Oenghus.

"You won't find any sympathy up here, Sprite."

"I don't need sympathy," she seethed. "I will, however, need you to restrain me from setting Marsais on fire."

"Get in line," Oenghus grunted.

CHAPTER 25

"Do you speak Suevi?" Acacia asked as the day darkened and their destination neared.

"That's an excellent question." Marsais scratched at the beginnings of a beard. "I'm hoping I'll remember when the natives start talking."

The sigh that issued from the scarred paladin was like a gust of wind, and the contempt was sweltering. "That isn't very reassuring, Seer. We're treading on foreign lands, into an unknown village, with a man who may or may not speak the language of heathens."

"I'm not here to reassure you, Sir Lucas. I'm simply stating a fact."

Isiilde wondered whether Lucas' wounds had made him disagreeable, or if he had always been ill-tempered?

Acacia held up a hand, silencing her lieutenant. "What do you mean you're *hoping* you'll remember? We're not faulting you if you don't speak Suevi, none of us do, but we're used to more... definitive answers."

"The only thing definite about Marsais is the unexpected. Trust me, Captain, I gave up long ago." Oenghus bared his teeth. "And I stopped counting the times I wanted to strangle his skinny neck."

Isiilde snatched up a flat stone, directed another glare at the indefinite mage in question, and tossed the stone to Rivan.

"Hmm, I've always believed your murderous inclinations were one of the contributing factors that made you such an excellent apprentice."

"Oenghus is your apprentice?" Rivan asked.

"*Was*," the ex-apprentice growled.

Surprise flickered across Acacia's eyes. "How exactly did that come about?"

Marsais glanced at his old friend.

"The Scarecrow saved my life," Oenghus answered vaguely, and promptly changed the subject. "What's it been now—working on eight hundred years?"

"I started having regrets after the proverbial twenty years of putting up with your hairy hide."

Oenghus snorted. "I should've strangled you as soon as I sobered up. Would have if you'd been carrying a weapon."

"You *tried* to strangle me."

Oenghus ignored the claim. "You see, in Nuthaan, a man without a weapon might as well be a man with no bollocks. Took 'im for a dandy."

"Until I turned you into a piggy," Marsais retorted.

"Shut your trap. It was a boar."

Isiilde snorted, Rivan gaped, and Lucas ignored them all.

"The two of you bicker like Oathbounds," Acacia said.

"Oen *has* kept me warm on more nights than I'd like to admit." The comment earned him a thrown rock, but the agile elf stepped aside.

Isiilde frowned at her guardian. "You could have hurt him, Oen."

"I know. That's why I was aiming below his belt."

She huffed, looked heavenward, and dropped back beside Marsais, who greeted his return to her good graces with a kiss to the hand.

"I'm still waiting for an answer," Acacia warned.

"I gave you an answer."

"Do you speak Suevi or not? A simple yes or no will do."

"But that's not the answer."

"You really can't remember whether you speak a language?"

Marsais scratched at the scar beneath his robe. "How many languages do you speak, Sir Lucas?"

"The trade tongue, obviously. Kamberian, Kilnish, a bit of Rahuatl, Celestial, and I know a few Southern dialects."

"Well, I'm not trying to boast, but at one time or other, I have spoken just about every language there is to speak—including dead ones. Words get muddled in this blasted mind of mine, and everything runs together after a time. Sometimes hearing a language will knock something loose, and I'll remember the rest of it."

None of them had anything to say to this—one could hardly argue with an elf born before the Shattering.

AT NIGHTFALL, they stopped beside the ruins of an abandoned longhouse —a charred, pitted thing that creaked with the wind.

"Keep the fire small tonight," Marsais ordered.

Isiilde frowned at the stream trickling through the trees. Fish was unlikely tonight, and her stomach growled in protest.

"Come, my dear. We'll find you something to eat."

He led her towards the ruin.

"In there?" she asked.

"Homesteads usually have gardens, even abandoned ones."

Rivan hurried to catch up. "There might be something dangerous inside. You'll need a guard."

Marsais eyed the strutting young man. "Guards serve best at the fore."

Rivan drew his sword and trotted ahead.

The longhouse was a burnt ruin that was slowly giving way to vine and bramble. Rivan stopped at the charred doorway, and edged forward, shield raised, blade at the ready.

The remains of a kiln sat on the far wall, blackness climbing like a disease from its center. The overgrown earth was covered with rubble and the debris of something that had once resembled life: a rotted cradle and bed, and a strangely intact jar, sitting on its shelf.

A noise drew their attention to the kiln, and Rivan stepped into the wreckage, tense for action. A moment later, a pointy, scaled face poked out of the kiln. Black eyes blinked into daylight, and a long slurping tongue tasted the air. Rivan bristled, and the creature ducked back into its nest.

"At ease, Rivan," Marsais said. "It's a trenggiling. They eat ants."

Rivan sheathed his sword with equal parts disappointment and relief. And Marsais smiled down at Isiilde. "Not everything in this realm is fearsome. Trenggilings curl into a ball when threatened—Reapers can't even crack their armor. Sometimes the best offense is to play along."

They left Rivan to sort through the rubble, and circled the longhouse to the rotted remains of a fence, where they found an overgrown garden.

They loaded their harvest into two scavenged clay pots: wild onions, turnips, carrots, two potatoes and a garlic bulb. A stunted apple tree shadowed a conspicuous patch of large, untouched strawberries. Isiilde fell on the berries, and Marsais left to gather mushrooms.

But Rivan soon approached with a wolf pelt in hand. She frowned at the tattered thing.

"It's not as bad as it looks," he said, cleaning it off.

A cloud of ash and dust flew in her face and she sneezed—three quick bursts of flame shooting from her ears.

"Sorry. It's not much, but it'll help."

"Thank you, but I have my cloak."

Rivan draped the pelt over his own broad shoulders. The others seemed unaffected by the cold, but she'd often caught Rivan shivering. He was staring longingly at her strawberries.

She did not offer any.

"I found more stones. I have two hundred now." He patted a bulging pouch hanging from his belt, and she sighed in resignation.

They ate their fill that night. Isiilde's stomach was full, her cloak warm, and a strong, steady heart beat against her back. Oenghus passed his newly finished pipe to Marsais, who unwrapped one arm from around her waist to accept the offering.

"Is that what I think it is?"

"Harsbane."

"Isn't that poisonous?" Isiilde asked.

Marsais puffed on the pipe with pleasure. "The leaves aren't, only the stalk."

"Less poisonous," Oenghus corrected. "Your dreams might be a bit off."

"When are they not?"

"Can I try?" Isiilde reached for the pipe hovering over her head, but Oenghus snatched it away.

"No."

"Probably for the best, my dear. I'm not sure how Harsbane will affect a faerie."

"Aren't you a faerie, too?" she whispered.

"An *ancient* one. Besides, your dreams are interesting enough without hallucinogens."

The tips of her ears heated, and she wiggled in his embrace. A pebble smacked Marsais on the head. "Ow! Blast it, Oen."

"Cursed squirrels," Oenghus said, pointing the stem of his pipe toward the trees.

"One more time—"

"What is that, Rivan?" Acacia interrupted the two bickering ancients.

"I found it in the longhouse." Rivan held the object he had been turning over in his hands towards the firelight. It was a small wooden horse.

"Do you like horses?" Isiilde asked.

"My sister loved them," he murmured. The figurine disappeared beneath his tunic. "What do I do with the stones now?" He posed the question to Isiilde, not Marsais. His willingness to learn from a mere nymph caught Isiilde off guard. No one had ever asked her how to do anything before.

Isiilde untangled herself from Marsais and climbed to her feet. "Before I can teach you to play King's Folly, I'll need to trace the runes. You can watch if you like."

As conversation drifted over the campfire, Isiilde traced each rune, muttering its name for Rivan's sake, who strived to memorize every word. But Isiilde barely noticed the paladin; she was lost in the runes, weaving with a flourish, until the stones swirled with a halo of bluish light that rippled like water.

When she'd finished, she looked up, startled to find herself the center of attention. The paladins had gathered around her, along with Oenghus and Marsais, his eyes gleaming silver in the night.

A shadow flickered across his gaze: unease, worry, but most of all, fear. She tilted her head, puzzled, and he smiled—a sad little curving of his lips that did not reassure her at all.

CHAPTER 26

WHO WOULD HAVE EVER SUSPECTED that the greatest enchanter in all the lands would be living in an alley behind a pleasure house? No one, save Isek Beirnuckle, who valued flapping tongues and curious eyes.

He fancied himself a spider on its web. Every strand was connected to something. A pinch of gossip here or a casual word there often led to a greater treasure.

Witman the Wondrous had never left the Isle; he had missed his boat. Finding the dwarf was the easy part. Sobering him up was difficult. And convincing Eiji that the crazed drunk was the legendary enchanter was another feat entirely.

But eventually, Isek had dragged Witman the Wondrous into the throne room.

"My, my, the laddie doesn't live too badly does he?" Witman smoothed the remaining strands of hair over his balding pate, and gawked at the vast chamber like a country peasant.

Eiji shot the dwarf a scathing look. "Kneel before the Archlord."

Witman did not kneel.

Tharios eyed the disheveled dwarf from his throne as Isek bowed at his feet. "May I present Witman the Wondrous."

Witman lifted his spectacles and squinted at the pale face hovering in shadow. "What happened to the laddie?"

"You haven't heard?" Isek feigned surprise. Witman would not have come willingly if Isek had told him that Marsais was no longer Archlord.

"*They* took him!" the dwarf shouted, wringing his hands, and backing up. But a knife's tip drew him up short, digging into his back. Witman hopped forward, swiveling to find Eiji with blade in hand.

"There's no need for violence, Eiji. Put your toys away." Tharios rose, gliding off his dais with a graceful swish of silk. "I am Tharios, the newly appointed Archlord. I assumed everyone would have heard by now."

Witman dug into his ear with a finger. "*They* put a bug in my ear. It steals words."

Tharios pursed his lips. "You are Witman, the enchanter, correct?"

"I might enchant a bit here and there, mostly there. So which took him?" Witman pulled a glob from his ear, flicked it on the marble floor, and leaned forward, licking his lips. "The others, or those—*Other* ones?"

"Others?" Tharios asked.

"Marsais was not taken," Isek explained. "The Blessed Order charged him with conspiring with fiends and using Bloodmagic. He fled with Oenghus and the nymph."

Witman leaned back and opened his mouth, releasing a bellowing laugh that echoed through the hall.

"It's hardly a laughing matter," Tharios cut through his amusement. "Bloodmagic is forbidden."

Witman wiped the tears from his eyes. "I was wondering when they'd find out about all that!" The dwarf continued to chortle, spittle misting his beard. "The laddie always did have odd tastes."

"What are you talking about?" Eiji asked.

Isek cleared his throat. "Witman—"

"Are you sure this is the enchanter?" Tharios demanded.

"Always being watched, we are. They're always waiting." Witman's mood shifted like mercury. He took a step forward, pinning Tharios with one bright eye. "If you find the laddie, he owes me coin."

"If it's coin you want, then I have it—in exchange for your services."

"I'm on a holiday." Witman grunted, hooking his thumbs in his waistcoat.

"You will be well compensated."

"For what? Shining those fancy boots of yours?"

Tharios took a deep, calming breath. "A ward. We need you to unravel a ward."

"A ward that the laddie left behind?" Witman whistled. "For that, I'd best be compensated very well indeed."

"I have coin."

"I don't want coin, Mr. Archlord."

"Then what?"

"A peek into the laddie's vault in that there Spine. And whatever I can carry out of it."

Tharios smiled. "Save for one item—a flask."

Witman patted a squarish bulge under his coat. "I've got my own, won't be needing one."

"The sooner the better."

Witman extended his hand and Tharios hesitated for the briefest of moments—a mere flutter of an eyelash. Rumors surrounded the enchanter, some wild, some fanciful, but all of them dangerous. No one double-crossed Witman the Wondrous.

WITMAN SQUINTED at a web of runes on a door. The stone underfoot had been scrubbed clean of blood. "Do you want me to get in this vault or do you want me to unravel the ward?" he asked the man at his side.

"I need to get into the vault," Tharios answered for the third time. His hands were clasped serenely behind his back, but there was an edge to his voice.

"So..." Witman tugged at his waistcoat. "You want me to get *into* the vault?"

A muscle twitched along Tharios' jaw, but he answered again, as if speaking to a particularly dense child. "We. Need. To. Get. Inside."

"Right then, leave it to me."

Witman clapped his hands and stepped towards the door. With wild ceremony and grand gestures, the dwarf waved his hands in the air like a man trying to move a stubborn donkey. Then he froze like a statue.

Everyone in the hallway held their breath, and waited. What would the legendary enchanter do next?

Abruptly, he grabbed the knob, and turned it. The door swung inward, leaving the ward intact.

Realization dawned on the others with varying degrees of teeth grinding.

"And that is why they call me Witman the Wondrous. The laddie always forgets to lock his doors." Witman chortled as he stepped inside the vault.

The flagon sat in a maze of priceless artifacts, on the same shelf that Isiilde had stood on to reach a chest of gems. Its companion was missing, stolen by curious fingers, and opened by a foolish nymph.

Tharios said nothing. The oversight was humiliating—no one had thought to try the knob. Most lords would rage and shout, proclaiming the stupidity of their underlings, but not Tharios. He was more concerned with the end result. He plucked the flagon off its shelf and cradled it like a man holding his firstborn.

"So that's it, aye? That's all you wanted?" Witman squinted at the flagon. "I'll just take what I can carry, then?"

"Yes, of course," Tharios murmured. "Thank you for your service."

"Archlord," a voice called from outside. It was Gabin Archer, yet another Wise One loyal to Tharios.

Isek had to hand it to Tharios. The man had built an enclave of Unspoken right under the noses of the Order—his own included.

They left Witman to his noisy rummaging.

"We've cleared Marsais' private chambers, but there's something... strange. An armoire. We can't move it," Gabin said.

"Show me."

Gabin led the way to Marsais' former chambers. The rooms were stripped of clutter and gleaming with polish. The charred bed was gone, and an aching memory reminded Isek of his failure—of the shimmering nymph sprawled on the bed.

How could he have missed it? All these years, one of the most powerful creatures in all the realms had been right under his nose.

Isek tore his gaze from the vacant spot and scanned the polished room. He approved of the order. Seeing the room uncluttered was nearly worth the price of disposing of his old friend. Yet, one piece remained: an elegant armoire stood defiantly in a corner.

Odd. That was an apt description. Isek could not recall having seen it before. As cluttered as the room was, he might have missed it, but it was large, too large to have missed. His eyes slid from the armoire's dusty surface, and he refocused his gaze on the doors, only to have his gaze slide right off again, landing on the wall. It was slippery—an enchantment.

Tharios passed the flagon to Eiji, and took a cautious step towards the armoire. His lacquered nails flashed, weaving a complicated weave, and a series of runes that Isek could not follow. Slowly, a runic pattern took shape, swirling around the armoire, creeping between the stone wall and wood. With a firm inflection, Tharios clapped his hands, and the illusion broke, shattering with a thunderclap. A solid slab of obsidian dominated the corner, pulsing with wards.

Tharios sucked in a sharp breath.

"Marsais did say it was a flask in his bedchambers, not in his vault," Isek reminded the three Unspoken.

The ward was as complicated as the Storm Gate, but when Tharios placed a hand on the stone, the Runic Eye of the Archlord flared to life on his palm. The stone blazed blue, searing and bright, and white hot.

Isek shielded his eyes. When the light dimmed, he lowered his arm, blinking past black spots.

The stone wavered, rippling with undercurrents. Its front swirled like liquid, parting, thinning. A hazy scene took shape: two thick tomes and a long-necked flask sat in the stone's center.

Tharios reached through the obsidian and snatched the three items from their nest. Stone returned with a grinding snap that extinguished the runes.

Eiji stood on her toes to study the items. "I will never understand Wise Ones and their fascination with flasks."

"Get Witman."

Eiji shot off like a dart and was back just as quickly. "The vault is empty. Witman's gone."

"Find him," Tharios hissed.

Every guard and Wise One lingering in the upper chambers fanned out to search for the enchanter, roaming through the storage rooms, libraries, and suite, but no one had seen the dwarf leave.

Isek stood in the vault's entrance. A dragon's hoard of treasure had simply vanished, along with a legendary dwarf. There wasn't even a copper left—only a crudely drawn circle of chalk on the floor.

CHAPTER 27

A SINGLE SNOWFLAKE landed on Isiilde's nose and she sneezed herself awake in the early morning light. In an instant, the skies spat down their fury, snuffing out the small campfire. As the bitter wind howled through the camp, the group scrambled to gather their supplies.

"The longhouse!" Acacia shouted over the storm, but Oenghus shook his head.

"We can't stay there all winter. On my back, Sprite."

Isiilde didn't argue. Her bare feet wouldn't last in the snow.

As the sun rose, the world transformed from emerald to white, and Isiilde huddled against her guardian for warmth, while Marsais braced against gusts of snow.

"Can you find the village in this weather?" Acacia shouted into the wind.

Isiilde couldn't see beyond five feet in the storm—the sky was as gray and white as the ground.

"There's nothing like a wee storm to stir yer kilt. Trust me, Captain."

"One moment, Oen." Marsais wove a quick ward, then tapped Isiilde's head. She stopped shivering as warmth spread through her body. He repeated the cold ward for himself and trudged after Oenghus, trusting to the berserker's instincts.

Sometime later, Marsais bumped into his back. They had stopped between two boulders. It was impossible to tell the time of day, but it was cold and dark, and the rocks perched on the edge of a ravine.

Oenghus focused on a small recess beneath a boulder. Then, at his sharp command, the earth shifted, widening the hollow. Marsais ducked inside to trace a fire rune on the rock. The stone glowed, and Isiilde crawled inside the crude shelter to curl against the heated surface.

"The village isn't far," Oenghus said. He possessed an uncanny sense of direction. Drop him blindfolded in the middle of the Great Expanse and he would unerringly lead the way to the nearest tavern. "Me and Lucas will scout it out. The Scarecrow isn't too good in close combat, Captain. Keep them safe."

"Drop the title, and stay out of trouble."

Oenghus' eyes crinkled in a smile. "Acacia it is. At least I'm making progress."

Acacia ignored the comment. Instead, she gave her lieutenant a nod of permission, and without another word, the two men vanished into the blizzard.

Isiilde huddled against Marsais, wrapping her cloak around them both and burying her nose against his neck.

"I don't suppose we could start a fire?" Rivan chattered, hugging his wolf pelt tightly around his shoulders.

"Be my guest."

Rivan stared into the blizzard, rubbed his snow scorched eyes, and blinked. It took a long time for him to realize there was no dry wood. "I think my armor is frozen."

"You'll warm up, Rivan. We have heat, Lucas and Oenghus don't."

"You're not upset that he ordered you to stay behind, sir?"

"To guard what he holds most dear? No."

"Maybe so, but I don't like it, sir."

"Part of leading, Rivan, is knowing when to listen—no matter who speaks. Now quiet, and keep your eyes open."

Marsais glanced at the woman by his side. Her pale gaze met his, and he inclined his head with respect. One sensible person was worth ten brutish warriors in any situation. The Knight Captain gave him hope.

THE TEMPERATURE PLUMMETED WITH NIGHTFALL, and Rivan's violent shivers turned to an alarming stillness. After Acacia elbowed him awake a third time, Marsais traced a delicate fire rune, and brushed his armor. The steel heated, but only slightly. If any other Wise One had attempted such a weave, Rivan would have been cooked alive.

"Thank you, sir," Rivan sighed, soaking up the warm cocoon with closed eyes.

"And you, Captain?"

Acacia was sitting cross-legged beside him with her sword laid across her knees. "Please."

Marsais tapped her shoulder. And although the set of her jaw relaxed a fraction, she remained alert.

"Most Wise Ones are tired after using the Gift, but it doesn't seem to bother you."

Marsais raised a shoulder. "Long practice."

"Can't you draw too much? What does your Order call it—a Backlash?"

Isiilde's ears perked up at the question. She lowered her cloak to study Marsais, waiting for his answer.

"I haven't had any issues yet."

When he raised a brow at her, she narrowed her eyes and pulled the cloak back over her head.

Marsais sat silently as visions appeared in the storm, flashing to life, then carried away by the winds: death, carnage, darkness. He'd seen it all.

With cool detachment, he stored each vision behind a locked door in his mind—in an endless maze of possibilities and time.

A touch shattered his visions, and he blinked, looking into a pair of emerald eyes. "Something is out there," Isiilde whispered.

The paladins were on their feet, swords held at the ready. "I hear howling in the wind," Acacia hissed.

"Wolves, maybe?" Rivan asked.

In answer, the wind died for a split second, and into that silence, a deep-throated moan rose in its place. It was a sound full of misery and pain. Then another moan overlapped the first, riding on its heels, ripped from some dark recess of an inhuman throat.

Marsais and Isiilde scrambled to their feet. His coins chiming a quiet warning as four enormous shapes emerged from the trees, lumbering through the swirling snow towards their position.

Marsais stepped in front of Isiilde. His fingers flashed, weaving an orb of light in the dark. The blue orb crackled to life and drifted forward, illuminating the four shapes. They broke through the trees, monstrous and macabre, with stitched flesh and iron lashings. Taller than Oenghus, their eyes gleamed with a ghastly light and a stench of decay clung to them.

"Golems," Acacia breathed.

Wrought from flesh and iron and willing spirits, golems were resistant to the Gift and to Time itself, making them tireless hunters.

"Guard her, Rivan!" Marsais barked.

Rivan moved in front of the nymph as Marsais slipped down the ravine and climbed up the other side to meet the charging golems. Acacia was a step behind him.

The four golems bellowed, inhuman and deafening, as Marsais wove a runic hand. He thrust out his own, and the ethereal form raced towards a boulder. Gritting his teeth, he plucked the massive stone off the ground and hurled it at the nearest attacker. The rock tore into the first golem, ripping its arm from its shoulder.

Acacia's chant matched her racing footsteps. A glow enveloped her shield, armor hummed, and her sword flashed with Divine fire as she stepped between two monstrous forms, weaving between their legs with biting skill.

Marsais grabbed another boulder, throwing it at the second's head. The rock struck, decapitating the golem, but the headless abomination kept charging.

Marsais dove to the side, rolled to his feet, and took a step back as a golem stomped its foot at him. With his left hand, he wove a blurring rune and with his right, he summoned his runic hand, grabbing the headless golem's leg and wrenching it back.

The monster crashed to the snow as the weave took effect, blurring Marsais' snaking form and making him indistinct. But Marsais struggled to maintain his hold on the thrashing construct as he threw a levitation weave at a nearby boulder. He bound it to the ground under the headless golem.

His coins chimed in warning, but Marsais was too slow. A rending force slammed into his ribs, sending him flying. His concentration slipped, but the weave held and the rock barreled towards its bind, falling with a squelch onto the golem.

Marsais smacked against a tree with a grunt. Shaking off the blow, he summoned a flame and hurled it towards the one-armed golem. The fireball ignited. But as the explosion roiled outwards, he stepped back into a tree, his flesh melding with the bark.

He hastily offered his apologies to the wood spirits for the intrusion, followed the twining roots to the next tree, and emerged behind his burning, one-armed foe.

Acacia was on the defense, losing ground and slipping in the snow as she dodged and twisted away from the killing blows of the third and fourth golems. Marsais brought his hand to bear with a growling incantation. The runic hand punched one of Acacia's golems from the side, knocking it off balance. And Acacia plunged her sword into a meaty thigh. But when the golem reeled backwards, her blade was ripped from her hand.

She shouted, summoning the blade, but before it returned to her hand, the fourth golem charged, sending her sprawling into the snow.

Marsais blasted the golem with a wave of searing heat, but it only slowed its progression as it stomped at the troublesome paladin trying to scramble away.

Two golems, one without an arm and the other headless, converged on him. Marsais turned to face his assailants, leaving Acacia on her own to fight her flaming foes.

With a clap, he completed a weave in time to catch the golems in a cage of runes. When they slammed into the runic shield, it rippled and collapsed, falling over the constructs like a net.

Straining to contain the two golems, Marsais shifted his focus, struggling against their bulk to bring his hands together. A moment more, and the golems would be crushed.

Marsais felt a surge of panic course through his bond with Isiilde. He twisted as much as he dared, still battling with the entrapped golems. The fourth, smoldering golem had abandoned the prone captain, and charged the ravine.

Rivan stepped forward to engage the monstrosity, but he was clutching his sword like a drowning man clinging to driftwood.

"Captain!" Marsais shouted, redoubling his efforts, channeling the Gift until a tidal wave of power thrummed through his veins. He didn't dare drop the cage now, not so close to victory. Arms straining, he clenched his jaw, and focused on bringing his palms together.

Acacia staggered to her feet, shield abandoned, arm hanging limply at her side. The third golem struck with a fist, delivering a glancing blow. She reeled, swinging her sword wildly, catching rotting flesh and ripping away decay without noticeable effect.

"Marsais!" Isiilde screamed.

Rivan's blade bit into the golem's flesh as he caught a pounding blow on his shield. But the golem didn't slow. It grabbed Rivan and wrenched him off his feet like a rag doll.

Trapped in a vise-like grip, Rivan hacked and swung, gasping for air as his armor crumpled with every expelled breath.

Isiilde screamed in terror. And then with rage. Her voice rose over the din of battle and spread its wings with thrumming power.

She burst into flame.

Fire swirled around her body with a hiss before slamming into the nearest golem and rolling over the others like a crashing wave. The golem dropped Rivan through a wall of heat into melting snow.

Isiilde's scream turned to something more—a haunting melody that froze Marsais' blood. Her voice fueled the flame, twisting it with white hot fury.

Marsais shielded himself against the power beating at his mind through their bond. With a final push, he brought his palms together with a smack, closing the Orb of Force around the trapped golems. Fire and flesh sprayed into the night, mixing rot with snow, and ash with iron.

Marsais turned to face his enraptured nymph. She stood barefoot and naked on the edge of the ravine, clothed in fire and lashing flame. An unnatural fire consumed the remaining golems, eating them like tinder, along with the surrounding trees.

Her voice continued to rise, gaining intensity, peaking with desire. Acacia and Rivan dove into the ravine, burrowing into the snow, as a wave of flame roiled over their heads. But Marsais stood his ground.

Mentally bracing himself, he yanked the veil from between their bond, letting Isiilde's spirit surge into his own.

It was pure, hot fire.

Stifling a wave of pain, he began to chant, his voice battling her own as he gathered the fires into his hands, rolling them into a blazing ball.

Isiilde turned her focus on him. She was seething with divine fury, an emerald blaze smoldering in her eyes. She fought him for control of her fire.

Her voice beat back the winds, chased away the snow, battering Marsais like a fishing boat on a churning sea. The storm was fierce, but short-lived. He snatched the last trailing wisps from her body and slapped his hands together with an explosion of energy. The shock wave ripped through the forest, felling trees with an earth-shaking crash.

Ash and timber and trailing brands fluttered to the ground, and in the aftermath of destruction, Marsais realized what he had done. The nymph collapsed in a pale heap. Her spirit flickered once through their bond, then vanished.

Time slowed as Marsais raced across the snow. With a curse, he leapt across the ravine to catch her body as it slid down the side. He pressed his palms against her breast, seized the Gift, and sent a jolt of healing energy into her heart.

Her body jerked. But nothing more. He tried again.

Acacia staggered over to place a hand on Isiilde's forehead. She bowed her head, beseeching the Guardians for aid, and a warm light traveled from the paladin's hand into the nymph. A fluttering spark ignited in her spirit.

Marsais focused on that tiny spark. With infinite patience, he nurtured it, channeling a finite strand of Life into its center. When her spirit flickered, Marsais withdrew, fearing he would snuff out her life a second time. His healing talents were limited. She needed Oenghus. Urgently.

After weaving another cold ward, he searched for her cloak. It was singed but intact. He wrapped it around her body, and gathered her up in his arms.

"Your pelt, Rivan. Quickly."

The young paladin's face was covered with blood. His helmet was gone, his armor crushed, but he pulled himself to his feet, only to fall face first in the snow a moment later. Acacia scrambled to retrieve the pelt, tossed it to Marsais, and checked on her soldier.

She looked into the seer's eyes. "Go."

Marsais wrapped the pelt around Isiilde and took off, leaving the Knight Captain and her wounded soldier in the middle of a burning forest.

CHAPTER 28

"Can you see anything?" Lucas whispered.

Oenghus could see enough, far more than he wished. These weren't the sort of men he'd let within a mile of Isiilde, and for that matter, he'd be dammed if he'd risk the captain and her fresh-faced young paladin either.

"You can't see anything?" Oenghus asked.

Lucas gestured at the scarring on his face. "My eyes aren't what they used to be."

The two spies lay on the bank opposite a village. It was fortified, surrounded by deep trenches and bristling stakes. Three longhouses sat on the river's bank, and canoes and longboats were tied to shore, guarded by fur-clad sentries who looked like grizzled bears in the storm —all normal enough, except that men and women were impaled on stakes.

After Oenghus told him, Lucas spat. "Heathens."

For once, Oenghus had to agree. The dead should be buried, not picked apart by carrion in the open air.

"We need supplies."

Lucas nodded in agreement.

The storm was both a blessing and a curse. On a night like this, most everyone had taken shelter, which meant fewer guards and a concealing storm. Unfortunately, the needed supplies would also be kept close at hand. The boats looked promising, though.

Oenghus eyed Lucas' armor. "Stay here, Tin Man. I'll see what I can scavenge without waking the dead."

"Not likely," Lucas said, unbuckling his armor.

Oenghus grunted, following suit. They unslung their shields, and stowed their heavier gear, moving upstream to ford the river with nothing but their knives.

There was a saying in the realm, and Lucas cursed himself silently for not heeding it: never follow a Berserker into battle.

Oenghus moved into the current, fighting the river and ice, and as they neared the opposite shore, he kept his chin to the water, eyeing the crude fortifications.

A lone guard leaned against a mooring post, but it was impossible to see his eyes in the storm of flurries.

The two warriors glanced at each other before crawling up the bank. Oenghus squeezed between the execution stakes, and slipped to the side of a longhouse. Firelight glowed from between cracks in the timber and a wave of festivities and raucous laughter hammered at the walls.

Oenghus stepped on a barrel, grabbed the under hang of the sloping roof, and hoisted himself up, peering through the gap between roof and wall.

From the outside, it sounded like a clan gathering, full of carousing and brawling, but thoughts of his homeland were quickly shattered. The Suevi were smaller than his own kinsmen, shaving the sides of their heads and leaving a long streak of black hair dangling down their tattooed backs.

They drank out of bleached skulls and the carcasses roasting on the spits looked too familiar for his taste. Wildness dwelt in the men's eyes, and their women cowered like dogs from their kicks, fighting for table scraps.

Oenghus dropped back to the ground. "Flesh-eaters," he whispered. Marsais was right.

In silent agreement, the two men crept from hut to hut, avoiding the sentries huddled around firepits.

The two spies peeked into dark huts until one proved promising. Coals glowed behind a heavy fur drape, illuminating a room filled with baskets and goods. A lone figure snored on a mat. He smelled of piss and mead.

Lucas and Oenghus moved silently into the room. The man didn't stir. While he slept, they plundered the goods, filling sacks with dried herbs, vegetables, and salted fish. A heavy blanket, cloak, a pot, waterskin, clay jug, a pair of trousers, and boots disappeared into their sacks.

Oenghus slipped outside into the shadows. Two furred figures dragged a third between them. Blood seeped into tracks of the two legs gliding over snow. When they had vanished into a gust of flurries, he tapped the curtain behind him, signaling Lucas to emerge. They moved on to the next structure, a wooden shed with a sloped roof.

The scrape of steel sounded from inside, and Oenghus put his eye to a gap. A squat figure sharpened a cleaver. Blood stained the butcher's block, and two scaled human-like shadows feasted on a heaping pile of entrails. It appeared they kept Reapers as pets instead of dogs.

Oenghus moved away in disgust. But a hide-covered structure caught his eye. Two sentries milled in front, huddled beside a flickering fire. They weren't guarding a house, or a hut, but a squarish shape.

Instinct prickled the back of his neck. Oenghus started for the structure, but Lucas caught his arm and jerked his head back towards the river.

They had what they needed. It was foolish to risk more.

Oenghus shook his hand free, and made his way towards the squarish shape. The hides concealed a cage of sturdy timber filled with miserable humans huddled in a knot for warmth.

"Bollocks," he cursed.

Lucas glanced inside, then jerked his head towards shore. The two moved away with their loot.

The longboats were guarded, but the canoes were ignored. Lucas stowed his sack, and climbed inside one. He turned to find Oenghus securing a canoe to his own with a length of rope.

"Get our gear and wait for me downriver."

"You're going back?"

"I'm not leaving those people in a cage."

"The lot of them are heathens. Leave them to their fate. Your nymph could be freezing by now."

"Not with Marsais about. Those captives are bound for the cleaver."

Before Lucas could argue, Oenghus stalked back through the storm. Stealth was no longer a concern. He materialized in front of the cage—a swift, hulking shadow charging from the sleet. A knife plunged into one fur-clad form, and a fist pounded the second. Before the stunned sentry could shout, Oenghus took the man's head in his massive hands and twisted. A limp body crumpled to the snow.

A spear struck wildly up from the ground. Oenghus stepped on the shaft, snapped it, twirled the spearhead and plunged it into the dying sentry's throat. The man's gurgles were lost in the wind.

Ripping his knife from his enemy's chest, Oenghus turned to the cage. The eyes of the captives were wide with fear. He raised a finger to his lips.

Oenghus gripped the iron lock, muttered the Lore of Unlocking, and wrenched it free. He swung open the crude door, but the captives stood frozen in place.

"Run, you bloody fools," he hissed.

His tone snapped them into action. A young man raced out, snatching up a spear and the rest followed, darting in all different directions.

Oenghus snorted at their stupidity. He couldn't help that, but he had given them a fighting chance. A long, urgent horn rose above the howling wind. The captives were escaping.

The longhouse doors were thrown open, warriors scrambled for their weapons and armor in a drunken haze and charged blindly into the night.

Oenghus stalked back to the shore unchallenged in the brewing chaos. Two captives had already cast off, and another two were trailing on his heels. He grabbed the edge of a canoe, pushed it out, and started to climb inside.

A Suevi charged from the darkness, cleaver raised. The captives on Oenghus' heels bolted, but the smallest tripped and fell in the snow. The second captive twisted and slipped, trying to reach the fallen form. Oenghus grabbed the canoe, lifted it with a surge, and hurled it at the attacker. The boat caught the man in the chest, knocking him to the ground. He ripped the cleaver from the Suevi's hand, and brought it down with a crunch, severing his head.

Oenghus heaved the canoe back into the water as the two captives watched in shock. The smaller of the two was a boy, and the other was covered in filth and furs. The thing met his eyes with a feral gaze.

Oenghus jerked his head towards the canoe, holding it steady. The two hopped inside as a knot of Suevi rushed into view. He planted himself between captives and warriors, and roared at the men. The first swung out of fear, and he swatted the blade to the side like a twig. A spear poked Oenghus' arm, and he swiveled, grabbing the haft and ripping it from the warrior's hand. With a skilled twirl, he plunged the weapon into its previous owner.

Oenghus grabbed the next man's neck, plucked him off his feet, and hurled him at his comrades. The remaining Suevi froze, then scattered in terror to look for an easier target.

That was disappointing.

He was surprised to find the bundle of furs and the boy waiting with paddles in the canoe. He had expected them to leave. Impressed, he pushed the canoe from the bank, and stepped in the center with a slosh of water and rocking uncertainty. The canoe held his weight. He snatched the paddle from the boy, and dug into the water.

Warriors with torches dotted the village, moving between huts, hunting for their escaped herd as Oenghus and the others were caught in the current. They moved swiftly away from shore until the sounds of horns and flickering torches fell behind a veil of snow.

Oenghus steered the canoe along the opposite bank until he spotted Lucas on shore. When Lucas grabbed the canoe, the bundle of furs in the front hissed in warning.

"What are these?"

"The only smart ones in the bunch."

THE BUNDLE of furs watched the two men as they hid the third canoe. He was surprised the pair hadn't bolted. Keeping his movements slow, he offered them a plundered dagger.

The wild captive snatched it from his hand.

"Go if you like, I have to—" Oenghus cut off when he caught sight of a glow on the horizon. Fire.

A panicked Whisper slammed into his ears, confirming his fears. "Isiilde is dying!"

Oenghus cursed and ran, leaving Lucas and the freed captives in confusion. Instinct guided him, and he charged heedlessly through the forest like a bull, crashing through anything that dared get in his way.

He nearly ran into Marsais.

The two men did not waste time with words. Marsais set Isiilde down in the snow and Oenghus pressed his palms against her forehead and stomach, summoning the Gift and plunging his awareness into her body.

The thin, wavering line of flame that was her spirit nearly shattered his focus. With careful skill, Oenghus fed his spirit into the nymph, bolstering, nurturing, sacrificing his own strength for the sake of hers. When he withdrew, he was weak, and shivering with cold.

"Four golems," Marsais rasped, holding Isiilde tightly to his chest. "She tried to help and lost control."

"And what?"

"I took her fire."

Oenghus' eyes smoldered, but now was not the time to pummel Marsais. "We have canoes. Where are the others?"

"Rivan is injured. The captain, too."

Oenghus staggered to his feet, pointed back the way he had come, and went to search for the others. He found them on their feet. More or less. Rivan leaned heavily on his captain for support. Most of Rivan's armor was missing. Blood matted his hair, and his leg dragged uselessly through the snow.

"He's bad," Acacia said in greeting. "Crushed."

Rivan was struggling to breathe.

Oenghus lowered Rivan down to the snow, and slapped hands to forehead and stomach. Bones mended, flesh closed, and the paladin's breathing evened. Without a word, Oenghus hoisted Rivan over a shoulder, and forged a path through the snow, noting Acacia's dangling shield arm and staggering gait.

They found Marsais at the river's edge, bundling Isiilde into a canoe, and padding her with pillaged goods. "This is Kasja and her brother Elam. They are Lome, and they are in your debt, Oenghus," Marsais said without looking up. "Kasja has invited us to her home."

Oenghus looked at the feral creature balanced on the prow of the boat—a woman. He grunted, lowered Rivan into a canoe, and checked on Isiilde. Her pulse was thready, but holding.

"Tell them we'd be honored."

Marsais spoke a few, flowing words to the woman, and she returned with a long string of fluttering replies. They sounded like twittering birds. Before Marsais could translate, Oenghus looked up. The forest fire had moved to the middle of the river, or so it seemed at first glance.

"Marsais!" he shouted, throwing himself between an approaching longboat and his daughter.

Marsais wove a lightning quick weave and tapped his human shield as a storm of flaming arrows flew through the sky. Acacia dove over Rivan with her shield raised. Lucas grabbed the boy's head, and pushed him to the ground, raising his own shield as cover while Kasja dove off the canoe.

Arrows rained on the group, bouncing off steel while others found flesh. Oenghus cursed and grabbed his hammer, but was too slow to attack. Marsais beat him to it.

He snatched the raging fire from the treetops and threw a bind at the longboat. A wave of flame rose over their heads, crashing like a wave over the Suevi's longboat and igniting it. Men dove into the icy river to escape the fire. But most were too late.

"There may be more."

"Hmm." Haloed by a backdrop of fiery death, Marsais shook out his hands and stepped into the canoe.

The Suevi had been caught by surprise. Scattered and drunk, their attacks had been clumsy. But morning might bring a more focused effort.

The ragged band paddled through the night, using Orbs of Light, bobbing like Will o' Wisps, to illuminate obstacles in the sluggish river.

"How is she?" Oenghus asked after the second hour.

"No worse, no better."

"Ask Kasja how far, and tell them there's food in the sacks."

Marsais translated, speaking to the woman rowing beside them with her brother. She replied with a string of chirping words.

"The Lome hold the lands along the south fork. The river becomes rough, but she'll navigate. We should be there by midday."

"So soon?"

"The current is quick."

Oenghus grimaced. He did not like boats, and since there was no other outlet for his frustrations, he focused his ire on Marsais.

"What did you do to Isiilde?"

"I told you, I took her fire."

"You nearly killed her."

"She would have burned herself out," Marsais argued, holding the unconscious nymph to his chest. "I had to do something. She's like a spark in a dry field. Fierce, but as soon as the fuel is gone, it burns out. I fear it controls her, and nothing she can do will stop it."

"That's what they say about berserkers."

Marsais twisted around to stare at his old friend. Oenghus was proof that anything was possible. With Marsais' help, the berserker had learned to channel his rage into something constructive. But Oenghus, for all his rage and strength, was human—or thereabouts. How could Marsais teach control to a creature of pure passion and instinct? That was the trick, and he had to do it fast—before Isiilde killed either herself or everyone within striking distance.

"You've taken her fire before, Scarecrow. What went wrong?"

"She fought me."

"And you fought back?"

"Of course I did," Marsais snapped. "It was all I could do to stand against her. Only... I miscalculated. I didn't realize how much of her was in the fire. Her spirit was snuffed out."

Oenghus surged forward, grabbing him by the neck, heedless of the rocking boat. "What do you mean, you *snuffed* her out?"

Marsais did not struggle, but surrendered to the vise-like grip. "Her spirit vanished. I sent a wave of the Gift into her, enough to produce a spark."

"You bloody bastard!" The roar slammed into the water, and bounced into the bleak sky.

"Oenghus!" The captain's harsh whisper snapped him from his fury. "Sit down before you tip the boat and drown the nymph."

Oenghus' jaw worked. His eyes smoldered, but he clicked his teeth together and sat, brooding like a grumpy bear.

"I don't care if you strangle the seer, but hand over the nymph first."

"Your concern is touching, Captain," Marsais coughed.

"Think nothing of it," she said in clipped tones. "And you should know, Oenghus, you have an arrow sticking out of your back."

Oenghus twisted, trying to glimpse the offending splinter. He reached an arm around, and ripped the arrow from his flesh. It was probably poisoned. He tossed it in the water.

"You have one in your leg, too," Marsais pointed out.

With a snarl, Oenghus wrenched the broken arrow from his calf, and threw it at the back of Marsais' head.

Marsais turned to face him. "Think," he urged, keeping his voice low. "How much brimgrog was flowing through your veins when you fathered her?"

Oenghus frowned, tilting the paddle so their canoe drifted to the side, away from the others. "Don't blame this on me."

"Morigan said it."

"Don't bring Mori into this."

"I know her wisdom rankles you, but she had a point about your brimgrog mixing with... *faerie* blood." He would not speak of Isiilde's mother. Not here.

"None of my other children burst into flames."

"No, but most of them grow up to be berserkers. Isiilde is faerie— not human. I'm willing to wager my fortune that the brimgrog affected her blood differently than the rest of your crazed brood. And Morigan agrees.”

Oenghus' mouth worked. He wanted to deny it, to slap his paddle across Marsais' face and swat the man into the water, but his good sense triumphed. There was no use arguing with Morigan, even when she wasn't there.

“What does it matter? *You* killed her.”

“Only briefly.”

CHAPTER 29

Snow and ice made the river treacherous. Kasja shouted directions to the others. She knew what currents to avoid, what forks to take in the river's course, and on which side of the boulders to pass. It seemed the woman could have navigated the river blindfolded.

Oenghus gripped his paddle, dragging it off the side, switching course with Kasja's expert hand. Eventually, the torrent spit them into a canyon with high cliffs and no shore.

Silence rang in his ears, eerie and foreign after a night and day of endless wind.

In a calm eddy, Oenghus called Kasja over, directing his boat alongside hers. Marsais and Kasja held the canoes close, as Oenghus reached into the cocoon of thick blankets to check Isiilde's pulse. It was thready and weak. He connected himself to spirit and body, and bolstered her strength with his own.

There was nothing more Oenghus could do for her, except find shelter and warmth, and a bed that was not rocking.

Eventually, the river propelled them around a corner into a wall of mist and thunder that stole Oenghus' breath—a waterfall, and something more. Docks floated at the river's edge, tethered to the cliffs. A maze of ladders and walkways climbed up the rock face. Nimble, fur-clad forms clambered up ropes, traversed dizzying walkways, and shot down ladders with a rush of cries and warning. The Lome.

Oenghus prodded Marsais with his paddle.

"Hmm?" Marsais tore his gaze from the sky and blinked at the masked men on the docks.

"We're here, Scarecrow."

"Where?"

"The Lome village—more like a city, I think."

Marsais still looked confused.

"You nearly killed Isiilde."

The statement nudged his memory. He looked abashed, checked on the nymph, then studied the cliffs.

The Lome reached towards the canoes with hooked poles, drawing the boats towards the dock. Oenghus didn't resist—he wasn't keen on going over a waterfall. But that didn't stop him from glaring at the fur-clad natives. They wore animal-like masks—from bears to wolves and eagles. And all of them had weapons, mostly pointed at Oenghus.

A man dressed in stitched wolf pelts stepped forward. Unlike the others, he wore a human skull mask, painted with bold, crimson slashes. He issued some harsh order, and jabbed a finger at Kasja.

The guards bristled in response, but before they could react, Oenghus batted away the closest spear, drawing their attention away from the wild woman.

It worked too well. The guards on the walkways drew their bows and pointed them at his head.

Kasja hissed at Wolf-pelt. The two exchanged a flurry of harsh words, rising in volume until their voices bounced off the granite cliffs.

Marsais leaned slightly back, speaking out of the side of his mouth. "They believe Kasja is dead—that she is an evil spirit disguised as one of their own."

The feral woman spat into the river and rolled up her sleeve, exposing a filthy forearm. She slipped a dagger from a sleeve and sliced her skin. The blade disappeared with equal speed. Kasja stood, balancing easily in the canoe, to raise her arm, letting the blood run free for all to see.

Wolf-pelt swiped the cut with his fingertips. He tasted her blood cautiously, and spat. More words were spoken, spears bristled, the argument heated, and finally, Marsais interrupted.

Oenghus didn't speak the language, but he knew his old master. And he knew that low, dangerous tone.

The Lome narrowed their eyes.

Oenghus and the paladins shifted uneasily. They felt like fish in a barrel. If a fight broke out, there would be blood.

A voice rang from the mouth of a cave above—a sharp, commanding voice. Wolf-pelt snarled, slapped a fist to his chest, and gestured at them with his spear.

"They're taking us to their chieftain to decide our fate."

"I don't like this, Scarecrow."

"Nor do I," Marsais admitted. "But we have little choice... unless you want to chance the waterfall."

"I'd rather be on solid ground," Acacia murmured.

Oenghus grunted in agreement.

"This is no mere village. And they don't like outsiders, most especially ones in armor." Marsais spared a pointed look at what was left of the paladins' armor.

Oenghus climbed out first, his size causing a ripple of murmurs as he bent to take Isiilde. "I was hoping Kasja was the chieftain's daughter," he grumbled.

"Because that worked out so well for you on the Isle of Winds," Marsais said, handing her up.

Wolf-pelt stepped forward to take the bundle from Oenghus' arms, but he moved away, throwing the bobbing dock off balance with his weight. Spears bristled, muscles tensed, and Oenghus growled low in warning.

Marsais thrust an arm between the two men. Quick words were exchanged, then Wolf-pelt gestured at the bundle. Marsais hesitated, but obeyed, peeling back the cloak to reveal the nymph.

The Lome pressed against walkways and stretched on ropes, straining to glimpse the unconscious faerie.

Marsais spoke again, his voice low and dangerous and full of warning. The warriors eyed the elf, and as one, they began to laugh. It was not a cheerful sound, but the braying of wild dogs.

The voice from above cut through the warriors' laughter, and Wolf-pelt gave a sharp command.

"We're to surrender our weapons," Marsais translated, handing over his eating knife with great ceremony.

More laughter rippled through the watching warriors.

Oenghus decided that Wolf-pelt would die first. At Marsais' arched brow, he grunted, and hefted *Gurthang*, passing the rune-etched war hammer over. With spears at their back, the paladins followed suit, and the group was ushered towards the ladders.

"Can you manage with your arm, Captain?" Marsais asked.

"I'm more worried about Oenghus and his size," she replied, eyeing the flimsy ladders.

"You wouldn't be the first woman to worry," Oenghus said, flashing a grin.

Acacia did not comment, but put her one good arm to the ladder and climbed. Marsais took Isiilde from Oenghus, shifting her to his shoulder. Time was of the essence, and he feared they had already delayed too long. Isiilde needed a warm bed to recover, not a bundle of furs in a rocking canoe surrounded by icy winds.

Kasja gestured towards the ladder. When Marsais began to climb with Isiilde balanced on his shoulder, the furred woman shot up a rope with squirrel-like ease, followed by her agile little brother. Oenghus waited until they stood at the cave's entrance before following. The ladder groaned under his weight.

The Lome watched, breath held, waiting to see if their craftsmanship would survive. It did. Oenghus climbed onto a ledge that had been carved into the cliff face. A deep cave led into the unknown, guarded by twin statues that were half eagle and half bull.

"The Lome worship the beasts of the land," Marsais explained as the group moved inside. Carvings covered the walls, from the smallest sparrow to massive bears. "They value a creature's strength and agility. If an animal can survive, then so can the Lome, but only if they mimic the animal's behavior."

Oenghus ducked his head as they filed down the passage, turning as the tunnel demanded to fit his bulk through the stone. He pointed to a depiction of a bear on the stone, and bared his teeth at the smaller men.

Their guards looked uneasy.

An iron gate sealed the end of the tunnel. It opened at Wolf-pelt's swaggering call, and shut after they passed the threshold. Another long passage twined through the rock, widening with every step. A constant theme ran throughout the art on the walls—the Lome's fight against Voidspawn and barbaric tribes.

At least this tribe didn't revere the Void.

Kasja half-crawled and half-walked like an animal she resembled, moving swiftly with the group. Oenghus leaned close to Marsais' ear. "Where does Kasja stand in the tribe?"

"She's touched in the head."

"A woman after your own heart."

"In more ways than one."

"Foresight?"

"Hmm, I'm not entirely sure."

"Madness, then?"

"Perhaps."

"Stop being so vague," Oenghus growled in his ear.

"Madness, foresight, or a brilliant deception—take your pick," Marsais said with a rueful twist of his lips. "Madness is feared, but foresight in a madman is revered. And if she has sense enough to feign such a gift, then that makes her brilliant."

"Well, you'd know, being an expert in matters of madness."

"So says the berserker."

A sharp, poking spear silenced the pair. Oenghus tried to twist around to glare at the offender, but the stone prevented the movement. Instead, he glared at the back of Marsais' head, trying to ignore the itch of threat along his neck.

They turned a corner, the passage opened, and Oenghus blinked. Stone steps spilled down the side of a cavernous valley. A sprawling city was nestled in its underground embrace, bustling with activity and light. Luminous vines, carefully cultivated in neat rows, climbed up stone structures and the valley's sides, glowing as bright and blue as a full moon.

"Amazing," Marsais breathed.

Oenghus couldn't be bothered with the view, not with a squad of armed men poking blades at his back.

They were led down the long winding stairs into a sea of Lome, who parted for the prisoners. The natives watched them pass with curious eyes. Underground, in their cavernous city warmed by natural springs, the natives shed their furs for simple black garments. The Lome were a black-haired, pale-skinned race heavily tattooed with spiraling art that glowed like the vines.

A chant rose among the watchers, rising in tempo with every passing step. Lips moved as one while their dark eyes and glowing faces followed the prisoners in unity.

"What's going on?" Acacia asked Marsais.

"I believe they're purging the evil we bring. You're not the first armored warriors they've encountered."

A ring of stalagmites rose in the center of the city like columns striving to join their twins high overhead. Each column bore the visage of a predator: eagle, bear, wolf, and cougar.

The prisoners were ushered between the pillars, and in the clearing beyond, a grizzled, one-eyed warrior whose skin glowed with tattoos sat on a throne of bones. The chieftain. He was a large man who dominated the bone chair. He wore a frost bear's pelt with pride, and his gnarled hand rested on a sharp axe.

A single bright eye looked from the prisoners to Kasja and her brother, Elam, then found a resting place on Wolf-pelt. The warrior stepped forward, talking and gesturing from Kasja to the prisoners.

Kasja scuttled out into the open, moving towards the throne, interrupting the exchange with a hiss. The chieftain said little, appraising the group and listening to the growing argument between Wolf-pelt and Kasja.

During the exchange, Oenghus studied the chieftain. The images on his bare scalp took shape: eyes. Hundreds of tattooed eyes covered his scarred scalp.

The chieftain gestured sharply, and the arguing Lome fell silent. For the first time, their leader spoke, his voice low and grating. There was, Oenghus noted, a jagged slice across his throat.

Marsais turned toward the group to translate. "This is a sacred city to the Lome. As outsiders, we cannot leave, but V'elbine, the chieftain, has granted us sanctuary. Our strength will be added to the clans."

V'elbine gestured towards the bundle in Marsais' arms. Wolf-pelt stepped forward, reaching out a hand, and Oenghus clamped down on the warrior's wrist before he could touch the nymph. With a growl, he shoved the warrior back.

Murmurs rippled through the gathered crowd. V'elbine said a sharp word. Silence descended and Wolf-pelt froze, quivering like a dog on a leash. The chieftain nodded to Marsais, who peeled back the cloak covering Isiilde's pale face.

V'elbine's eyes widened, and the other Lome leaned in for a look with varying degrees of surprise and a ripple of excitement. The chieftain gestured at the nymph in a grandiose manner as he spoke. Oenghus did not like his manner at all.

"V'elbine," Marsais translated, "will take Isiilde as his own and the captain will be given to another worthy warrior. Since Kasja owes you a Blood Debt, Oenghus, you are now her master, and the boy's."

"Bollocks." Oenghus vowed to never rescue another group of captives as long as he lived.

Marsais turned back to address the chieftain. Whatever he said, it elicited a roar of laughter from the natives.

"I have informed them that Isiilde is my Oathbound and the captain is yours. He has graciously allowed you to keep your woman."

The fate of Isiilde stole the humor out of the statement.

"And you?" Acacia asked.

"I have informed our hosts," Marsais began, placing Isiilde in Oenghus' arms, "that I will not give her to another, and if anyone attempts to take her from me, I will kill every last one of them without mercy."

That explained the laughter. But the paladins had witnessed Marsais' powers—they did not laugh, and neither did Oenghus.

Marsais addressed V'elbine again, then translated the exchange. "He says that their tribe is honorable. They respect the Oaths between man and woman. I must fight to the death for her. The chieftain will honor the outcome."

"Well, don't bloody play around this time, Scarecrow."

"I wouldn't dream of it."

Marsais stepped into the center of a hastily formed circle of Lome. Several warriors stepped forward to volunteer, all seasoned and eager and strong. Wolf-pelt slapped his chest and bellowed a boast, strutting into the circle with a threat that did not need translation.

The chieftain nodded to the puffed-up rooster, and the warriors fell back in line. Another stepped forward to offer Marsais a spear and sword, but he shook his head and pointed to the Lome who held their weapons.

When he selected his eating knife, the crowd laughed again, but their amusement was cut short by a sharp gesture from V'elbine.

Marsais stood at the opposite end of the circle and pointed his little knife at his opponent, folding his other arm behind his back. Wolf-pelt hefted a spear, and the two combatants waited for the chieftain's signal —whatever that might be. While most were focused on Marsais' knife-hand, Oenghus watched his other. He was weaving one-handed—without the Lore.

V'elbine raised his fist, then brought it down.

Wolf-pelt lunged, Marsais thrust out his hand, clenched his fist, and the spear point faltered. The warrior gasped, stumbling back, dropping his weapon in shock. Before the audience registered what was happening, Marsais jerked back his arm, ripping Wolf-pelt's heart from his chest.

The crowd shrieked in horror and shock. As the warrior crumpled, Marsais caught the bloody organ and turned to the chieftain. Blood rolled over his outstretched hand and dripped onto the stone. He addressed V'elbine.

Oenghus did not know what he said, but Marsais' tone sent a shiver down his spine. V'elbine did not reply. The grizzled chieftain only nodded—one curt gesture that held fear.

Marsais dropped the heart at the chieftain's feet, withdrew a dingy handkerchief, and methodically wiped his hands clean.

"We'll worry about leaving later," he said. "For now, we have sanctuary."

CHAPTER 30

Isek Beirnuckle gazed down at the town of Drivel with revulsion. Yet another storm was battering its walls. He'd watched humans for centuries, and he would never understand them. They walled themselves up, living like rats in their nests, fighting over morsels of food.

Why did they insist on gathering in filthy cities? There was plenty of room in the realm. But they did like to feel safe. Even when numbers only brought betrayal, murder, and grief.

A lashing wind whipped at his cloak as he placed a steadying hand on his nervous mount. His destination was within sight, nestled between the Viscount's reserve and a cliff side that plunged into the ocean's surf. The manor belonged to Tharios.

Isek reined his horse in front of a heavy gate. The property was surrounded by whitewashed walls topped by artful renditions of twining iron vines. The outside wall was warded. Only a truly foolish thief, or a very skilled one, would risk robbing the manors on the hill. Wise Ones were always in high demand for their wards.

The gatekeeper emerged from his house, squinting through the sleet from beneath a hood.

"Isek Beirnuckle for the Archlord," he shouted over the winds. "I have urgent news."

"The Archlord is not to be disturbed."

"This cannot wait."

The gatekeeper narrowed his eyes and dipped his bushy chin, leaving Isek to wait and shiver in the restless wind. Tharios did not surround himself with fools.

A Whisper would have been enough, but delivering a message in person would remind Tharios of his usefulness.

The gate soon opened, and Isek nudged his horse into the walled refuge. Victer was waiting for him inside—a former merchant guard of the Golden Road with broad shoulders and a stiff spine.

"It best be important," Victer rumbled. "But I figure you're smart enough to know that."

"Your confidence is not misplaced."

Victer led the way around the manor to the back of the estate. A neat row of trees, interspersed with garden squares and fountains, remained untouched by the weather. An enchantment, Isek surmised; a very skilled one. Tharios liked order and things in their places, defying nature and leaving nothing to chance.

Isek followed Victer into a stone shed, and down a gaping staircase that led to the heart of decay. There must be, he thought, a way to mask the small building. Or the Inquisitors had never bothered to look inside what appeared to be a lowly gardener's shed.

Fresh air became a thing of memory as his boot hit the bottom step. Incense assailed his senses with a sharp odor of lye that failed to mask the sickly rot of death. Isek pressed a handkerchief to his nose.

An immense ritual chamber lay beyond, typical of any Bloodmagi, save for its size. The corrals were empty of victims, but the scent of their slaughter lingered. A ritual chamber was never fully cleansed—no matter how many times the walls were scrubbed.

Guards were stationed around the walkways, alert and professional, and a crimson-clad man stood in the ritual circle tracing in the sand. Tharios drew one's eye like a light in the darkness. He wore a half-robe of silk in the Xaionian style that displayed a sleek chest and a maze of tattoos flowing over alabaster skin.

Isek and Victer skirted the ritual pit, then waited in silence for the Archlord to acknowledge them. Tharios did not look up, but remained focused on his work. The pattern of runes was familiar in that vague way that shadows in darkness take shape, more imagination than reality.

"I suspect you have a good reason for coming here. Or so you think." Tharios never took his gaze from the sand. "Let us hope I agree with you."

"Morigan received a message from a priestess in Drivel. The priestess needed help with a boy who showed up at her orphanage, near death: blow to the head, gouges on his wrists, and a Weave of Silence on his throat."

One symptom without the other would not have been alarming, but all three together had perked Isek's ears. Suggestive, to say the least. Marsais would have agreed, and by Tharios' reaction, he did too.

The current Archlord looked up from his work with a thoughtful gaze that settled on Victer. "The boy who ran."

"He was killed."

"One was killed, yes, but it appears another may have slipped through the cracks in the chaos."

"Impossible. He could have escaped from another situation."

"I have never liked coincidence." Tharios straightened, folding his hands behind his back in thought.

Victer did not argue, though it was clear from his stance that he placed little value on the information.

"Take care of this, Victer," Tharios glanced at Isek, "and you as well —if you have the stomach for it."

"What if the boy has already talked?" Victer asked.

"*If* the boy has informed the priestess and Morigan of the ceremony, then remove the women, quietly." Tharios paused and tilted his head, as if listening to someone whispering in his ear. "On second thought, I don't want Morigan killed. She's far too valuable as a healer, and she'll give us little trouble. Put them in the dungeon."

Both men bowed, and turned to leave.

"And Isek... Would you like to be present when we open the flask?"

"Of course, Archlord." Truth be told, Isek wanted to be as far from this ritual chamber as possible when the flask was opened, but this was another test of loyalty.

Tharios dismissed him with a wave.

SIX SHAPES RIPPLED in the night, shimmering like a disturbed pond as the wind tore at their invisible cloaks. Isek was not worried. There was no one to see them in the slums of Drivel, and if any eyes did, they'd look away. He slid his hand along a stone on the back of the orphanage, searching for the hidden rune.

Marsais loathed the obvious. He had always avoided front doors like the Blight. And Isek knew all his secret entrances—and exits.

The teleportation rune was faded, but still functioning. The ward recognized his hand and unraveled, revealing its secrets. Stone rippled like the invisibility weave that encased his body, and Isek ushered the five hidden men inside, sealing the gate on their heels before walking to the front of the building.

There were too many men, too many voices and boots and opinions. Isek would have preferred to carry out this assignment alone, but Victer was a strategist who liked to give orders to underlings. So the plan was complex, whereas Isek's had been simple and direct.

But now was not the time to argue with one of the Unspoken—not until Isek's position was firmly established.

Isek dropped his weave and pounded on the heavy front door until the slat slid to the side and a pair of green eyes searched the night.

"What do you bloody want?"

Isek pushed back his cowl, revealing his bald pate and a wide smile. "You might remember me, Priestess. I handed you the key to this place some years back. I'm Isek Beirnuckle."

The priestess glared at him. Isek feared his betrayal had been uncovered for a moment, but she was simply dredging up memory.

She recalled his face a moment later. "And I've been thankful ever since."

The door opened, revealing a tall, busty Nuthaanian. Brinehilde had not changed. Isek let his eyes linger briefly on the bosom that was eye level with his gaze, because human men noticed such things. Details were imperative.

"What brings you here, sir? Not gonna take it back, I hope?"

"Wouldn't dream of it," he said, weaving a coin over his knuckles. "I have other news."

"What is it, then?"

"The Blessed Order seized Marsais' properties and holdings, but I've arranged matters so ownership will pass to you."

"The Sylph bless you."

"It's the least I can do." He smiled, a perfectly rehearsed smile that always touched his eyes, but rather than put the priestess at ease, the gesture made her take a slight step back.

What had betrayed him? He pushed the question away for further study, and continued with his ruse. "Given recent developments, I want to search the manor—in case he might have left anything dangerous behind."

"The Blessed Order already searched the place. I'm sure the Sylph would have helped me find it by now."

"Marsais was well known for his trickery."

Brinehilde crossed a pair of arms that would make any man envious. She had a reputation for cracking skulls. "Morigan and I don't believe one word of this nonsense, but you can look if you like."

"Have you spoken to Morigan recently? I've not seen her in the infirmary."

"That's 'cause she's here. Been lookin' after a boy for me."

Right on cue. "She is?" he asked with surprise.

"Aye, you want to see her? The boy's still out cold, so you'll have to keep your voice down."

As easy as that, Isek had the answer he sought. The boy had not talked. "I don't want to disturb her."

"It's not a problem. She's probably bored out of her mind. It's likely the most rest she's gotten in ages."

Brinehilde was already walking down a corridor, leading the way to the upper floor. Isek followed. Murder was messy—the more bodies that piled up, the higher the risk of discovery. Fortunately, the boy would not be missed.

Morigan sat in a chair beside the bed. Her hands were folded in her lap, but the moment he entered, her eyes snapped towards the door. She never slept deeply.

Isek smiled in greeting, his gaze flickering over the boy on the bed. He was a skinny, brown little runt, and his shaggy hair was plastered to a fevered brow. The room smelled of sickness and hovering death. No one would suspect foul play when he died.

Morigan got to her feet. She was short for a Nuthaanian, but still dominated a room. "What a surprise, Isek."

But she did not appear surprised as she ushered him out of the room. The two women did not trust him. Isek realized Brinehilde brought him here so she'd have help.

"A surprise for me as well. I came to stop the Blessed Order from snatching the orphanage."

"And did you?"

Isek flashed a grin. "Do I ever fail?"

"Not that you've ever admitted."

Morigan Freyr was not a woman to underestimate. Few knew of her history—the full of it, at any rate. Her dark gaze was shrewd and appraising. She'd never warmed up to him.

"Well, I haven't in this case either," he said lightly. "It's the least I can do."

A shift of air slipped in the door behind him.

"There's something more you can do," Morigan said. "This boy in here... someone put a Weave of Silence around his throat. Would you know anything about that?"

Brinehilde suddenly stiffened. And Isek knew a failed gamble when he saw one—something had pricked the women's instincts. She barreled past Isek into the room, and punched at an invisible assailant hovering over the boy. Her fist connected with flesh.

Gabin Archer's invisibility weave unraveled, and the priestess dragged the dazed man out of the room, and ran his head into a wall. His life ended with a sickening crunch.

A chant rose from a Wise One at the end of the hallway, but Morigan hurled a weave at the invisible foe.

Brinehilde charged down the hallway with a roar, slamming into an invisible guard and knocking him against the wall with another crunch of bone.

A second guard attacked, popping into sight with a sword raised to strike. Morigan stepped into the chop, driving her palm into the guard's nose. Her next strike crushed his windpipe. Before he'd dropped to the floor dead, she spun, throwing a bind at another chanting voice. The Unspoken gagged on the Lore, and his weave unraveled, sending a backlash of energy through his body. His skin hardened, cracked, and he fell over, shattering on the floorboards.

Victer threw a lightning bolt at Brinehilde, but she shrugged it off, and charged. Nuthaanians were notoriously resistant to weaves. She slammed Victer against a wall, and the two went down. Brinehilde came out on top; one hand locked around his throat, and the other repeatedly punched at his face.

Isek darted into the room, grabbed the boy off the bed, and dragged him into the hallway. "Stop, or the boy dies!"

His threat stilled the two women. Brinehilde's bloody fist remained poised above an unrecognizable face. The hallway looked like a battlefield.

"It was you," Morigan stated. She did not sound surprised, only hurt. "How could you, Isek?"

"Let Victer go," he ordered.

Brinehilde looked from Isek to the boy, and dropped her foe. As soon as he was free, Victer hurled one more spiteful bolt at point blank range. Brinehilde was blown off her feet, landing on the men she'd killed.

"Stay where you are, Morigan," Isek warned, giving the boy a shake.

She looked on the verge of charging. And he knew none of them would be able to stop her. The boy was their only bargaining chip.

"I don't want to kill these children anymore than you want them to die, so here's what I propose: you're going to walk downstairs and tell the children that everything is fine. Victer will be standing by, so don't think about warning them."

"Let the boy go."

"As soon as you do as you're told."

"You'll kill us anyway," Morigan said.

"No, I won't," he countered. "I'll put you in a comfortable dungeon with Brinehilde and the boy. You can heal them."

"Your word means nothing."

"True, but I have my orders."

"From Tharios?" she asked. "Why would he do that?"

"Because you're useful, Morigan. He values you for your healing talents. Why would he waste that?"

Isek suspected it had more to do with having a hostage to barter with if Oenghus should return. But he personally thought her too dangerous to keep alive.

Morigan seemed to come to the same conclusion. Better a hostage than an orphanage of dead children. "I'll tell the children we're headed to the castle to treat the boy. Will that do?"

Isek dipped his chin.

"Six men for two women and a boy," she said, glancing at the carnage. "You picked the wrong side to be on."

"I am my own side, Morigan."

<hr>

Twenty cowled Unspoken ringed the walkway. Isek Beirnuckle did not join the circle, but stood politely off to the side, silently weaving a crown over his knuckles as he tried to put names to the concealed faces.

Nearly every one of them had a quirk—the way each moved or stood or breathed—but the robes were heavy and black, obscuring most of their tells. Eventually, the cloaked Unspoken would make a mistake.

Sidonie had already made a mistake. Isek had picked her out by the way she moved when she joined the circle, all elegance and grace—so innate to her highborn blood. Victer was easy to spot. His military training never left him. And Eiji was known to all—the spiky-haired gnome couldn't be bothered with robes. As for the rest, they might as well have been Thira.

The circle chanted in a low drone. Not the Lore, but another tongue —a familiar, skin-crawling language that was distinctive to Bloodmagi. The guards opened the corrals and began dragging out silent prisoners for the slaughter. The first offering hit the slab, was sliced, gutted, bled and discarded with efficiency.

Blood flowed down the slab, pooled, and spilled out of the statues' mouths.

Tharios stood in the center of the ritual circle, weaving a complicated series of runes that hung in the air and began to glow red when the blood pooled.

Isek raised a hairless brow at his efforts.

Tharios was mixing the Lore with Bloodmagic. Theoretically, the two drew from the same source, but he had never seen the two disciplines used in tandem. Tharios was using the perverse on something pure. Isek was both impressed and appalled, and he studied the smooth-faced Wise One with new respect. The current Archlord possessed knowledge beyond his years.

When the last thrashing body stilled, it was tossed into the waiting cart. Blood ran through the sands, filling a maze of runes. The last drop fell from the spout, and the enchantment flared to life—a barrier that swirled with power.

Tharios withdrew the flask they had found in Marsais' bedchamber and set it in the center of the maze with ceremony. The ritual swept the flask up, plucking it from the ground, so that the vessel hovered at waist level.

Without hesitation, Tharios raised his palm, summoning the Runic Eye. The Archlord's mark flared to life and the cork dissolved.

The air turned frigid. Frost crept from the opening, climbing down the metal onto the ritual circle, freezing the blood with a spiderweb of icy tendrils.

Isek's lungs burned. The air was hollow and stinging, and he fought for breath as a thick mist seeped from the flask. It buried its chill touch into his skin like a cloak of needles.

The chant died. Those gathered began to choke on the frozen air, but their boots were rooted in place, stuck to the layer of ice that had crystalized in the fog.

A creaking exhale filled the room like a slab breaking from an iceberg. When the breath hit this realm, a Greater Elemental born from the Frozen Wastes of Isiikle surged into being. A thing of ice in its purest form blinded the onlookers and froze the air.

Tharios struggled to breathe, to form a word, but he managed a single gasping word. It activated the circle.

Copper runes clamped around the elemental, burning into its icy form with vise-like brands. A powerful ward pulsed on its monstrous shape. It fought and bellowed, and thrashed with a ferocity that shook the walls.

The frozen blood of the sacrificed began to boil and churn, moving with sluggish purpose through the pattern below, but the crystal creature fought on, moving like gossamer through the blood.

"*Silence!*" Tharios shouted.

The elemental stilled, but its breath creaked in the air, raining shards of ice into the room with every exhalation. It shifted in its prison, ancient, powerful, scratching at their sanity.

The thing was a cloud of ice, shaping, solidifying, turning to gas, and back to its solid form without rhyme or reason and taking no discernible shape. The constant transformation hurt Isek's head—and his eyes. The elemental's clear light was painfully brilliant.

Tharios sucked in a breath, then shifted with a crack as ice fell off his robes. Moving painfully slow, he plucked the flask from the air and turned the container upside down. Something small, the size of a coin, fell into his palm.

The Archlord peered at the object for a moment, then curled his fingers around the trinket in triumph.

CHAPTER 31

DEATH WASN'T what she imagined. The Spirit River was warm and the water soft. Isiilde had never associated the reassuring pop and hiss of flame with the ol' River.

A warm touch informed her she still had a body—a hollow, numb one that seemed far away. A feather drifted over her ear, leaving it tingling with warmth to ward off a sudden chill. She tried to open her eyes, but failed.

Isiilde didn't have the strength to fight the darkness. But another presence kept it at bay. A sun burned fiercely inside her breast. For her alone.

It stood guard as faces leered from the darkness with reaching hands. But she was drifting farther away from the light—drowning in a sea of blood.

Isiilde drifted for eternity. But a pang of loneliness brought her back, and a touch reminded her of love.

Marsais.

She opened her eyes to a pair of silver ones that shone like stars overhead.

"Stay here, my dear. Stay with me." His voice soothed her fear and his hands warmed her face.

"Marsais," she whispered.

"Drink this."

A gentle hand lifted her head, pressing something warm against her numb lips. She swallowed. The liquid burned down her throat. Exhausted, Isiilde closed her eyes again.

"Stay with me, Isiilde."

But she was already retreating into the darkness.

THE PEACEFUL CRACKLE of a fire lured her awake. She was no longer cold. Isiilde opened her eyes and raised her head from Marsais' chest.

They lay on a bed of white furs beside a fire set deep in a pit. The cave should have been oppressive, but a forest scene was etched into the stone and climbing vines glowed with a soft blue light that set off veins of silver streaking through the stone.

It was peaceful. And Isiilde could almost feel a breeze moving through the carved leaves.

Marsais was asleep. But he stirred with a murmur, scratching at the scar on his bare chest. She touched his cheek, and his eyes snapped opened, filled with relief. He caught her hand, and pressed it to his lips.

Isiilde gave him a weak smile, and returned to his chest, but he would not let her rest. He slid to the side, reaching for a waterskin, and supported her head as he pressed it to her lips.

Cool water slid down her throat.

"Not too much."

Marsais took the skin away and lowered her head onto the furs. He brushed the hair from her brow as she studied his face—the firm line of his jaw, his sharp cheekbones, the slightly amused tilt of his long lips, and the gentleness in his eyes.

"Everyone else is asleep."

"Tell me the rest," she whispered.

Marsais did not have to ask—he knew. He smiled easily, and settled beside her, taking her into his arms. Isiilde found his voice reassuring and his touch soothing as he finished the tale of the sea god's daughter.

When his voice fell silent, she sighed against his chest. All that trouble for a woman he did not know.

"Am I that much trouble, Marsais?" she asked. Her eyes were heavy.

"No one compares to you."

Isiilde smiled, strangely pleased, before she surrendered to sleep.

CHAPTER 32

THE NYMPH DANCED around a blazing bonfire in a realm where fire roiled in the sky. Hot tendrils licked her flesh, and her moans fed its hunger. With a hiss and a sizzle, a dragon of fire was born, emerging from the embers, slithering up her legs, climbing higher, twining around a silky thigh and igniting fire.

Isiilde awoke with a gasp.

Marsais arched a brow. "Hmm, I think you'll live." He sat cross-legged on a fur beside her bed, and was dressed in simple clothes of black that hugged his body.

Hot and panting, she pushed the heavy fur blanket off her tingling body. After her heartbeat slowed, she stretched with a sigh, gazing at the strange cavern with wonder.

"We've taken refuge with the Lome," he explained, reading her thoughts. He picked up a wooden mug that held a foul smelling concoction and helped her drink. "Drink slowly, you've been—" he faltered, "asleep for two days, on and off."

"Two *days*?" It seemed too long a time, but she was having trouble remembering from what beginning, or why. "What happened, Marsais? I remember a storm, but nothing else."

"Finish drinking this first, then we'll talk."

There was an ominous sound to his words, so she distracted herself by appreciating how the long winter underclothes hugged his body. Marsais looked like an acrobat. A tired one, with dark circles under his eyes.

"Is everything all right?" she asked when she had gulped the last drop of gruel.

"Not really." He rubbed his short goatee, causing the coins to chime.

"What's wrong?"

"I'm wondering what to do with a certain nymph."

"You could start by getting into bed with her."

His lips twitched as he slid beneath the blankets and gathered her into his arms. "Is that better?"

"Hmm. You took a bath," she noted. His familiar scent was mixed with exotic oils.

"Oenghus eventually chased me out."

"You were worried about me?"

"I still am. What *do* you remember?"

"I told you—the storm."

"Nothing else?"

"I don't want to talk about it."

Marsais pulled back to look her in the eyes. But before he could breach the uncomfortable silence, Oenghus pushed aside a fur curtain and ducked inside the room.

"Get your sack o' bones out of—" He stopped mid-sentence and changed his tone to one of relief. "Look who finally decided to join the living."

"Not much choice was involved," Isiilde said.

Oenghus grunted. "You hungry?"

"Marsais gave me that... slop."

"Oh, did he now?" She felt Marsais tense. "How bloody thoughtful of him. I thought I told you to stay in bed."

"He is in bed."

Oenghus snorted. "Don't think you're escaping the grog, ye ol' Bastard."

When Oenghus disappeared behind the curtain, she pulled away to study Marsais. "Were you injured?"

"I'm not sure which is worse: Oenghus yelling at me or mothering me. He's worse than a fretting old woman."

Marsais had not answered her question. Before she could press him for one, the 'fretting old woman' returned with a mug in hand.

As the curtain opened and fell, she spotted other people moving in the bluish light. "How'd we get here?" she asked.

Marsais untangled himself, and sat up, wrinkling his nose as he accepted the mug. And since he was otherwise occupied with gagging down the potion, Oenghus answered, "While you were burning down the forest, I picked up some strays."

"How is your Oathbound?" Marsais asked between gulps.

"Shut it." Oenghus tugged on his braided beard. "I want nothing to do with that crazed woman, and she doesn't want a thing to do with me. All that bloody hissing—"

Isiilde feared Oenghus would rip out a braid.

"I meant the captain," Marsais said.

Isiilde's eyes widened in surprise. Her guardian had been busy.

"She's not my Oathbound."

"Marsais!" Isiilde warned. He froze, halfway to pouring the mug into the firepit. At least he had the decency to look ashamed. "I had to drink it. Surely you can, too."

"I've been drinking this for two straight days."

"Then you should be used to it."

"Stop being a dandy," Oenghus muttered.

"If you had taken the time to learn how to brew a proper potion, then I wouldn't be complaining."

"I brew them better than your forgetful arse."

"As if you're not forgetful."

"Would you two stop it?" Isiilde growled, rubbing her temples. "What happened?"

Marsais gulped down the rest of the potion as Oenghus answered her questions. All in all, Isiilde was glad she'd missed the trip down the river. But as Oenghus described Marsais' recent duel, her stomach turned queasy.

Marsais cut the tale short. "She doesn't need the details."

"Is that how you got hurt, Marsais?"

"This brings us back to my earlier question, which you don't want to discuss."

Isiilde plucked at the white fur blanket. "Is this a frost wolf?"

"It's a winter wolf," Marsais answered.

"What's the difference?"

"The frost pelt would still be cold, not warm."

Oenghus knocked the two back on topic. "Why don't you want to discuss it, Sprite? You either remember, or you don't."

"I—" Isiilde faltered.

The carvings on the cave wall no longer reminded her of the forest. She was trapped in a cave. Suffocating.

The room grew smaller, the air stale, and a surge of panic clutched her throat. Flames retreated, drawing in on themselves, feeding the coals at its base until the firepit glowed molten.

It whispered to her with a soft hiss.

She focused on Marsais. "You took my fire."

"I did," he said.

"So you lost control again and tried to kill him?" Oenghus asked.

"You're one to talk!" Isiilde bristled. Her eyes flashed, and the fire in the pit surged with fury. But Marsais was ready.

He leapt to his feet, and plucked the flames from the air as they roared outwards, gathering the heat into a ball.

"Stop it!" she screamed.

Oenghus grabbed her. The Lore was on his lips, even as the nymph's skin seared his palms, but he didn't let go, and a moment later her world went dark.

MARSAIS HURLED the fireball against the cave wall. He cursed as a backlash of sparks sprayed into the room. Outside, footsteps pounded down the tunnel, and the fur drapery jumped aside as Acacia charged into the room, sword in hand. She frowned at the drifting sparks and then at the unconscious nymph.

"It's all right, Captain. Isiilde is having a... difficult time."

"I've never seen her like that," Oenghus whispered, staring at his daughter in shock.

"Your hands."

Oenghus looked down at the blistered skin, and cursed. But it wasn't for pain or injury, it was for his daughter. "She's always had a sharp tongue on her, but nothing like this."

"Did she attack you again?" Acacia had been roused from sleep, and wore the clinging black underclothing of the Lome. Shocked as he was, Oenghus didn't even notice.

"More or less."

The captain took each of Oenghus' hands, examining his injuries. "You had to knock her out," she surmised.

Oenghus grunted.

"I'm not surprised at her behavior. She's as undisciplined as you."

"It's not as if we haven't tried," Oenghus growled, snatching his hands away from the captain's scrutiny.

"Oenghus is right," Marsais said. "Other Wise Ones, including myself, have tried to teach her control—to no effect."

"And yet you continued to teach her your Lore."

"This isn't the Lore."

"Then what is it?"

"It's her blood," he explained. "Nymphs are creatures of passion, as you well know, Captain. They live in the moment, with no thought for the past or present. We're, in effect, asking her to change the way she thinks, the way she *feels*. We want her to behave as a human, but she is faerie—never forget that."

"That's not an excuse."

"No, it's her *nature*. You might as well tell Oenghus to stop eyeing women." As he was now.

Acacia shot a warning look at Oenghus. "I understand, Marsais, but out here we can't afford her whims."

"No, we can't, but for what she has gone through this past fortnight —" Marsais ran his hands over his face, seeking to erase the past. "Her rage and fear are understandable."

"She needs rest," Oenghus said.

"Yes," Marsais agreed. "With time, I think she will calm down."

"That could take years. We don't have years."

"We certainly don't."

"And every day she remains in this underground city, she is at risk—we all are. Bonded or not, a nymph is still a tempting prize."

"I think the precautions you've taken are wise," Marsais said.

Acacia had ordered Rivan and Lucas to perform a cleansing ritual on their food and water stores. The Lome chieftain might fear Marsais' power, but poison was quick, silent, and above all, easy.

"We need to plan an escape."

"Let's not be hasty."

"Marsais, we can't rely on someone else to stop the threat on the Isle. The stronghold is guarded by powerful enchantments."

"I agree."

"I've not pressed you."

"And I appreciate your patience."

"Lucas is not patient."

"I've noticed." Marsais stood, moving away from the sleeping nymph. "What would you like to know?"

"How long will it take Tharios to free Karbonek? What is protecting the tomb? And what is in the flask?"

"I don't know the answer to the last, so I can't answer your other questions."

"By the gods," Oenghus swore. "I know you, Scarecrow, and I know when that mind of yours is scheming. You've been scheming something fierce these past days. What are you brewing?"

"Your confidence in me is frightening."

"That's not an answer."

Marsais ignored the observation. Instead, he clasped his hands behind his back and began to pace.

"Has he forgotten we're here?" Acacia asked.

Oenghus reached for his pipe. "Probably."

"That's convenient."

"The Scarecrow's like a burr. He eventually works his way beneath the thickest hides."

"Why do you call him Scarecrow?"

"You don't want to know. Just don't interrupt him when he's like that." Oenghus jerked his chin at the tall elf who had stopped dead in his tracks to stare at a crack in the wall. "It can take him years to find his way back."

"From where?"

"Who the Void knows. You might as well make yourself comfortable. I swear I'll behave."

Acacia sat cross-legged beside the fire. "Hard to imagine."

Oenghus settled beside her, and began filling his pipe. "I thought I had been behaving myself."

Acacia ignored his flirtatious tone. "Lucas told me what happened. I'm surprised you went back for the captives."

"Why would you think that?"

"You're a berserker."

"What of it?"

"I believe the saying goes, *the strong survive until they die.*"

"I gave them a fighting chance—nothing else." He plucked a tinder from the fire and paused before lighting the tobacco. "You and your lot would've left women and children to rot because they don't bow to your bloody Blessed Order."

"Some might, yes," she admitted.

"But not you?" he asked, puffing on the stem until the weed caught.

"Is a paladin who helps the weak really as rare as a berserker who heals?"

"In my experience," he said slowly, "it is."

"You seem to have met as many unworthy paladins as I've met careless berserkers."

"I never said the rest of my kin were careful."

"No, they certainly aren't." She looked at the sleeping nymph. "You are exceptional."

Oenghus inhaled a mouthful of smoke. "Excuse me?" he coughed.

"It means rare."

"I know what it bloody means," he grumbled. "Just never thought I'd hear it from your lips. And a lovely set they are."

"Don't get cocky, Oenghus."

"I'm always cocky."

"You weren't cocky in the camp." He narrowed his eyes, and she went on to explain. "I would have likely freed the captives immediately. But you showed exceptional restraint in securing the supplies and returning. You didn't place my lieutenant in danger for a side errand."

"An impulsive paladin," he whistled low. "A woman after my heart."

"I don't like cages." Her pale gaze focused on him, and she stood to walk over to Marsais, who was now staring at his toes.

"Your Order doesn't share your views," Oenghus noted.

She changed the subject. "I'm surprised you haven't taken up with one of the Lome. The women certainly seem eager where you're concerned."

Oenghus scratched his beard. He wasn't sure how to take her comment. So he took it lightly. "Tribes consider me good breeding stock. My size gets them all excited."

"Is that what happened with Isiilde's mother?"

His beard twitched, and he tensed, holding himself still and dangerously quiet.

"You're a man. Isiilde is a nymph. I've been around enough nymphs to know how they affect men, especially ones like you."

He found his voice, a rougher one than normal. "You don't know a thing about me."

"I know enough."

"I cared for Isiilde's mother as the emperor's healer. I was with her when she gave birth, and I was with her when she died holding her infant."

Paladin and berserker locked eyes, one pair gleaming with emotion, and the other cool and calculating. "That must be it," she said at length. "Because if you *were* her father, Oenghus—the consequences would indeed be grave."

"Worse than being charged with Bloodmagic?"

Acacia smirked. "Lies are easy to unravel. Truth is not."

"Good thing it's just my caring nature, then."

"Good thing," she agreed.

"Good things are always good," a voice murmured distantly.

"You back with us, Scarecrow?"

"Had I left?"

"Aye, you bloody left."

"Where'd I go?"

"To a harem with a hundred virgins."

"By the gods, no wonder I'm exhausted."

"Before you left for your harem, you were going to share your plans with us," Acacia said.

Oenghus glanced at the paladin in surprise. It appeared she could stretch the truth when it suited her.

"Was I?" Marsais asked.

Acacia didn't answer directly. "You mentioned the Shadowed Dawn earlier. Why that day?"

Marsais scratched at his chest as he gazed around the room, until his eyes fell on the sleeping nymph, where they remained fixed. "A night and a day of darkness. It's suitably dramatic, don't you agree, Captain?"

"You pulled that out of a hat to placate me?"

"Not precisely," he said. "All paths show three moons."

"The moons align in the summer, too," Acacia objected.

"Ah, but the veils between realms are thin on that night, when the Dark One's moon, as you call it, smothers the sun."

"But Tharios has Soisskeli's Stave. You said he can open a Gateway with it. Why would he need to wait for the veil to thin?"

"I don't know, Captain."

Acacia pressed her lips together, eyeing the vague seer. She didn't believe a word he said.

"So what's your plan for getting our hides back on that Isle?" Oenghus asked.

"I know someone who may be able to help."

"Who?" Acacia asked.

"An old acquaintance in Vlarthane." Before Acacia or Oenghus could ask who again, Marsais continued, "I've been speaking with Kasja. I believe I can pinpoint where we are in Vaylin. With the rivers, we should make good time."

"Who is in Vlarthane?"

"Someone with unscrupulous ties."

"Details," she pressed.

"That's all I'm willing to share. You and your men are free to choose your own path."

"Iilenshar has decided for me."

Marsais inclined his head. "Then you should know the road is dangerous."

"What road isn't?"

Acacia turned on her heel, but Oenghus stopped her at the curtain with a call. "If you get cold at night, feel free to join me."

"I'm sure you'd make an excellent rug." She left without a backward glance, leaving the two ancients with their secrets.

"I THINK I'm winning her over." Oenghus chuckled, but Marsais didn't share his amusement. "So this friend of yours—someone I know?"

"Have I ever mentioned Saavedra?"

Oenghus plucked his pipe from his lips. "What the Void!"

Marsais quickly wove an Orb of Silence, cutting off his bellow. "I'll take that as a yes."

"You *are* insane."

"Was that ever in question, Oen?"

"Didn't she try to kill you?"

"Hmm, kill is such a permanent word."

"Are you going to bloody warn the paladins?"

"I did," Marsais defended. "In a roundabout way."

"What aren't you telling me?"

Marsais pinned Oenghus with a steely gaze that made him feel like a mouse. His fingers twitched in thought, and at last, they stilled when he came to a decision.

"I need you to trust me."

"You know I've never given a copper's worth of muck about your visions, but it'd be nice to have a clearer picture of what you plan, and what to expect."

Marsais pressed the tips of his fingers against his temple. "How many times have I explained my visions to you? My presence alone makes you privy to things that you would otherwise be in the dark about. Tharios and his plans, for example."

"But you want me to trust you. You always expect me to follow you blindly. I don't follow anyone blindly."

"What would you do if I weren't here?"

Oenghus opened up his mouth, paused, then clicked it shut. "Wait for Isiilde to heal."

Marsais spread his hands.

"But it's not just me you're dragging around this time."

"I know, Oen." His voice was quiet and full of ache. "I'm well aware of that, but we can't leave the realms to this. A wise man once said that we cannot hide from our Fate. Isiilde must choose hers in the end."

Oenghus glared. "I hate it when you quote yourself. Answer me this." He jabbed the stem of his pipe at his old master. "You knew the golems were after us, didn't you? That's why you ruined our only route of retreat."

"Logic told me something was after us, yes. But I'm blind to constructs—Time holds no sway over golems."

"But you weren't blind to the men at the camp."

Marsais looked sharply at Oenghus, hearing the words he did not say. "I admit, it was a risk letting you scout the village. But I did not foresee her... brush with death. I never know what she'll do, which is why we must remain here."

"For how long?"

"Long enough for her to calm down, and learn control."

"What do you think we've been trying to do for the past eighteen years?"

"I wasn't bonded to her then."

Oenghus clenched his fists. "Don't you dare bind her."

The focus of his seething rage blinked.

"Blast it!" Marsais barked. "Is your opinion of me so low? I would be no better than Stievin if I used our bond to control her." He abruptly turned his back on Oenghus.

"Look here, Scarecrow. Of course I have a low opinion of you, but I didn't mean—"

Marsais raised his hand, demanding silence. "Control," he murmured at length.

"Aye, it's bloody obvious. She has none."

"I used to think that, but now I'm privy to her thoughts, her feelings, the way her mind works."

"You always understood her better than anyone."

"And yet both you and I, her only friends, doubted her." Marsais faced Oenghus. "Every time she lost control, every time we tried to teach her to rein in her fire, we were asking her to do the impossible. It's akin to handing a child a rope and telling her to tame a lion, and every time she failed or someone was hurt, we blamed her."

"I don't follow."

"Isiilde *tries*," he said. "She truly does, but we've been asking the impossible of her. I've *felt* her power—the source she draws from is boundless. Most Wise Ones dip a bucket into the Gift, draw it out, and manipulate that small portion. Whereas a truly Gifted Wise One wades into the currents. But with Isiilde, she *is* the riverbed. And when she's angry or frightened, her defenses are lowered. The river rises, overflowing like a flood. She can't control the power flowing through her veins anymore than the earth controls the river."

"Maybe so, but she can't continue on like this either."

"No," Marsais agreed, tapping his chin in thought.

Oenghus frowned at his daughter. If Marsais was right, which he usually was, then they had been demanding she do the impossible for years. They had unknowingly corroded her confidence. He felt sick.

"If she's channeling the Gift like a riverbed, then what do we do?"

"We need to strengthen the channel, build up the embankments until they're cliffs."

"And just how are you gonna do that?"

Marsais settled himself beside Isiilde, folding his long legs easily. He brushed the curve of her ear. There was sadness in his touch. "I'm going to make use of our Knight Captain and her martial training. Isiilde needs an instructor."

"You're going to ask the captain to teach Isiilde to *fight*?"

"Yes," Marsais said simply.

"You *are* bloody mad."

"Madness is so often a companion of genius."

Oenghus snorted. And Marsais' eyes danced in the firelight.

CHAPTER 33

THE COALS WERE ASH, the hearth cold, and Isiilde was alone in the glow of subterranean vines. Voices seeped from a tunnel. A heavy hide covered the opening, its edges promising a fire beyond and the company of others.

Isiilde rolled onto her stomach, pulling the fur over her head. The past days were blurry and nightmarish. She closed her eyes, resting her cheek on the silky fur, imagining better days. That she was back in Marsais' study, lounging on his rug, carefree and... *Foolish*.

No, not that, not entirely. Innocent was the word. A part of her wanted to be that girl again—when the world had been a kinder place.

The ground no longer felt solid. She curled into a tight ball to keep from falling, but she still fell into a memory of fevered eyes and torture.

Another presence flared to life inside her, chasing back the memories, the hopelessness and despair, infusing her bones with warmth. She was loved.

Marsais thought she was worth something.

Moving like an old woman, Isiilde dragged herself off the cushion of furs, and pulled on the clothes waiting at her bedside. The long under-clothing and supple buckskin hugged her like a glove. She pulled on a lambs-wool shirt and laced up a jerkin of elaborate stitching.

The feel of clothing against her skin was bliss. How long had it been since she had destroyed her own clothes? Surely, the Gateway had stretched time, turning days into years.

Isiilde frowned, trying to count, but shied from the blur of horror. Instead, she focused on the leather footwear that sat nearby. Boots. At last.

They fit like a glove, and she nearly wept.

Weak with hunger and exhaustion, she used the rock wall for support until her legs cooperated. The tunnel was short, and the curtain hid an unworked cavern veined with silver. Stalagmites and stalactites intermingled, creating a lattice of stone, and fur curtains hung over the openings that branched off like cells in a honeycomb.

Everyone was gathered in the common room. Lucas, Rivan, and a wiry boy were sparring, a sheen of sweat coating their bare chests as they worked through their maneuvers.

The others were sitting with a dog by a firepit. As Isiilde neared, the animal moved, and she faltered. It was not a dog, but a human, or at least human in shape, with bright eyes and a filthy nose, garbed in a hodgepodge of furs.

Rivan's gaze flickered in her direction. A mighty crack split the rhythm of swords, and Rivan cursed, clutching his arm.

"Focus!" Lucas barked. He nudged Rivan with his boot, pushing him to his knees.

Isiilde nearly fled back to her cave, but Marsais and Acacia stood up from their game of King's Folly.

"Good morning, my dear." Marsais bowed over her hand, brushing his lips across her knuckles. "You look well."

She favored him with a smile.

"Aye, just like usual, Sprite," Oenghus said. "Always waking up in time to eat."

"Is there meat in there?" she asked, sniffing at the stew.

"Not a bit," Oenghus said. "There's bread and cheese in that bag."

Isiilde spared an uneasy glance at the bundle of furs crouching on a rock and rifled through the provisions. The bright eyes watched her the entire time, but did not move. She retreated to the fire with bread, butter, cheese, and goat's milk and sat beside Marsais, who was studying a swirling pattern of rune stones.

"What is that?"

"Kasja. She's Oathbound to Oen."

Oenghus flicked a pebble at Marsais.

"Oh, it's a woman?" Isiilde tilted her head, staring at the feral shape.

"Supposedly," Oenghus grunted.

"Are you feeling better?" Acacia asked.

"Much better, thank you. Is Rivan all right?"

"If that had been an actual fight, he'd be dead. So, yes." Acacia resumed her seat across from Marsais and narrowed her eyes at the rune pieces.

"You're losing, Captain," Isiilde pointed out between mouthfuls.

"I gathered as much. Marsais has been indulging me."

"You're far from the worst player I've come across."

"Thanks," Acacia said dryly. "Any help would be appreciated, Isiilde."

"Really?"

"I thought you enjoyed King's Folly?"

"I do, it's only... No one's ever asked my help before."

"Only a fool declines help when faced with a superior foe," Acacia said.

Marsais chuckled around the stem of his long pipe. The tobacco was fragrant, and Isiilde sat closer to him as she assessed the captain's position. Acacia still had her fire rune. That was always a good sign. But the Queen was in danger; Marsais would take her in five moves.

"May I?" Isiilde asked.

"By all means." Acacia scooted over, making room for the nymph.

Isiilde plucked up the ice rune and set it atop Marsais' stone. The runes rippled, the enchantments clashed, and the ice rune slid off the stone, falling beside Marsais' water rune.

"You can do that?" Acacia asked in surprise.

Isiilde nodded absently, then looked to her opponent, raising a delicate brow in challenge. Marsais leaned forward, studying the game with renewed interest.

The bundle of furs crawled off her rock, steadily closing in on the nymph. Kasja hissed at Oenghus as she passed, and he growled back. "Blast it, Marsais. Would you tell this woman that I'm not going to touch her?"

"Hmm, I have. Honestly, I'm not sure her hissing is meant to deter you."

Kasja shambled closer and Isiilde smiled uneasily, gazing into the slash of dirty flesh that was crisscrossed with scars.

"Hello," she ventured.

The woman inched closer. Marsais said something in a fluid tongue, and Kasja reached out a tentative hand to poke Isiilde in the shoulder. She flinched away like she'd been burned.

"Are you all right?" Isiilde asked.

In answer, the woman plucked a long strand of hair from the nymph's head and shambled back to her rock.

Isiilde wondered if she should be offended. What on earth was the feral woman going to do with her hair? She looked to Marsais in question.

"The Lome think she's touched in the head," he explained, "But she seems sane enough to me."

Oenghus roared with laughter.

Isiilde watched as Kasja studied her plunder, caressing the long strand of red hair. In her opinion, every human was touched in the head.

Marsais made his move, placing a bind stone atop a power that crushed her iron. Together, the two made a formidable combination. She would have to destroy the bind, or lose her Queen. She made her next move, and he answered; back and forth, shifting strategies with a swirl of cycles.

"Marsais."

"Hmm?"

"You've had a bath."

"In a lovely underground spring."

"Is the water cold?"

"It's a hot spring."

She nearly purred. "Can you show me after breakfast? I think you could use another."

Marsais looked up from the game, and she held his attention with a smile while she nudged a rune to the side.

A surge of desire rippled through their bond. Her newly positioned deceit rune took his bound power rune, and he never noticed.

"Of course," he said.

"She just cheated," Acacia noted with a frown.

"Who?" Marsais cast around in surprise.

"Isiilde," the captain blabbed.

"Marsais didn't see me."

"My eyes were elsewhere," he agreed.

Isiilde shrugged. "Then I didn't cheat."

"King's Folly mimics life," Oenghus explained, as he dished up the stew. "Not everyone plays fair—just like a battlefield. There is no honor in King's Folly. If you're fool enough to get distracted, then you won't last long."

"Noted."

"And you weren't supposed to say anything," Isiilde said. "I'm on *your* side. That makes you a turncoat."

Acacia clicked her mouth shut. And for the rest of the game, she observed in silence, watching nymph and seer plunge into a game of wits.

Isiilde matched Marsais without hesitation, attacked and defended, and reworked her strategies with flawless focus in a complicated cycle of runic power.

Oenghus leaned over to whisper in Acacia's ear. "No one ever taught her. She was watching me and Morigan play one afternoon, and when I went out to piss, I found her in my chair, playing my circle. At first we were amused, but—" He jerked his chin at their swift hands, the swirl of runes, and the ever changing game. "Then this. Two weeks later, she beat her first novice on the Isle. She was only six."

The others wandered over to watch, but Isiilde and Marsais ignored their questions, leaving Oenghus to explain the basic cycle of runes.

Acacia had left Isiilde in a bad playing position, and Marsais was a formidable opponent at the best of times, but what was worse, he knew her weakness.

With a flourish, Marsais plucked up his water rune, let his air rune hurl it to another circle, and placed the deadly stone within striking distance of her fire rune.

Isiilde looked up at him sharply. If she moved her fire to safety, it would disrupt the cycle and leave her Queen ripe for the slaughter. "I'm done," she announced.

"You can have the ol' Bastard in three moves," Oenghus said. "I have a wager on you."

"I don't want to play anymore."

Marsais arched a brow, studying her in the fire's light. "Hmm, perhaps we'll call it a draw." He unfolded himself and stood, offering his hand.

She did not accept, but rose and waited for him to lead the way to the hot spring, leaving Oenghus to grumble over his lost wager.

Isiilde stopped in the arched doorway of their lodgings. Two guards flanked the exit, but she barely noticed the armed men. A cavernous valley with homes carved into rock walls glowed at her feet. When she finally remembered to breathe, Isiilde ignored Marsais' offered hand and walked lightly down the steep stairway. Silently, the guards fell in step behind them.

"Are we prisoners, Marsais?"

"More like new additions to the tribe. This is a sacred city."

"We can't leave?" she asked.

"No."

The valley was vast, lit with luminous vines, its walls carved with monstrous beasts. The city was full of strange, tattooed faces and watching eyes that stopped and followed her as she passed. Whispers followed too, hushed and fearful. Mothers pulled their children into houses and men took a hasty step back.

The weight of stone pressed on her senses, and her throat clutched with panic. "I don't feel well."

"I know."

Marsais slipped her hand through his arm and led her up a series of winding stairs and into a tunnel that looked no different from the rest.

The passage narrowed, her world spun, and Marsais squeezed her hand. A gate waited at the end of the tunnel, flanked by fur-covered guards with spears.

The warriors bristled as they approached, and the two men behind them closed in. Marsais addressed the guards in their flowing tongue. Words were exchanged, the faces blurred together, and Isiilde swayed. A strong arm wrapped around her waist, and she buried her nose against leather and fur and supple cloth.

It seemed they stood waiting in that tunnel for an entire day. A touch calmed her and voices flowed over her ears, until a gust of wind brought her around.

Marsais led her through the gate. Snow swirled madly into the passage, blinding white, pushed by howling winds. They pressed forward, emerging into an icy wilderness. She filled her lungs, stood straight, and turned her nose to the open sky, letting the wind cool her mind.

Her anger seemed foolish now. It was only a rune.

When she'd calmed, they stepped back into the shelter of the tunnel. The wind let go of her cloak and the blizzard screamed sideways through the air. She stepped into Marsais, slipped her arms around his waist, and caught his eyes with hers.

"I'm sorry."

"Apology accepted." He warmed her cheek with his hand and she pressed into his palm. "We need to talk."

"Could we go somewhere warmer?"

"I think this is the perfect place."

"Oh."

Isiilde thought for a moment. There was only one reason Marsais would want to converse out here in the cold. Abruptly, she stood on her toes to press her lips against his with an aching moan. And Marsais forgot where he was and who he was, losing himself in the moment.

Isiilde pulled away, and smiled.

"What—" he stammered.

"If our discussion has to do with what I think it does, then that was an advance apology in case I get angry again."

"I see." She doubted he did. His eyes had lost focus. "In that case, I should warn you—I think you'll be furious."

"Then exhaust me first," she whispered.

Marsais' last shred of resolve was thrown to the winds. "An excellent idea."

THE SUBTERRANEAN GROTTO hissed with steam. Blue light danced in its waters, and its stone held the memories of passion. Marsais lounged against a rock, eyes closed, half-dozing with his nymph resting limply in his arms.

Marsais cracked an eye towards the entrance. He could not recall setting a ward or sealing the grotto from prying eyes, but apparently he had—an illusion of stone covered the tunnel. He sighed with relief and closed his eyes, listening to the fall of water and the moans that still lingered in the air long after Isiilde had stilled.

There was no need to silence her in the water.

"What did you want to talk about?" The lilting voice, along with a delicate touch tracing his scar, nudged him from the edge of sleep.

"I can't remember," he admitted. His heart was still racing. "Hmm, wasn't I supposed to exhaust you?"

"You did, but you could try again to be safe. That was—" Words failed. "I don't think I'll ever tire of making love to you."

"You will be the death of me."

"Did you have a vision?"

"If only I were so lucky. Dying in your arms would be bliss."

"I'd rather you not die."

"Hmm, that brings us to the elephant in the room."

She sat up in surprise. "Where?"

"Not here."

"An elephant is going to kill you in the future?" she asked.

"A figure of speech."

She rolled her eyes. "It must be a human expression."

"It means the subject we've been avoiding."

"You're going to die?"

"By the gods, no, not if I can help it. But I nearly did. And so did you. Do you realize how close you came to killing the both of us?"

"I wasn't trying to kill you, Marsais. I wanted to help. Nothing more. Rivan was being crushed. You were surrounded. The captain was on the ground. And then my fire came, and before I knew it—I couldn't tell friend from foe, only that someone was taking my fire. I don't like it when you do that."

There was no anger in her words, only honesty.

"Why not?"

She lifted a slim shoulder. "It feels like a part of me is being taken."

His fingers trailed lightly down her spine, dipping below the water to caress her lower back. "Are you sure it's not the opposite?"

Isiilde tilted her head. "It's taking me?"

"Yes. It caught you in its currents and swept you away."

"I tried, Marsais."

"Tried to do what?"

"To help, to control it."

"You were afraid."

"Of course I was afraid!" Her skin heated, the water steamed and hissed, and Marsais cupped her face, searching her eyes.

"You were afraid. And now you're angry and frustrated and your fire is stirring, rising to your defense—like a guardian."

This brought her up short. "I've always thought of my fire as alive," she admitted.

Marsais brought his hand up, studying the fiery head of a dragon that rested in his palm. "I've seen your mark—our bond—move as if it were watching me."

"Really?" She took his hand and studied the dragon, but it didn't move.

"When we first bonded, it slithered down my arm, and later blinked at me."

"It seems so long ago, and yet—" She shivered despite the heat. "I still feel trapped in the washroom with him. And the others... in the dungeon."

"Some horrors never leave us. Not fully. One day, you'll learn to live with the past, but more importantly, you'll learn from it."

"Like your wound?" Her touch made him sigh.

"This wound is of a different nature. Time will help yours, but mine is a reflection of a larger one. I'm afraid nothing can erase what was done."

"But what was done?"

"The Shattering."

"What does your scar have to do with the Shattering?"

"Everything," he said. "But we have another matter to discuss. One we've spoken of before, although not in such an intimate setting."

"Control." The word left a sour taste on her lips.

"More or less."

The nymph opened her mouth to reply, but Marsais held up a hand, stalling her arguments. "Hear me out, Isiilde. We've been approaching your power from the wrong angle. I've been treating it as something that should be controlled—that *can* be controlled."

"You're saying I can't control it?"

"If your fire is alive, as we both suspect—" Marsais paused at her sudden tears. His words were vindication and his support a balm to her fears. He smiled in understanding. "It *is* alive—for you. And it protects you. Do you understand?"

She nodded, wiping at the tears with her palm.

"Let's use your flesh and blood guardian as a comparison. Can you control Oenghus?"

Isiilde snorted. "Not likely. But if I'm careful, I can get my way."

A surge of warmth flooded their bond. "As exquisite as your beauty is, it pales in comparison to your mind. Hmm, now I'll put another question to your keen intellect. How does that knowledge help you?"

"To give my fire free rein?"

"You could, but if that were the case, your fire would have killed me. I would like to believe you didn't want that."

"Of course I didn't, but you were trying to take it away."

"Exactly. I was trying to *control* your fire, to rip it out of your hand, away from you. I feared you would burn yourself out. And in attempting to control a part of you, I nearly killed you."

"Is that possible? To burn myself out?"

"I don't know."

"It would be a wonderful way to die."

"I'd rather you not."

"So what do you suggest?"

"When Oenghus is in a rage, using force feeds his fire while calming him takes manipulation. Sometimes it helps to point him towards something he can bash."

"Surrender," she murmured.

"Certainly not. That would be akin to giving your fire free rein."

"Not really," she argued. "Not if one surrenders, and then manipulates." She met his gaze with an arched brow. "I know how you use the Gift, Marsais."

He froze, startled by her insight. "Do not attempt what I do."

"I wasn't going to. I'm not that foolish. You surrendered long ago, didn't you? You threw yourself into the river and never looked back. You're always connected to the Gift. That's why you don't need to speak the Lore. You only need to trace the runes."

Marsais pressed his lips together in silence, and she gave him a knowing smile.

"I've seen your eyes when you weave. You have the same look in them when you're between my thighs. You're just as fond of your runes as I am of my fire." She moved closer, straddling his lap, pressing her breasts against his chest to whisper in his ear. "You caress it. You surrender to its currents and let its power wash over you. It's your passion. Now why can't I do the same?"

Marsais cleared his throat. "Self-control." His voice was hoarse with a lack of it.

The nymph wrinkled her nose and drifted to deep waters, slipping beneath the surface. Another word she didn't care for. Controlling the Gift required concentration, and controlling herself long enough to control something else was a monumental feat.

She surfaced in the middle of the hot spring, gazing warily at him through a cloud of steam.

Marsais stretched his arms along the rim. "I propose a pact, Isiilde."

"What are your terms?"

"I swear I will never take your fire again. I will gather it if need be, but never snuff it out. King's Folly doesn't count," he added quickly.

"What must I do?"

"You must start applying yourself, whether or not you like it." He held up a finger, stalling her complaint. "I realize there are limits with a faerie, but you must try to learn some degree of self-control—more now than ever. We face dangers enough without your fiery temper. I can't have you combusting on every whim, certainly not where we're headed."

"What are my options?" she asked.

"Short of binding you, through our bond, not to use your fire—" Her throat clutched with panic. "I won't do that, I swear it," he assured, stretching out to seize her hand.

It was possible, she realized in horror. Their spirits were intertwined and his was far more powerful than hers.

"Not ever, Isiilde, trust me, please," he whispered.

She stared into his eyes, saw the truth in his words, and slowly calmed. "I believe you," she finally said. "But what other choices do we have?"

"The only alternative is risky: I won't ward myself or silence you during our lovemaking in hopes that you'll find a way."

"That's insane," she hissed.

The charred corpse of Zander, Miera Malzeen, and the burning flesh of Zianna flashed in her mind.

"There are few options left to us."

"We could leave this place and hide, just you and I—like the druids and their nymphs of old. I'm so tired of humans, Marsais. Of their eyes and their constant fear."

"Do you remember when I told you that there was very little in this realm that I would not do for you?"

"How could I forget?" she whispered.

"I have a responsibility to this realm. I cannot, in good conscience, leave them to flounder in the approaching darkness. Fyrsta is on the verge of tipping into chaos. This realm needs you. And so do I."

Isiilde stared at Marsais, dumfounded. If they were not bonded, she would have thought he was joking, but the conviction in his words rang like a gong through their bond.

"Do we stand a chance against Tharios?" she asked.

"Nothing is written in stone."

She did not believe him for a moment. "Then I agree to your terms." She sealed the oath with a lingering kiss. "But I don't know where to begin," she admitted against his lips.

"Were my lessons ever tiresome?"

"Never."

"Let's start here, then."

"Here?" She shifted on his lap.

"Precisely here." He was serious, and she laughed, her curiosity aroused. "Your lovemaking, although intense, is—" Marsais searched for an elusive word. "Short-lived."

Isiilde pulled back. "Oh." Heat rose to her ears. "Are things supposed to last longer?"

"I'm not complaining by any means, but perhaps you could try to... prolong the experience. You might find it more enjoyable."

"I doubt that."

"A wager, then."

She smiled, slowly. "I think I'll like this lesson."

"I hope it won't be too torturous for you."

"Marsais?"

"Hmm."

"Can we begin right now? I'll need a lot of practice."

"I was afraid you were going to say that."

CHAPTER 34

Novices scattered, apprentices bowed, and even seasoned Wise Ones fled as the Mistress of Novices approached. She had taught most, and the lot of them were lazy and uninspired. Few were worth the effort.

Thira stalked straight for Leiman. He had kept his nose in a book during his entire time as a novice, was never late, never out of turn, and always handed his papers in on time. The man had absolutely no ambition and no backbone.

"Where is Morigan?" Pleasantries were a waste of time. She didn't care how Leiman was, and he knew it.

"She's still tending the children at the orphanage, Mistress."

"It's been a week."

"Yes, Mistress, it seems they're having a bad fever outbreak. She sent a message requesting more supplies."

"Let me see that note."

Leiman left his patient to retrieve it.

The note was in Morigan's handwriting and the supply list was for the proper herbs. Everything looked in order.

"Is there something else I can help you with, Mistress?

"Not unless you know her recipe for Crumpet's medicine." Thira kissed the top of her companion's head and received a few affectionate licks in return. "His joints are stiff from the cold."

Leiman muttered something under his breath about moving to a warmer climate.

Thira narrowed her eyes. "And have even more incompetent louts like you running around? Doubtful." She turned on her heel and strode out.

It could very well be a fever outbreak. Oenghus usually responded to requests for healers in the surrounding towns, and with his sudden disappearance, it seemed logical that Morigan would take his place. So why was Thira worried?

There was so much activity in so little time. New novices were being accepted by the day, fresh soldiers were being recruited to bolster their guard, and the Spine hummed with activity—as it should.

Ordinarily, she would have approved. But years of catching novices in the act of every kind of mischief imaginable had given her a nose for trouble, and this business stank for various reasons.

Thira remained adamant that Marsais had no business leading the Order of Wise Ones. He treated it, like everything else, with the casual air in which he excelled. Without a doubt, Marsais was gifted, suspiciously so, but that did not make him an ideal Archlord.

Did he consort with fiends? Probably.

Did he have knowledge of Bloodmagic? Undoubtedly.

Unfortunately, as much as she'd like to push the matter aside and return to her research, there were too many nagging questions. The nice and tidy report that the Inquisitor was so eager to put his seal on was full of inconsistencies.

Thira did not like holes. And an absent Morigan was a rather gaping one.

Marsais was a lot of things. But of all the things that he was, and all those habits she detested in him—he was not a man who was careless with the important things. Not with lives, not with knowledge, and definitely not with power.

Thira strode through the castle, passing newly stationed guards and lost novices, and hurried into her suite of rooms. She sealed the door with its usual ward and walked into her workshop, scanning the shelves of orderly potions.

"It's time for a bit of work, my dearest."

Crumpet's ears perked up, and she scratched his chin before selecting a small green vial.

"Go to the orphanage in Drivel and show me what you see."

Crumpet barked once in eagerness and she upended the vial down his throat. The transformation was flawless. It always was.

Thira opened the window to the swirling storm, and Crumpet took flight—a strong, black crow. She watched his avian shape disappear into the snow with a fondness that she held for no human.

That was the wonderful thing about animals. You could trust them. And if her suspicions were correct about the events that transpired after the duel, then one thing she could not afford right now was placing her trust in the wrong person.

THIRA ATTACKED the winding stairway with relish. When she reached the top of the second highest tower in the castle, she paused, glancing out the arrow loop with barely a hurried breath. She envied Rashk her rooms, but they were too far away for her to keep a proper eye on the students.

The door opened to her knock, and a bronzed-skinned Rahuatl narrowed her dark eyes. "Thira."

"Rashk," she said with equal contempt. "You were friends with the nymph, weren't you?"

Rashk raised an ivory studded brow, tapping her finger claws on the edge of the door. "What do you want?"

"I want to come inside."

Rashk's eyes flickered from Thira's empty hands to the ground around her feet, and behind.

"Crumpet isn't with me."

"Too bad." She bared her sharpened teeth. "I want a snack." Rashk turned lazily from the door and sauntered into her chambers.

"And I'd have your eyeballs for one if you touched him," Thira returned pleasantly, letting herself in and closing the door behind.

Rashk plucked a grisly bone from its bowl and sucked on the marrow as Thira wove an Orb of Silence. With a breath, she took the plunge, risking all.

"Morigan is missing."

Rashk sucked and licked the bone clean with her forked tongue, and casually tossed the bone into a pile of similar bones. Thira waited, watching the Rahuatl. They were a hard race to read.

"And so is N'Jalss," Thira added, switching tactics.

Rashk hissed. "What is he to me?"

"I think he is your enemy."

The woman shrugged a shoulder. "Everyone is my enemy."

"But not the nymph."

A ritual scar twitched near Rashk's black lips.

"You don't trust me, Rashk, and I can't trust anyone. But I'm going to confide in you—otherwise, we will be paralyzed by our mutual distrust. Morigan left on an errand to the orphanage in Drivel and hasn't returned for a week. She sent a note to the infirmary requesting supplies for a fever outbreak—yet she isn't at the orphanage."

"Maybe she is somewhere else helping the sick."

"Along with the Priestess of the Sylph who runs the orphanage?"

Rashk shifted with a clink of piercings.

"Morigan was under suspicion."

Rashk snorted. "For what?"

"She was close with Oenghus and Isiilde."

"What of it?" Rashk asked. "You can't believe she was involved in Bloodmagic."

"I don't. But others were whispering. It's no secret she's taken multiple Oaths with Oenghus—that she raised the nymph as her own. Her loyalty was in question."

"Morigan was never loyal to this Order," Rashk hissed.

"Did you speak with her?"

"Words are a waste. It's written plainly on her heart."

"Exactly," Thira agreed. "She didn't believe the charges laid against Marsais and Oenghus."

Rashk turned towards her worktable, dipping a claw into a bowl and stirring, checking the consistency. "And do you agree with her?"

"I wouldn't be here if I didn't doubt the charges."

"They *are* lies."

"What makes you say that, Rashk?"

"Grimstorm is no Bloodmagus, and the Fire Imp's master would never hurt her."

"I agree."

Rashk turned, surprised at the admittance.

"There are too many holes in the story, Rashk. Surely you see that, too?"

"It's obvious," Rashk snapped. "Isiilde does not like dark places. Marsais would not have taken her down into the dungeons. And Grimstorm could kill three paladins in his sleep."

"To say nothing of Marsais, even wounded as he was. The entire story hinges on one account—the only survivor of the carnage—Isek Beirnuckle."

"He has always smelled tricky," Rashk confided.

"But no one questions him, do they? And why would they? He's been Marsais' friend far too long for that."

"The Fire Imp was ripe."

"Trouble always follows a nymph," Thira agreed. "The creatures seem to bring out the worst in men."

"Or they simply uncover what is hidden," Rashk mused. "What do you want from me? They are all likely dead, gone in the Gateways, lost."

"Perhaps. And perhaps not. It *is* Marsais, after all. We need to find Morigan first, or at the very least, her body."

"I can help with that."

"Why do you think I came to you?"

"For my power of persuasion," Rashk purred, dragging a claw around the rim of the bowl. "I will question Isek. He will talk."

"I came to you because you're discreet and you can hold your tongue."

"I'll hold my tongue very well when I slit Isek's throat."

Thira huffed in exasperation. "We need answers before we jump blindly into whatever is brewing."

Rashk shrugged. "We kill first, eat quickly, and question later."

"And if there are more tigers lurking in the jungle?" Thira shot back. "Why the dungeon? And how did Isek lure them down there? He must have had help."

"Have you searched the dungeons?"

"I went down there with the Blessed Order. They're in disreputable shape. Did the nymph say anything to you, anything at all before this business began, about her master's plans?"

Rashk turned back to her worktable, unscrewed a jar, and picked up a slimy pinch of entrails, dropping it into her mortar. Thira let her work in silence, knowing the female was anything but inattentive.

"Isiilde asked me for teeth—the morning she destroyed the Relic Hall." Dark eyes slid sideways, and Thira clenched her fist, bristling at the memory of that day. "She said her master needed teeth."

"Why would Marsais need teeth?"

"That is what Tharios asked her."

"Tharios was here? Why?"

Rashk tapped a claw on her worktable. "My expertise."

"What did he ask?"

"It is his matter."

"Tell me," Thira snapped.

Rashk pressed her black lips together, defiant. Intimidation was lost on a Rahuatl.

Thira took a calming breath. "I understand you have professional obligations, but this is important—please." The word was more hiss than supplication.

Rashk smirked. "Tharios showed me a detailed sketching of an artifact. He wanted my opinion on how it might function."

"What artifact?"

"Soisskeli's Stave."

And just like that, all the missing pieces clattered into place.

CHAPTER 35

"AGAIN!" Acacia ordered.

Half a fortnight into her pact with Marsais, daily baths and nights excluded, she was sorely regretting her agreement.

Isiilde picked up the heavy practice sword, and steeled herself, holding the wooden sword before her like a talisman.

Unfortunately, the talisman didn't deter Knight Captain Acacia Mael.

"That's not the stance I showed you, Nymph."

Isiilde shifted her feet.

Acacia advanced slowly, and Isiilde twisted her wrists, batting away the thrust. The clacking grated on her ears.

"Good. Now attack."

Isiilde squeezed her eyes shut and swung. The jarring impact rattled her bones and loosened her grip. Her sword clattered to the stone.

"Wait!" she squeaked at the advancing paladin.

Acacia's sword connected with her ribs, and Isiilde doubled over in agony. A boot planted itself on her backside and shoved, sending her sprawling onto the stone.

"An enemy doesn't wait, Nymph."

"My name is Isiilde," she seethed through clenched teeth.

Combustion was not an option. The last time her skin heated, Marsais had dumped a waiting bucket of icy water over her head. They'd skipped their afternoon bath that day.

"When you stop closing your eyes, I'll start calling you *Girl*. I've seen five-year-olds fight better than you."

"Perhaps you should find one to beat," Isiilde shot back. Acacia's swift sword smacked her thigh. She scrambled to her feet, putting her back to the stone. "Paladins have always excelled at beating the helpless." The sword struck again, but this time, Isiilde skipped to the side. "Oh, wait, everyone knows they can't hit a thing unless it's shackled!"

Acacia pressed her attack.

Isiilde wrenched her sword up, parrying two blows before a strike slammed into her knuckles. Her sword clattered to the ground, and the captain hooked the nymph's leg, sending her sprawling backwards into the wall. A sword tip pressed against her throat, pinning her to the floor.

"If only your sword were half as sharp as your tongue," Acacia said.

"You're cruel, like every other human."

Acacia withdrew her sword and crouched. "Not half as cruel as an enemy would be," she whispered. "Here you are lying on the ground, whimpering over bruised knuckles. If your enemy shows you an ounce of mercy and stops short of the killing blow," she jabbed a finger at Isiilde's heart, "it will be because you're a nymph. Do you want that again?"

Every muscle in Isiilde's body shook. The blood drained from her face, and pain was replaced with a crawling presence that made her want to shed her skin.

"Captain," Marsais warned.

"Don't interfere. She's mine for another hour."

Isiilde glanced at Marsais in alarm, but Acacia gripped the nymph's chin, forcing her to meet her pale gaze. "Don't look to Marsais or Oenghus for help. They weren't there in the washroom."

Isiilde swallowed down the bile that rose in her throat.

"Do you want that again? To be a helpless nymph?"

"No," Isiilde rasped.

"Then pick up your sword and fight!"

Isiilde shook free of the woman, and stood. "I did!" she screamed.

"Then stop acting as if you didn't."

The words knocked the breath from her lungs. The stone beneath her feet rippled strangely, her bones quaked, and she swayed. "It only angered him," she whispered.

"But you *fought*."

"I was useless."

"Useless?" Acacia took a step forward. "Because you were defeated by overwhelming odds? Am I useless, Nymph?"

"I didn't say that."

"I have scars." Acacia ripped at the laces of her jerkin, tugging down her underclothing to show the scars crisscrossing her collarbone. "I fought, and I lost. And so did he." She thrust a finger at Oenghus. "Look at the scars on his body—his face, his legs, his arms. And what of your Bonded? Look at his back!"

Isiilde looked at Marsais, who held himself very still, and very straight, bracing himself against those long ago lashes that had scarred his back.

"And my lieutenant—" Acacia bit back her words, saying no more. "We have all fought. And failed. And we bear scars, just as you do. Yours are deep, but that doesn't mean they aren't worthy."

"I'm a *nymph*," she bit out. "I have no worth beyond a bedchamber."

"Then drop your sword and walk away."

Isiilde narrowed her eyes. She stood on her own two feet, connected to the earth, felt the breath enter her lungs and anchor her to this realm. She was a warrior of Clan Freyr.

Her knuckles tightened on the hilt. "No."

Acacia's pale eyes flashed. "I didn't think so." She raised her sword and Isiilde moved to counter. "Good, now we'll see if you can last the hour."

"You're still a cruel woman."

"That's my job, Girl."

Isiilde limped beside Marsais, leaning heavily on his arm. She had lasted the hour, and her body had paid for her willpower. Acacia had treated her like a recruit. And somehow that made the bruises and blood tolerable. But Isiilde's heart was numb.

Silence stretched between the pair as they walked through the familiar tunnels. Nymphs were not made to live underground, and Marsais and she had discovered that she needed to breathe fresh air at least once a day, or the stone began to suffocate her.

Isiilde hid beneath her cowl as they walked, eyes downcast, watching the movement of her boots.

Sharp air brought her back to her body. The storm had sated its rage, leaving winter in its wake. The sky was a bright blue and fresh snow sparkled under the sun.

They fought through snowdrifts to stand on the ledge. She slipped in the fresh powder, before steadying herself on Marsais' arm to peer over the edge. The river was sluggish and clear, rolling over an icy waterfall. The mists had cleared with the ice, revealing a valley of white that stretched towards rising cliffs and jagged mountains.

She watched the falling sun, burning red in the snow, but it was as cold as her heart and so very distant.

Marsais tilted his head, closed his eyes, and let the snow cool his face. Delicate flakes gathered on his long lashes. With the burning sun that was his spirit, Isiilde half expected the snowflakes to melt, but they lingered on his skin.

She tried the same, but the snowflakes only made her sneeze and three bursts of flame shot from her ears.

The guards took a hasty step back, hoisting their spears in fear. Marsais reassured the guards with a few words, and they lowered their spears, but continued to eye her warily. She preferred it that way.

Isiilde pointedly ignored the pair and frowned at her hands, poking at the black bruises on her knuckles.

"Are you all right, my dear?"

"No."

"If you decide to yell at me, I'd appreciate some warning," Marsais said, scooping up a handful of snow.

"Why would I yell at you?"

"I'm the one who asked the captain to train you. Perhaps I deserve your anger. Your silence is worrisome."

He took her hand, and pressed the snow against her knuckles. A shiver zipped up her arm, but he held her hand with gentle strength, keeping it in place. Gradually, the pain turned to a numb ache.

"I agreed to your terms."

"It doesn't make it easier."

"For you, or me?"

Marsais sighed. "If only we could take the pain from those we love."

"You are," she said, softly. "But I'm foolish, Marsais. All those years in the castle... I look back at that girl with disgust. And I pity her innocence."

A pang twisted Marsais' heart. He caressed her knuckles with his thumb, tracing the bones and bruises in soothing circles. "Do you pity a flower for its beauty? Knowing that it will wither and die in a short time?"

"It's a flower, Marsais."

"Precisely." He gave her a small, sad smile. "In all my long years, I've never tired of their beauty. As fleeting and delicate as a flower is, such things make life worth living."

"They are useless."

"Not to bees, or to young men in love—shall I go on, or would you like to replace flowers with the word in your heart?"

"*Nymphs* are useless. What purpose do we serve other than living 'gifts to the gods'? I don't want to be anyone's gift."

"You're not like other nymphs, Isiilde."

"Yes, I know," she said through her teeth. "I'm—how did you put it —slight?" She gestured at her breasts.

"Your breasts are proportionate to your body. You certainly haven't heard me complaining, and that's not what I meant." He rubbed the bridge of his nose. "By the gods, you're confusing today."

"No, I'm tired and sore, and I have no idea what I'm supposed to do now. Why did Oenghus rescue me from Kambe? Why did you bother teaching me the Gift? And why the Void is Captain Mael treating me as a squire?"

"We have talked about this—"

She cut him off, throwing words at him without pause. "Do you know what the captain told me about King Syre's harem of nymphs—they barely talk, Marsais. They sit around in an enclosed garden enclave, giggling and swimming all day. A month ago, that would have sounded like bliss, but now it disgusts me."

"Isiilde."

"I do not belong anywhere!" Her eyes flashed.

The guards' gazes gleamed from behind their masks, and Marsais sensed their interest. The nymph was alluring, but her fury made her divine. He gripped her arm gently and steered her towards the tunnel with a whisper. "Not here."

She relented, and let him lead her down the tunnel, slipping her arm through his. As they walked the familiar path towards the grotto, he continued, "Nymphs aren't useless. They are—"

"Flowers that men pollinate?"

Marsais cleared his throat. "True, you're not human, but then neither am I. We're faerie. But everyone, human or faerie, must find his own path. I've walked so many paths that I've forgotten where I've walked."

Isiilde snorted.

"You've held up very well, my dear."

"Only because of you."

"You would have managed on your own."

"Then prove it, and leave me."

"I'm not leaving you alone for a moment in here."

"*Inside*. Our bond, Marsais. I'm not even sure what is me and what is you."

"Hmm, no."

She bristled. "I thought you were supposed to cater to my every desire?"

"Not the unwise ones."

"You're stubborn."

"Perhaps you're confusing me with your own emotions?"

"I'm positive it is you."

"And why is that?"

"You share so many other traits with a mule."

The edges of his lips twitched. "You know, my dear, I think the captain was on to something—if your swordsmanship fails, you could always try taunting an enemy to death."

"Are you trying to provoke me?"

"Hmm, a small price to pay to see the fire in your eyes."

"You can watch my eyes from dry ground today. I'll take my bath alone."

"Oh, thank the gods," he breathed.

Isiilde frowned. Her words had not had the desired sting.

"You're progressing very well in that area."

Isiilde smiled, slowly. "Why, thank you, Marsais. I was going to suggest that you start working on your faltering self-control."

Marsais looked sharply at her, cleared his throat, and did not say another word.

THE GUARDS TOOK up their customary position outside the grotto as Isiilde and Marsais entered the luminescent spring. The Lome who were there already scrambled to collect their things. Some were naked, others half-clothed; their pale skin glowing with tattoos. They reminded Isiilde of fireflies.

Isiilde smiled at a woman who was hastily wrapping a robe around herself. She snatched up her child, and ran out. The others followed, while a bare-chested man planted himself between the women and the strangers, waiting for the last to leave before following.

The Lome feared Marsais. When she had asked why, he told her that madness breeds caution, foresight is revered, and power is respected, but all three together are feared.

"Did you ever look like that, Marsais?" she asked, eyeing the last man to leave. He had the musculature of a bull.

"Hmm, my tattoo ran away."

Isiilde tilted her head, decided she didn't want to know, and clarified. "I meant the rest of him."

"Save for extreme youth, I was never that short, and as for the rest of him—I've always been on the lean side. Although my hair was black once upon a time."

"Really?" she asked, as she circled the spring, searching the twisting stone and shadows with a careful eye.

"It turned this lovely shade of white when the Orb shattered," he said, weaving a mirror rune and an Orb of Silence over the entrance.

"Is that when you started having visions?"

"I've always had the curse of foresight, but after the Shattering things... fell apart." He frowned, head bowed, gazing at an unseen spot.

Isiilde wished she had not asked; unfortunately, words could not be taken back, so she pressed forward. "How so?"

"Do you remember the ocean storm that washed away entire sections of Drivel?"

"There was a Blood Moon."

Marsais gave a slight nod, sending his coins echoing against the stone. "The waves were my visions, and I was the part of the city that was dragged out to sea."

"How did you find your way back?"

"With help, eventually."

"Who helped you?"

He smiled. "A good man."

"With no name?"

"A wise Cleric of Chaim," he said. "But a number of odd things happened during the Shattering. The disaster affected entire races—the fiends, the Fomorri, the Afarim."

"Is that where Reapers and Grawl came from?" Isiilde asked, pulling off her clothes.

"No one knows for sure."

"You don't know?"

Amusement flickered through their bond. "I don't know everything, my dear."

"But you've lived so long." She dipped a toe into the pool.

"Hmm, the younger you are, the more you know."

Isiilde's laugh echoed in the grotto, dancing with the trickling water. She grinned and dove into the pool, slipping beneath the surface. When she came up for air, she pressed on, "I'm serious, Marsais."

"The young are blissfully unaware of what they don't know, so they know much more."

"Your reasoning has several cracks."

"Was that ever in doubt?"

She splashed him.

"Was that an invitation?" he asked, shedding his wet jerkin.

"No." She folded her arms on the edge of the pool, letting the swirling current tug at her feet as she watched Marsais strip off his clothes. "Tell me where Grawl and Reapers came from."

"You are so sure I know."

She stared at him, waiting.

And he relented. "There's plenty of wild speculation, of course, but there are two theories that seem plausible to me. The first being that they're the offspring of fiends and faerie, or fiends and human, or whatever lurid fantasy the theorist favors."

"Is that possible—a fiend and a human?"

Marsais paused. "As possible as faerie and human." He cleared his throat and changed the subject. "The second belief is that Dagenir, after taking the Orb's power, twisted the Gift and created the Grawl with the Void. It's said Death did the same with Reapers. I do believe Reapers are called Death's children for a reason."

Isiilde squeaked, pushing away from the edge of the pool. There was a creature perched on her boot. "Marsais!"

"It's a lizard."

"Lizards have scales." She wrinkled her nose, studying the clawed creature. At least it wasn't black. "I can see inside of it."

"That's because they are subterranean creatures. They live in the vines." Suddenly, the grotto didn't seem so peaceful. "Why don't you cast a bolt at it, and scare it off?"

"I don't want to kill it. Can I burn it instead?"

Marsais opened his mouth to reply, thought better of it, and closed it with a click, gently picking the lizard up by its tail and moving it to the vines.

Isiilde retreated beneath the water, deciding that it was too hot for anything to live in the spring. "I was serious," she said at length.

"If you really want to burn the poor lizard to a crisp, you'll have to catch it yourself."

"I meant about our bond, Marsais."

"I was too."

"But I need to know how much is me and how much is you."

"You're still recovering from your near death."

"It's been seven days."

"And I kept you alive by giving you my strength. I still am."

"I'm *still* dying?"

"No, you're not dying," he said. "But there isn't a drop of blood in you that isn't faerie, and nymphs were never meant to live underground."

"Oh, yes, I nearly forgot. We're bed slaves for the gods."

"You don't seem to mind my bed."

"You're different. And no, you cannot come in."

"I didn't ask."

"You were going to," she said. "Is that why you've been so tired?"

"Sharing my bed with you—yes."

"Lending me your strength?"

"In part, and our baths, and your late night stirrings, and let us not forget your early morning appetites as well."

"You never put up much fight."

"Hmm." The water's reflection danced in his eyes.

"I could let you sleep, if you wish," she said with a flutter of lashes. "It's not as if I need you."

He snorted.

Her grin vanished. "You're tired because of your visions?" she asked, turning serious.

Marsais nodded in answer.

"You've been having one nearly every other day."

"Yes." Despite the heat, he shivered. "Sorting through my visions is an exhausting process."

"Then come in here with me, and I'll make you forget everything."

"You can, and do, but no—not today, I think. The captain's lesson this morning shook you."

"You felt everything, didn't you?" she asked. "That's exactly what I mean. You know what I feel more than I do myself."

"Isiilde, trust me, please," he implored.

She wanted to—she truly did. But today, when she'd stood her ground, was that because of Marsais' strength or her own? Where did she end and he begin? She no longer knew. He had not left her, had not held their bond at arm's length since he had been healed.

Their connection was not equal. She did feel strong, sudden emotions from him—but rarely. The rest of the time, Marsais' spirit was as brilliant as the sun surrounding her. What did she feel like to him?

Had she even tried to explore their bond?

Isiilde frowned in thought. Between vile Wise Ones, traitors, blood-drinking Reapers, and Blighted, there hadn't been a lot of time to ponder much of anything except survival. *It's not as if you've tried*, a tiny voice inserted. Isiilde had basked in the sun's glow, but never studied it.

Floating on her back, she drifted in the spring, letting its bubbles tickle her ears and massage the ache from her bones. Her focus turned inward, towards Marsais' glowing spirit. How did he push her away and withdraw so easily? Shouldn't she be able to push him away as well?

If one could poke at her own thoughts, the nymph began to do so—only it wasn't herself she prodded, but the bind that tethered Marsais' spirit to hers. A bind. That was exactly what their connection was.

Every weave could be untangled, but she didn't want to untangle their spirits completely. It was only that there was so much of him inside of her. If she didn't trust him so completely, the bond would be terrifying.

Isiilde focused on it as she would any weave. Their bond took shape in her mind's eye—a twining dragon of fire, curled around the sun. She tugged gently on the dragon, easing it away, as carefully as she might coax an air rune to water.

The sun was bright, and she thought of privacy, of shelter from the heat. Without warning, the dragon slipped from the sun and a wall of darkness snapped into place.

Isiilde was slammed to the ground, shards of pottery sliced her back, and a weight pressed down on her. His breath was close. Pain laced up her arm. She screamed. But it was silenced by water. Isiilde broke the surface, choking and gasping, flailing in confusion and terror.

It seemed an eternity.

Marsais' spirit burned away the darkness and reclaimed the dragon, even as he darted around the pool. He yanked her out of the pool and she flopped onto the stone, coughing up a lungful of water.

Marsais crouched beside her, watching and waiting patiently with a comforting hand on her back as she fought for air. As soon as she could summon the strength, she turned, wrapping her arms around his neck. He held her tightly.

"That was unwise of me," she groaned.

"Hmm."

"There's nothing left of me."

"You need time," Marsais soothed.

"For what?"

"To heal."

"I was weak to begin with," she growled.

Marsais pried her arms from around his neck, so he might look her in the eye. "Stop this, here and now."

"Stop what?"

"You're a newly awakened nymph, Isiilde. Your blood is stirring with a fierceness to match your fire. You are confused, you are lost, you are growing, and it is all quite normal. That's why the Sylph entrusted her daughters to the druids."

"Were you a druid, Marsais?"

"I am now. And as your druid, I have an obligation to watch over you and support you, in whatever way is needed. Nymphs draw from their druid's experience, from their strength, because quite frankly I doubt they'd learn a thing on their own."

"How do you know all this if you weren't a druid before?"

He ignored her attempts to distract. "With that said, I am going to order you on your bond—"

"No, please!" She tried to break free, but his grip was like iron. He had sworn not to take her fire.

"—not to worry about anything."

As the words sank in, she stopped struggling, and eventually relaxed altogether. Isiilde tilted her head, searching his eyes for deceit.

"That's it?"

"Yes."

Isiilde opened her mouth to argue, but clicked it shut in defeat. She felt strangely... lighter. "Nothing at all?"

"That's correct. Not Tharios, not myself, nor Oenghus. Not the past, the future, or even the now."

"That's a very odd order, Marsais."

"I'm a very odd man."

"You are," she agreed. "But a wonderful one."

CHAPTER 36

"The storm has blown over, Seer," Lucas Cutter said, blocking the entrance to their cave.

Every day for the past seven days, the scarred paladin had asked Marsais when they planned on leaving. And every day, Marsais had asked the same question: Where did he intend to go in a blizzard? Lucas was restless today.

Elam and Rivan glanced up from their game of King's Folly. The small boy appeared to have a better grasp of the game than the paladin. The thought of Rivan and runes made Isiilde's head ache. She had spent most of her evenings trying to teach him the basics. And she vowed never to volunteer Marsais for anything ever again.

"I find your small talk on the weather tedious, Sir Lucas."

Marsais made to step around the paladin, but Lucas grabbed his arm. "It's not small talk."

Marsais glanced at the hand holding him in place. A flash of irritation rippled through their bond, but she was not altogether sure it wasn't hers. There was no sign of Acacia, and Oenghus had offered his healing talents to the tribe, so he was rarely present.

"These heathens won't let us near the river running through their valley," Lucas said. "There's a stairway beyond a heavily guarded gate. It must lead to the other side of the waterfall."

"A wise assessment," Marsais noted.

"Then we're leaving?"

"I never said we'd leave once the storm blew over."

"You used it as an excuse."

"No, Sir Lucas. I simply pointed out that there was a blizzard. You took that as the reason for our delay."

"What is our delay?"

"I'm waiting."

"For what?"

"An opportunity."

"We can make our own opportunity," Lucas growled.

"And the guards?"

"We'll fight our way out."

"And afterwards?"

"We'll keep going to Vlarthane, as you said we would."

"With a tribe of furious Lome, who know every corner of the valley on our heels? That is suicidal."

"Then what is your plan?"

"I'm not at liberty to say."

"Curse you!" Lucas spat.

"Oh, I've been cursed plenty. I doubt one more time would matter."

Lucas yanked Marsais forward to growl in his face. The veins in the paladin's neck pulsed. "There's a Bloodmagi on the verge of opening a portal to a dark god and you'd rather lay about plowing your nymph."

Isiilde took a step back.

"Do not speak of Isiilde in such a manner, *swine*." His words cracked with power. A weave clenched around Lucas' throat, dropping him to his knees. The paladin doubled over and clutched his stomach, frothing with convulsions.

Rivan scrambled to his feet, but one look from Marsais froze him in place. Elam darted out of the cave, but Isiilde stood her ground.

Lucas' clothes became loose while he shrunk, twisting and thrashing, fighting the enchantment. Runes swirled around his form, obscuring him in a bluish glow, until he disappeared. A scarred, black little piglet scrambled out from beneath the pile of clothing. It darted away with a squeal.

Rivan dropped his sword.

"Sorry about that, my dear. It was rather rude of him." Marsais kissed her hand, slipping it into his arm, and led her to their room.

Marsais' heart thumped against her ear. Isiilde trailed her fingertips through the hair dusting his wiry chest. She traced his ribs, and moved to his hip. He chuckled, squirming at her touch.

She rolled on top of him. A waterfall of fire fell around their faces, and she smiled, bringing his hand to her throat.

"Oh, forgive me," he whispered, brushing her throat and lips, tugging his weave away. The pleasant, tingling warmth of the weave vanished, leaving a lingering memory of his touch.

Voice restored, she moaned and stretched along his body. "You're so warm."

"Anything for my nymph."

"I think we dozed off," she murmured. "Are you going to change Lucas back?"

"Hmm?"

Isiilde laughed, free and easy. "Have you forgotten, Marsais?"

"I'm quite sure I forgot everything when we fell into bed."

"You turned him into a pig."

"Did I?" Although his lips were on her neck, his voice was far away, and his touch was distracting.

"Maybe it was a dream," she conceded. "But if it wasn't—I don't think it was wise of you."

"Probably not."

Confirmation came in the way of Knight Captain Mael. Acacia stepped through Marsais' mirror weave without hesitation. Her brisk footsteps hit the other side of the Orb of Silence, followed by a towering berserker. They both looked displeased.

"More than likely," Isiilde sighed, sliding off her Bonded onto the furs.

"What in the Nine Halls did you do to my lieutenant, Marsais?"

"I thought it rather obvious."

"Scarecrow," Oenghus warned.

"You had no right," Acacia pressed.

"Your lieutenant was rude," Marsais explained. "And so is barging in unannounced."

Acacia clenched her jaw. "You would drive a monk to rudeness, Seer."

"She has a point," Oenghus grunted.

"Sir Lucas was rude to Isiilde."

"What the bloody Void did that bastard do?" Oenghus' eyes blazed. "Maybe we should have pork tonight."

"Rivan said Kasja has already tried to slaughter my lieutenant," Acacia snapped. "I don't care what he did or said. It's no excuse for your childish antics. Unravel your enchantment, now."

The tension in the room was palpable, and the captain's pale gaze was ice. Isiilde melted back beneath the covers, holding her breath, waiting for Marsais to respond.

As calm as could be, Marsais slipped from beneath the covers and casually stood without a scrap of clothing on his lean body. "If you will catch your lieutenant for me, Captain, I'll be out shortly." She turned on her heel and strode out.

"Gods, I love that woman," Oenghus grunted, as Marsais tugged on his trousers. He turned to leave, but stopped when Marsais called his name.

"Lay off the mead for a few nights, my old friend." The two men regarded each other silently. Then Oenghus nodded in understanding.

"You gonna bloody do your usual?"

"As much as I tire of it," Marsais sighed.

Bare-footed and bare-chested, Marsais strode into the common room, scratching his scar as he surveyed the scene, trying to recall why he had come out here.

Isiilde frowned at the tension in the cave. Elam had returned, and Rivan was standing guard over a pig while Kasja circled the pair. Oenghus sat on a rock, preparing a pipe.

Acacia pointed at Lucas, and Marsais' fingers flashed. Isiilde watched him trace, focusing on the runes and committing them to memory. With a soft murmur, he tapped the pig on its head and ripped the weave from its skin.

Isiilde had witnessed Marsais perform a transformation on various Wise Ones over the years. She'd never liked it, but now she found it fascinating.

The pig writhed and squealed; bones cracked and shifted as runes unraveled, swirling in tatters over the air. In moments, a naked man trembled on the stone.

Isiilde could not look away.

Lucas was covered in scars, and the extent of his injuries were horrifying. He was also a eunuch. And there was an unmistakable pattern to his scarred flesh—it was deliberate. Torture.

Acacia tossed a cloak over his shoulders, but when the man found his feet, he lunged at Marsais. Fist connected with flesh, whipping Marsais' face to the side. He staggered back and took another fist to the ribs before Acacia grabbed Lucas' arm.

"That's enough, lieutenant," she warned.

Lucas shook off her grip, and snatched up his clothes. "You owe me an answer, Seer."

Marsais wiped the blood from his nose. "You owe Isiilde an apology."

"No, you owe me one."

"Look here, Lucas," Oenghus said around his pipe stem. "You can pummel the Scarecrow all you like, but when it comes to Isiilde, you best treat her with respect."

"I do not *want* his apology," Isiilde said, handing Marsais a handkerchief.

"Get your clothes on, Lieutenant."

"I want a straight answer from him, Captain."

"Marsais was just about to give us one before you belted him."

"Answering your seemingly simple question is a complicated matter," Marsais interrupted the paladins, his voice muffled by the handkerchief pinched to his nose.

"What is so complicated about our question?" Acacia asked. There was strain in her voice. And she looked as if she'd like to punch Marsais, too. Isiilde quickly stepped between the two.

"I don't know when we're leaving. I'm waiting," Marsais said.

A muscle in Acacia's jaw twitched. "For what?"

"I'm a seer, not an astrologer."

Acacia looked heavenward.

"I told you he was insane," Lucas growled, tugging on his clothes.

"I could have told you that," Oenghus rumbled.

"So you've had a vision?" Acacia pressed.

"When have I not?"

"Well, what have you seen?" asked Rivan.

"Aha!" Marsais exclaimed, beaming at the young man. "Therein lies the problem. Let me endeavor to explain what you will undoubtedly not understand. I owe you all that much."

A number of eyes narrowed.

"Rivan, as riveting as your game of King's Folly is with Elam, I'm afraid I must use the runes to explain."

Rivan backed away from the jumbled pieces and everyone gathered around the circle of runes, even Kasja, who crouched at the edge of the area. Isiilde wondered how much the wild woman could understand. And what she and Marsais talked about when they conversed.

"I'm only going to explain this once, because I've tired of explaining it in both past and future. So listen." Marsais paused, making sure he had everyone's attention. "I'm going to tell you of my visions and why I can't speak of them."

Lucas flexed his fists.

"Hmm, Time does not flow like a river; it's an ocean of moments, brushing together like waves. Choices cause diversions, they stir the ocean like a wind. But old mumbling crones and impassioned young oracles would have the populace believe that Time is unchanging, that fate is set in stone. That is not true. The future is made up of possibilities, and my visions are pathways that have not yet been walked.

"Imagine, if you will, a mountain shrouded in mist. You're perched on a precipice, gazing at the bleakness. The mists part, and for a moment there is a flash, and you glimpse the world at your feet." Marsais gestured at the rune stones. "Here is the world." The runes flared to life, the cavern fell away, and each stone was burned into their eyes. "And here are the mists." With a sweep of his hand, the brightness died and the stones moved, swarming and clacking together into a jumbled mess.

"I see flashes of Time, but I must separate those visions, and reassemble them. Now, who of you can piece this game back together, just as it was?" Marsais looked expectantly at the gathered audience, but no one volunteered.

Finally, Isiilde shrugged. "I can."

Marsais focused on her like a hawk. "By all means, my dear."

Isiilde began sorting the chaotic rune pieces, nudging one here, and the other there with a deft touch. It wasn't much different from unraveling a Ward, only she was putting one back together, trusting her instincts. When the runes created a swirling tapestry of stone on the cave floor, she leaned back to survey her work.

Marsais circled the group slowly, studying the complex pattern from all angles. "Perfect as always, my dear," he said, brushing her knuckles with his lips. "The next part is more difficult. I see a handful of possible moves, but which one will Rivan take? Hmm, that is what sets seers apart. Choice is unsteady. I, however, know what move Rivan will make based on observation—my knowledge of the past." Marsais glanced at the uneasy paladin. "Whisper to your captain what move you'll make."

Rivan hesitated, but did as Marsais asked. When the message was delivered, he nodded, and Marsais pinned a rune with a long finger, moving the iron rune beside the ice. A foolish move on Rivan's part, but based on the answering gasp, it was clearly the move he had intended to make.

"Since Elam can't understand a word we're saying—" Marsais gave the boy an apologetic nod. "Captain, would you be so kind as to whisper your next move to Sir Lucas?"

Acacia did, and Marsais moved the Death rune into the inner circle, altering the cycles. He predicted their moves for five more turns, and finally, Lucas had had enough. "It's a neat trick, Seer, but what does this have to do with my question?"

"You haven't grasped my dilemma."

"The only dilemma you have is your head."

Oenghus chuckled.

"Hmm, I can't disagree with that," Marsais admitted, scratching his scar. "But no, that's not what I was trying to show you. Let us switch angles. Rivan, if I were to tell you that the captain's next move will take your ice rune, what would you do?"

Rivan blinked and leaned forward, studying the cycles with knitted brows. Clearly, he had missed the obvious, so Marsais answered for him. "You would alter your planned move, would you not? And you, Captain, in response, would change your plans to match his. Am I correct?"

"Of course."

"So my point, Sir Lucas, before your temper gets the better of you—if I tell you what I know, then what you know would change, altering the knowing that I came to know after countless hours of exhausting contemplation."

Confusion settled on the paladins as they tried to unravel his words. "Hmm, in short, your knowing would waste my energy." He held up a finger. "And I'll point out that in knowing me, you are all privy to more matters than you should know."

The paladins gaped, Oenghus' beard twitched, and Isiilde chewed on her lip.

"He's insane," Lucas spat, surging to his feet. "We're in the middle of Vaylin, with a berserker, a madman, and a combusting nymph." The paladin turned on his heel and stalked down a tunnel.

Marsais beamed. "Clarity is such a beautiful thing."

CHAPTER 37

Isiilde stirred against Marsais, coiling herself around his long, lean body as coals whispered in a nearby firepit. His fingers were tangled in her hair.

The cave was as cool as the soft blue light, but she welcomed the contrast, nudging the heavy fur blanket down, letting the air brush her shoulders. She drifted in a haze of lazy pleasure. Her body was bruised, her bones limp, and yet she felt wonderful.

She smiled against his skin, breathing in his scent, thinking of the salt and sea, and his strong hands. Marsais made her toes tingle.

"Oh, gods," he groaned. "You're going to be the death of me."

"I know, you're already stiff."

Marsais snorted, gripped her hips and switched positions, pressing her against the furs. "And how are you feeling this morning, my dear?"

"You tell me."

"Delicious," he purred.

His lips touched her neck, exploring its intricacies, while his hands slid down her body. She melted beneath his touch. He tugged the fur over his head and disappeared beneath, trailing fire down her flesh.

Their bond pulsed with desire and need, and Isiilde moaned,

burying her fingers in his hair. But another noise interrupted her pleasure.

"*Isiilde!*" a voice barked.

Marsais jerked in realization, and for a hasty second she felt the Lore whispered between her thighs. Marsais straightened with a weave on his fingertips, but he was too late. Captain Mael stepped into their room as his weave snapped in place behind the intruder.

Isiilde nearly screamed with frustration.

Acacia crossed her arms. "You're late for practice."

"Must you barge in unannounced?" Marsais bit out.

"I announced myself three times."

"Surely you can wait?"

"No."

Isiilde moaned.

"Captain—"

"This is not a pleasure house, Marsais. You asked me to train her. Up, Isiilde, the sun rose an hour ago." Without waiting for a response, Acacia turned on her heel and left.

"I'm going to kill her," Isiilde growled.

"You can try during practice," Acacia shouted through the curtain.

Isiilde threw the covers aside and tugged on her clothes. "I hate that woman."

Marsais frowned at something in her tone, then quickly hopped to his feet.

Frustrated, hungry, and irritated beyond words, Isiilde stalked outside with Marsais on her heels. She snatched up her practice sword and charged the captain. Acacia spun, caught the sword in her hand, and disarmed Isiilde before tripping her.

Isiilde hit the ground with a jolt.

"Anger has no place in battle."

Isiilde snatched up a pan resting by the fire and swung two-handed. Iron hit wood, and Isiilde swung again. But Acacia's sword rapped against her knuckles. She dropped the pan with a clatter, put her head down, and rammed the woman's stomach. Or tried to at any rate.

Acacia stepped easily aside and cracked the practice sword against Isiilde's thigh.

Isiilde grabbed the second sword and charged, swinging wildly, forcing her opponent to retreat. Acacia parried and deflected, then struck Isiilde's hand. This time, Isiilde did not let go; she gritted her teeth and continued to swing.

"By the Pits O Mourn, if you ever interrupt me in my bedchamber again, I'll burn you to a crisp, you whore's son of a drunken swine!"

Rivan's mouth fell open, Lucas arched a hairless brow, and Elam and Kasja skittered into the shadows. Marsais' coins gave a low chime as he rubbed the bridge of his nose.

"Really?" Acacia asked.

"Does Zemoch have bloody bollocks?" she spat.

Insulting the Knight Captain was tolerable; however, defaming a Guardian's name was another matter entirely. Acacia snatched up a shield and surged forward. The practice sword smacked against Isiilde's ribs, then arm before a boot connected with her backside, pushing her to the ground.

Isiilde called to her fire.

Coals roared to life, licking the stalactites, rolling and crashing towards the captain. Acacia deflected the fireball with her shield, grunting at the heat. Sparks exploded in the cavern, but Acacia did not falter. She sped towards the prone nymph, grabbed her by her hair, and pushed her head into a bucket.

Isiilde feared the woman would drown her.

Acacia brought her up for air, and a calm voice spoke in her ear. "I wonder where you got that mouth of yours. Never use a Guardian's name in vain, Girl."

"Kiss my faerie arse!" Isiilde spat, sucking in a breath as her head was forced into the bucket again. She struggled against the iron grip, and then purposefully went limp. She had not spent hours in the bath for nothing. Isiilde could hold her breath for a full turn of the hourglass.

A surge of concern filled her bond, but she refused to call to Marsais for help. This was between the captain and her.

Isiilde readied herself, biding her time. When Acacia yanked her up for air, she was ready, gasping for her flame. It stirred with a fury.

Acacia abandoned the nymph, diving to safety, hitting the stone, and bracing her shield as a wave of heat slammed into the steel. The

Lore throbbed in the air and Isiilde's fingers flashed, throwing a bolt of lightning in the fireball's wake.

Steel crackled with energy, but the captain held fast. "Is that the best you can do, Girl?" Acacia stood, brushing the ash from her arm.

"Ladies…" Marsais began, but both women pinned him with a cool gaze and he drew up short.

"All part of training. Isn't it, Captain?"

Acacia dipped her chin.

"I know what you're doing," Isiilde said, circling the woman cautiously. "But I'm not one of your mindless, dim-witted recruits."

Acacia matched the nymph step for step.

"I've watched drillmasters before. I know their tactics. You want me to fear you, but you will settle for my hate."

"I don't settle, Girl."

"I won't give you anything. You have no control over me."

"Apparently, I've been too soft with you. It's a shame Marsais put restrictions on me."

"Is that an excuse, Captain?"

Marsais gestured sharply, hinting strongly for silence. But Isiilde ignored him and focused on her opponent, who smiled at her challenge.

It was the first time Isiilde had seen the Knight Captain smile during their training, and she suddenly wished she had not.

Quick as a snake, Acacia charged. Isiilde barely managed to weave a shield. Without thinking, she added fire instead of a feather rune. Heat rippled over her flesh as Acacia struck, connecting with her gut.

The blow knocked the breath from Isiilde's lungs, and an unexpected occurrence, but not altogether ill, flared to life as an arcing flame. Fire sped up the captain's arm.

Isiilde coughed, scrambling back. "Is that the best you can do, you sheep-buggering crone?"

Acacia plunged her arm into the bucket, snatched it up, and tossed the contents at the nymph. Isiilde was too slow. Water drenched her, sizzling on her flesh, and a split second later, a sword hooked her legs, whipping them out from under her. She hit the stone flat, gasped, and croaked out a word.

Fire rippled from the pit, slamming into Acacia, who twisted to deflect the blast. The distraction was enough. Isiilde recovered her breath, her fingers flashed, and she sent a bolt, one after another, crackling towards the paladin's exposed side.

Acacia grunted, stumbled, but pressed on. Exactly as Isiilde had expected. Acacia hit her grease enchantment and slipped on the stone. The woman pounded onto her back, shield raised, and Isiilde was on top in an instant, ripping the sword from her slippery grasp.

Isiilde brought the wooden sword sideways against Acacia's throat, but it wasn't the woman's face beneath her.

"Don't you ever touch me again, you puking, slimy bastard!" Isiilde screamed through a haze of hot tears. It was Stievin and his fevered eyes.

Isiilde's skin sizzled, the water steamed, and the firepit flared in anticipation, waiting for her call. She opened her mouth, intending to burn them both, but Acacia slapped her palms against Isiilde's ears, stunning the nymph.

Isiilde slid off the shield, gasping, rolling into a painful ball. Marsais started forward, but Acacia thrust out a hand. "I have another two hours, Seer," she rasped.

"You've done quite enough."

"If she wants your help, then she can ask. Otherwise, stand back."

Isiilde bit her lip against the pain. It would be so easy to ask. Marsais was so close, so willing and ready to rush to her rescue, but determination tore at the thought. She would die before she gave the Knight Captain the satisfaction.

Ignoring her shaking limbs, she climbed to her feet, and faced the woman. "You're still a sheep-buggering crone."

"Since that's impossible, I'll let that curse slide until you come up with a better one, Isiilde."

She blinked in surprise.

"And next time you start throwing your fire around, I'll stop going easy on you."

"Likewise, Captain." She raised her chin.

"Good. Now pick up your sword."

CHAPTER 38

Oenghus strolled behind his pint-sized guide, savoring his first pipe after a long night. He didn't speak the language, but he understood clans. And when the chieftain invited a guest to a feast—you went. But last night had been different.

A woman was in bad sorts with twins, and Oenghus had offered his talents. Mother and children had survived and V'elbine was pleased.

Oenghus passed his pipe to Elam. The boy had no other family besides his crazed sister, and he made for refreshing company compared to the tension brewing in their dwelling.

Marsais was best tolerated in small doses. Prolonged contact with the skinny bastard would drive anyone to murder.

Elam flashed a gap-filled grin and handed the pipe back. With the excitement of a ten-year-old, he began conversing. Language was never a barrier with children. The boy's gestures said everything as he described what could only be a battle.

"Aye, sounds fearsome," Oenghus grunted, pressing himself against the side of the passage to make way for two women.

Their pale faces glowed with tattoos that swirled enticingly around their eyes, dipping beneath their collars and spiraling down their arms.

The women openly admired his physique, and Oenghus offered a charming smile, watching their hips sway as they passed.

Elam held up two thumbs. The boy was intent on finding him a good woman.

"Aye, you've got good taste," Oenghus said.

They exited the passage, climbed down the steep winding steps that spilled into the valley, and entered the bustle of the underground city. Oenghus towered over the populace and the Lome greeted him with wide smiles. News traveled quickly in a clan. A fighter of Oenghus' size was a prize, but a healer was a treasure. The Lome would not part with him easily.

Blood would be spilt whenever Marsais decided to leave, and he didn't much care for the idea of fighting their way out—not after the Lome had been so hospitable.

Unfortunately, there was nothing for it.

Oenghus ducked under an arch, stepped through the brief passage into their common room, and froze.

"Bastard!" Elam swore. It was the boy's favorite new word in the trade tongue. And Oenghus had to agree.

Isiilde and Acacia faced each other, practice swords in hand. His daughter looked on the verge of collapse. Blood trickled from her nose, and fresh bruises blossomed under a layer of sweat and grime.

The captain looked ruffled.

Marsais stood off to the side, tight-lipped and sharp-eyed, while Rivan and Lucas watched from the wall. The common room was in ruins. Scorch marks stained the carvings, the firepit appeared to have exploded, and the pans were scattered, along with an overturned bucket.

"What the Void is going on?"

Isiilde's eyes flashed. "We're sparring."

"Are you sure that's all?"

"Yes," Acacia said. "And we're done. Aside from that tongue of yours, you did well today, Isiilde. Don't make me wake you tomorrow."

"I was already awake," she argued.

"Wait, what tongue?" he asked, pushing away the bundle of furs sniffing at his legs.

"She has your foul mouth," Acacia explained.

"Since when?"

"I have something to curse about now." Isiilde set her practice sword aside, snatched up bread and cheese and limped towards her room.

Tension bled from the cave the moment she vanished behind the curtain. Elam said something to Marsais.

"Hmm, the boy wonders why we are fool enough to travel with an elemental spirit."

Oenghus eyed Acacia's stiff movements and scorched shield as she limped to her quarters. "You know, Marsais, before you got to my sprite, she was a docile little thing."

"Oh, really?"

"Aye, that's right, timid as a mouse."

"With fangs," Rivan muttered.

"DO YOU NEED HEALING, ACACIA?" Oenghus called through the curtain.

"Lucas is seeing to me."

"Aye, but I'll have your sword arm good as new."

There was silence, and finally, "Come in."

Oenghus pushed the curtain aside and crouched, ducking into a room that was little more than a hollow. Isiilde and Marsais had taken the largest nook in the stone hovel.

Acacia sat on a bed of furs with Lucas at her side. He had helped her out of her jerkin, and was trying to peel away her scorched shirt, but the wool was stuck to flesh. Acacia shook with pain, sweat glistening on her brow.

"Not like that, Lucas." The hollow would have been crowded with just Oenghus, but with all three, it was cramped. "Get out of the way."

Lucas glanced at Oenghus.

"It's fine," Acacia said.

Lucas was hesitant. "Are you sure?"

"Your captain's honor is safe with me," Oenghus said with a hand to his heart.

"But not my temper," she remarked, dismissing her lieutenant with a nod.

"Bring me my kit and water, would you?"

Lucas squeezed past, and Oenghus settled himself at her side. The paladin returned a moment later with the requested items: mortar, pestle, a waterskin, and herbs. Oenghus grunted his gratitude, withdrew a narrow knife, and waited for the captain's permission. She nodded, and he began slicing through the fabric, leaving the bits that were stuck to flesh.

"I didn't take you for the type to have a watchdog."

"He's my lieutenant, I'm his captain."

"I was wondering about that."

"You can keep wondering."

Oenghus grunted. She watched him work in silence, grinding herbs, mixing and sniffing at the contents. "What is that?"

"I can mend your flesh, but I can't do it until the wool is out of those burns."

"Won't water do?"

"Aye, but this is better. Takes longer, too. It means I get to spend more time with you."

"You don't give up, do you?"

"I'm stubborn, remember?"

"More like pig-headed."

"I'll take what I can get."

"I'll save you the trouble. I have an Oathbound."

"Paladins make horrible liars—the good ones, anyway."

"I thought there were no good paladins?"

"About as many good paladins as there are good berserkers."

"Rivan told you, didn't he?"

"I cornered the poor lad."

"And you wonder why I think you a brute."

"Aye, but I'm a lovable one."

"The lies we tell ourselves are the most convincing."

Oenghus chuckled. "Well, you haven't run yet." He brought the mortar to his nose and wrinkled it, turning serious once again. "You ready?"

Acacia nodded.

"In case you're wondering," he said, dipping his fingers in the salve, "this is not an excuse to get my hands on you."

"Is this your idea of charming?"

"How am I doing?"

"How do you think?"

"Making progress."

Acacia clenched her jaw as he slopped the mess over her burns.

"So what was your Oathbound like?" he asked, trying to distract her. "Another paladin?"

She did not answer straightaway, but slowly, she relaxed, frowning at the yellowish mixture. "My arm is numb."

"It won't hurt as bad when I scrub off the wool."

"No, he wasn't a paladin. He was a Wraith Guard in Iilenshar. My daughters still live in Easthaven."

"What happened to him?"

"The Keening took him while I was in the Fell Wastes. We were bound for fifty years."

Oenghus frowned. There was tension in her voice, but it wasn't from the water and cloth he was using to scrub her wounds. "Not an easy thing to lose someone to the Keening. Let me guess, he was up to two hundred?"

"No, he thought I'd been killed."

Oenghus might be a brute, but he knew when to let a subject lie. Acacia nudged the conversation onto another path. "But you're right—few seem to have the will to live past two hundred."

"During the first hundred, you figure out how to live, and during the second, you figure out there's not much to live for."

"Unless you find a purpose," she finished. "And what about in the ninth century?"

"Life is just getting interesting."

"You mean you're still looking for the perfect ale?"

"Aye, let me know if you find it."

"And what about you? I suppose you have four Oathbounds, being a Nuthaanian."

He shook his head. "That's our women. They can have as many Oathbounds as they like."

"I always assumed the men could, too."

"Goes back to the Shattering. One of my daughters, the Clans Head, has five Oathbounds."

"Your daughter is the Clans Head of Nuthaan? Why am I not surprised?" she muttered.

"I see you've met my sweet little girl."

Acacia eyed him. "In the Wedamen invasion about thirty years back."

"You were at the Plains too?" That had been one of the bloodiest battles in nearly two centuries.

"Yes, I discovered, quite brutally, why it's never wise to follow a berserker into battle."

"I hope you weren't following me."

"No, I'd remember. Is that why your women take more than one man?"

"Because we're so keen on dying?" he asked with a chuckle. "No, it's one of the wiser things my people have done, actually. After the Shattering, there was hardly a soul breathing. Women were scarce. So, while the other lands took what they wanted and treated their women like cattle for breeding, we barbarians took a more civilized route. Figuring we menfolk would muck up things, we gave our women the very best of everything we had, and made them our clan chiefs. That's why a maid can go walking in any part of Nuthaan, during any part of the day, and not be harmed. There isn't a Nuthaanian alive who'd take advantage of her." The pride in his voice was unmistakable. "And your Order thinks we're all brutes."

"No," she corrected, "we view you as useful weapons in our fight against the Void."

"Aye, well, I never said we're the brightest bunch. Point us at a fight and we'll be first in line."

Acacia chuckled. "And how did a mindless brute become a Wise One?"

Oenghus frowned, rinsing out his cloth and soaking it with fresh water. "I lost my first Oathbound in childbirth. Terrible way to die, that. Took the both of them three days, and I could only sit there and watch. We were snowed in, far from a healer."

With large gentle hands, Oenghus scrubbed the wool from her flesh. He was silent, lost in memory for a moment, before he continued, "I wasn't much good for anything after that—so I took my chances with the grog. It kills most men who risk it, but I was already dead."

Oenghus leaned close, eyeing Acacia's wounds. When he was satisfied that the burns were free of contamination, he settled a blanket on her shoulders. "I went looking for death with a passion, and do you know, Death fled with her bloody tail between her legs. I'm not exactly sure how I got where I did—everything is muddled—but eventually, I woke up in some cage in the Bastardlands. Drunk as piss and fighting in the pits."

Acacia swallowed her surprise. The Bastardlands were a brutal place. Arena fighters were thrown into pits for money, and few survived for long.

"I loved it," he said, flashing a grin. "All the free ale I could drink, and all the women I could, uhm—"

"Plow," she finished.

"And plenty of fights. Then one day, some dandy bastard comes and takes my grog away."

"Marsais?"

"Aye, I swear he was looking for me. Once I sobered up, I did what any self-respecting barbarian would do—I tried to kill the smug bastard. Bad mistake."

"That's when he turned you into a pig."

"Boar," he corrected. "For a whole fortnight. I think he forgot about me."

Acacia laughed, abruptly. He hadn't heard her laugh before, and he liked the sound of it.

Oenghus scratched his beard as she eased herself onto her uninjured side. "Anyway, the Scarecrow sorted me out eventually, as much as I can be, at any rate."

"And he discovered the why," she said, softly.

Oenghus gave a stiff nod. "A man can fight for those he loves, but there's only so much a hammer can do."

"You trust Marsais because of this?"

"Let me tell you something about the Scarecrow. When he dragged me out of that pit, I didn't know his motives. I still don't half the time, and I don't bloody well agree with his methods either, but the end results—well, you can't argue with them. If he's wasting time, it's for a purpose."

"But has he had a nymph before?" she asked. "I've seen good men turn into layabouts and cowards because of a nymph."

"Not the Scarecrow," he said with complete conviction. "He's been battling the Void for longer than I like to think about. Have some faith."

"My faith is with the Guardians."

"You sure it's with the Guardians and not the Sylph?"

She narrowed her eyes up at him. "Why do you say that?"

"Just a hunch." Oenghus slipped his hands over her furrowed forehead and taut stomach. "Now relax."

His hands were warm and heavy, and his palms rough, but his touch was polite. He waited for her to relax. A healing was intrusive, especially for the distrustful. When the tension bled from her body, Oenghus summoned the Lore, as easily as taking a step. After flesh was mended, he stole a peek at Acacia's spirit; it was a column of light. But it did not radiate warmth. Frost crept up it like a window pane. The Keening.

Oenghus wrapped the Gift around her spirit like a warm blanket, bolstering it with his own, taking the sting from her grief. There wasn't much else he could do but hope it was enough.

The tight control with which the captain carried herself was gone, her features relaxed, and her breath evened. He placed a hand on her short hair. "Sleep well, lass."

Stretched beyond his limits, Oenghus picked himself up, and went to fall into his own bedroll.

CHAPTER 39

A YOUNG GIRL floated in an underground spring, white hair drifting like a cloud around her head. Voices droned around the girl, but her ears were submerged, dampening the noise.

She was bound to the pool by chains with a manacle on each limb. Anchored while the rest of Time shifted and flowed past her.

Beneath the water, she was at peace.

A rattle of chains shattered her peace. Her limbs were pulled taut, and she rose to the surface of the pool, body stretched to the four corners, until her back skimmed the water.

The chained girl opened her eyes, sightless and white, to the cave. Men surrounded her, bodies covered with chalk, rocking and chanting with harsh voices. A man with fangs and claws, and ivory studs embedded in his copper flesh stood off to the side. He was the stranger who'd arrived some time ago. The chained girl convulsed, and a bent Shaman shoved the stranger back against the wall.

The chant reached a crescendo and the naked forms around her rocked violently, reaching out to touch her flesh. She tugged at the chains, screaming to return to her watery refuge, but the chains kept her anchored in place.

The Shaman accepted something from the stranger—a strand of

white hair. He edged forward like a wary animal testing a hole. When he was within arm's length, he dropped the strand of hair into the pool. It swirled with the water's pull, polluting the chained girl's refuge. The water churned, the girl screamed and fought until her mind was rubbed raw against the currents of Time.

With a final tug, the currents caught her form, and her eyes opened to the realm. She flew over mountains, creaking like an old wind; restless and searching, sweeping over frozen wastes and up impossible cliffs, diving into a black maw and speeding down its throat. Blue light embraced her and she swirled over a pale city beneath the earth, unseen and free, searching for the source of the pool's disruption.

Flying through twisting tunnels, over a glowing valley, and finally, into a stone dwelling. The presence she sought stood at her shoulder. It seared her vision.

Time greeted her with silver eyes, and as the girl always did, she fled, speeding away in fear, snapping back into her body and its torment.

CHAPTER 40

Isiilde slept in the arms of her druid. There was nothing beyond him, no stone, no fire, no hatred. Only the nymph and her glowing sun. Hunger nudged her from slumber. She stretched with languid pleasure along Marsais' body, and realized he wasn't there. Not his mind, anyway.

Marsais' eyes were white, tension radiated from his body, and he murmured restlessly. Their bond felt distant.

Isiilde rested her forehead in the crook of his neck, listening to half-muttered words. He was not speaking Common, but another language she could not name, both familiar and foreign.

She caught the hand scratching at his jagged scar and whispered his name. He did not snap out of the vision.

Isiilde waited, holding his hand to her breast as he ground his teeth. His muscles spasmed and his veins stood out stark on his flesh. He clamped down on her hand. And she nearly cried out.

Marsais gasped, and finally his body released its hold, dropping him back to the furs. His eyes were no longer white, but grey and tired and ever so pained.

Isiilde pressed her lips to his damp brow. "You're not alone," she whispered.

He pulled her close. "I am here."

It was an odd thing to say, but she understood. "Yes, you are," she reassured, sensing his fear. "And I love you."

"I am not an easy man to love." His voice was hoarse, cracked, and full of despair.

"Maybe not. But I'm still here."

"For now," he murmured.

Isiilde pulled away, but his eyes were closed, and his arms relaxed their hold. Exhaustion had claimed him. She watched him sleep for a time, smoothing the creases from his brow.

Another time, long ago, she might have sung to ease his slumber, but not now. Not ever again. Isiilde pulled the blanket up to his shoulders, and slipped out of the cavern in search of food.

The common room was quiet. Lucas and Rivan conversed by the fire as they cooked. A sharp burst of laughter from Rivan nearly sent her back into the room, but she squared her shoulders and stepped into the light.

The paladins fell silent, and Rivan hastily rose, gawking at her as she rummaged through a sack.

"Please don't stop on my account," she said, gathering an armful of edible faerie food. "Oenghus raised me. There isn't much I haven't heard."

"No, that's not it at all," Rivan stammered. "It's just—you're so—"

"Rivan," Lucas warned.

Isiilde arched a brow, waiting.

"You don't look real," Rivan blurted out.

Isiilde stared at the man for a second before bursting into helpless laughter. Heat rose from Rivan's collar to the top of his broad brow.

"Sit down," Lucas growled, tugging at the soldier.

"I'm sorry, Rivan," she said, wiping her eyes. "It's just that if I'm not real, that means you've been losing to yourself at King's Folly every night."

"I'm just bad enough to do that, aren't I?" He gave her a lopsided grin.

"I've seen worse."

Lucas smirked. "You're a good liar, Nymph."

This pleased her no end.

"Can I get you some water or mead?" Rivan asked.

"No, thank you."

Isiilde was keenly aware of the men, of their eyes, of their presence and threat. She hesitated. It would be easier to retreat to her sleeping chamber, but she was tired of hiding. She settled beside the firepit to eat, studying the pair across a barrier of flame.

Rivan wasn't much older than she. Strong, square, with tightly curled black hair. His eyes reminded her of chocolate.

"Just so you know, the captain is tough on everyone," Rivan said, poking at the coals with a stick.

"Is she all right?" Isiilde asked. She actually cared to know. And that surprised her.

"It would take a lot more than you to stop the captain," Lucas said. "Knight Captain Mael has led armies, fought Voidspawn, and stood against fiends. I have no idea why she's taking orders from that seer."

Isiilde frowned at her bread. "If you trust your captain, Sir Lucas," she said, looking up to meet his eye. "Then you would not question her decisions."

"Not a question. It's a statement. You and your lot aren't worth her time."

"Not fit to shine her boots?"

"That's right."

Isiilde flashed a smile. "Good. I dislike cleaning boots."

Rivan snorted into his mug. And much to her relief, Lucas ignored her presence while she ate. When she'd finished her meal, Lucas nudged the younger man with an elbow and Rivan finally breeched the quiet. "Would you feel up to helping me with King's Folly again tonight? I think I'm making progress."

"You are," she admitted.

"I appreciate it. So uhm... Does Marsais ever tell you about his visions?"

Not a very subtle pair, she thought. "Why would he?"

"Well, you're..." Rivan shifted. "He's, erm, you and him—aren't you?"

Isiilde rescued Rivan from his fumbling attempt at spying. "I don't really want to know the future, do you?"

Having been Marsais' apprentice for four years, she was accustomed to people trying to wheedle information out of her about the recluse. What did his chambers look like? Did he sleep? Did he have a temper, consort with dark fiends, trail his fingers through cat guts, and splatter its blood over runes—the nymph had heard it all. And she had enjoyed spinning bizarre stories, feeding rumor.

Isiilde had once convinced a group of Wise Ones that the Archlord never physically left his chambers. His body was floating in midair, in an empty room of swirling runes. And that what they saw of Marsais was only an elaborate illusion. She had thought nothing of her tale until one of them was overcome with curiosity and threw an apple at his head.

That had not ended well for the Wise One.

"Enough of the future to know what he's planning, yes," Lucas said.

"You've made that clear," Isiilde said. "But generals aren't expected to share strategies with their troops, are they?"

"The seer isn't my general."

"And yet the Hound respected him."

"Aren't you a smart-mouthed nymph?"

"No, just a logical one."

"I prefer your kind when they're silent."

"You mean chained."

"Gagged works, too."

"Lucas," Rivan hissed. "By the Sylph, please just leave her alone."

The lieutenant muttered a curse, set down his mug so hard it cracked, and stomped out of the common room.

"Is he always so polite?" she asked Rivan.

"Yes, actually. Don't take it personal. He's restless. Doesn't like tight spaces or waiting, or... well, much of anything."

"Was he like that before his injuries?"

Rivan shrugged. "Don't know. Lucas and the captain go way back, though. Just, whatever you do, don't ask him about those scars."

"I gathered as much." She met his eyes across the fire. And Rivan shifted, picking up the bag of runes. He sat on the edge of his fur and began placing them in their swirling cycles on a smooth patch of stone. She edged closer, meeting him halfway.

"You know you don't have to worry about me," he said, without taking his eyes off the runes. "I wouldn't ever hurt you."

Isiilde was surprised he'd noticed her unease. "I'm sure you believe that." She corrected his rune placement, and he followed her example, shifting his cycle.

"I don't expect you to." His hand stilled and he looked up suddenly, his gaze haunted with memory. "The Fomorri took my sisters during a raid. The captain found me under my mother's body."

"What happened to your sisters?"

"I don't know. I try not to wonder." He dropped his eyes to the game and nudged a rune stone in place. "The captain is my family. Has been for a good long time."

"I'm sorry, Rivan."

"She's a regular drillmaster."

Isiilde smiled at his attempt at lightness. "I meant your family before."

"I know." He smiled, shy and crooked, but it vanished as he admitted, "I couldn't do anything. I didn't even try—I hid."

"How old were you?"

"Eight, or thereabouts."

"You were *eight*, Rivan."

"But I hid, and I remember."

There was nothing more to say. They played in silence, manipulating runes to shift cycles, concentrating on the pattern under their eyes. After a time, Rivan began to talk, describing Mearcentia, its sun and fruit and crystal oceans. And she told him of her time on the Isle, which led to darker matters: the Unspoken, foul gods, and madmen.

"Are you worried?" Rivan asked. "That Tharios will open a portal to the Nine Halls?"

Isiilde chewed on her lip, sliding her fire rune towards her air. The rune swirled with fire and burst over Rivan's earth rune, burning it to a crisp. A moment later, the illusion faded, and the stone reappeared, unharmed. She plucked it up and added it to her growing pile of captured runes.

"I try not to worry about the future, Rivan."

"Hmm," a voice mused from the shadows. "You've been spending far too much time with me, my dear."

As Marsais walked out of the tunnel, she watched his long-legged stride with appreciation. For a split second, she caught Rivan watching him, too. Then the paladin hastily jumped to his feet, looking guilty.

"Oh, don't stop on my account." Marsais waved an elegant hand, and Rivan sat back down at its command. Marsais bent to kiss her hand. Something was troubling him; she could see it in his eyes.

"I think you're hungry," she said.

Brows rose in surprise. "Ah, yes, have I not eaten?"

"No, not at all."

"An excellent place to start, then."

Marsais appeared lost, so she rummaged through the sack, brought out cheese and bread, and pressed it into his hands. He sat beside her and ate, but didn't appear to notice.

"Marsais," she said, touching his arm. "You're in the Lome city."

Grey eyes fixed on her. "I am, aren't I?"

"I hope so."

"I do too." He placed a hand over hers and tightened his grip, blinking away confusion. "Hmm, that's right. We're bonded, and you are an enchanting vision, whom I am currently frightening."

"That's about it."

"I thought you weren't supposed to worry?"

"Where you're concerned, that isn't possible."

"Are you up to practicing weaves today?"

"After you finish eating."

"You're worrying again."

"I have a vested interest in your stamina and health."

His eyes twinkled, and he took another bite.

Isiilde faced Marsais across an expanse of stone. "Will you teach me to weave a more powerful bolt?"

"No, we're going to work on your less than average ability to concentrate."

Isiilde glanced back to the firepit. They had been working on her less than average ability to concentrate every afternoon. She'd rather keep teaching King's Folly to Rivan. With a sigh, she returned her attention to Marsais.

"Have some faith in your former master." Marsais picked up a stick from a pile of wood and held it over the fire. She brightened.

Fire made everything better.

Marsais traced a rune around the end of the brand, tethered it with a bind, and crooked a finger. The flame left the stick to hover in midair at his command.

"We're going to levitate fire?" she asked.

"Ah, I see I've captured your attention."

"You usually do."

He beckoned her closer. "Something more interesting, my dear. Your weaving has progressed, and so has your control." His eyes glittered, and she nearly abandoned her self-control and dragged him back to their bed.

"I'd rather spend the afternoon perfecting it."

Marsais cleared his throat. "As tempting as that suggestion is, I have something else in mind—I'm going to teach you how to defend yourself against other weaves."

Isiilde frowned, watching the flameling's dance. "You mean Barriers?"

"Yes."

"Aren't they advanced? Oen can't even defend against weaves."

"He has a natural resistance to weaves. The Hound possessed a number of Barriers woven into his armor and flesh. It took me a while to find his cracks."

"Is that why you were able to kill the Lome barbarian so easily?" Rivan asked.

"Yes, and I completed the weave before we began."

Rivan narrowed his eyes. "That's not—"

"Honorable?"

"Not really."

"But preferable to my blood on the stone, and Isiilde handed over to the chieftain as a prize, I hope?" He arched a brow at the paladin, who nodded. "Hmm, now the problem with Barriers is you have to know what your opponent is throwing at you; otherwise, you can't adjust your weave. That's where King's Folly comes into play—the rings of cycles and interaction of runes. Weaving a Barrier and manipulating the Gift during a battle is exactly like King's Folly, only faster, deadlier, and *far* more challenging."

Her emerald eyes lit with excitement, and Marsais knew he had her undivided attention.

"I swore to you that I wouldn't snuff out your fire, but this time, Isiilde, it's up to you—you must protect your fire from my water rune." His eyes shifted to the hovering flameling, and she looked at the trembling heat with the affection that a mother would feel for an infant.

Isiilde nodded. "Where do I start?"

"The base for a Barrier is the same as the first cycle in King's Folly: wind, fire, earth, and water. You'll need to bind them together with spirit."

"You can't bind them together, Marsais. They're all opposites."

"You're right, they can't be bound; however, a cycle requires constant shifting and sustained concentration. Let me show you."

Marsais selected two apples from their stores, tossed them up in the air and deftly began to juggle one-handed. "These are wind and fire." He snatched up two more, juggling the new additions in his left hand. Both hands moved with a blur of intersecting green.

Isiilde stared, mesmerized, and even Acacia emerged from her nook to watch.

"Earth and water, and air can stir them all." He switched the cycle, all four apples circling from hand to hand and into the air, in one constant ring of motion. He stole a bite, and she beamed with delight. "Shall we add spirit?" he crunched.

Isiilde's eyes went wide. "Another?"

Marsais shifted on his feet, nudged an apple from its pile with his toe, and flicked it upwards, adding it to the cycle. "I think that apple was wormy," he coughed. "Now, here comes the hard part. Say you were to petrify me. It involves a binding of stone, much like armor, but with malevolent intent. What would you use to counter the weave?"

"Do I want to deflect it or destroy it?"

"Oh, gods, you're absolutely brilliant." There was ache and longing in his tone, and it warmed her to her toes. "Most Wise Ones don't think beyond unraveling a weave, but deflecting one, especially back at your opponent, is extremely useful. For the time being, let's focus on destroying the weave."

"An iron would break the weave, but it might not be strong enough... No, it would be difficult to insert into the cycle." Isiilde chewed on her lip in thought. "A power rune mixed with water?"

"Perfect as always," he purred. With a flick of his foot, he added yet another apple. The circle widened, nearly brushing the tip of a stalactite. "Now we have a Barrier against petrify." That was a lot of apples to juggle, but Marsais made the feat look easy.

"I get to do this part," Oenghus said. She had not noticed him enter. He picked up an apple with a ruthless grin, tossing it from hand to hand.

"One crown." Marsais started the time-honored tradition of wagering on anything and everything with Oenghus. "From the back wall."

"Make it two, ya smug bastard. Remember, I'm up one hundred crowns."

"Ten crowns to me for the singed beard," Marsais corrected the standing debt. "And the ocean counts as two."

Oenghus turned to the captain. "What's your ruling?"

"Sorry, Marsais, but I'm going to have to give that to Oenghus. In the future, I'd suggest only angering smaller kingdoms."

"Don't forget that Oen owes you a hundred and eighty crowns, plus interest."

"That's right!" Marsais nearly dropped his apples. "You ruined that tavern in Drivel while I was gone."

Oenghus grumbled at Isiilde. "Turncoat."

"Ten crowns interest?" she asked.

"That's cutthroat, my dear."

"Make it an even twenty, since it involved my paladins," Acacia suggested.

"Aha!" Marsais beamed. "You owe *me* a hundred and ten crowns."

Oenghus glared at the paladin. "I'm not asking for your help again."

Acacia smirked.

And Oenghus threw.

Six apples flew in various directions as Marsais abandoned them to catch the one with a resounding smack. "Curse it!" He clenched his teeth, dropping the apple to clutch his stinging palm. An apple that was more juice than fruit plopped on the stone.

"You owe me, Scarecrow."

"I caught it," Marsais defended. "I'm up one hundred and *twelve* crowns."

"You dropped your balls."

"He caught it, Oen. You really must iron out details before you wager —especially with Marsais."

"Very wise, my dear."

"Bollocks. You're just defending him because—" Oenghus ground to a halt, tugging his beard.

"Because of what?" she asked, with a flutter of lashes.

"Never mind. I'll win it back." Oenghus planted himself beside the captain to watch the enfolding lesson.

"Now," Marsais shook out his hands, "for the real thing. Don't get frustrated, Isiilde, this isn't easy. Watch carefully."

"Or there will be ill occurrences."

"Precisely. I'm going to show you how to add a power rune to air, to deflect a bit of water."

Isiilde followed his exaggerated movements. It was a complicated weave which resulted in a swirling shield of shimmering air. The air in front of Marsais was distorted, as if he were standing behind a veil of water.

"Got it?"

"I think."

"Never think, my dear. One more time." He tugged on an ethereal strand and the weave unraveled, falling to the stone floor with a splash of runes. This time, as he wove the Barrier again, she caught what she had missed. He bound power to air last, to keep the cycle moving.

Isiilde nodded. "I've got it."

Oenghus climbed to his feet, standing at the ready. Ill occurrences indeed, she thought.

"Don't hide your runes. I need to watch you weave."

Isiilde summoned the Lore, weaving without worry or thought, feeling the currents of the Gift stir with her words. But when she tried to weave the final rune with the shifting cycle, everything unraveled, slipping through her fingers.

The air imploded. Something rammed into her body, and she opened her eyes. Warm hands cupped her face, attached to a worried face and moving lips.

She tasted blood.

Isiilde coughed and jerked, her muscles spasming. She was on the floor, crunched against a stone wall. She dimly remembered the squashed apple.

"Sprite?" Oenghus snapped his fingers in front of her eyes.

The cave spun, and she groaned. "What happened?"

"You put a foot in the current, my dear, but a bit more is needed, I'm afraid."

Isiilde stared at Marsais who crouched by her side, studying her with a careful eye. "More?"

"Yes."

"But what if I draw too much? What if I crack?"

Every Novice was warned about drawing too much of the Gift—a backlash. And every Wise One feared doing it one day. Those who drew too much died. They bled out from every crevice and pore, until there was nothing left but a dried husk. Not for the first time, Isiilde wondered how Marsais did what he did with the Gift.

"Do not try what I do," he warned, sensing her scattered thoughts. "You can draw more, Isiilde, trust me. Try again when you are able."

When the room stopped spinning, and spots stopped dancing, she climbed to her feet and steadied her nerves, focusing on the lean man standing opposite. The flameling still flickered in midair, waiting for her leisure.

Taking a breath, she tried again.

Three attempts (and one very battered nymph) later, she finally produced a Barrier, though somewhere during her celebratory jig, it collapsed. "Blast it!" she cursed from the ground.

Marsais helped her up. "Concentration, my dear. That is where your fire comes to play. I'm going to cast a simple water bolt at it. If you want it to survive, then you will need to protect it with a Barrier. Your failure means no more fire and it won't be my fault."

"That's a loophole, Marsais."

"But it's one you didn't think of."

She narrowed her eyes. "Oen, you may want to wager on this."

"Make it another two crowns. For ten seconds."

"Agreed," Marsais said. "And since you're learning, I'll be a gentle-man, and allow you to weave the Barrier first."

"An enemy wouldn't be so kind."

"No, but I really don't want to scrape any more of your blood off the stone."

Isiilde took a deep breath and focused on the floating flame, putting its hypnotic glow between Marsais and her. She summoned the Lore, and began her weave, wading into its currents. Power flowed through her veins, pushing against her flesh like a rushing river. It was the farthest she had ever ventured into the Gift's currents, but there was no temptation to wade farther, no thirst for power.

Fire was her passion, her temptation.

Her Barrier rippled into place, protecting the flameling. She looked at Marsais through the shimmering veil, and decided that he would not have it.

Marsais' fingers flashed, gathering moisture from the air. With a casual flick of his wrist, he hurled the watery missile at her flame. The clash of energy caught her off guard, and the impact shattered her focus. The missile snuffed her flameling with a sizzle and drenched her in the process.

"Bollocks."

"I hope you're a rich man, Oenghus," the captain said. "You owe him one hundred and fourteen crowns."

"I can add numbers. Thank you very much."

Rivan snickered.

Isiilde ignored the lot of them, feeling lost and bewildered without the little fire's light.

"It's all right, my dear. Remember, this isn't easy. Most Wise Ones will never manage a Barrier."

"Aye, I can't bloody weave one," Oenghus admitted.

"You can't?"

Oenghus glared at Rivan. "Shut your mouth or I'll shut it with my fist."

Rivan closed his mouth with a click.

Isiilde wiped her nose. Her hand was wet, and she sneezed. Marsais snatched one of the flaming bursts with a hand and a weave, binding it to the air between them. She steeled herself for another round.

"I'll wager a hundred and fourteen crowns on myself," she said. "Oen will front the coin."

"Sprite!"

"Don't you trust me?"

Oenghus groaned.

"Make it a hundred fifteen," she corrected.

"Why the extra?" Marsais inquired.

"I owe you one, remember?"

"You don't want to wager more for yourself?"

"I want us to be even."

The moment the words left her lips, she realized that would never be possible. A burst of sudden awareness took root in her mind, and Marsais saw the chasm of time in her eyes, of experience and knowledge that stretched between them.

We cannot be. There is too much at stake.

His words from the King's Walk came back in stark clarity. And yet they had bonded. Marsais had ignored his own warning and damned his own visions. But at what future cost?

"Come, my dear," he said with a gentle smile and soft words. "Focus on the present and not the future. It will come when it comes."

Isiilde braced herself and focused on the present. The moment her Barrier snapped into place, a water missile slammed into her shimmering shield. It didn't disperse as she hoped it would. Instead, the water swirled and drilled, turning against her shield.

Marsais pushed against her Barrier, hand outstretched, directing the Orb of Water.

Her weave was unraveling.

Isiilde looked from her runes to the flame, wading deeper into the Gift's current, drawing more power from its river.

Marsais would not have her fire.

The cavern disappeared. Marsais vanished along with his destructive weave. All she saw was the dancing glow of something that she loved more than life itself. Isiilde thrust her arms out, shaking as she braced against the attack, pushing Marsais' power back with every ounce of will.

The more she pushed, the more power he drew, forcing her to wade into treacherous waters.

The two combatants stood poised with outstretched arms, facing each other over an expanse of churning energy, water and fire and clashing runes. The air beat with fury.

Marsais changed his strategy. Keeping one hand straight, he brought the other around, splaying his fingers with a twist of his wrist. The water spread, flanking her flame.

Isiilde adjusted her focus with a gesture, shifting the Barrier to meet his charge. Her body shook with strain.

"Scarecrow…"

Marsais thrust both hands towards the Barrier.

"Stop it!" Oenghus barked.

Marsais ignored the order. A clash of power flared between the two, knocking the audience back a step, and still Marsais pushed.

With a rush of air, her Barrier shattered. Water surged around her flame with a steaming hiss, and Isiilde screamed. In rage.

Her cry turned to something more. A voice filled with power rose in the cavern. What she chanted, no one knew, but it sounded like a fire's roar. The flame surged, fueled by her voice. It rolled and churned and grew as the water weave battered at its reddish hue.

Marsais stood his ground. Water and fire fought, coiling like warring snakes, hissing and spitting, one churning over the other.

Isiilde's chant beat in their ears.

The fire exploded, sending a wave of rolling heat from the point of origin. Marsais ducked beneath the wave and Oenghus threw himself backwards, dragging Acacia down with him.

Steam filled the chamber, blinding them all.

Isiilde collapsed in a trembling heap. Something warm oozed from her nose, and she gagged at its coppery scent. Blood. Panic seized her. She had drawn too much.

"It's all right, Isiilde." Marsais was there, handkerchief in hand, pinching her nose and wiping away the blood.

"You bastard!" Oenghus untangled himself from the captain, and rushed over to his daughter. Blood was leaking from her ears, too. "You pushed her to Cracking."

"Hardly," Marsais hissed. "Quiet, Oenghus."

Isiilde's chest hurt, as if a weight had settled on her ribs. Marsais cupped her face, forcing her to meet his eyes. "You're fine, my dear. You're all right. Every Wise One must learn her limits."

"She's not a Wise One."

"You're right, she isn't, Oen. She is so much more."

"I don't feel well." A cough clutched her throat, and a spray of red misted a patterned kilt.

"You drew a bit too much. But you'll live. Though I'm afraid you'll wake up with a splitting headache."

Her head was throbbing already.

"And you won Oenghus a hundred and fifteen crowns minus one."

"No," she managed. "*I'm* up a hundred. He can have fourteen for fronting the coin. And one for you."

Marsais gave a sharp laugh. "I owe you a hundred, then." But his words were so very far away, in a language she could not understand—a black spot seeped over her eyes, spreading inwards, until the world closed.

CHAPTER 41

THE WINTER NIGHT WAS STILL, and stars were its only light. Fur-clad sentries huddled at their posts in the dark. Their eyes gleamed through slitted masks and their breath mingled with the chill.

Far below the guards' cliff-side perch, the river moved sluggishly towards frozen falls. Canoes bumped against their buoyed docks, and the gentle creak of ice moaned against the granite cliffs.

Elquin watched the night through the hollowed skull of a bear. Its pelt kept him warm, and its spirit watched over him as he listened to the song of ice. The bear had taken Elquin's arm in exchange for its life, but the bear's fierceness remained, and the warrior was still a force to be reckoned with. It was an honor to stand at the gates and guard his people through the long nights.

Thick sheets of ice drifted down the river, shifting and creaking in the heaviness of snow. The ice bumped against the Lome's floating docks, clogging the sides of the sluggish river.

Elquin frowned behind his mask. The ice would pull the docks from their moorings. He nodded to his companion, handed his spear over, and twined his arm around a rope, slipping down to the docks.

His boots hit the planks and he rode the river's swell, bobbing on its surface. Elquin's companion dropped the spear down to him and he caught it easily, turning to push the sheet of ice away, but he froze at what he saw: a spirit drifted beneath the glazed surface of ice.

Elquin stepped back. But a spear followed him, surging from the frigid waters, piercing fur and flesh. Impaled at the same spot where he had slain his bear.

The spirit took shape in the form of a man, who pulled himself out of the water with the barb stuck in Elquin's ribs. More spirits emerged from beneath the ice with blood on their hands and fury in their eyes. Painted men, white as snow and wild-eyed. Spears sped through the night, pinning the other guards at their posts.

The spirit of the bear stirred in Elquin's dying body as Ardmoor savages slipped from the river and crawled up the cliffs. Elquin gripped the horn at his side, and with his last breath, sounded the alarm.

CHAPTER 42

A HORN BLAST jerked Isiilde from sleep. Hundreds of them were echoing through the city. There was urgency and death in the alarm. She fought her furs and aching bones, dimly aware that her main source of heat had vacated the bed.

Marsais was on his feet, every muscle of his lean body flexed with tension as he tugged on his clothing. He glanced down at her with an unspoken command before sprinting from the room.

The horns died and sounds of clashing swords and screams replaced their echo. She scrambled to her feet and nearly collapsed when her head gave a throb of pain. Still weak from her training, she managed to yank on her clothes, but fatigue and fear made her fingers clumsy. She struggled with the laces of her shirt.

"Void!"

The curtain was shoved aside so abruptly that flame sprang to her hands. It was Marsais. She shook the flame back into the pit with a relieved breath.

"Time to leave, my dear," he announced. "The Ardmoor have breached the city."

His words barely registered over the sound of battle. The laces on her boots had become impossibly slippery and she fumbled over the ties with growing frustration. "Blast it," she growled.

The dying embers in the firepit stirred fitfully.

Marsais paused while stuffing a pack full of supplies and crouched in front of her. He held her gaze with his own. "Stay close to me," he said calmly as he laced her boots, "and all will be well."

She could only nod.

When the final lace was knotted, Marsais finished packing her supplies and slung the pack over his shoulder. He offered a hand and she stared at it, frozen. Every instinct she possessed screamed at her to flee. To stay hidden behind the curtain. But in the end she took his hand and he pulled her towards the battle.

A grunt and crunch welcomed the pair into the common room. Oenghus' hammer caved in a man's skull. He shoved the dead warrior backwards, into a knot of wild, naked men covered in chalklike paint and blood. The hammer swung again, taking chunks of flesh and bone, and Oenghus slammed his shield into the last of the intruders, knocking his opponent down the stone steps that led to the valley below.

Marsais threw a weave at the entrance, concealing their cave with an illusion.

The Ardmoor warriors were as large as Oenghus. One was still breathing on the cavern floor. Acacia impaled him through the heart before wrenching her sword free.

Isiilde turned from the sight, from blood and slaughter and organs that were never meant to see the light. Reapers and Blighted were not human. These men, no matter how wild, were. Marsais kept an iron grip on her hand as she fought an urge to bolt.

"Bloody Void," Oenghus cursed, flicking a chunk of clinging brain matter from his hammer. "They've overrun the city."

"A perfect time to take our leave," Marsais said.

The paladins stood at the ready, weapons drawn, shields poised. Fear widened Rivan's brown eyes, but he stood his ground, steeling his shoulders for what was to come.

With a flash of fingers, Marsais wove an armor weave, then tapped her on the head. Tingling warmth spread to her toes.

"Is this what you were waiting for, Scarecrow?" Oenghus growled.

"Now is not the time," Marsais said, slapping a weave onto the bristling berserker. "Stay with us, Oenghus, and by the gods, don't bring this mountain down on our heads."

An Ardmoor charged the entrance with a rush. Oenghus stepped aside and swung, catching the man on the chin. His head and body snapped back, and his feet flew forward. The stone stopped him and Oenghus stomped on the man's head, stilling the warrior with a jerk.

"Like the Void I will. You'll get in my way. Guard Isiilde, or I'll have your hide, Scarecrow." He ripped the cork off his Brimgrog, took a long swig, and jammed the flask back in his belt.

Smoldering eyes focused on Marsais, and for a moment, Isiilde feared Oenghus would pummel him. Instead, he turned towards the illusion and began beating his hammer on his shield. With a growl, Oenghus stepped through the weave.

"Stay out of his range," Acacia ordered her men. "Form around Marsais and Isiilde. Stay together. We'll head towards the falls."

A thundering rhythm rose over the din of battle. It was Oenghus beating his hammer on his shield like a herald of doom.

Armor and shields surrounded Isiilde, and she gripped Marsais' cloak, as the group moved towards the illusion. Fear clutched her. They were going out into the valley, into the screams of women and children, and towards the dying—into the thick of the slaughter.

Isiilde was dimly aware of Rivan at her side, muttering a frantic prayer. Marsais pulled her on the captain's heels, and with a breath, they pushed through the illusion.

ARDMOOR SWARMED THE VALLEY, clashing with surprised Lome and chopping down the defenseless like wheat. Clusters of warriors fought, but the valley was vast and the Ardmoor numbered in the hundreds. And into the chaos, Oenghus waded, beating his hammer against his shield in challenge.

Time was indecisive, hurrying to outline the naked fighters, raging and chopping, and then slowing down for every sickening slice of their axes. Isiilde was pulled into the slaughter, buffered by steel and shield, fighting to catch glimpses of her suicidal guardian.

The Ardmoor heard Oenghus' challenge and the painted barbarians swarmed him like moths to fire. A roar shook the valley, and then an earthquake. Oenghus slammed his hammer onto the valley floor. The rock cracked. A chant beat the air and a wave of stone rippled, rising like a wave, crashing over the warriors' heads. Oenghus charged in its wake, slamming into the Ardmoor with fury and death and bone rending force.

But he was lost in the surge of battle, and Isiilde was battered like a leaf caught in a raging river as the Ardmoor charged. The attackers were human, but their eyes burned with feral thirst.

Acacia matched their ferocity with an efficient grace. Axes battered her shield, but her sword tip struck with precision, bringing up blood with every strike. Lucas cleaved at painted flesh with methodical persistence. Blood and bone sprayed into the air, and slipped beneath Isiilde's feet.

Rivan struggled at her side, frantically parrying and swinging at the rushing forms. Cleavers and spears and hammers bit into the paladin, seeking chinks in his armor and encountering stone. Despite Marsais' powerful weave of protection, the enchanted paladin staggered beneath the onslaught of blows, fighting to hold his own.

Marsais murmured under his breath, weaving a masterpiece of runes with calm finesse. "Pardon me, Captain."

Acacia instantly stepped to the side, and Marsais thrust out his arms, fingers splayed. A wave of crackling death rippled from his fingertips, arcing from one barbarian to the next, leaving a path of charred, broken bodies and burnt flesh.

The Ardmoor dropped like flies. But more rushed to fill the void.

Isiilde's world drained of color. Only black and white existed, with vibrant slashes of crimson that sprayed in the dark. She walked in a dream, detached, floating high above the valley, watching it all with a cold heart.

A shock of pain shattered her stupor. Events rushed in like a crashing wave, snapping her back to her body. She tripped onto a slippery step, blinking with surprise.

The stairway was cut into a rock face that circled a churning pool—the waterfall at the end of the valley. Marsais steadied her, and Rivan clambered behind, helping a wounded woman. Acacia and Lucas held the base of the stairs, ushering several Lome up its winding path.

Arrows soared in the air, zipping through wind and mist, aimed at the stairway. Marsais gestured sharply. The air in front rippled, and the arrows bounced away, but some pierced his weave, pinning the fleeing Lome and dropping them into a watery grave.

Another roar shook loose rock. A massive stalactite cracked from the sky and fell. Then Isiilde saw her guardian, bloodied and enraged. He stood against a tide of painted bodies. The stone shifted and cracked beneath Oenghus' feet and lightning crackled from his hammer. There were so many Ardmoor. He would surely drown in death.

"Curse you, Oen," Marsais growled, weaving a message that hopefully contained more than irritation. With a sharp gesture, he sent the Whisper fluttering to the berserker's ears. But Oenghus was lost in battle. He would stand until there was no one left to fight, or die with his hammer swinging.

A bonfire on the valley floor caught Isiilde's attention, one that was burning flesh and whatever else the Ardmoor could throw in the stack. Smoke billowed, clouding the ceiling. Isiilde did not think. She reacted, calling to her fire with a frantic command.

Flames surged, exploding, washing over Ardmoor and Lome alike. A timid, frightened part of her was aware of Marsais shouting, but her voice drowned out his words as a hot wind stirred her hair, beating against her skin. The flames swirled, coiling, and sprang, cutting through the air with a maddened hiss of heat.

Fear vanished, and her vision sharpened. The chaos lacked one thing: fire. All the blood, screams, and death would vanish beneath a cleansing flame.

The flame sensed her desire.

A wave of fire slammed into the Ardmoor surrounding Oenghus, and as they burned and scattered like ants, she saw what Oenghus had been fighting for. Elam was there, helping a wounded woman who carried two bundles. And over their heads, Oenghus fought.

Her words transformed into a song that thrummed in the air with a flame's roar. Her voice fed the fire, skipping from one painted form to the next, licking skin like tinder. It ate the blood from the stone and drowned out screams with its hunger.

Isiilde's fire danced from form to form in a whirlwind of death and glory. She ached to feel its touch. One human blurred with the next. It no longer mattered who burned.

Oenghus caught a fireball with his shield, enduring the scourge as the fleeing Lome were caught in a wave of heat. She was blind to it all. Her fire would cleanse the blood and carnage, and bring peace to chaos—

A hand clamped over her mouth. Isiilde thrashed against the grip, biting down with vicious teeth and a gurgling call. Flames arced towards the stairway. And her attacker. Marsais thrust out a hand, sending a wall of air into the flame, directing it downwards, into the pool. His concentration broke.

Arrows slid through his weakened shield. One after another slammed into the stairway. An arrow pierced Isiilde's skin, snapping her from rapture. A trail of heat burned on her arm, but others weren't so fortunate. An arrow pierced a child's neck, sending the girl reeling into the pool, and as Isiilde watched her tiny form plummet, realization slapped her soundly.

The valley floor was littered with the smoldering corpses of Ardmoor. And Lome.

Revulsion rose in her throat.

Marsais slammed her against the stone as another hail of arrows pelted the stairway. A sting of pain pierced their bond, but his fingers were already flying. Another barrier snapped into place in front of the stairway and its cowering occupants.

"Hurry!" Marsais shouted, snapping off the shaft of an arrow that protruded from his shoulder. A veil dropped over their bond, numbing his pain.

"But Oen—"

"Will be fine." Marsais nudged her, and Isiilde's feet obeyed.

She stumbled the first few steps, fighting to keep her footing as the press of fleeing bodies closed in on her. In the current of fear, she was separated from Marsais and corralled into the narrow tunnels. The cave closed in, her head swam in confusion. Isiilde pushed forward, slipping between bodies, struggling to control panic and the rising temperature of her flesh.

Fire would clear the way. It whispered to her, aching for release, to drown the cries and screams in one roaring wave.

An old woman brushed against the nymph and cried out in pain, as her skin was scorched. Isiilde could not stop, did not dare slow to help her. She rushed towards an open sky.

A RIVER of Lome flooded into the night. But the waiting paths were slick with ice, and many slipped off the edge, spiraling into the roaring mist of a waterfall.

The path opened to trees and a clearing on the mountainside. Fresh snow was trampled underfoot, and the virgin white had turned red. Isiilde glanced down in confusion until a gap opened in the press of fleeing Lome.

Ardmoor stood in the clearing. They held torches, snatching up women and children as they fled. The men were killed, and the old were tossed to a pack of feasting Reapers.

The Lome in front turned, slipping on snow, trying to run back into the mountain, but the wave of humans could not be stopped.

A blur of movement alerted her to a swinging axe. Isiilde threw herself onto a snowdrift. The woman at her side was cloven in two. A one-eyed warrior caught sight of the nymph in the torchlight. Desire burned, and he reached for her.

Isiilde tried to scramble away but was yanked off the ground by her hair. The warrior howled in triumph. Isiilde's fingers flashed, and a bolt hit him square in the chest.

He snarled, barely fazed.

She called to the fires on the torches and they leapt at her command, slamming into her attacker. His howls took on a frantic note, and he flung Isiilde away, rolling onto the snow. Her skin cooled with a hiss, and she was sliding, twisting and clawing, as the ice took her towards the edge of the waterfall's gorge.

A hand clamped down on her ankle, halting her slide. The warrior was blistered, and spitting oaths in a rough tongue. She opened her mouth to call to her flame but was silenced with a fist. He pulled her up by the hair, tucked her under his arm, and began trudging towards the other captives.

Isiilde reeled, dazed and dangling. A split second later, she was falling.

The smell of seared flesh filled her nostrils, burning down her throat. Blood splattered on the snow and the one-eyed warrior fell on top of her as a powerful lightning bolt crackled from warrior to warrior, dropping the men like flies.

The remaining Ardmoor turned to their challenger, and the Lome scattered, fleeing down the treacherous pathways. Three axes flew towards Marsais at once. Coins chimed as Marsais twisted. An axe grazed his arm, but the others flew harmlessly by. His fingers moved faster than she could follow. Another wave of pounding force slammed into the charging barbarians. The knot of warriors was thrown back, sliding on the slippery slope.

"Behind you!" Isiilde screamed.

Marsais stepped aside with unnatural speed. A curved sword met air, but there was no time for weaving—the warrior had caught him by surprise. Too close, with nowhere to run, Marsais drove his shoulder into the thick warrior.

The two men went down, and the barbarian came out on top, driving the haft of his axe into Marsais' face. His head snapped back, and the Ardmoor pressed his attack, raising the blade to strike again. Isiilde wove a bolt and hurled it in the barbarian's face. The blow hit him square, knocking his axe from his hand.

Marsais choked out a half-formed weave as the rest of the Ardmoor converged, but it was sloppy and incomplete. The unraveling was violent. Raw energy rebounded in the air, booming from Marsais like thunder. Ardmoor and Lome were thrown into the air and the impact washed over Isiilde, plucking her from the earth.

The edge of a rock stopped her flight. Head pounding, vision dancing, she struggled to regain her senses. She was slipping. She clawed at the snow, at the ice and the rock underneath. Finally, her boot caught a slippery wedge, and she clung to its side, afraid to move as the battle raged on.

A chant rose in the air, coins chimed, and a blast of energy shot from high ground. But it wasn't Marsais' weave. It blasted him as he struggled to stand. He crumpled into the snow.

Paladins charged with steel and shields, and Lome fled, risking Ardmoor and Reapers for the cover of trees.

Isiilde could not feel Marsais, only a dark, cold pit through their bond. She summoned the Lore, tempting death, tracing with a trembling hand as she slipped. Her levitation weave caught, pushed her upwards, and she scrambled forward, slipping and sliding on ice towards Marsais.

A rush of bodies clashed, wild men and furred defenders. A hand gripped her arm, and yanked her upright. Instead of chalky flesh, her eyes met a golden sunburst. Rivan pushed her behind him, catching a spear on his armored ribs. He chopped with his sword, sliced the haft, then rammed the edge of his shield against the barbarian's thigh. Acacia leapt to his side, fighting an onslaught of enemies.

Lucas stood over Marsais, defending the fallen seer. Isiilde scrambled over to Marsais' side. He was breathing and stirring and trying to rise.

A savage roar crushed the carnage of sound. Cold wind battered their faces, and ice swirled to life. A massive, dark shape swooped down from the falls, tearing into the knot of fighters with a monstrous growl. Jaws descended, Isiilde screamed, and a maw of teeth clamped down on a painted warrior, devouring him in three crunching gulps.

A wyvern.

Marsais yanked her onto the trampled snow as the beast raged over their heads. Clawed feet pounded the earth beside their cowering bodies, and a whipping tail impaled a Lome warrior.

An answering roar challenged the wyvern. Oenghus. The monster twisted and lunged at the charging berserker. Oenghus met the beast with hammer and shield and crackling energy, pounding the wyvern's snout to the side with a bone-splitting strike.

Marsais pulled Isiilde along as they slithered from beneath the beast, emerging near the tree-lined slope. He spun, his fingers weaving, before aiming a beam of searing white energy at the wyvern's side. It bellowed in rage, lashing its tail to crush the pest.

Marsais ducked beneath barbed death, and Isiilde scrambled forward, taking cover behind a tree.

All was chaos and death; Ardmoor and paladins fought, and Reapers waited in shadows. There was nowhere to hide.

The wyvern lunged at the hammer-wielding flea. Oenghus caught the jaws on his shield, but the force sent him reeling. He was slammed against the rock face, and trapped by chomping jaws. His hammer battered the beast's skull, but fangs continued to gnash.

Marsais sent another searing stream of heat burning into the creature's side, but the attack only angered it. Oenghus' shield splintered. He swung his hammer against the wyvern's nose, but it persisted, pinning him to the rock, and forcing him to abandon his weapon. He gripped the beast's jaws.

Man and wyvern struggled in a contest of brute strength.

A sound caught Isiilde's attention. Nearby, in the trees on a snowy slope, stood a cowled, chanting figure. Coins chimed, and Marsais spun, throwing up a Barrier. He caught the weave with deft hands and hurled it back at the sender, but the robed figure stepped to the side.

A warrior came out of nowhere, blindsiding Marsais and ramming him against a tree.

The robed figure summoned lightning, his hands crackling with energy and illuminating the shadows under his cowl. It was N'Jalss. Heedless of who he killed, he threw the charge at the combatants. It slammed into the man grappling with Marsais, and he dropped into the snow dead.

Isiilde scrambled to her feet, climbing the slope, and using the trees as cover, moved swiftly over the slush towards N'Jalss.

A clash of power crackled between the Wise Ones, of shifting runes and ill effects, shredding the nearby trees with force. Isiilde's fingers flashed, mixing earth and stone and fiery death. With a final breath, she hurled a bind at N'Jalss. A wave of molten rock flew through the air. He gestured sharply, deflecting the weave. It slammed into the mountainside. And he countered with one of his own.

His weave worked its way past her lips and crawled down her throat, paralyzing her tongue.

Before Isiilde could react, an arm caught her, carrying her swiftly through the trees. She struggled against her abductor's strength as Marsais raced in her wake.

An ethereal hand appeared before N'Jalss, knocking him off his feet with a bone-crunching blow. But the Rahuatl had his own shield, and he recovered, sending a weave spiraling at Marsais' feet. Ice erupted from the earth, as sharp and lethal as spears.

Isiilde's abductor ran towards a near-naked woman covered in scars. She raised a curved dagger, finished her ritual with a twisting word and slashed the neck of a captive. An inky portal opened over the body as blood spilled into the snow.

"No!" Marsais' shout was the last she heard. He thrust out his hand a moment before the Ardmoor dove into the Blood Portal. A tingling sensation sped down Isiilde's throat.

The world went silent and still. But the hands holding her were real. The Ardmoor dropped her onto a stone floor, and a figure stepped into view. The last thing she saw was the snarling mask of N'Jalss, followed by a fist.

CHAPTER 43

THE PORTAL SNAPPED SHUT. Marsais blinked at the space. Chaos reigned, and its winged manifestation thrashed, trying to dislodge Oenghus, who had its jaws locked shut with bulging arms. He could not risk letting go.

Marsais sent another bolt ricocheting into the Ardmoor, dropping eight men, leaving a trail of seared flesh, before the energy slammed into the scaled monstrosity. The wyvern's tail slashed, felling trees and ice with a thunderous smack. It reared, ripping Oenghus off the ground. He held fast.

The wyvern rammed its unwanted rider into the rocks. And Oenghus' grip loosened. He fell to the snow, utterly exposed. As the wyvern tensed for the kill, Oenghus twisted, driving his fist into the stone cliff with a word.

The mountain shifted, snow slid, and the world cracked. Oenghus threw himself to the side as an avalanche tumbled down the mountain, burying the beast. But Oenghus continued to slide, clawing at the ice.

He disappeared over the edge.

Silence throbbed in Marsais' ears. He rushed to the edge, weaving with trembling fingers. He slid to a stop on his stomach, hanging over the edge of a mist-shrouded gorge. Oenghus was dangling from a ledge. Bloodied and battered and clinging precariously. But he was there.

Marsais shuddered with relief.

Then the ice cracked.

Oenghus looked up at his old friend. "Find her," he hissed.

A heartbeat later the cliff side gave way. Oenghus plummeted, and then stopped, as Marsais plucked him from the air with a levitation weave.

The two friends grinned at each other. But their relief did not last long. A bloodied, burnt, and angry wyvern exploded from the rubble, shaking loose the churned earth. A wave of stone pelted Marsais. His concentration wavered, his hold slipped.

Oenghus disappeared beneath the mist.

CHAPTER 44

When the winged monstrosity hatched from the snow, Acacia plunged her sword through a barbarian's gut, and spun him around, putting the man between her and the wyvern. Bloodied, burnt, and enraged, the wyvern snatched the Ardmoor off her blade like meat from the bone. Wings beat, stirring a blizzard to life, as it leapt into the air with its prize.

Acacia exhaled, scanning the remains of the battlefield.

A knot of Lome continued to fight, battling the last of the Ardmoor who had not taken flight. Lucas was in the thick of pushing them down the trail. Her eyes fell on Rivan, who rushed to the edge of the cliff with Elam on his heels. They began digging in the snow.

Acacia staggered over. Marsais was buried in the rubble. Blood streamed down his face from a gash on his forehead and his eyes rolled with confusion and pain. Together, they dug him out.

Acacia gripped his shoulders. "Where is your nymph?"

"Who?" he rasped, fighting to rise.

"Isiilde. Where is Isiilde?"

"Gone. All gone."

"And Oenghus?"

At this he laughed, a maniacal, spine-crawling sound. "I won," he wheezed. "I won the wager." Laughter turned to silent tears as he gazed at the falls.

The three pulled him to his feet, and Marsais swayed like wheat in the wind. She gripped his head in her gauntleted hands and caught his darting eyes with her own. "Where is Isiilde, Marsais?"

"Who are you?"

Acacia grit her teeth. "Where is *your* nymph?"

"Nymph?"

Acacia shook the man, but instead of shaking loose memory, she shook out the last of his strength. His knees buckled.

With a curse, Acacia ripped off her gauntlets, unlaced his jerkin, and slipped her dagger from its sheath. "Light, Rivan."

She chanted a prayer, bathing Marsais in warmth. Rivan turned him onto his side, and she probed the arrow wound on his shoulder. Moving with skill, she slipped her knife into the muscle and freed the arrowhead from its nest. Marsais groaned.

Acacia placed her hand on his chest, over his scar, bowed her head and prayed to the Guardians. Warmth spread from her heart, to her palm, and into the unconscious elf. She sucked in a sharp breath. Marsais' spirit was vast, and his mind was a maze. It was terrifying.

Dizzy and reeling in confusion, Acacia mentally scrambled back to her own body. She tore her hand away, and fell back into the snow, staring at the madman in shock. But she'd healed him. The blood gushing from Marsais' brow dried and his breathing evened.

When she raised her eyes, Elam was gesturing towards the wreckage of fallen trees. The boy rattled on in a language she could not comprehend, but Acacia had children, and she had played this game before.

The boy drew a knife from Rivan's belt, held it aloft, poised grandly over his head, and plunged it into a nonexistent form. He gestured at the blood staining the snow, then drew a circle, mimed two big ears, and pretended to dive into the circle.

"A Blood Portal?" Rivan asked.

It had been on the tip of Acacia's tongue. "And Oenghus?" she asked.

Elam's lip quivered. He pointed down.

"Are you fit, Rivan?"

"Thanks to his armor weave."

Acacia glanced at the bloodied elf. Another wave of dizziness rushed over her, and she shoved the memory of Marsais' spirit aside.

"You're hurt, Captain."

She shook her head, slung her shield over a shoulder, and bent to hoist Marsais to his feet. Rivan hurried to help.

"We have to leave, Captain!" Lucas shouted as the last invader's head dropped at his feet.

She nodded, and together, they dragged Marsais down the treacherous path with a knot of surviving Lome.

"The Ardmoor scattered when the wyvern came, but there's plenty left," Lucas said when they caught up to him. "As long as the Ethervenom runs through their veins, they'll be back."

"Did you see a Bloodmagus?"

Lucas shook his head. "Where's the nymph and Oenghus?"

"I lost sight of them in the battle. According to Elam, she was taken through a Blood Portal, and as for Oenghus... he fell."

"Oenghus said the seer knew of the attack. Why the Void did he wait?"

"Would you have preferred meeting this army on open ground—after escaping from the Lome?"

Scarred lips twisted downwards. "You have a point, but he could've warned us."

"Remember his explanation. If Marsais had prepared us for the attack, everything would have changed."

"That doesn't make a lick of sense," Rivan pointed out.

"That's because he's a fool."

Acacia stopped, fixing a severe eye on her lieutenant. "Marsais may be mad and broken, but he's no fool—trust me."

The tone of her voice silenced his retort.

"But how did the Ardmoor track us?" Rivan asked. "*We* don't even know where we are."

"There must be a traitor," Lucas growled.

Acacia frowned, turning over possibilities. A traitor in the tribe was certainly a possibility. What of Kasja? Strangely absent on the day of the attack. Marsais' words swirled in her head, shifting like the pile of stone runes. He had clarified nothing, only sowed confusion and headaches.

"A traitor, or a scryer," she realized aloud.

"What is that?" Rivan asked.

"Seers, soothsayers, and oracles," Acacia explained.

Lucas spat. "Nothing more than raving madmen."

"Not all of them, Lucas. Wars have been lost because of a scryer's sight."

"With respect, Captain, I disagree. In my soldiering days, we had another name for them—scapegoats."

The shadows shifted ahead, and Lucas hefted his sword.

"But why did the Ardmoor come after us? Was this all for Isiilde?" asked Rivan.

"Tharios knows we're alive," Acacia reasoned, shrugging her side of the load off on Rivan. She unslung her shield. "If we make it to a Chapterhouse alive, then word will reach the Isle—Tharios' scheming will be over. There's likely a bounty on our heads in Vaylin. I just didn't expect an entire army to come collecting."

"How are we going to find Isiilde?"

"First things first, Rivan. Stay with the seer, protect the women and children. We'll make for the river."

Without a word, Acacia and Lucas trotted ahead, towards a knot of Lome warriors. Acacia summoned light to her shield, and illuminated a waiting line of Ardmoor and collared Reapers at the end of the path. A battle cry rose into the night, and the paladins charged, followed by a ragged group of refugees.

SOMEWHERE IN THE NIGHT, in the blood and carnage, their little band of refugees touched the valley floor, hounded and ambushed, skirmishing as they limped away with women and infants and wounded men in tow. A scout hissed, and the group took cover in trees.

Acacia, tense with exhaustion, searched the shadows, listening. A warbling call pierced the din of the river. It was answered by another.

The fur-clad scout at her side relaxed, and so did she. A shadow detached itself from a tree, then was joined by another. The two men embraced. And the Lome emerged from their concealment, flocking around their massive, one-eyed leader.

Lucas looked at Acacia. She gripped Rivan's shoulder, keeping him in place before he could rise, but the scout pointed back towards the paladins.

"This can't end well," Lucas said, adjusting his shield.

"Steady," she warned, and stood.

V'elbine greeted them with a growl and three long steps that took him within striking distance. Elam shot in front of the grizzled warrior, holding up his hands, but the chieftain swatted him aside like a fly.

Acacia stepped up to meet the one-eyed warrior. And Elam yelled from the snow, words pouring from his raw throat. Women and wounded stepped from the crowd, adding their voices with the boy's, and finally the warriors, who nodded and gestured—all the Lome they'd fought with through the night.

The chieftain continued to glower, casting his eye from the unconscious seer to Acacia. With a sharp, dismissing word, he thrust his spear towards the river.

"Supplies will get us farther," she ventured. She mimed food and hugged her cloak. V'elbine snarled, and Acacia slowly backed away, inclining her head.

They'd get nothing.

Silently, the Lome vanished into the darkness, leaving three paladins and a seer in the middle of nowhere.

"It was worth a shot, Captain," Lucas said.

Movement caught Acacia's eye. They had a follower. Elam stood nearby, watching and gesturing. "We may have something better." She pointed at the boy. "A guide."

Lucas hoisted Marsais over his broad shoulders, and the group limped after Elam's hurried steps, trudging through the snowdrifts. The walk was exhausting, and they had to stop more than once to catch their breath.

"Where did that crazy sister of his get off to?" Rivan puffed in the chill.

"I didn't see her during the attack, did you?"

"No," Lucas grunted. "She left after the nymph nearly killed you."

"It was barely a scratch, Lucas. I needed the exercise," she said dryly. An answering *harrumph* shattered her boast.

Acacia stopped, scanning the trees. "Where did the boy go?" she whispered.

Trees and flurries and the distant river's drone greeted them. A short shadow waved them over. Elam stood at the base of a towering sequoia. A mound of fresh snow hugged its broad base, and when they were within sight, he scrambled up the mound, digging in the snow.

"Help him, Rivan."

Rivan exhaled, dropped his shield where he stood, and trudged up the hill with dragging steps.

"If I had any energy left," Lucas said, setting down the seer. "I would chew him out for that."

Acacia looked at her soldier's discarded shield. "I'll remind you to yell at him later."

Together, with Elam digging like a dog, and Rivan using his sword as a shovel, the two uncovered a hole. Elam beamed, lifting and shaking a covering of fur to reveal a round door. He opened it, and climbed in. Rivan looked at his captain.

Acacia rolled Marsais onto Rivan's shield, gripped the seer's arm, and dragged Marsais up the mound on the makeshift sled.

The snow-covered dwelling was cozy and bare, but the real surprise lay in the back, at the base of the tree. Elam shot through a fur curtain, and the paladins followed. The sequoia was hollowed on the inside. Herbs hung from racks, furs covered the floor, and a firepit sat in its center.

"Thank the Sylph," Acacia breathed.

MARSAIS REGAINED CONSCIOUSNESS AT SUNRISE. He sat up with a start, throwing off his furs, confusion clouding his eyes.

Acacia stirred from sleep. "There was an attack on the Lome city," she explained from the other side of the coals. She rose and handed him a mug and a chunk of dried meat. "We're in a scout's hut, or something of the sort."

"Oenghus," he breathed, staring at the food.

"He fell."

"I dropped him." Pain cracked his voice.

"Do you remember Isiilde?"

"Of course I do, Captain," he snapped, tossing the jerky aside and springing to his feet. He downed the water in one long gulp. At his harsh tone, the others woke, reaching for their swords. Marsais launched himself at the supplies, rifling through stores and sacks.

"Do you know where Isiilde is?"

"Yes," he hissed.

"Where?"

"I don't know," he barked. Marsais upended a large sack, spilling its contents onto the floor. He snatched a furred pouch from the crude table, upended that too, and brushed aside a pile of skulls and clay bowls, knocking them onto the floor.

Elam jumped to his feet, chattering madly at the seer. He ignored the boy, working quickly, but stiffly. His white hair was stained with blood, one eye was nearly swollen shut, and creases lined his face.

"You're not fully healed, Marsais. You need to rest before you go after her," Acacia urged.

But Marsais ignored her. He muttered the Lore, his nimble fingers tracing the larger sack, over and over, weaving a swirling net of glowing runes. His fingers shook. But whether it was pain, exhaustion, or desperation, she could not tell. Slowly, he teased a thread from the ethereal weft and coaxed it into the smaller pouch. Inch by inch, he pulled, as if sewing a piece of delicate lace.

The paladins watched in wonder as the larger sack disappeared into the smaller. When the two merged, Marsais snatched up the pouch, and reached for a waterskin. Elam's mouth fell open as the large skin disappeared into the small pouch. A cloak, flint, knife, vials, rations, and a spare set of furs disappeared inside, too.

"We'll help you get her back, Marsais."

He shot out the exit. The paladins followed, emerging to a white world, glittering beneath a rising sun. It was blinding.

Marsais tugged off his tunic, and then his shirt in the chill. He rolled them into a bundle and stuffed them into the pouch.

"Where are you going?"

"Where I go, you cannot follow." Marsais tugged off his boots, and then his trousers, stripping down to the flesh. Bruises and half-healed wounds marred his wiry body. He stuffed the last of his clothes into the pouch, cinching it tightly, and looked at Acacia.

"Vlarthane," he chattered.

And then he did not look at them again. With trembling fingers, he unwound the coins from his goatee, attached them to a leather cord, and slipped it over his neck.

The coins chimed in the early morning light, and his fingers flashed, voice rising with power. A chant stirred the snow. Runes swirled to life with the flurries. Marsais jerked, his muscles spasmed, and his neck arched towards the sky like a bow about to snap.

The pouch fell to the ground, and Marsais followed. Bones cracked, and feathers as white as snow emerged. In a blinding flash, all went still. A tall owl stood on the ground, blending with the whiteness. A cord dangled around its neck, and its noble head swiveled. Two large, luminous, grey eyes locked on the paladins. With a beat of wings, the owl took flight, snatching the pouch with its talons.

"By the gods," Rivan breathed.

Elam appeared to agree. He was crouched in the snow, head buried, murmuring a frantic prayer to whatever gods he served.

"I hate Wise Ones," Lucas growled.

"You hate everyone." Acacia glanced at the scarred man.

"I liked the berserker."

"So did I."

CHAPTER 45

Two cloaked figures bent their heads together, creating a barrier against the wind and sleet. Rashk steadied her restless mount before uncurling her fingers, checking the skree's direction.

The stone arrowhead floating above her palm pulsed with runes, spinning aimlessly. "The storm," Rashk hissed to her companion.

Thira's lips moved, but her words were lost to the Rahuatl. With a decisive hand, Thira wove runes in the air, and swept them aside dismissively. They swirled to life, and the snowstorm stopped blowing into their faces.

Rashk did not know what Thira wove, but then there was so much about the woman that she did not understand. Knowledge and mystery, however, went both ways—Thira did not understand Rune-etching, only weaves and potions.

The skree stopped spinning, pointing solidly towards the sea and the group of manors perched on the hill. Rashk was not surprised. She curled her numb fingers around the skree, feeling the pillaged strands of hair wrapped around its weight.

Thira nudged her horse forward, oblivious to the cold, while Rashk shivered beneath her heavy fur poncho. The Rahuatl were not made for the north. The jungles of Rraal ran through her veins, not the Frozen Wastes.

The skree led the two women to Tharios' estate. It was surrounded by white-washed walls and a heavy gate. Rashk hissed the Lore, and when she opened her eyes, what was dormant became visible—the walls were covered in warding runes.

Rashk uncurled her fingers again, checking the skree's tip. It quivered at the gates. She frowned at the wards, and looked to Thira. The woman had no scent, save for tea and dog; therefore, Rashk could not sense a thing from the Mistress of Novices. The lack of a scent made Rashk uneasy, made her want to gut the old woman and peek inside her body to see what made her tick.

"Are you sure, Rashk?" Thira asked.

"The skree does not lie. Are you sure you gave me the right hairbrush?"

Thira raised a sharp eyebrow. "The hairbrush was in Morigan's rooms. So it is hers unless someone sneaked into her chambers to use the brush, or switched brushes. I think that highly unlikely, don't you?"

"Maybe Morigan is visiting Tharios."

"Don't be an idiot, Rashk," Thira snapped, dismounting. "I'm already surrounded by enough dim-witted fools."

"Look at those wards." Rashk thrust her chin towards the walls. "What are you going to do, walk up to the gate and knock?"

"What else would I do?"

Rashk hissed. "Hunters do not shout into a Reaper's lair."

"Oh, but I do, and I yell loudly." Thira set Crumpet down, and the useless animal shivered in the snow as his Mistress crooned over his poor little paws.

"We should speak with the Lord General."

"And tell Ielequithe what, precisely?" Thira looked up at Rashk in question. "That Marsais' spymaster betrayed him, chased him from the castle, framed him with Bloodmagic, and that the current Archlord may or may not be a mad Bloodmagus holding a healer prisoner? Should we ask her to ever so politely interrupt the Nine's Council so she can interrogate the new Archlord?"

Rashk ran her forked tongue across her teeth in irritation.

"Go if you like," Thira said, opening her long coat and selecting a slim vial from a pocket. "You've found Morigan; nothing more is needed."

Rashk eyed the woman, who was weaponless, save for her potions. She had the look of an old one who intended to walk into the jungle and never return.

"We should find a secret way," Rashk suggested. "A hunter strikes from the shadows."

"Unless you are a mammoth with the disposition of a Pomeranian." Thira poured the vial down Crumpet's throat, and the furball lapped at the liquid greedily. When the vial was empty, Thira swung onto her horse, and urged it towards the gate, leaving Rashk with a transforming dog. The swirl of runes was powerful, the light blinding, and the shape that emerged—mammoth.

The ground shook, the furry beast reared, and Rashk's horse danced away from the tusked horror.

"Come along, Crumpet," Thira called

As the earth shook with Crumpet's mammoth gait, Thira summoned the Lore, weaving a Barrier of runes around her pet.

Rashk abandoned her horse, and sped after the charging mammoth, drawing her kukri from its sheath. Cries of alarm rose as Crumpet slammed his tusks into the gate, triggering a chain reaction of wards. Lightning struck the mammoth but bounced harmlessly off as he charged the guards with a bellow.

Rashk hurried through the ruins of the gate, keeping to shadow and silence as Thira trotted on Crumpet's heels, cloaked in a swirl of runes and protective Barriers. Arrows zipped through the air, and Rashk moved quickly, slipping behind the crossbowmen. Her blade struck kidneys, quick and brutal, dropping three guards.

A clash of runes rose from the center of the courtyard as a Wise One challenged Thira, but she deflected the weave, sending it hurling back. With a flash of energy, he dropped dead. A stream of guards flowed from all corners and Crumpet greeted them with a clash of tusk against flesh and crushing hooves.

A guttural chant pricked Rashk's sensitive ears. Bloodmagic. Rashk hurled herself to the side as unnatural darkness washed over the courtyard.

The earth quaked, the blind mammoth rampaged, and Rashk landed, coming up in a crouch, ears straining. A hunter did not need her eyes. Unfortunately, another hunter had his.

A lash of energy bit her arm, and Rashk rolled, summoning the Lore, pressing her palm to the earth, listening, as best she could between strikes of thunder and lashing runes, to the slight tremor of footsteps. She twisted, and threw her kukri. The enchanted blade spun end over end, a deadly swish of steel in the darkness.

She heard a grunt, and moved towards its source, surging forward and ducking beneath a sword's edge. With a shout, her blade returned, slapping into her palm in time to bite flesh again.

The darkness lifted with the man's death, and Rashk stood over the body of Victer. She sneered down at the traitor.

Thira was also off her horse, and Crumpet romped around the courtyard, charging anything that moved. Thira stepped over a corpse to join Rashk. She finally had a scent: revulsion.

"If there is one thing I hate more than a Bloodmagus, it is a Wise One who turns to the practice," Thira said. "Victer was an uninspiring apprentice."

Rashk scanned the ravaged courtyard and the lights glowing from the manor house. When no apparent threats revealed themselves, she removed the skree from its pocket and opened her hand. The stone pointed down.

Thira eyed the ground around Victer, and began following the obvious footprints in the grass, leading them to an unexceptional outbuilding. The two women walked to the structure, but their arcane eyes revealed nothing more. Thira shoved the door open, rushing inside with a weave at the ready. But it was just a garden shed.

Something crashed and shook the earth. Rashk poked her head outside to find Crumpet ramming the manor house. She would never again think of that dog as useless.

Thira made a slow circuit of the shed, then tapped her foot in the center. "Bloodmagi are clever. They leave elaborate temples for the Blessed Order, making them difficult, but not impossible to find. So the Blessed Order always looks for the grand, while the real enclaves are overlooked for their modesty." Thira unsheathed a thin stiletto, and pricked her finger, letting a single drop fall into the earth. A squarish void materialized at their feet.

Thira gathered up her skirts and stepped into the void. Rashk followed on her heels.

The air was colder than the air above. Ice clung to the stone and steps, coating the underground lair with crystal brilliance. A creaking, rasping rhythm echoed off the stone, raising Rashk's hackles. Something fathomless and ancient drew a restless breath.

Thira stopped, listening. "What has he done?" She summoned the Lore, weaving a powerful ward. Thira tapped Rashk, and needles prickled over her skin. It felt like falling into a frozen lake.

"It will pass."

When Rashk found her breath, Thira moved forward into the tunnel. The ice flowed into a massive ritual chamber and a terror from time immortal. Rashk stepped back into the passage. A monstrous elemental creaked in the chamber's center, pulsing with red and blue energy, straining against its runic chains.

Thira stepped into the chamber, skirting the walkway and the elemental. The skree led them down a side passage, past cages full of frozen corpses, and eventually, to a dungeon set apart from the rest.

A crossbow bolt zipped down the hallway, hitting Thira in the throat before bouncing harmlessly off her armor weave. In answer, Thira hurled a weave. The attacker clutched his throat, choking and gasping for air.

Rashk stepped up and rescued him from suffocation with the blade of her kukri. He fell over dead. She retrieved a set of keys and the women moved forward into a dungeon lined with metal doors and thrumming wards.

"I'm relieved to find you alive," Thira said.

"Healers make for useful captives," Morigan said from inside.

Rashk bared her teeth at the woman. She looked unharmed and well rested.

The keys deactivated the wards. The lock clicked, the door swung open, and Morigan stepped out, nodding to the two women. "I certainly didn't expect you two."

"If you had not let yourself be captured, we wouldn't have had to come."

Morigan snorted, caught the thin woman in a hug, and set her back just as quickly, before moving to the cell opposite. Rashk handed Morigan the keys.

A little boy stepped out of the cage, throwing his arms around the healer. "I told you we'd find a way out, now didn't I, Zoshi?" She pressed her lips to the boy's filthy hair, and spoke over his head. "The boy saw Tharios use Bloodmagic. Isek and Victer were the ones who captured us."

"As I thought."

Morigan moved to another cell, looked inside, and with a tight-lipped grimace, unlocked the door and rushed inside.

A battered, redheaded Nuthaanian woman was chained to the wall. Morigan knelt beside her, unlocking the chains. Brinehilde's wrists were raw and bleeding and her lips were cracked.

"Get the water from my cell," Morigan ordered. Rashk jumped to obey, and Morigan pressed the jug to the injured woman's lips. She stirred, and drank.

"Get on your feet, Priestess," Thira urged. "We need to leave at once."

Morigan shot Thira a glare, but the order roused the priestess to her senses. She gulped down the jug of water, and stood, wavering on her feet. The ring finger and pinky of her right hand was a bloody, bandaged stump. Morigan put a shoulder under her.

"I assume you have a plan?" Morigan asked. "Tharios will know we're free soon enough—if he doesn't already."

Thira plucked the empty jug from the ground. "We'll inform the High Inquisitor, but I'll not wait for his incompetence. Let us hope the Lord General is loyal to the Order, and not to Tharios."

"And if she's not?"

Thira frowned at the jug in her hands. "Then we'll drag them all with us into the ol'River."

THERE WAS NO MOON, only the wind and an endless swirl of snow as the women and boy rode through the main gate into the inner bailey. Thira dismounted, tossed her reins to a stablehand, and mounted the steps.

Lord General Ielequithe was waiting in front of the Storm Gates with a company of Isle Guards.

A sleek crow swept from its perch on a guardian statue and settled on Thira's shoulder. She hushed Crumpet's demanding squawk with a word. He hated being a bird, but instead of transforming him again, she shooed him back to his safe perch.

"Lord General, I see my message was delivered." Thira held her breath, and the jug in her hand, fearing the soldier was here to arrest rather than aid her.

"Your charges are not light, Mistress Thira." Dark-haired, sharp-eyed, and stern as a crag, Ielequithe did not waste time with pleasantries. Thira had always worked well with the general.

"I have a witness." Thira gestured to Zoshi.

"You will need more than a boy."

"Morigan and the priestess were taken prisoner by Isek Beirnuckle and Victer, along with a number of your own guard."

A muscle in the Lord General's jaw twitched.

"Rashk and I rescued them from Tharios' manor house," Thira explained. "From a Bloodmagus ritual chamber beneath his property. I've sent a message to the High Inquisitor."

Ielequithe looked at each in turn, who nodded confirmation. Decided, she placed her helm on her shaven head, and nodded to her soldiers. They moved into formation.

"The Nine are in Council."

"An excellent place to lay charges against the Archlord."

The Lord General nodded her agreement.

Morigan turned to a soldier. "Guard the boy."

"But I want to come," the boy protested.

Morigan pushed him into the guard's hand and the group passed the Storm Gates into the outer sanctum of the main hall. Thedus, naked and sunburnt, stood in the center, beneath the dome, gazing at the cycle of constellations blazing on the ceiling. He did not glance at the new arrivals. They passed beneath Lispen's Folly—the churning whirlpool of chaotic energy—and barged into the Council Chambers of the Nine.

Tharios sat in the Archlord's chair. Shimei Al'eeth, Isek Beirnuckle, Eldred, Yasimina, Tulipin, Sidonie, Eiji, and Taal Greysparrow sat around the massive stone table.

All eyes turned to the intruders with varying degrees of surprise, save Tharios, who smiled in greeting. "I was expecting you, Thira."

"Not surprising. Your eyes and ears are everywhere."

"And yet you came willingly."

Thira turned to the assembled Nine. "We've been fooled. Marsais and Oenghus were betrayed by Isek Beirnuckle, who was working with Tharios."

Eldred's brow furrowed, and Tulipin sputtered.

"Tharios used Bloodmagic," Morigan said, watching the Nine's reaction. "A boy witnessed a Blood Portal being opened. He escaped the ritual chamber and ran to Brinehilde's orphanage. I was called to heal him, and we were captured there—ambushed by Isek and Victer and taken to Tharios' dungeon."

"What do you say to these charges, Archlord?" Ielequithe inquired.

Tharios spread his hands. "I admit to everything."

All the Wise Ones save Isek and Tharios stood, backing away from their chairs and the accused. "You are under arrest," Ielequithe said, drawing her sword. "I suggest you come quietly."

The guards fanned out.

"As with all things, let us put it to the Nine." Tharios looked at the assembled Wise Ones. "Cast your say—shall I be removed as Archlord? All in favor?"

"The charges are preposterous!" Tulipin said.

Tharios smiled. "But true," he said, simply.

The gnome bristled so badly with outrage that his levitation weave faltered, but he raised his hand along with Eldred.

Rashk scanned the remaining six—all silent. She smelled approaching death, her own.

"Surely not all of you?" Morigan nearly spat. "*Taal?*"

"All opposed?"

All six raised their hands.

"You see, Lord General—I have the majority."

"There is no room in this Order for Bloodmagi," Ielequithe said.

Tharios stood, meeting her gaze across the stone table. "We are not Bloodmagi, Lord General. We are Wise Ones who seek to restore this Order's glory."

"There is no glory at the end of your path," Ielequithe said.

"Yours, I'm afraid, is at an end."

Tharios nodded to the soldiers, half of whom formed a protective ring around their Archlord. The other half took sides with their Lord General. "Most everyone has a weakness, Ielequithe, save you."

Realization cracked her stony face. They were outnumbered and surrounded.

The guards tensed in preparation. The Wise Ones stood at the ready, but before Tharios could give the order, Thira pulled a trick from beneath her long coat.

"Here is your glory, Tharios," she hissed.

With a casual gesture, she hurled the clay jug onto the stone table. Pottery shattered, binding runes flared and swirled, and winter itself howled into the chamber.

A storm of frost blasted the assembled, flinging them against the walls, stealing the air from their lungs and turning their veins to ice. Wise Ones and guards scrambled, fighting one over the other to escape the frozen terror. Ice crawled over the great stone table of the Wise Ones Order. The greater ice elemental bellowed a freezing breath that cracked the stone beneath its foundations.

The timeless granite table shattered, and the flowing words of the Order—*We protect the past to safeguard the future*—crumbled to frozen shards.

Tharios slapped his palm against the stone and melted into the Archlord's preparation chamber. He gasped, sucking in warm air, and stumbled to the other side, pressing his palm against the marble.

"That crone," he snarled.

The castle was shuddering with the elemental's immense power, but the stone still welcomed him. He stepped outside, into the Hall of Judgment. The others ran out of the doors, ice creeping in their wake.

Runic energy surged, a battle of steel and word, as the Wise Ones and his Unspoken clashed in the main hall. Weaves went awry, slamming into stone pillars, arcing into the dome, disrupting the enchanted paintings. All Tharios' plans were in ruin.

His eyes locked on the gates of titan metal and the two statues that stood guard—the faithful hounds of the Archlord, warning off all those who entered with ill intent. It was a lie.

Tharios knew what would trigger their rampage. He had no choice, save one.

Tharios raced across the Hall of Judgment. A weave blasted his shoulder, singeing his flesh. Thira was on his heels. He summoned the Lore, mixing Bloodmagic, creating a Barrier for her weaves, shifting them as he ran. There was no time to deflect, only absorb.

The greater elemental surged into the Hall of Judgment along with a tornado of icy shards. He threw up a hand to shield his eyes as the shards sliced his skin. A moment later, he passed through the threshold, and closed the Titan Gates with a gesture.

They slammed shut. Silence replaced the raging battle. Tharios stood in a place of emptiness, a dimensionless universe of obsidian, all polished darkness and glossy reflection. Shadows drifted in the stone's reflection.

All had not gone to plan, but not all was lost—events had only moved his plans forward. Tharios took out a ring, and slipped it over his finger. It was the same ring the ice elemental had been guarding. It was a key. He stood in the center of the Nameless and steeled himself with a breath, then unhinged the ring and tipped it towards the floor.

A single drop of blood fell from the small container. It hit the stone like a pebble splashing into a pool. The glassy reflection rippled beneath his feet, sending waves rolling outwards, up the walls, and over the ceilings. Darkness bled from the stone, bringing the mist and fear, and releasing a thousand trapped souls from their prison.

THIRA SLAMMED her fist against the Titan Gates with a snarl. Tharios had escaped. A blizzard raged inside the main hall. And if she remained, frostbite would rot her fingers. She ducked behind a stone column and traced a quick weave to ward against the onslaught.

Bodies were buried in ice, but she could barely see them in the whiteness, save for a single glowing form in the center of the storm.

Thira squinted at the glow. There was a man in its center. Thedus. He appeared unbothered by the raging elemental, a pinprick of heat in the blizzard. All at once, the naked man turned towards the Titan Gates and broke into a run, stopping at the gates. His sun blinded eyes focused on her.

Time stopped, chaos fell away, and in that instant, all was still. She could see every shard of crystalline ice, and every facet of the elemental, the bodies in the snow, and the Wise Ones and soldiers fleeing for their lives, but she remained. She felt as if she stood there for eternity, eyes locked with his, until he turned away, splaying his fingers against the gates.

The stone shuddered, and a spiderweb of dormant runes flared to life, traveling over the marble, flaring from the gates, breathing life into the guardian hounds.

Thedus had activated the castle wards. Impossible. For the first time in over three thousand years, the castle came alive.

Thira grabbed Thedus, yanking him away, and dragging him along as she fled, sorely regretting her decision to bind a greater elemental to a clay jug.

CHAPTER 46

THE WORLD SWAYED, back and forth, with a creaking rhythm. Isiilde cracked open an eye. And instantly regretted it. Her gut twisted and bile rose in her throat. She shut her eye. The other didn't seem to work.

Memories washed over her, chaotic and bloody, full of fire and pain. Her sun was gone, she was cold. Her cheek rested on metal. She smelled rust. And heard laughter, mingling with screams.

Those screams warned her not to move. Not yet. Better they think her asleep. She studied her prison through her lashes. It was dark, but she could see bars beneath her. And sand.

A suspended cage.

She had a brief image of a trapped bird under a covered cage. With the upward swing, she glimpsed stone. Her cage dangled over a sand pit ringed by a stone floor.

Clumsy with pain, she slipped her arm through the bars, searching for a seam in the hide covering her prison. When she found it, she pulled back the edge, gazing through the slit. A stony visage glared at her from a hewn wall. Its mouth gaped and its tongue lolled, nearly touching the sand. The mouth and tongue reminded her of the drains decorating manors.

Isiilde let the drape fall back in place. She tried to ignore the screams. She tried not to think about the future or how helpless she felt. Instead, she watched the sand sway beneath her and tried to wish the world away.

THE WORLD DID NOT GO AWAY. It returned in the form of footsteps. The screams and laughter and terror had gone silent, and now the soft hiss of shifting sand grated on her ears. Someone was pacing around her cage.

Isiilde wanted to disappear. She knew what was coming next. But why the sand and why the cage? She swallowed down fear, and forced herself to think. What could she do?

The movement of her throat and tongue slapped her mind into action. Marsais had thrown a weave at her, right before she disappeared through the portal. It had tingled down her throat in a familiar way.

She had her voice.

The drape over her cage was pulled aside. Isiilde forced herself to remain still, to keep her eyes closed and pretend to sleep while she studied her captor through her lashes. He was as large and muscular as Oenghus, covered in scars, chalk, and tattoos. The Ardmoor's hair was a matted clump of braids and his fierce eyes studied her. He wore a leather loincloth, decorated with trophies: scalps, knucklebones, and shriveled pieces of flesh that Isiilde did not want to identify.

"Don't spoil the sand, Fell," a familiar voice hissed from beyond.

The Ardmoor glanced at the new arrival. "Do not give me orders, Rahuatl." His voice was harsh, the common language foreign and clipped on his tongue.

"You are no Bloodmagus," N'Jalss replied. "If the sand is spoiled, we cannot open a gate."

"That is for your kind to worry. I get you cattle, and I get you this creature," Fell snarled, ripping the drape off her cage.

Isiilde did not move. It helped that she was frozen with fear.

"But not the seer," N'Jalss said.

Fell crossed his arms at the accusation. "The others are dead."

"So says your scryer."

"*My* scryer led you to the mountain after your rotting men were defeated," Fell boasted.

Isiilde's heart lurched. She focused inward, on the darkness, searching for any sign of life beyond the thick veil that Marsais had thrown up after he had been wounded. Would she know if he were dead? What would become of their bond?

"The price was for their heads."

"Their heads are at the bottom of the gorge. If you will not pay us, then I keep this nymph." Fell tasted the word on his tongue. He stepped towards her cage, thrust his arm between the bars, and grabbed a handful of her hair. She bit back a scream, swallowing even the slightest noise. "Go home, Rahuatl. Your fangs are little ants in Vaylin."

Fell ran a rough hand over her face and shoulder. Isiilde squirmed away from his touch, but he crushed her to the metal grate with ruthless strength, working a hand beneath her jerkin and shirt to pinch her breast. She bit her lip.

She would not betray her voice. They must not know… Not yet.

N'Jalss walked down a set of steps carved into the stone pit. "Ants supply you with your venom, Fell. Don't forget that."

Like all Rahuatl, he was predatory by nature: copper-skinned, black-haired, with ivory studs decorating his brow and cheeks and pointed chin. N'Jalss had always made her skin crawl, and more so now. His bite lingered on her neck. The cruelty he'd shown her. The savage glee in his eyes. His betrayal of Marsais.

She would never forget.

"There are many ants," Fell snickered. "What is this nymph to you?" The groping hand squeezed her breast, and Isiilde jerked with pain.

"Have her if you wish. I'll take my venom elsewhere. There are other tribes, other warlords, who would pay dearly for my vials."

Fell's grip loosened for a moment, and Isiilde threw herself backwards, scrambling to the opposite side of the cage. Fell tilted his head, matted hair brushing his shoulder as he studied her through the gaps. She met his eyes, defiant, and his lip curled. He gripped a bar and pulled, sending the cage spinning on its chain.

She drifted closer to the warlord, and hurried to the opposite side, but this time, he gripped the cage and heaved. She could not escape his grasp. An arm thrust through the slats, seizing her neck, yanking her against the bars.

"Why is this faerie so important, Rahuatl?" Fell's breath crawled in her ear. He smelled of lust and blood and rot. The hand on her throat was strong; he could crush her in a moment.

"My master has obligations," N'Jalss hissed. "As do you to your men. How long can they last without their venom?"

"There are fewer men to supply now."

"A hazard for any mercenary," N'Jalss said, glancing at his sharpened finger caps.

"You did not tell me these men were so powerful."

"I hired your company to kill *two* men and three paladins. Did you think them an easy kill—like the nymph?"

Fell's hand tightened around Isiilde's throat. If she had wanted to make a sound, she could not have managed one. "I think you are frightened of these men. But they are dead, Rahuatl, so you have no more to fear. Give me the venom, or leave, and I will keep the spoils of war."

N'Jalss glanced at Isiilde, whose freckled skin was turning mottled and purple under Fell's hand as she clawed at his fingers. "I'll need more cattle for the portal to Vlarthane."

"Lazy," Fell spat, releasing her. "You could walk."

Isiilde fell to the cage floor, sucking in air, filling her lungs around the pain in her throat.

"Can your men wait that long?"

Fell did not reply. He grabbed the cage and heaved, sending her world spinning before stalking up the stairway.

N'Jalss reached out, letting the claws of his finger caps scrape the rusty metal with every turn. A cold heart beat in her breast, and she met his gaze with each revolution. As the cage slowed, he gripped a bar, stopping the spin so she was facing him.

"If I had my way, Nymph," he hissed. "I'd leave you to Fell."

Never wavering from his imperious gaze, Isiilde hugged her knees and rested her chin on top, smiling ever so slowly. The future stretched in front of her with perfect clarity, like the runes that Rivan had clumsily maneuvered every evening.

Men were predictable. And she was tired of them.

N'Jalss frowned at the knowing nymph. With a growl, he tugged the hide back in place, and left.

FELL RETURNED IN THE QUIET. Whether night or day, she did not know. He paced like a restless tiger around her cage, lust burning in his eyes.

Isiilde followed his path. Memories whispered of her future, of pain and humiliation. She retreated deep inside herself, where the memories could not find her, to a cold, unfeeling place. From a safe cocoon, detached from her body, she focused on the man and the moment.

His eyes were wild. His focus clouded. Fell could not look away from the ethereal creature. She seemed a dream.

Isiilde parted her lips in invitation and the man lurched forward, gripping the bars of her cage. His body was tense, his desire apparent beneath the leather loincloth.

She reached through the bars to run her fingers up his thigh. The man's chest heaved. He grunted at her, reaching into the cage. Isiilde pressed herself against the opposite side as he strained to drag her closer. But she stayed just out of reach.

Frustrated, Fell growled, spun the cage, and stopped it at the door. He ripped a key from his belt, thrust it inside the iron lock, and ruthlessly twisted. The chains fell to the ground, and he lifted the iron bar, dropping it to the sand.

The moment Fell swung the door open, he triggered Isiilde's ward. The iron crackled with energy, melding his hand to the iron bars. Muscles spasmed, his body convulsed, and the paint on his skin sizzled. Burnt flesh filled the air, sharp and noxious.

Isiilde watched Fell die from the center of her cage, safely wrapped in an earth weave.

The warlord dropped to the sand with a thud and his men rushed to the side of the pit, gazing down at their fallen leader with raised torches. N'Jalss hurried down the steps, followed by the woman who had opened a gateway and another man, grizzled and bent and covered in scars.

The Shaman bent over his fallen lord, studying the bulging eyes, charred skin, and black blood in the torchlight. "A trap," he declared.

Isiilde pointed at N'Jalss.

Their voices rose in a grating tongue. The warriors above shook their spears and brandished swords.

"I set no ward," N'Jalss hissed. Then he looked at Isiilde, realization flashing in his slitted eyes.

N'Jalss started weaving, but Isiilde was faster, her weave was waiting, and she traced the final rune. N'Jalss hurled a silence weave at her, but it hit her shield, and rebounded, slamming into N'Jalss. His eyes widened in shock as he choked on his own gag.

Isiilde called to her flame. It leapt from the torches, gathering at her call. A whirlwind of heat and fire swirled around its mistress, snatching up thrown spears and spitting them out as ash. Her voice rose with the firestorm.

She spoke the language of flame, of passion, and of destruction.

N'Jalss turned and fled, with the Bloodmagus and Shaman on his heels. A lash of flame whipped from the whirlwind, catching the Bloodmagus in a coil of fire, devouring her scars and flesh with a flare.

Isiilde's lips parted, tendrils of fire toyed with her hair and the wind beat on her flesh, rendering cloth to ash. The power in her veins burned and there was no one to stop her. She let it carry her away, far from the cruel earth, to a realm of heat and cleansing fire, riding the currents like a bird on the winds, stretching her wings until she was a part of the storm. Her voice wrapped around the flickering flame, seducing it like a lover.

As her clothes fell away, and the cage heated, Isiilde unfolded herself and stepped onto the sand. It was hot and burning and she curled her toes gleefully at its touch. The fire took shape, mirroring the fiery dragon on her back, and with a roaring lash it twisted through the cavern, devouring everyone in its path.

Amid a chorus of screams and smoke and glowing stone, Isiilde moaned. She was free, and men fell at her feet in fear and writhing death.

Isiilde stretched in the silence. She floated on warm waves, exhausted, but dreamy with pleasure. Flames lingered over smoldering bodies that were little more than husks of ash.

The sand was hot, and she was tempted to lie down and sleep. But she had not forgotten where she was. Or who had fled. She wove another armor ward, adding fire to the cycle, and climbed the steps, alert for survivors.

The cavern was filled with smoking corpses, twisted in death, littering the floor like a forest of burnt trees. Isiilde felt nothing for the humans.

The cavern walls were scorched and black, covering the chaotic patterns and horrific visages etched into their surface. Everything was in ruins, except for the stones of a large firepit and a few crumbling pieces of timber.

She stopped at the remains of a human, and kicked what was left of his wrist. A charred knife fell from his brittle grasp and she picked the blade up, knocking it against the stone. The leather around the hilt fell off, but the blade was sound. She would have liked to wipe it clean, but there wasn't any cloth left that she could see.

Moving in a dream, Isiilde wandered through the cavern, walking on a cloud of warm ash and smoldering coals. A gust of wind prickled her skin, reminding her of a world of waiting snow.

And more humans.

If she were to leave this place, she needed water, food, and clothing.

There was a noise like thunder in the distance. The sound came from a side passage, carved with writhing forms of pain and pleasure. Averting her gaze from the images, she walked towards the sound, aware of the blade pressed in her hand.

Mist tickled her throat, and the noise of a waterfall drowned the blood rushing through her veins. Her fire had not touched this stone. It opened to a cave of luminous vines and a waterfall plunging into darkness. Water drained into a shallow side basin. The pool was not empty. A pale girl floated in the water, ankles and wrists bound with chains, stretched to the four corners of the pool. Her skin glistened, her eyes were as white as her hair, unseeing but moving.

Isiilde pressed herself against the stone, clutching her dagger with horror. The girl's lips moved, murmuring in a foreign tongue. Her body arched, her jaw cracked opened, and she spat out words.

The water began to churn.

Shadows moved in the ripples, taking shape with each raving word. The girl foamed at the mouth, tugging, ripping at her chains, but she was bound tightly, spread-eagled and helpless.

Isiilde saw herself in the pool's reflection, but it was not her present self. This reflection was crouched at the edge of the pool. A shadow detached itself from the wall, stepped behind her, and drew a claw across her throat.

A vision. And a warning.

Isiilde screamed for her fire, but it was too far and the air too moist. A warning pricked at her instincts. She spun in time to see N'Jalss lunge from the shadows. Isiilde threw up her arms. Claws bit into flesh. Her armor weave flared, searing N'Jalss. The clash sent her reeling, and she slipped on the slick stone, falling into the water.

N'Jalss stepped into the pool and grabbed her by her hair. Isiilde twisted in his grip, striking with her knife. Her blade pierced the meat of his forearm, and he released her. She dropped into the water, scrambled under the thrashing girl, and came up on the other side, weaving.

Defenseless without his voice, N'Jalss launched himself over the girl at Isiilde, disrupting the weave. The backlash hit them both. White hot pain slashed through Isiilde's bones as energy crackled between the two, hurling them apart.

Isiilde slammed onto the stone floor. Her head felt cracked, her heart skipped and started, she could not draw breath. An eternity later, air filled her lungs, cool and sweet. But N'Jalss recovered first.

He seized her by the throat, dragging her back into the pool. Her armor weave sizzled as his claws raked her flesh. Isiilde ignored the pain, searching blindly for her knife. It lay on the stone. Her fingers curled around the hilt and she stabbed at his side. It slipped between his ribs. His grip tightened for a moment, then weakened.

N'Jalss staggered backwards, pressing a hand to his side. Blood bubbled from his lips, and with a final wheeze, he fell forward into the pool, floating beside the chained girl.

Isiilde crawled out of the water. On hands and knees, she watched a cloud of blood spread over the surface. She saw her future self in its crimson reflection, lying limply at the edge—bruised, swollen, and bleeding. A vision.

It came true a moment later. She collapsed at the pool's edge, too weak to move. As her vision narrowed, and spots danced in the growing darkness, the pool churned with another vision: a snowy owl soaring through a charred cavern.

CHAPTER 47

AN OWL GLIDED over a mountain fortress. Harsh winds and sleet battered its ice-covered walls as the owl swooped closer. The sun was falling, yet the fortress walls were empty of guards and the braziers unlit.

The owl landed on a twisted altar at the top of a steep stairway cut into the mountain. Its head swiveled, surveying the fortress. Snow-covered lumps littered the ground and threat lingered in the air.

The owl ruffled its feathers, settled, and stepped to the side, away from the pouch it had carried for miles. The coins around its neck clinked and chimed, reminding the owl that he was a man. A spark of memory took root. The weave unraveled, and the owl jerked and spasmed. Snowy feathers swirled in the wind, leaving a lean, shivering man lying on the altar.

Marsais rolled off with a groan. His feet hit ice and ash, and he slipped, catching himself on the sacrificial stone. With trembling limbs and a spinning head, he grabbed the pouch, and staggered away. His skull throbbed with pain, but it was not his own.

Marsais strode into the temple. Its entrance gaped like a maw of icy fangs, but its throat bore signs of scorch marks. Ash partially obscured carvings that roiled and moved beneath his eye, transforming the stone into a writhing mass of snake-like images.

The Ardmoor were fond of hallucinogens, and their sacred carvings inspired terror and madness. But Marsais was not drugged, and he was already mad, so he moved forward without hesitation, coins chiming gently against his throat.

Isiilde was in pain, but alive. And strangely unafraid. He searched the cavern for her, the ash and death and destruction. The carnage gave him pause. He stopped beside a giant, phallic-shaped pillar, reached into his pouch, yanked out his trousers, and tugged them on. Moving swiftly, he cinched the pouch around his waist, and followed the pull of their bond to his nymph.

An entire tribe littered the floor. He skirted their burnt corpses on silent feet, hands ready to weave. But no one was left. Not a soul stirred. She'd slaughtered them all. He went cold with dread.

It went against a nymph's nature to kill. But Isiilde was no ordinary nymph—she was the daughter of the Sylph. And Oenghus.

Still, this would mark her. He could feel the coldness creeping around her heart. It was a dangerous path. One taken before by another: Pyrderi Har'Feydd, the first Fey, who set the realm on a path of destruction.

How far down that path would Isiilde go?

Marsais did not like the looming end. He pushed the future aside and focused on the present—his nymph, who was no longer the innocent. Their bond led him to a tunnel, past a ritual pit and corrals, where captives had been cooked alive in their cages.

The drone of a waterfall drew him deeper into the cave. Isiilde was there, lying naked beside a pool, her fiery hair mixing with a cloud of blood and the body of N'Jalss.

Marsais did not look at the child chained in the water. The scryer screamed her visions, and he closed his ears to her prophesies as he circled the pool, careful not to touch the water.

Isiilde was alive, he knew, but she was bleeding from numerous wounds. Gently, he lifted her head from the water, turned her over in his arms, and cradled her to his chest. Her eyes fluttered open at his touch. There was a smile in those eyes.

"My sun," she whispered.

A knot unwound in his heart. There was hope.

"I feel I should say something in return, but words fail me at the moment."

"You *are* saying something, Marsais." Her voice was thready and weak.

"It's not a very good something." He pressed his lips against her forehead, whispering his love on her skin.

"I thought you were dead. What of Oenghus?"

Marsais pulled away, meeting her gaze. "We need to leave."

"Tell me," she demanded, struggling to rise.

"He fell off the edge—into the mists."

Isiilde closed her eyes. A tear slipped down her cheek, trailing through blood and ash. He felt her heart fall with her guardian, but the girl's thrashing in the water brought them back to the present. Isiilde clenched her jaw, and pushed herself to her knees, shoving N'Jalss aside to reach the tortured girl.

"We must help her."

Marsais averted his eyes. "Yes."

"I saw visions in the water, Marsais."

"The girl is a scryer. The Ardmoor have been using her to track us."

"Help me get her binds off."

"There are clothes inside this pouch. Wait for me in the tunnel."

"Why?"

The girl thrashed, moaned, and the water churned. Isiilde looked into the bloody swirl and her eyes widened in horror. "You can't. We can save her."

"*Go!*"

Isiilde blinked at the harsh order. She stared at him, stunned and appalled, and for a heartbeat, she saw what others saw—why they feared him. But she was not afraid. In that moment, they were equals.

"It is a mercy, Isiilde." Marsais closed his eyes. "I was collared and chained for years. By the gods, you must believe me."

His hoarse confession cooled her skin. He could not meet her eyes, could not bear her pity. Marsais thrust out the pouch. "Wait for me, please."

Isiilde staggered out of the pool, retrieved the pouch in silence, and limped into the tunnel, leaving the seer with his tortured kin.

Marsais turned to the girl and looked at her then. He picked up a knife from the ground, his fingers numb, and waded into the water. He touched the girl's wrist, uttering the Lore of Unlocking, and then to the other, before moving to her ankles until she floated free.

"Grant me peace," she pleaded.

"May your spirit drift free." Marsais slipped a hand behind her head, exposing a pale throat. "Be at peace, child."

The blade bit flesh in one clean jerk, unburdening her from Time.

MARSAIS PLOWED through thick drifts as Isiilde staggered on his heels. She was injured. They needed rest. But not all the Ardmoor had been killed. Eventually, the warriors would return. But most of all, more than any threat, they moved because neither Marsais nor Isiilde wished to remain in the fortress a moment longer.

Isiilde stumbled, and he turned to catch her, then helped her onto his back. She was so delicate, so frail, and yet so powerful. As light and fierce as flame, he thought. Pulling his cowl lower, Marsais put his head down, and walked as far as his long legs would take him from the chained girl.

The temperature dropped with the sun, and in the light of two moons, Marsais walked down the mountainside and into a valley. He adjusted the nymph on his back, and pressed his hand against a twisted tree trunk, marred by wind and axe and scarred by flame. The sequoia's branches swayed, its needles shivered, and the wind moaned in greeting.

"We need shelter, old ones," Marsais beseeched. A gust of wind caught his breath, chilling his bones, and he stepped into the forest, coins chiming like a herald announcing his presence. The trees whispered in answer, and he followed their quivering needles.

The wood spirits guided him to a clearing. He wove an orb of light and sent it floating ahead. It illuminated a cabin buried in snow.

"Isiilde," he whispered.

The nymph stirred at his call, and opened her eyes. Without urging, she slid from his back, and he steadied her until she found her feet. They moved towards the cabin, climbing a snow drift. Marsais kicked in a shutter and sent his orb inside, until every crevice was filled with light.

The cabin was abandoned.

Marsais folded his long body through the window, turned to help Isiilde down, and moved to the large, river rock hearth, brushing off the snow and cleaning it of debris. He traced a fire rune on its back wall, then reached into the pouch to pull out blankets. Isiilde limped over, and lowered herself on the furs.

They ate in silence, in the glow of heat, and when their bellies were full, Marsais rummaged through their supplies. Isiilde watched him as he added yarrow leaves and honey to a small bowl, crushing and grinding the leaves into a poultice.

"I can't risk using the Gift to heal you," he said, breaking their silence. "I only heal as a last resort." There was always a risk that a vision could seize him in the middle of a healing. A loss of focus would be lethal.

Isiilde unlaced her jerkin, peeled it off, and pulled her shirt over her head. She moved in a daze, not even flinching as the cold air brushed her shoulders. Marsais eyed the bruises on her neck and breasts. She yanked off her boots, shimmied out of her trousers and underclothes, and sat on the fur. Wrapped in a blanket, her eyes turned towards the glowing fire rune.

"How long did you wear a collar?" she asked softly.

"Long enough to stop counting."

A shudder swept through her body. He gathered clean snow from a corner into a bowl, then knelt beside her and warmed the water with a delicate weave. Marsais offered her a cloth, but she did not take it, so he dipped it in the water and began to clean the blood from her body. She was a battered mess, and he shuddered at the pattern of bruising along her bones. It had the mark of a lightning weave. The claw marks and gashes hinted at her battle with N'Jalss.

After she was clean and dry, he reached for the poultice.

"I killed them, Marsais."

He paused at her whisper.

"You were taken captive," he said. "You did what was needed to survive."

But she was shaking her head.

"The Lome. I killed so many trying to help Oen." Her voice cracked and tears shimmered in her eyes as she looked at him. "You knew, didn't you? That a scryer was tracking us. You *knew* the Ardmoor would attack—that's why you waited." The accusations rang in her voice. "We could have left, Marsais. We could have run and left them in peace."

"Yes," he agreed.

She stared at him in confusion. "Did you know Oenghus would die?" The question was wrenched from her heart.

Marsais looked into the hearth, following the flowing lines of his rune, feeling the power coursing through its shape as surely as he felt the blood pumping in his veins. "I have glimpsed a thousand deaths, all vast and varied and brutal. You cannot chart Chaos, my dear."

"But you keep trying."

"That is all any of us can do."

"I wish I hadn't tried," she whispered. "Oenghus might be alive—we would not have been separated, you would not have been wounded, we would have left together." A sob tore at her throat, but she fought it, swallowing back grief.

"So many paths," he said, tracing the curve of her ear. "There is nothing I can say to ease your heart, but I know that Oenghus would not regret his path. You are, after all, alive. And you, my dear, made his life worth living."

Isiilde squeezed her eyes shut. Tears broke free, slipping from her lashes, falling freely down her cheeks, sizzling as they fell. She took refuge in his arms.

"May the ol'River take him," Marsais recited the last rites of a berserker. "May it choke on his blood and spit him out. Do not weep over death—weep for his return, for the earth will tremble in fear."

Isiilde wept herself into exhaustion, and Marsais sat, cradling her head against his heart, listening to her ragged breath.

"Why would the ol'River spit Oen out?" she wondered after a time. Her voice was distant, drained of emotion.

"A Nuthaanian is more likely to spit in the face of a god than worship one. Drifting peacefully in a spirit river tended by a benevolent god isn't exactly their idea of bliss."

"I never liked that idea either."

Marsais smiled. "I'm not surprised." He nearly told her of her blood, of Oenghus—her father—but he stilled his tongue. Her world was already shaken. And he was not sure she could bear the truth, for it would lead to other questions—ones he had no right to answer.

"Perhaps there is a spirit river of ale for Oen."

"What is ale without women?"

"I suppose he'll come back, then."

"Hmm, he usually does." Marsais bit his tongue into silence. Fortunately, Isiilde was too rattled and drifting towards sleep to question him further.

After her breathing evened to a gentle rhythm, Marsais eased her to the fur, tucking a blanket around her. He refreshed the fire rune, and rose to set wards. The years weighed on him, and he moved stiffly under the burden.

Frowning at the sleeping nymph, he turned his back to her, and climbed out the window. The air was icy, and its bite cleared his head. Marsais raised his eyes heavenward, gazing at the silver crescent and its faithful red moon through a gap in the canopy.

Time stilled with the earth. Alone with the eternal stars, the throbbing ache of his scar, and eons of memories, Marsais focused on his heartbeat—on the present. His focus turned to the nymph's bond and her spirit surrounded by shadow. It no longer flickered in the darkness, but burned steadily. She had found her flame.

Marsais exhaled. His path was set, but he hesitated. His heart was not in this journey. He inhaled, chest rising, lungs burning with cold.

Three deep breaths and a heartbeat later, he clenched his fists, straightening his shoulders with resolve. Turning towards the cabin, he slipped through the window, and retrieved an empty vial and knife from his supplies. He thrust the blade through his belt, held the vial aloft, and traced an intricate pattern of runes over its surface with a murmur. When the glowing runes had faded into the clay, he knelt before the sleeping nymph.

Marsais traced a quick weave over Isiilde, numbing her senses, lulling her into a deeper sleep. He gently pulled her arm from beneath the blanket, exposing bruised flesh to the cold air. He removed the leather cord from his neck, cinched it tightly around her forearm, and placed a bowl under her hand.

"I don't expect your forgiveness, but I *am* sorry for everything I am about to do," he whispered, bringing the blade to her wrist.

The knife pierced her flesh as he dragged it lengthwise over her vein. Blood blossomed from the slice, and he caught it in the vial, filling it to the brim. The holding weave flared, and activated, then subsided.

Moving quickly, he stuck a cork in the top, pocketed the vial, loosened the cord, and placed his hands over the bleeding wound, summoning the Lore. Flesh mended, and he quickly withdrew, loath to risk a more intrusive healing. Visions came at the most inopportune times, and one came now—a fist flew at his face, and scarred knuckles as hard as iron slammed into his nose.

Marsais blinked away the disorientation. "Thank the gods," he murmured.

CHAPTER 48

A WHISPER TICKLED HIS EAR. *My rock.*

Soft as a sigh, silk trailed down his broad chest and a kiss touched his heart, bringing warmth.

My earth. Fingers combed through his hair. *Not yet.*

A figure of silver, full of hip and breast and longing lips, stretched along his body. Hot breath mingled with his. *Rise, my love.*

Oenghus Saevaldr opened his eyes to a silver moon, and darkness. He was being shaken. The surrounding shadows moved with a hiss and a lunging strike. A furred creature at his shoulder struck back with a gleaming blade, returning hiss for hiss.

Another shadow neared. Oenghus caught the Reaper by the throat and hurled it into the lake. With a cracking of ice, he rose from the frozen bank, pounding his fist into a leaping shadow.

He staggered, shook the dizziness from his head, and kicked another. Shadows swarmed, claw and fang bit his flesh, and Oenghus roared with pain, reaching for a broken branch and snapping it from the tree. Half-blinded with weakness, he swung wildly at the writhing shadows, until none moved save one. He raised his club, and the shadow yelled, cowering at his feet.

A pale hand reached from beneath the furs, touching his shin.

Oenghus fell to his knees on the ice, breathing hard. He tugged his flask free, bit out the cork, and took a long draught of Brimgrog. Its bite seared his veins and his body warmed.

The woman in furs edged closer, two eyes gleaming in the moonlight. She gripped his arm, covered with ice, and pulled.

"In a minute, lass." Oenghus closed his eyes. But it was more than a minute.

When he regained consciousness, Kasja was cinching a cloth around his abdomen, speaking in his ear. Oenghus didn't understand her words, but he understood the urgency in them. He stirred, ice creaked and cracked on his kilt, and he pushed himself up, staggering forward, barreling over a lurking Reaper before catching himself on a tree. Snow fell on his head, joining a bandage on his forehead and the layer of ice on his beard.

Oenghus gripped the tree, leaning heavily against its strength for support. His head lulled forward, chin resting on his chest, shoulders shuddering. He was wavering between life and death. By all accounts, he should be dead.

Kasja pulled on his hand. This time, he followed. Twice he staggered and fell, and twice his guide urged him forward, along the bank. A canoe appeared, and he fell inside, nearly tipping it over. Kasja wrestled his legs into the canoe, threw a fur over his bulk, and pushed out into the lake, hopping inside.

As they drifted over calm waters, Oenghus watched the silver moon and the wild, red guardian trailing in its wake. His heart ached, and he shook off his longing with a growl.

"Where's Isiilde?"

The woman said a single word in her tongue, one he knew. *Gone.*

"Did the Scarecrow tell you I'd be here?"

She tilted her head.

He exhaled, closing his eyes.

When he opened them again, the moon was in a different position. The canoe was caught in a current, drifting towards the mouth of a river. Oenghus swallowed, silently assessing his wounds, but his body was numb and distant. He fumbled for his flask, fingers trembling over the cork, until it opened, and he took another swig. His head cleared.

"Kasja."

The furred woman leaned forward. He pointed to his eyes, and then to his chest. "The Scarecrow?"

The wild woman shook her head, pointed to her own eyes, and then to his chest, smiling proudly. Teeth gleamed white and feral in the dark.

"*You* had a vision?" he asked.

Kasja nodded.

Oenghus did not much care where he was going, but the river was gentle, and the moon bright. Its silver light caressed his cheek, and he closed his eyes, dreaming of the Sylph in his arms.

CHAPTER 49

Acacia Mael frowned at the boy. He was wedged in the narrow exit, refusing to budge and rattling on in a language none of them understood. Then, finally, she caught one word in the jumble: Kasja.

As usual, Lucas quickly lost patience. He grabbed the boy by his collar, and pulled him aside. The paladin tossed his pack through the exit and climbed outside.

Elam fell to his knees at Acacia's feet. "Kasja," he repeated over and over, pointing to the ground.

"We can't wait for her, Elam. You can stay here if you like."

The world was white and smelled of evergreen. It sparkled under the sun. Acacia squinted past the blinding snow, searching the quiet.

"Do we even know where Vlarthane is?" Lucas asked.

"We'll head east. Eventually, we'll come to the coast."

The three paladins hoisted their packs and started their long march, but Elam ran ahead, flying over snow drifts like a sparrow, waving his arms, and pushing on Lucas, trying to force him to turn around. When that did not work, Elam threw himself at Acacia and latched onto her leg.

She dragged him through the snow for a few steps, then stopped with a sigh. "Hold up, Lucas."

"You want me to toss the little imp?"

Acacia looked down into a pair of pleading eyes framed in a filthy face, and pointed back towards their shelter. "You want us to wait?"

Elam nodded. "Kasja, Kasja," he repeated.

"She could be dead, boy," Lucas said.

But Elam shook his head.

"What do you think, Rivan?"

Rivan started in surprise. The captain had never asked his opinion before.

"You've spent a good deal of time with the boy."

"He doesn't scare easily," Rivan said. "It seems like he knows something we don't."

"Maybe his sister was the traitor, and now she's leading the Ardmoor back to us."

"A possibility." Acacia was not one to wait. And worse, there were Ardmoor lurking in the forest. She had men for whom she was responsible, a task ahead, and a seer to meet. And yet, the boy was so adamant. Against logic, against sense, the Knight Captain listened to her heart. "I don't much like the idea of waiting inside the tree. There's only one exit. We'll wait over there."

"For another day?" Lucas asked.

"Does it matter at this point?"

In answer, Lucas planted himself beside a fallen log, settling in for a long wait.

"Can I wait inside where it's warm, Captain?"

Acacia looked at Rivan. "No."

THE PALADINS DID NOT HAVE to wait long. Something pelted Rivan on the back of his dented helm. He glanced up, around, and behind, looking for birds or a squirrel. A furred figure slipped from behind the trees on silent feet, and Acacia and Lucas turned in surprise.

Elam rushed forward to hug his sister. In the torrent of words that followed, Acacia caught mention of Oenghus in the jumble. Elam slipped free, pointing and motioning with urgency at his sister, who moved back through the woods.

Acacia sprinted after the wild woman, straight to a wide river and a canoe, half bobbing in the water and half stuck on the bank. The boat carried a heavy load—one Kasja could not drag ashore.

Acacia pulled back the fur. "Chaim give him strength," she breathed.

Over seven feet of Nuthaanian muscle lay in the canoe, seven feet of wounds, of jagged gash and bruise. She put an ear to his ice-burned lips and a hand over his heart. Oenghus was alive. Barely.

He had lost his shield and hammer in the falls, and his broad chest was bare. Kasja had removed his breastplate and bandaged his wounds. The bandages were soaked through with blood.

"Thank Zahra," Rivan said, touching fingers to lips.

"Can he wait to be healed?" Lucas asked. "Even with all of us, I doubt we can drag him to the tree."

Lucas had a point. Oenghus was not a man who was simply carried. She shook him, calling his name. "Oenghus, can you walk?"

His eyes opened, then closed. His hand rested on his chest, gripping his sacred flask. She pried his fingers back, uncorked the flask, and put the Brimgrog to his lips.

Oenghus sat up with a growl, knocking her to the side. The canoe tipped, spilling out its load onto the shore. He stumbled to his feet, searching for his flask.

Acacia held it out.

"Where's Isiilde?" he rasped, snatching the flask from her hand.

"Marsais went after her," Acacia said, laying a hand on his arm. He looked at the hand, and the wildness left his eyes. "Can you walk?"

"Course I can walk." To prove it, he took three steps, and promptly dropped to his knees, then fell face first into the snow.

"Void," Lucas spat.

"Indeed."

Between the five of them, using two shields strapped together as a sled and a lot of effort, they wrestled the giant berserker inside the tree. Acacia unwound his filthy bandage and grimaced. His side was torn open. His eyes opened at her touch.

"Looks like you collided with a rock or two on your way down the river, Oenghus."

"Or three, and a hungry wyvern," he grunted. She pressed a water-skin to his cracked lips, and he swallowed. "Long as I 'ave me bollocks, I'll be fine."

Acacia frowned, looking down at him severely. "I'm sorry, Oenghus, but you were in the snow a long time."

As sure as a shot of Brimgrog, he reached for his crotch. When he was reassured that everything was where it should be, he glared at Acacia, whose face betrayed none of the amusement dancing in her eyes.

"You're a cruel woman," he huffed.

"I know." She placed a hand on his chest, pushing him back to the ground. "I'll get you right."

"Those hands of yours can do anything they like."

"I'm tempted to shove you back in the river," she warned.

Before he could answer, she bowed her head, silently thanked the Sylph, and placed her hands over his wound, praying for the skill to mend his ruined flesh.

CHAPTER 50

A STEADY STREAM of travelers flowed into Vlarthane, walking over a long bridge that dipped its arches into a bay. A painted barbarian pushed stragglers aside, clearing the way for his line of slaves. His chalk-covered hair was pulled behind his head in a topknot. The sides of his scalp were shaved, and his beard was twisted into three thick braids. Bones and trinkets hung from his belt, weighting the loincloth between his powerful thighs. The barbarian was sorely missing his kilt.

Oenghus Saevaldr adjusted the shield bumping against his back, and eyed the tiered battlements that wound up the mountain. Sailboats and rowboats flittered over the water, traveling between towns, avoiding the oared monstrosities and their lethal ship-breakers.

"It's huge," Rivan gawked from the slave line. "Are you sure this is going to work?"

"If you wanted sure, boy, you should have been an acolyte," Lucas growled from the back of the line.

Oenghus glanced over his shoulder, studying the group in their stolen costumes. Convincing the paladins to ambush a caravan of slavers had not been difficult. But convincing those same paladins to trade their arms and armor for looted clothing had not been easy. He'd had to sacrifice his own kilt—the Saevaldr tartan cloth was too recognizable, even in Vaylin.

In the end, Acacia had compromised, scratching out holy symbols, and ordering her men to discard their golden tunics in exchange for furs. Then they tarnished the armor's sheen with grease and dirt before putting the bundle on a horse. Their line of slaves—Rivan, Kasja, and Elam—were easily freed if needed.

"This had better work," Oenghus grumbled, grabbing Rivan by the neck for show. "My fist has a bone to pick with the ol' Bastard."

"At least wait until we're out of Vlarthane," Acacia murmured.

"You just want to hit him first."

"I'm sure you would let me."

Oenghus bared his teeth at her, and turned his attention towards the gate, to the crimson guards with their scaled armor, crossbows, and bristling spears. Vlarthane's banners billowed in the wind: a black circle on crimson.

Three days ago, Marsais had sent a single message via Whisper: *Vlarthane, the Crooked Man*. No word about Isiilde.

One would assume the Crooked Man was a tavern, but one never knew with Marsais—his mind worked in mysterious ways, and he was always suspicious of people standing around all day snatching Whispers from the air. But just because Marsais found the pastime amusing, didn't mean everyone else did.

A trio of guards stopped them at the gates. A line of crossbowmen on the battlements lowered weapons, their deadly missiles aimed at the towering barbarian who looked like a volatile Ardmoor.

"Slave tax," a guard ordered.

Oenghus dropped three dented coins into the guard's hand, one for each slave. The visored helm tilted down as the man hefted the little coins. He held out his hand for more.

"They're runts. We won't get much for them," Acacia said in flawless Vaylinish. But the guard persisted, and Oenghus dropped three more coins into his hand. Finally, Oenghus and his group were waved through, shoulders tense as they followed the flow of travelers and traders down a spacious road.

The snow was trampled and black beneath Oenghus' boots, pushed to the sides of the cobblestones, where muck-covered drains unleashed nauseous smells. Vlarthane was vast and varied, and traders from the Bastardlands flocked to its markets. Long lines of slaves, driven by men with whips and cudgels, marched down the street towards the market district.

The Vaylinish were not particular when it came to slaves. Anyone brought to Vaylin's markets was sold to the highest bidder. No questions, scruples, or regulations involved. Lords or ladies could find themselves on the viewing block as easily as a street urchin.

Oenghus turned down a side street where sprawling rookeries clouded out the sky, then down an alley. His slaves shed their collars and chains, and he stuffed the discarded items under a refuse pile. "Remember, stay within sight of each other, and unless you speak Vaylinish, don't talk." He put his hand on Elam's shoulder and steered the boy back into the street.

Lucas followed with Kasja, and Acacia and Rivan trailed far behind, keeping Oenghus within sight. Two travelers warranted little notice, but a group of six would attract attention.

Oenghus stepped aside for a squad of soldiers escorting a gilded litter that whip-scarred men carried on their shoulders. He followed the twisting streets, making his way steadily up the mountain, passing a guarded gate at each tier. The buildings, built from stone blocks that were as thick as the battlements carved into the hill, rose in quality with the tiers.

On the third tier, Oenghus kept to the winding path around the mountain, moving towards the Bitter Coast, while keeping a discreet eye on his group. He'd been to Vlarthane before, long ago, and the city had not changed. It was as formidable and as well defended as he remembered. And although the Knight Captain would not say why, or when, she had also visited Vlarthane. She stopped to question the occasional grocer or urchin, but every time he caught her eyes, she gave a slight shake of her head.

"To the Pits with Marsais," Oenghus muttered.

Searching for The Crooked Man in a city of brothels, taverns, and boarding houses could take a fortnight. It would also attract attention.

With an oath, he stomped into the nearest tavern, and had his first ale in a week.

AT NIGHTFALL, Oenghus began to climb down tiers, moving into rougher districts where they were less likely to attract notice. They took rooms on separate sides of the street, in the shadow of the great walls that lined the bay. Oenghus left Elam in their shared room and went down to the tavern to nurse another ale.

Acacia walked into the common room. Firm-jawed, armored, and armed, she earned glances, but none lingered for long. Oenghus pushed out a chair, grunted at her, and signaled the barkeep for another ale. She sat, leaning close to ward off prying ears.

"Kasja ran off," she said into her mug.

"Bloody Void."

"Lucas would agree. Elam?"

Oenghus shrugged. "He was sleeping when I left him. They can do whatever they like. I'm not responsible for those two."

Acacia hid a smile in her mug. "She might have had a vision of Marsais."

"If I never hear the word 'vision' again, I will die a happy man."

"In a city like Vlarthane, there is a rather good chance of dying before that happens."

As if her words had sparked the fight, two men erupted from a nearby table. One drew a sword, and the other threw a knife. The knifer won. Blood pooled on the stained planks. The corpse was stripped in a matter of moments, and dragged out back into the alley.

"The city has a certain charm to it," Oenghus agreed.

"And Grawl."

Oenghus turned in surprise. "What?"

"Rumor has it they've come for their yearly tributes."

Oenghus spat in disgust, hitting a man's boot. The squat man snarled, reaching for his cudgel, but Oenghus beat him to it, rising from his chair and grabbing the man's wrist. Oenghus spoke Vaylinish well enough, but in all taverns there was a common language in which the hulking berserker was fluent. He lifted the man off his feet, and tossed him towards a newly cleared spot on the floor.

The man did not return.

Oenghus resumed his seat, feeling the eyes of Acacia on him, neither disapproving nor amused. "I am trying to behave," he explained.

Acacia shook her head. "You're favoring your left side."

"Your healing was fine."

"But not good enough."

"I'm alive, aren't I?" The chair creaked in protest as Oenghus leaned back against the wall. "If you like, you can try again. I'll submit to your healing hands any time."

"I knew that was coming," she said dryly.

"Women can't resist a barbarian."

"Although you pass as an Ardmoor, the look doesn't much suit you."

"I'll put on a kilt as quick as can be if you stay the night with me."

"I doubt you could find a kilt in Vaylin."

"I'll sew one if I have to."

She leaned in close. "We have a seer and a nymph to find."

Oenghus sobered. "I've been mulling over the Scarecrow's Whisper."

"Haven't we all?"

"Sometimes he's a bit too cryptic—for my mind, anyway."

"Is there a possibility that the Whisper was tampered with?"

Oenghus shrugged. "I've heard it done, but I have no talent with Whispers myself."

"Too heavy a hand?"

"Too loud a voice," he purred like a rumbling storm.

"Are you sure Marsais said *The Crooked Man*?"

"That's what I heard."

"Could it have been something along the lines of the Hooked Hand?"

"I think I would have noticed the difference," he growled.

But her eyes were focused elsewhere. Jerking into action, she pushed back her chair and stood, racing out of the tavern. Oenghus was slower than usual, but his long stride and bullying size made up for his lapse.

Oenghus stepped out into a bitter night on the captain's heels. She stood alert, gazing at a spot across the way as falling snow gathered on her head and shoulders. Drunken patrons jostled her, stumbling down the steps, and Oenghus stepped behind, forcing them to go around his formidable presence.

"What is it?"

"I thought I saw something."

"Something?"

"A winged-something."

Oenghus frowned, and stepped down the stairs into the street, turning around in time for a rock to pelt him in the face. A greasy monkey with a misshapen mouth and leathery wings flapped and danced on the tavern's top.

Oenghus threw a knife with more irritation than skill. It hit the roof, and Luccub shot into the air with a cackle as the blade rolled off.

"Cursed imp," an old man spat from the shadows.

"Has he been here long?" Acacia asked.

The old man peeled back his lips, displaying several gaps. "Long enough. The Crimson don't dispatch pests. Not until the beast snatches a lord's tooth."

Acacia dropped a copper in the man's hands. "Have you heard of the Crooked Man?"

"I'm straight as a stick," he slurred.

Oenghus swore under his breath, and Acacia stilled, tilting her head at the old man. With a jerk of her chin, she motioned Oenghus to the side, under the eaves and a curtain of icicles.

"The message," she said when he joined her. "Was it in the trade tongue?"

"Aye. What of it?"

"I should have realized sooner." The barbarian standing before her bristled with alertness, ready to charge off in a direction at a moment's notice. "In the trade tongue, crooked usually refers to a street, or a shady deal, but in Vaylinish, it means bent."

"And?"

"The bent man—an old man."

"We've been assuming it's a tavern or a street."

"We've spent the entire afternoon asking after an old man."

"I'll strangle the Scarecrow." Oenghus' chest rose, muscles flexed, and Acacia placed a hand on his bulging pectorals.

"Not yet, Oenghus. Think this through."

He looked at her hand. "You're not helping me think."

Acacia started to pull away, but he caught her hand, pressing it to his muscles. "Might help a little."

"I'm sure a few pints would, too."

The closeness, her hand on his skin, and the meeting of their eyes brought to mind their conversation in the Lome city. About the past, their losses, and the Keening. It also sparked a thought.

"Of course," she breathed. "If you were traveling with a nymph, would you risk staying in a tavern or an inn?"

"An inn would be best, but Isiilde draws attention wherever she goes."

"But old men, dying men consumed by the Keening, would be less likely to notice."

"That's right," he said. "The Vaylinish don't tolerate infirmities, or weakness. They send their old off to die, out of sight, out of mind."

"And there is a place where they go to die in Vlarthane, in the shadow of the walls by the catacombs."

"Takes a nimble mind to unravel the Scarecrow's ways."

"You sound as if that's a bad thing."

"Not at all. You just have me wondering if the rest of you is as nimble."

"You're not wearing a kilt, Oenghus." She patted his chest, and trotted across the street to update her lieutenant.

CHAPTER 51

Figures moved through the gently falling flurries, drifting through the streets, detached from one another, hurrying towards shelter in the early morning snowfall.

Snowflakes gathered on Oenghus as he walked beside his only companion in the bleakness. Acacia was tense with expectation. It felt like the whole of the city was holding its breath. The feeling was palpable, thick as the snow, and a mystery to the foreigners. Oenghus hoped it was nothing more than an approaching storm or the grim reality that followed a night of revelries.

Their boots crunched underfoot, approaching the first tier gate and the Crimson guards, who were bright slashes of color on the walls.

The gate stood open, and they passed under the portcullis and swinging gibbets without challenge. As soon as they moved beyond the walls, a gust from the Bitter Coast slammed into Oenghus, bringing snow and ice, and a churning world. Trudging down the hill, Oenghus and Acacia braced themselves. They found refuge in the flatlands, amid creaking rookeries and narrow streets—empty streets.

"Why do I feel someone is about to plunge a dagger into my back?" Acacia muttered.

"It's likely the cold." He sounded unconvinced by his own words.

"The whores aren't even out."

"Bit early yet."

"Not for the hungry and desperate."

Oenghus had nothing to say to that. They walked through the sleet, until it opened to a square, to thousands of people bowing in the shadow of a titan's heel.

"Zahra protect us," Acacia murmured. Oenghus could feel the tension in her body, the muscles flexing, preparing to fight, and the unease rippling beneath her skin.

"Just don't burst into divine light and we should be all right."

The titan Dark One rose over their heads, towering over city and sea. Oenghus and the others had caught glimpses of the monolithic statue all throughout the day before, had moved around its shadow, but never within range. The titan's face was lost in the swirl of snow, save for the burning fires of the Dark One's eyes, far above, guiding ships into the harbor and fear into sailors' hearts.

Oenghus glanced around, noting the position of the guards and the buildings lining the square. He plucked Acacia's sleeve, motioning with his chin, and they headed towards a lane, but before they could slip between buildings, the Crimson guards sank to their knees, too.

Acacia yanked Oenghus down.

Out of the falling snow, monsters emerged with a thunderous chant. An entire horde of Grawl marched through the square, winding down the road on its way to the bay.

The voidspawn were over eight feet tall. Their crimson flesh as hard as steel and wicked claws filled the space between fingers. They had no mouth or nose, only eyes that brought madness to anyone who dared meet their gaze. The horde was followed by slaves, driven by masters with whips and jagged chains.

Oenghus raised his eyes from the snow, watching the line. A Herdsman marched with the Grawl, driving them with a barbed, black whip that moved unnaturally, as if alive. The general of the Dark One was as white as snow and hairless as a worm. He wore a cloak of shadows that writhed like a nest of snakes.

"Blood and ashes," Oenghus said between his teeth.

It was hard to focus. Difficult to remain kneeling. The Chant was unnatural—a power that wormed into a person's mind and drove them to insanity. Its power had broken armies without a fight.

Acacia grabbed Oenghus' hand for support as they fought against the wave of horror that the chant invoked. It thundered inside his skull. Oenghus wanted to rage, to charge, to roar at the Voidspawn in challenge.

Overcome, a handful in the assembled crowd darted, screaming with madness, only to be hunted down and impaled by a Grawl's claws. Others were snatched from the snow by the Crimson guards, chained and thrown into line with the other miserable slaves.

Acacia pulled Oenghus back, and together they inched into the lane. In the shadow of buildings, they retreated through twisting lanes and alleys until the Chant faded to a distant drone.

Oenghus clenched his hand into a fist, searching for something to drive it against. He had stood against Grawl, but never run.

"Focus on our task." Acacia's voice broke through his building rage. "We're two against a horde, and your death won't help your nymph."

"You're with the bloody Blessed Order," he growled. "Aren't you keen to smite a courtyard of Voidspawn?"

"You have me confused with an Inquisitor—they're the ones who send soldiers to the slaughter."

He grunted. They turned, moving farther into the lane, following twisting alleyways, working their way around the square. But their progress was soon halted by a winged visitor. Luccub landed on a roof, dislodging a small avalanche of snow on their heads.

Oenghus glared at the imp. He broke an icicle from its perch, but before he could throw the icy missile at the imp, it chucked a rock at his head.

This time Oenghus ducked.

The winged imp flew into the sky, disappearing into the sleet. Acacia bent to retrieve the rock. When her fingers touched the stone, they activated a rune. Light flared, runes swirled, forming a scrawl of words in the air. Acacia squinted at the jagged lines and severe slants interspersed by chaotic loops.

"Can you read this?"

"It's Marsais' handwriting." He tilted it sideways, and squinted. "Says *Maiden's Court*, I think."

Acacia rubbed her head. "Is Marsais always so cryptic?"

"You don't know the half of it."

MAIDEN'S COURT was far from maidenly. Its bricks were filthy and the drains were clogged with rot, both animal and human. The snow that fluttered between building tops touched the ground as black as the muck surrounding it.

Oenghus frowned at the enclosed courtyard, gazing at vacant windows and scorched stone walls. A crash turned them around. A hidden gate tucked into the archway dropped, cutting off their exit, and windows bristled with barbed bolts, all aimed at them.

Oenghus adjusted his shield, and Acacia put her back to him.

A voice echoed off the stones. "If you come quietly, we'll spare your three friends."

"I don't suppose this is another one of Marsais' schemes?" Acacia murmured, counting barbed bolts and the eyes gleaming from windows and sewer grates.

"Not a scheme, but I'm pretty sure this is his fault."

"The scarred fellow put up a fight," the voice continued calmly. "The young man pissed his pants, and the boy—well, you can see for yourselves."

A man appeared high overhead on a rooftop, hoisting a bound boy over the side. Elam screamed and fought and raged against the ropes, kicking the dingy brick with his boots.

Oenghus growled, and dropped his axe and shield with a clatter. Acacia followed, raising her hands in surrender.

CHAPTER 52

Isiilde stretched on the bed. It wasn't plush and it wasn't filled with feathers, but it was clean and the blankets were warm. She rolled to the side, searching for her bedmate, but found his spot empty and cold. A steady rhythm of footsteps told her where he was.

She lowered the covers. Marsais paced by the window in his trousers, turning the already threadbare rug into tatters. The window was frosted, and the world beyond was grey with early morning light. She did not want to leave her cocoon just yet.

"No sign of them?" she yawned.

"None."

Isiilde could tell he was worried. Waiting was taking its toll on her, too. Marsais had seen Oenghus alive in a vision, but Isiilde needed confirmation. They both did.

The wait had given her time to recuperate, and this morning, she found she could move a little easier than the day before. Or she'd simply become accustomed to the ache of healing injuries. She rubbed at a painful bruise on her wrist, and rose from the bed, dragging the blanket with her to squint through the frosted window.

Snow covered the filth of the street, and a few brave travelers trudged through the thick snowfall. Isiilde shivered, pulling the blanket closer around her shoulders. "Should we risk another Whisper?"

Marsais sighed. "I fear the first might have been intercepted."

"But how could one Whisper be snatched from the air unless someone was expecting it?"

Marsais whistled, and she looked at him, cocking her head. He whistled again, a different tune, like that of a bluebird, and then a creaking chirp like a swallow. She laughed when he made the mocking call of a seagull.

"Shall I imitate a rooster in the henhouse next?"

Marsais pulled her close, and she wrapped her arms around his neck to stretch towards his lips. "Only if you tell me why you're making bird noises at me."

"Whispers, my dear," he said, pulling her down onto the bed, "have their own signature, like a scent, or a voice, or a whisper in a lover's ear." This last was said against her own ear. His purr made her shiver, but she would not be distracted. This time.

"Only if one recognizes it," she said.

Marsais stopped kissing her neck to lie back on the pillow, staring up at the creaking rafters. "Indeed," he sighed.

"So who would recognize your Whisper in Vlarthane?" she asked, propping herself up on an elbow to look down at him.

"Do you remember when Oenghus mentioned the notches in my belt?"

Isiilde narrowed her eyes. "You mean other women."

Marsais cleared his throat. "About that..."

A persistent tapping saved him from the uncomfortable subject. As one, they looked towards the window. A familiar face smeared with dirt stared back.

Marsais rushed over and threw open the window. Kasja hopped to the floor with a gust of wind and a flurry of snow. She shook herself like a wet dog, and smiled up at Marsais.

Words passed between the two in a musical language, quick and flitting as a bird on snow. It was too quick for Isiilde to follow.

"Blast it," Marsais barked. "The giant, block-headed imbecile!"

"What is it?"

"I told him the *Hooked Hand*," he growled, pulling a shirt over his head. "The *Hooked Hand*, not the bloody *Crooked Man*."

Isiilde sighed, closing her eyes. Oenghus did not have the best hearing—he'd been in one too many battles.

"But he's alive?"

"Yes, for now."

"How did Kasja find us?" Isiilde looked at the shuffling bundle of furs sniffing her feet. The woman did not smell good at all, and she vaguely wondered when Kasja had last bathed.

"From your hair."

Resigned to answers that were both direct and vague, Isiilde pressed the subject. "My hair?"

Marsais gestured at his own with a waving, sporadic gesture. "Kasja pulled out a strand of your hair in the Lome city."

"Oh. I thought it was for a love potion or something." Isiilde stood, pulling on her own warm clothes, while the woman sniffed her leg. Isiilde patted her on the head, and the woman looked up with bright eyes.

"Kasja is an augur, a tracker of sorts, who uses physical components to divine things about her surroundings. And sometimes the future as well."

At the sound of her name, Kasja dug deep in her fur tunic. She brought out a little redheaded doll made of twigs and waved it in triumph. Isiilde frowned at the doll. It looked nothing like her.

"She'll lead us to the others." Marsais cinched his boots, and stood. "Now, my dear, do you want to try your illusion weave?"

"I'd rather try a transformation." Rather than risk the guards noticing her at the gate, and seeing through an illusion, Marsais had turned her into a bird for a glorious afternoon.

"Start with an illusion."

"All right."

Isiilde straightened from her boot laces and closed her eyes, focusing on the runes that Marsais had been weaving around her for the past week. Once they were firmly in her mind, she pictured the illusion: the shape of the face, the color of eyes, the roundness of ears, and the mop of hair.

She was borrowing the face of Coyle, or close to it at any rate. She thought it only fair, considering he'd asked for her urine. *Nymph's piss.* His request still made her seethe.

Isiilde summoned the Lore, tracing runes. Fire around stone, adding water to the wispy threads, then a pinch of spirit to draw the man's image from her mind and place it into the mix. With a final word, and a flourish, she bound the illusion to her form. Coyle's likeness settled over her with a tingling touch.

"Perfect," Marsais breathed. And he kissed her, hard and long and as desperately as if it were their last. When he pulled away, she was breathless. He tore his eyes from hers. "We should go."

Isiilde stared at his narrow back as he wove his own illusion, wondering at the surge of emotion rippling through their bond. But Marsais was an endless puzzle—one never fully understood. And she loved him for it.

Isiilde looked in the mirror, at the handsome human face with green eyes, and hoisted her pack.

THE INN WAS NOT FAR. Kasja walked at their side, uncomfortable in the open, but blending in with the other fur-covered travelers. She led them to an inn: *The Dancing Pig*. The place was quiet and nearly empty, newly opened and scrubbed from the previous night's festivities.

They followed the feral woman upstairs. Kasja began pacing restlessly in front of a door. It opened at Marsais' knock, but instead of Oenghus, a masked man greeted them with a crossbow.

"I wouldn't, Seer." Two men stepped into the hallway, both leveling crossbows at the nymph. "If you want to see your friends, come quietly."

Kasja hissed.

"I'll come," Marsais said, stilling Kasja with a hand.

"The Jackal wants all of you."

Isiilde could feel the fire dancing in a lantern at the end of the hallway. It waited for a simple command. She had only to give it.

The man sensed her thoughts. "You might very well kill us, but when we don't come back, your friends will have their throats slit."

"No binds or gags," Marsais said.

"Your word, I am told, is good enough."

Marsais inclined his head. "My word then."

THE MEN DID NOT TAKE them out the front, but led them out the back, into a snow blanketed alley. The trio were dressed in identical leathers and masks. Silver short swords hung from their hips, and their crossbows were sleek and light. Isiilde had little experience with the criminal element, aside from the usual lot of humans, but she recognized wealth and organization.

One man opened a hatch buried in the garbage, and stepped into darkness. Isiilde backed away from the hole in panic, but Marsais placed a steadying hand on her shoulder. His hair was short and black, and his face as red as a drunkard's, but an illusion was only a veil, and she looked past the weave until she saw the man beneath.

She squeezed the hand on her shoulder and climbed down. When the entire group stood at the base of the ladder, the hatch above closed. One of the masked men opened his palm. A light stone flared to life, illuminating the passage with a soft blue haze. The surrounding passage was not so pressing anymore, but the stench was overwhelming.

They hurried through a maze of twisting sewers, skirting the depths of filth on narrow walkways. At times, they popped above ground, like rabbits from a warren, scurrying to the next hole. It seemed they walked forever, and with every step, a knot wound tighter between Isiilde's shoulders. Where were the men taking them?

The sewers soon fell away, the tunnels widened, and they began to climb a long, winding stair. A landing gave way to a spacious hallway, marble floors, and two ornate doors at the end. The doors opened in invitation, and Isiilde stepped into another world.

CHAPTER 53

Marble, silk, and luscious steam welcomed Isiilde. Silk-robed attendants stepped silently from alcoves on slippered feet. They shuffled forward with heads bowed, hands tucked in their robes.

"Guests of the Jackal should be presentable." The guards closed the door, leaving Marsais, Isiilde, and Kasja with a small army of servants.

"This way." One woman gestured Marsais towards a screened door, and another bowed to Isiilde, gesturing in the opposite direction.

Marsais said something to Kasja, and she hissed in return, backing towards the exit. A third servant stepped behind the wild woman, swift as a viper, and flicked her wrist. A dart pierced Kasja's neck, just under her ear. The woman screeched, hissed, and fell forward, landing on the floor.

"Sleeping," the attendant said in the trade tongue.

Isiilde glanced uneasily at the women, all exotic and lethal, wearing meekness like a mask. At Marsais' reassurance, she was led through a screened door, into a small bathing chamber.

The attendants converged with casual efficiency, pulling off her illusion weave with a deft gesture. "Your clothes."

Isiilde glanced at the waiting bath.

"They will be cleaned and returned," a woman explained. Isiilde removed her cloak, and the trio stepped forward, helping her shed her filthy clothes.

The woman bowed, slid back a screen door in the wall, and disappeared, carrying away her clothes. Isiilde stepped into a waiting bath. The heat nearly made her moan, but the pampering could not conceal her unease. They were captives.

Isiilde was scrubbed and soaped and dried with an impersonal touch. When her hair gleamed and her skin glowed with oils, an attendant helped her slip into a silk robe that matched her eyes and was trimmed with a sash of gold. Isiilde stepped into slippers, and exited the bath chamber at the woman's gesture.

Marsais was waiting. His hair gleamed white against a black and silver threaded robe. His eyes brushed hers, but he did not speak. Kasja was carried in a moment later. Isiilde had never seen the woman without her layers of fur. Her black hair was chopped short, tattoos covered her exposed skin, and she bore numerous scars.

An attendant waved a vial beneath Kasja's nose, and she gasped, sitting upright. She hugged the silk robe, shivering with fear, eyes wild and darting. Marsais crouched, placing a careful hand on her shoulder, speaking softly.

A pang of sympathy twisted Isiilde's heart. Kasja did not belong here; she belonged in her forests and mountains. Taken out of her element, she looked naked and small in the opulent palace. Isiilde reached for Kasja's hand, and the woman took it, edging closer to her for comfort.

"This way, please."

Politeness had never sounded so demanding. A section of screened wall slid to the side, revealing a wide corridor lined with gold sconces and impossible flower arrangements.

Guards, large and domineering in silver armor and jackal masks, waited at the end of another corridor. The doors swung open, and they were ushered into a domed hall, into the very center of a space surrounded by a dizzying mosaic.

Isiilde craned her neck to look up at the ceiling. It was covered with a painted paradise of cavorting men and women—and creatures, both fiendish and beautiful.

Alcoves and a high walkway ringed the chamber. Light streamed through stained glass windows, creating pools of shadow and prismatic light. A wall slid quietly aside, and Lucas emerged from an alcove. The next two alcoves spewed forth a blushing Rivan and an indignant Elam. All three were clean and chained, and wore nothing but a slave's linen loincloth.

A wall in an alcove on the opposite side opened, and Acacia shuffled out, similarly clothed. When the captain caught sight of the others, relief filled her eyes. Oenghus was shoved out next, and Isiilde ran to him. He could not hug her back, but he bent, so she could throw her arms around his neck. Heedless of the watching guards, she squeezed him and he kissed the tears rolling down her cheek.

"I thought you were dead," she breathed.

"It takes a bit more than a wyvern and a cliff to finish me, Sprite," he said gruffly in her ear.

"How touching," a voice purred from the shadows above. The accented voice sent a shiver up Isiilde's spine. She released her guardian, searching for the speaker.

A cloaked figure swayed on the walkway, drifting in and out of shadow with a predatory gait. A little flapping fiend skipped on the railing in the speaker's wake, tossing pebbles at Oenghus' head.

"Traitor," Oenghus growled at the imp.

"You never held his allegiance," the voice hissed. A pale, clawed hand reached from the shadows, stroking the imp on its head. Luccub purred and lashed his tail, then stilled as the woman left, perching on the railing like a miniature gargoyle.

"Hello, Saavedra," Marsais said, revolving with her steps.

"Marsais." The voice sounded from all corners, brushing their ears, savoring the name with a sibilant note.

"I did not wish to meet under these circumstances."

"I doubt you wished to meet at all."

"On the contrary," he said.

Something lashed in the shadows. Saavedra's cloak moved, and Isiilde narrowed her eyes, trying to make sense of the woman's shape.

"There's a bounty on your head," Saavedra said. "A considerable one. Only a fool would seek me out. And you are no fool."

"I have business with you."

"Prisoners have no business with me."

"Then why are we speaking?"

"I wanted to see what all the fuss was about."

The woman on the walkway leapt over the railing. With a snap, giant black wings unfolded from her body, catching air, slowing her descent with a single wind-churning flap. Isiilde gasped in shock. The paladins backed up, Elam and Kasja pressed their heads to the floor, and Oenghus cursed under his breath as Saavedra landed in front of Marsais.

Sanguine whorls spiraled over an ivory body that was generous in hip and breast. Her ears swept up and back in a magnificent arc, and her fingertips were tipped with talon-like claws. Saavedra stretched her powerful wings and lashed a whipcord tail. It snaked around Marsais' leg, slithering under his robe.

Saavedra was a fiend.

The fiend pinned Isiilde with golden eyes. "*This* appears to be the fuss." Unwinding her tail from Marsais' thigh, Saavedra sauntered towards the nymph. The fiend was unencumbered by clothes, and at the juncture of thighs where most women had hair, she had a fine triangle of minuscule scales.

The fiend reached out a talon, and Isiilde flinched. Saavedra stopped, moving no farther, but her tail whipped around, tugging at the back of the nymph's robe, exposing Isiilde's nape and her bond. Saavedra leaned close, peering over Isiilde's shoulder to look at the fiery mark.

"How quaint."

Isiilde trembled at the proximity of the fiend. The creature tilted her head, inhaling the nymph's scent.

"Leave her alone, Saavedra," Marsais said.

"Never tell me what I can and cannot do in my own house!" Saavedra hissed. Her lips parted, revealing four pearlescent fangs and a black tongue. Her golden eyes flicked to Marsais and back to the nymph, and her lips, as rich as the darkest wine, curved in a sumptuous smile. "Did Marsais tell you how brilliant you are?" Saavedra purred in Isiilde's ear. Her breath was cool, and her eyes hungry. "Did he tell you how beautiful you are—that he lusts after your ears?"

The words stung. But that had been her intent.

Isiilde swallowed down her fear, and found her voice, steeling herself to meet the reptilian gaze. "Of course he did," she replied. "I'd hardly expect him to share his bed with anything less. Would you?"

Saavedra smiled, delighted at her reply. "O, Marsais, she has spirit. I'm sure this little nymph will try to kill you in the future."

Isiilde smiled. "I already have."

Saavedra made a sound that sent slivers of ice under Isiilde's skin. When its echo died, Isiilde realized Saavedra had laughed.

"What fun. I might keep you for myself." Saavedra's tail curled around Isiilde's neck as the fiend gazed at her in appreciation. "A pity we can't bond. But there are other pleasures to be had."

"Saavedra, please," Marsais said softly.

"I do whatever I like." Saavedra said, caressing Isiilde's lip with the tip of her tail.

The thorn-like tip looked lethal, but Isiilde stayed perfectly still, waiting, plotting what weaves she would wield first.

"Have you forgotten where I found you, Vedra?" Marsais asked. "Chained to a pillar—"

"Enough," Saavedra hissed. She unwound her tail, and shot towards Marsais with a snap of wings. "I no longer hold a Blood Debt to you."

"I never asked for one."

"I never wanted your pity," she said to his face. "Despite your charity, I am honorable—I pay my debts."

"And you enjoy your freedom. Even here, in Vlarthane, you're unmatched in the criminal underworld."

"Yes, I am," she moaned.

"You live in luxury."

"I do." Her tail slashed the air like a satisfied feline.

"People fear you and your Jackals."

"Beyond a doubt."

"And yet..." He paused.

Saavedra narrowed her eyes.

"In the Nine Halls—your realm—you're nothing but a slave. A mere step above vermin such as Luccub."

Saavedra growled.

"A lesser caste from the lowest class of whores," he said.

A clawed hand snaked towards Marsais' throat, lifting him off his feet. "Not *here*," she said with a click of fangs.

"Then help me," Marsais gasped, grabbing her forearm, pulling himself up to ease the pressure on his throat. "Or your realm will bleed into this one."

Saavedra released her hold. Marsais fell to the floor, coughing and gasping for air.

"Leave us," the fiend ordered. Concealed doors slid back in their alcoves, and the guards disappeared. "Tell me more."

"Karbonek."

Saavedra swiveled, the black slits of her eyes widening. "What?"

"The man who put the bounty on our heads intends to invite the god into this realm."

"Impossible."

"It has been done before."

"He is chained!"

"And he can be released," Marsais said. "Help me, Vedra."

She turned away, tail flicking irritably on the marble.

"We want nothing to do with this filth!" Lucas spat.

"Silence!" Marsais hurled a tongue bind on the indignant paladin. Acacia tensed, but his eyes flashed in warning: *Not now*.

Another spine-chilling laugh echoed in the chamber. "Oh, Marsais," Saavedra moaned. "You're in deep waters, as the saying goes." She turned and sauntered over, ignoring her audience, trailing a clawed finger down his cheek. "But then, you always were."

"Some things never change."

"And others do." A hint of sadness melted the ice, but only for a moment. "My help comes with a price."

"Taken only from me, whatever it may be. But only after."

"You might be dead."

"If I fail, a lack of payment will be the least of your worries."

"Still, a price is a price, therefore I'll name my terms." She dragged a claw down his bottom lip, drawing blood. "Don't worry, I'll think of something suitable. What do you need?"

Marsais wiped the blood away. "A portal to Mearcentia."

"Marsais..."

He held up a hand in warning.

"Oh, don't silence your noble paladin. I'm enjoying this little show."

"We don't have time for your amusement," Marsais said.

Saavedra batted her scaly lids. "You always amused me before."

Isiilde pressed her lips together, willing the fiend's wings to catch on fire.

"Let me see if I understand you correctly," Saavedra mused, wrapping her tail around his waist. "You want me to open a Blood Portal to Mearcentia, so you and your company of paladins can walk through."

"We will have no part in this," Acacia protested.

Marsais ignored her, speaking only to the fiend. "Yes."

"As much as I'd love to fulfill your request. I'm afraid it's impossible. A portal to Mearcentia would take at least a thousand head of cattle. While the Crimson are tolerant of Bloodmagic, someone would surely have an issue when an entire quarter was emptied of occupants."

"Leave it to me, Vedra." The fiend opened her mouth to speak. "No questions." She closed it with a thoughtful click.

"I admit, I'm intrigued, but not near enough to waive my price." She tapped a thoughtful claw on her chin. "I'll have to blindfold all of you. I can't have your shiny paladins tattling on an enclave of Bloodmagi. It's bad for business."

"Understandable."

"And as for my payment..." She let the words linger in the air. "If I'm a whore, my dear *godling*, then so shall you be, too."

CHAPTER 54

Before the words even registered, Saavedra clacked her claws together with a snap.

"This is madness," Acacia said.

Isiilde bristled, her fingers flashed, weaving a bolt. With a shout, she hurled it at the fiend.

Saavedra waved a bored hand, deflecting the jolt, which hit Rivan, searing his skin. He screamed and dropped to the floor, stunned and twitching. Isiilde looked on in horror.

"You have a lot to learn, little faerie," Saavedra said with a wink. "And don't worry, Mars is sturdier than he looks. I'm sure he'll last the night."

The alcoves opened, and guards stepped in with weapons readied. Saavedra wrapped her tail around Marsais' neck, and yanked. He stumbled, but kept his feet as the two disappeared into an alcove.

The door swung shut. Pain sliced through their bond, and Isiilde staggered. Before the next slice came, Marsais dropped a heavy curtain between their spirits, cutting her off from his light.

THE OTHERS, save for Rivan, struggled as they were dragged away, but Isiilde barely noticed the hand on her arm. They were taken to a chamber of opulent prison cells and shoved into separate cages.

"If you want your chains off, back against the bars."

No one turned down the offer. A guard pressed a vial to Rivan's lips, and it revived him.

Isiilde ignored the comfortable bed, the gurgling fountain, and the plush carpet to pace in misery, mind churning over the unknown.

What was Saavedra doing to Marsais?

"Are you all right, Rivan?" Acacia asked.

"I think I can feel my fingers again," the young man groaned. "I'm just a bit raw. Whatever the guard made me drink helped."

Acacia nodded with relief and called across the circle, "Can you break us of here, Oenghus?"

He eyed the Kilnish steel bars, the waiting wards, and the witch-wood underfoot. The pinprick holes in the ceiling were the most ominous of all. "Marsais made a deal."

"I'll have nothing to do with his pact."

"We don't have much choice, Acacia."

She clenched her jaw, speaking through her teeth. "Can you get us out of here or not?"

"This cage is built for a mage," Oenghus said. "And even if I could break the bars, I'm not sure I would."

"But thousands of lives will be sacrificed, sir," Rivan said with a grimace.

"The Scarecrow said he has another way."

"Blood Portals require sacrifices," Acacia argued. "Marsais said leave it to me—not that he had another way."

"He wouldn't," Oenghus defended.

"Are you so sure?"

Oenghus gripped the bars. He did not reply.

"They know each other—how?"

Oenghus shifted from foot to foot under the weight of the captain's gaze. "Not really my place to say," he muttered.

"Isiilde, do you know what he's planning?"

Isiilde stopped pacing. She looked at her companions, all waiting for an answer, and shook her head.

Acacia turned her glare on Oenghus. "He has a history with the fiend. What do you know of it?"

"Not my place to say."

"Another notch in his belt?" Isiilde asked.

"I tried to warn you."

"*Exotic* is a bit of an understatement, Oen."

Pinned between two hard stares from opposite sides, Oenghus shifted uncomfortably.

Rivan finally caught on. "That's *disgusting*."

"You knew Marsais had consorted with—no, bedded—a *fiend*, and yet you said nothing."

"He's bedded a fish woman, too," Oenghus defended. "And no, I didn't bloody say anything. What he does, and who he does it with, is his own business."

"There must be limits," Acacia argued. "By the gods, she's a fiend from the Nine Halls. There are laws against such... unions."

"I'm sure your Order could find a loophole to excuse it," Isiilde remarked. "You could just deem fiends as property."

"My Order is far from perfect, Isiilde, but at the very least, we try to defend this realm against the Void. We do not plow Voidspawn."

"Fiends aren't Voidspawn," Isiilde corrected.

"Where you find one, you often find the other."

"Or in bed with the Scarecrow," Oenghus muttered.

Isiilde shot her guardian a withering glare. Acacia looked heavenward, turned, and walked to the fountain on the wall, splashing her face with water to cool her rising temper.

"Look," Oenghus relented. "He told you he was going to meet an old acquaintance in Vlarthane."

"If I'd known it was a fiend, I would have objected."

"Which is probably why he didn't confide in you."

"Did he plan this, too?" Acacia gestured at the cages.

Isiilde frowned. It was an excellent question. Circles upon circles of runes spun in her mind, shifting cycles and endless strategies. Had Marsais maneuvered and manipulated her and the others to this point?

Oenghus ran a hand over his beard. "Maybe," he grunted.

Silence settled between the cages. Isiilde stood, hands on the bars, chewing on her lip in thought and moving events around like rune pieces. Had it all been a carefully constructed strategy to get them here, in these cages, unable to resist? Had Marsais instructed Luccub to find Saavedra and misled Oenghus on purpose? But then she thought back to Marsais' reaction when she was taken, when he found her, and even to this morning, when he paced in front of the window. There had been sincerity in his eyes, and yet—he had whispered the same things to Saavedra once upon a time.

Marsais was an excellent liar.

Isiilde poked at the heavy barrier between their spirits, wondering what was going on behind the blackness. Pain, or pleasure; fear or rapture? And suddenly, what had been a black curtain, became a chasm of gaping darkness.

Their bond had been severed.

The nymph's sun was gone, her bond fluttered loosely, unattached, incomplete. Without the sun, her heart turned cold, and she was left all alone with past horrors.

Isiilde clutched the bars as her body trembled with the memory of Stievin's hands around her neck. His body on top of hers. She shut her eyes, but memory persisted, until she felt the stone digging into her back again. Trapped.

Darkness converged, and another memory sang a song of sweet allure, of fire and heat and cleansing breath. Its power roared through her veins, burning away memory. A dragon of fire lashed at the darkness, burning bright in her mind, and with a flare of power, the dragon latched onto its own tail, binding itself to fire.

Her bond no longer fluttered loosely.

Isiilde's eyes blazed with emerald fire, fed by the ouroboros dragon on her back.

"You all right, Sprite?" Oenghus asked. But she barely heard his question with the power flowing through her veins.

"I'm fine." Her voice was distant.

"What happened after you were taken?"

She met his gaze through the bars. "I killed them."

"N'Jalss?" Oenghus asked with surprise.

"You killed him?" Acacia repeated.

"Yes," she said, dispassionately. "I killed the Ardmoor. Everyone. It was beautiful—the most beautiful thing I've ever seen."

Isiilde did not notice the worried glances that followed. Or the questions. Instead, she curled up on a pile of cushions and pondered the man she was no longer bonded with.

CHAPTER 55

IT MIGHT HAVE BEEN DAWN, it might have been dusk. Isiilde had not known when the guards would come next, but eventually they did.

"Your rags were filthy," a guard explained as attendants filed in, placing a fresh set of clothes in the slot of each cage.

Isiilde dressed without care, barely registering the fine wool and linen and leather garments hugging her body. The clothes were fit for kings and queens, but none of the party felt like royalty.

When they were dressed, the paladins stood defiantly in the center, and Oenghus looked distrustful.

"Backs to the cage, please," a jackal-masked guard ordered. No one moved. "Allow me to explain. Your clothes are coated with poison—a delayed poison that has already seeped into your skin. When you walk through the Portal, you will be given the antidote. Drink it then and not before—or die. The choice is yours."

"A paranoid bunch, aren't you?" Oenghus growled.

"We are accustomed to dealing with dangerous guests. If our mistress wanted you dead, then you would already be dead. As agreed, the nymph will not be bound or gagged. Backs to the bars, please."

There was little choice. Isiilde stood in her cage watching the guards chain her companions. Taking no chances, the guards took them first.

And then one returned, swinging her cage door open. Saavedra was a fiend of her word.

Isiilde was taken by a different route, one that ended in a ritual chamber. Oenghus, the paladins, Elam and Kasja waited on the opposite side. Isiilde stood alone.

The stone walls were polished to an obsidian sheen. Gargoyles perched in front of slabs on a circular walk, tongues lolled, dropping towards the pit of pristine sand. A maze of deep grooves twisted through the sand, gathering like a whirlwind in the center. Cage doors covered the back wall of numerous alcoves. There was no torch or flame, only runes, glowing dimly in the space.

A donkey laden with supplies and packs was brought in, waiting on the walkway beside Oenghus.

"Your gear," the guard explained. "You'll be blind-folded, and led through the Portal. The waiting enclave will lead you away. They will give each of you a vial. I suggest you drink the antidote at once. Your chains will be removed and you will be free to go on your way. I strongly suggest silence during the ritual, or you will be silenced permanently."

The eyes behind the mask looked at each in turn. When no one said a word, she turned to the guard at her side. "Inform the Jackal that her guests await her leisure."

Saavedra's leisure was not overly long. The fiend soon sauntered into the ritual chamber. She paused on the edge of the sand beside Isiilde, and stretched her wings languidly.

Marsais was hauled out by two guards, and dropped on the floor. He was naked, battered, and bleeding from numerous cuts. A guard dumped a pile of clothes on the ground.

Isiilde rushed to his side.

"Oh, he's fine." Saavedra's eyes slid sideways, smirking down at the nymph. "Don't feel too humiliated, Marsais. At least you command a princely sum."

Marsais coughed and raised himself up stiffly. Isiilde helped him find his feet, and he steadied himself on her shoulder. "I enjoyed every second," he rasped, wiping his mouth.

"That's what all the good little whores say." Saavedra smiled and lashed her tail against his backside. He grunted and nearly fell forward, but kept his feet.

Isiilde seethed with fury. Saavedra stepped towards her, but Isiilde didn't back away. She stood her ground, eyes blazing up at the fiend.

"Try it, little nymphling," Saavedra hissed. "Break his word, and I will break every one of you."

"Isiilde," Marsais warned. She looked at his pale, drawn face, and the lines of pain tugging at his mouth. He shook his head, ever so slightly, his grey eyes beseeching.

"One day," she said to Saavedra instead. "One day I will gut you."

Saavedra's tail lashed with pleasure. "Until that day." The fiend spread her wings and stirred a wind with their strength, leaping off the walkway and landing softly in the center of the ritual pit.

"Now, my dear old master..." Saavedra turned, studying her lines in the sand. "What surprise do you have for me today?"

Marsais did not reply. Instead, he pulled on his trousers, but stopped with the single garment; he was in too much pain to bother with the rest. He limped to the mule and rummaged through the saddlebags until he found his old clothes. The enchanted pouch was there, and his hand and forearm disappeared inside the space, searching for something in particular. He pulled out a vial etched with faint runes and tossed it towards the fiend. She caught it easily.

"What's this?"

"The needed sacrifice."

"An enchanted vial the size of a well?"

"No," he grimaced. "It will be enough blood for the Portal."

"I doubt that."

"Trust your old master."

Saavedra lashed her tail as she turned the vial over. She uncorked it, and sniffed at it carefully. Her eyes widened in shock, and flickered from Marsais to Isiilde.

"So tempting," Saavedra moaned.

"You gave your word."

She inclined her head. "Well played. Don't worry, godling, your faith in me was not misplaced."

"Just most of it," Marsais said, dryly, stuffing the rest of his clothing into the pouch.

"I'll miss you."

"We have a madman to stop, Vedra."

"I know you'll succeed." She raised the vial with a wink. "You're the only one I've ever had faith in." With an alluring chant, she began the ritual, pouring the vial into the circle. Blood, bright and vibrant, pooled in the sand, seeping into the grooves.

Isiilde narrowed her eyes at both vial and blood, and her right hand stole to her left, rubbing a bruise on the inside of her wrist. A moment later, before realization could fully dawn, a Portal burst to life, feeding off the blood of a goddess.

CHAPTER 56

THE CARRIAGE ROLLED TO A STOP. The driver's seat creaked, and boots touched the ground. Isiilde tensed, listening. A hood covered her head. She was blind to the outside world and found it unsettling.

The carriage door swung open. This was their third carriage exchange since walking through the Blood Portal. Her skin still crawled at the ritual's touch, with both revulsion and familiarity.

Marsais stepped out of the carriage. "We're here." His voice was strained. She felt his touch on her arm, and she shook it off, feeling her own way down. Sunlight warmed her skin. Vibrant scents filled her senses. The air was humid and bursting with life.

Chains jostled as the others stepped down.

Somewhere close by, she heard flowing water. And birds. Flitting about the trees, singing with joy—a far cry from the bitterly cold city they had recently left.

The carriage sped away, and Isiilde pulled off her hood, squinting against the brightness. The earth was red, the sky clear and blue, and everything in between was green. Towering palms basked in the sunlight, and red and orange fruit weighed the branches of bushy trees. Isiilde tilted her head at the birds. Parrots, she thought, but she had only ever seen them in books.

Marsais freed the others, then pressed a vial into each of their palms. "Drink this—all of you." No one argued.

As soon as Elam finished with the vial, he darted towards the trees, and raced up branches to pluck fruit from their leaves. Kasja sniffed at a coconut, turning it around in her hands, searching for a crack in its shell.

Caught between wonder and anger, the group settled on momentary silence. After Acacia emptied her vial, she riffled through the mule's saddlebags, recovering her gear.

They stood at a crossroads. Red earth stretched in four directions, one road looking much the same as the next. But as soon as Marsais pulled the silence weave from Lucas' throat, the peace was shattered.

Lucas punched him in the face. "Never silence me again, Seer!"

Kasja hissed at the paladin with a feral sound that defied her clothes and cleanliness.

"There was a line for that," Oenghus grumbled. He shook out a handkerchief and handed it to Marsais, who was sprawled in the dirt. "But I was going to wait till he was healed."

Isiilde eyed Marsais dispassionately. He looked old and worn beneath the sun. But she did not go to him. She did not trust herself.

"Do you want me to heal you?" Oenghus asked.

"Spare me the shame," Marsais snapped.

Elam froze at his tone.

"Suit yourself," Oenghus said lightly. "At least they didn't knock all your teeth out."

Marsais flinched.

Oenghus narrowed his eyes at Marsais' arm, then looked to Isiilde in surprise. He'd noticed. The fiery dragon mark was gone from Marsais' arm. Their bond was broken.

The air crackled with tension, churning around the elf sitting in the dirt. Oenghus shifted to the side, shielding Marsais from mutinous stares. It did the trick. Rivan and Lucas followed their captain's example, and began donning their battered armor.

"Why Mearcentia?" Acacia finally asked.

"I believe you know King Syre?"

"I handle the Law when there's a dispute with his nymphs, yes."

"We need a ship, we need warriors, and we need to sail to Fomorri."

Shocked silence answered this declaration.

Oenghus was the first to recover. "What the Void for?"

"You had best start talking, Marsais," Acacia warned, strapping on her sword belt.

"We had a scryer tracking us. I couldn't share my plans with you." Marsais sighed, lowering the bloody handkerchief. He glanced at Isiilde, but she looked away.

"But why *Fomorri*?" Acacia pressed. "Tharios is on the Isle of Wise Ones."

"He's also Archlord. He knows its secrets. And its walls have never been breeched by an invading force. With good reason. All paths end in destruction, save one. My visions stop at Finnow's Spire."

"The Unicorn's Horn?" Acacia asked.

"Yes."

"That's a myth," Lucas said.

"It's not a myth," Marsais said, climbing slowly to his feet. "Tharios has Soisskeli's Stave. But he only has one of the end caps—the artifact that can open a Gateway."

Acacia narrowed her eyes. "And the other end cap is in the Unicorn's Horn, in the middle of Fomorri?"

"Yes."

Lucas ground his teeth together. "What good will that do us?"

"It's the binding artifact, isn't it?" Acacia asked.

"Oh," Rivan realized aloud.

"The Cleric of Chaim I spoke with is aware of my plan, and supports it," Marsais said, glancing pointedly at Acacia. "Wraith Guards are being sent to the Isle, and while visions of death are never set in stone, any fool can tell you that sailing to the Isle and challenging Tharios and an unknown number of Unspoken would be suicidal. I do not wish to leave things to chance."

"And Fomorri is somehow safer?" Rivan demanded. "You can't possibly be thinking about taking Isiilde there?"

"Isiilde is no longer bonded to me. She may do whatever she wishes."

Surprise rippled through the group. Acacia was the first to recover.

"King Syre is a good man, Isiilde. I'm sure he'll give you sanctuary—along with Kasja and Elam."

Isiilde said nothing.

"And to be absolutely clear about where you and I stand, Marsais," Acacia continued. "After this is over, I'll have you stand trial for consorting with the likes of Saavedra."

Marsais inclined his head. "After, Captain, that's all I ask. I'll stand and answer for my crimes. And if you wish, you can personally draw and quarter me." There was a plea in his words, as if he wanted the deed done now, to escape some misery.

Acacia shook her head. "I will stand, too."

"What the Void did you do?"

"I haven't dragged him to a Chapterhouse yet."

Oenghus grunted.

Gathering what dignity was left to him, Marsais limped towards the source of water, but was stopped short by the captain's voice.

"What was in the vial you gave to the fiend?"

Marsais stiffened at the captain's question. He waited for half a minute, bruised shoulders braced for another blow, but when no attack came, he limped out of sight.

"Blood," Isiilde bit out. "*My* blood. Taken without my knowledge—without my permission." The air smoldered around her form, wavering like a mirage in the desert. She looked at the captain. "Where is the palace?"

Mearcentia was as white as the sands. Tall spires climbed like trees towards the azure sky, buildings overflowed with greenery, spilling from windows and sweeping arches. Canals, sparkling with clean water, flowed through the city, running down tiers, creating waterfalls and misting fountains.

Guards in shining silver and flowing blue rode on white horses escorting the group through the city—not as captives, but as guests.

Isiilde rode in a carriage with Acacia and the Lome strays. She stared out the window, pondering pathways and the myriad of ways that a life could take. What, she wondered, would have happened if King Syre had won her with his bid, instead of the brutal course her life had taken?

Acacia was studying her.

"What is it?" Isiilde asked.

"Your bond."

She tore her gaze from the window. "What of it?"

"Only death or another man can sever it."

"The bond was broken when he... bedded that fiend."

"Perhaps it has to do with the fiend, then."

"Perhaps."

"They are foul creatures."

Isiilde frowned in thought. "Your Order thinks that of my kind, too."

Acacia didn't argue the point. "If I may ask, what does your bond feel like now?"

Isiilde raised a slender shoulder. "I have my fire."

"Are you all right, then?"

"I am perfectly fine."

While the city was grand, the palace was an oasis of elegance in paradise, a blend of sculpted beauty and strength. It reminded Isiilde of the sea. But the palace paled compared to the real thing.

Isiilde stepped out of the carriage, and froze. The sea around the Isle of Wise Ones was grey and moody, but this ocean was vast and blue, and sparkled like a gem under the sun. It took her breath away.

"Wait until you swim in it," Rivan said at her shoulder. She looked over at him, and he smiled, eyes alight. "You can see the bottom of the ocean, the sand, the canyons, and even the fish. They're as bright as parrots."

"How could you ever leave this?" she breathed.

"Because I wanted to protect my home."

His words touched a nerve. A thought stirred in the back of her mind, but it fluttered just out of reach when the palace doors opened. A tall, elegant man in flowing blue robes came down the stairs. The sun glinted off his silky black hair, and his bronzed skin glowed with health.

His shoulders were broad, and he carried an air of confidence that was unmistakable. King Finn Syre II didn't need a crown; he wore nobility on his brow.

Acacia stepped forward and bowed, but he seized her hand with both of his, shaking it with surprising warmth. "Always an honor, Captain."

"The honor is mine, Your Majesty. Thank you for seeing me on such short notice."

"I am happy the rumor of your murder was highly exaggerated."

"Rumor is so often twisted. May I present Marsais, the former Archlord of the Isle."

Syre stiffened ever so slightly. He eyed Marsais warily for a moment, before inclining his head. "You're a mythical figure in Mearcentia. I hesitate to say it is an honor, but just so."

"I understand, Your Majesty," Marsais said, returning the gesture. "Considering our mission, I think Nereus will not look unkindly on you and your people for welcoming me into your lands."

Syre glanced at the sea with a thoughtful eye, clearly intrigued and concerned by Marsais' words. "Then, welcome," he said, and turned to Isiilde.

Surprise stirred the green depths of his eyes, and Syre stepped forward, bowing deeply. Isiilde did not return the gesture. She was tired and wary and heartbroken. The thought of bowing to any human made her sick, much less one that had partaken in a bidding war over her body.

Acacia frowned at her rudeness. "May I introduce Princess Isiilde Jaal'Yasine?"

"I gathered as much." He straightened with a shift of the ivory tokens woven into his long hair. "Welcome to my home, Your Highness."

"Isiilde will do," she said.

"Finn for me then, too."

"I'd rather not, Your Majesty."

"As you wish, Isiilde."

Syre turned them over to his servants, so they might rest before discussing business. As they were escorted to separate rooms inside the palace, Isiilde kept her distance from Marsais. She did not look at him. Not even a glance. And he did not try to catch her attention.

CHAPTER 57

A POLITE KNOCK interrupted Isiilde's turmoil. She turned from her view of paradise and walked into her vast chambers. The luxury seemed out of place, a dream after the weeks of horror and flight.

A servant entered, bowing low. "Lord Oenghus Saevaldr to see you, Your Highness."

The title felt uncomfortable on her shoulders. It scratched at her ears, and they twitched. Apparently, Oenghus shared her dislike of ceremony—he stomped in without invitation. In another time, Isiilde would have run into his arms and taken refuge, but now she only stood, unsure what to say.

Too much had happened for words.

Oenghus looked around her chambers. "You got a better place than me," he said, walking to the balcony. He glanced over the balustrade, at the sea far below, and quickly took a step back, planting his hand on a solid stone column. Isiilde hopped on the top, settling herself on the precarious seat.

"Why don't I affect you, Oen?"

He shifted, reaching for a pipe. She studied him intently as he took a pinch of tobacco, tamped, and puffed, until a sweet fragrance mingled with the tropical flowers.

"That's a complicated matter, Sprite."

"As complicated as I suspect?"

Eyes as bright as the sea met her own. "Aye," was all her father said.

Her heart lurched. Yet another lie. All these years she had been too oblivious to see the truth. The stone beneath her seemed to quiver, as if the foundations were not as sturdy as they had been a moment before.

Oenghus sat in a chair that creaked under his weight, and he smoked, letting the fact settle in her heart. After a time, he studied the pipe in his hand. "I'm sorry I didn't tell you sooner, Isiilde. I only wanted the best for you."

"Words without actions are meaningless, aren't they?"

"Blood and ashes, you *do* listen," he said with surprise.

"Sometimes."

His lips twitched upwards in a smile.

"Why should it matter?" she asked, softly. "You've been a father to me in every way except word." The sea misted, and her heart melted. She slid from the balustrade and buried herself in his arms.

"Gods, Sprite, this is not what I wanted for you. Never wanted you to—" His gruff voice caught.

"I know," she finished for him.

Oenghus pressed her head to his chest. He could crush skulls with those hands, and yet he cradled her with tenderness. She felt his lips brush the top of her head.

"I understand why you couldn't risk telling me."

"Stays between you and me, right?"

"Of course," she said.

"It's not all that bad being a princess, is it?"

"I am happier being your daughter, Father."

Tears slipped from his eyes, and he sniffed, wiping them away with a rough hand. When he found his voice, it was hoarse with emotion. "Careful with that word, all right?"

Isiilde nodded. "And Marsais, did he know?"

"Aye," Oenghus admitted.

Isiilde sighed, pulling away to curl in the chair across from her father. Marsais was a complexity, and she kept puzzling over his actions versus words, over visions and schemes, and only the gods knew what else the man had done.

"What of my mother—was she like other nymphs?"

Oenghus scratched his beard. "Uhm, not really."

She arched a brow.

"I mean, not that I've had a lot of experience with other nymphs—just her."

"How was she different?"

Oenghus blew a long breath past his lips.

"Oen," she warned.

"She was unique."

"Could she summon fire?"

"No, not exactly—about that, Sprite," he said, pointing his pipe stem at her. "Floating with Brimgrog as I am, Marsais thinks it was my fault. You got a fair amount of berserker in you."

Isiilde tilted her head. Everything clicked, and suddenly, without warning, she began to laugh—long and hard, until her belly ached and tears streamed down her cheeks. When her laughter died, and she wiped her tears, she looked up to find her father staring at her with worry.

"A *nymph* berserker," she said with a grin. "Do you have any idea how relieved I am to find out why I am the way I am?"

Oenghus chuckled, worry draining from his face. He sobered and leaned forward with a dangerous glint in his eye. "What did you do to those bloody bastards in the fortress?"

Isiilde told him, but her tale lacked boast. Oenghus, on the other hand, was mightily proud, slapping his knee at the conclusion. "Wait until you meet your brothers and sisters," he growled. "You'll have an epic tale for the clans meeting."

"And I'll get to visit, won't I?"

"Aye, you're free to do as you like."

"I am, aren't I?" She smiled at the thought, but it was filled with sadness.

They were interrupted by the servant's return. "Knight Captain Mael to see you, Your Highness."

"Show her in, please."

Oenghus rose hastily as Acacia entered. The captain had shed her customary armor in favor of a light, flowing wrap. Despite the woman's shorn hair, her scars and callouses, and warrior's physique, she appeared relaxed in the native dress.

"Am I interrupting?"

"I was just talking to Isiilde about finding myself a kilt."

"You'd likely die of heat exposure in this climate."

"It'd be worth it," he purred.

Acacia ignored the comment. "His Majesty, as always, has been generous. We sail with the tides tomorrow."

"Good."

"And, Isiilde, he's offered you his protection. Fomorri is no place for a nymph—any woman, child, or man, for that matter." A quiver shook the steel in the warrior's voice.

"Aye, Sprite, you've already been through more than most. Leave this nasty business to us. Besides, someone's got to look after that feral woman and Elam. Keep an eye on them for me, will you?"

Isiilde looked towards the endless horizon. "It is beautiful here."

"You can lounge about in the sun all day, like you've always dreamed," Oenghus pointed out.

"With other nymphs," Acacia added. "His Majesty said his nymphs are eager to meet you. He wondered if you would like to do so now, and —one of them is ill. I've vouched for you, Oenghus."

"Don't worry, there's only one woman in this palace I want to carry off."

WALLS WITHIN WALLS and ornate gates separated the nymphs from the rest of the palace. Grand pillars supported tiered walkways with wide trees and lush vegetation. Isiilde gaped at the construction, the canals of flowing water, the sculpted pillars and flourishing splendor.

Children ran through the pathways, laughing and playing, while their mothers tended the plants. It did not feel like a prison.

"I wanted them to feel safe, but not trapped," Syre explained as he led them through the cultivated wilderness.

"Did you build this before or after you started collecting nymphs?" Isiilde asked at his side.

"I know how this must appear to you, Isiilde."

"You have no idea, Your Majesty."

Syre smiled sadly. "When I came of age, as is our custom in Mearcentia, my father sent me to sea. When I returned alive with a number of successful sea battles under my sash, he purchased a nymph from a slave market, thinking I would find amusement with the creature."

There was a rumor that Finn Syre II had hired the Widow's Own to assassinate the late king. Hearing the distaste in his voice, Isiilde wondered if rumor was fact.

"I found no amusement, only sympathy." He gestured towards a wide archway of jasmine, and they followed a winding path that flowed downwards. "Alara had been kept on a leash, passed from owner to owner like a dog. I could not bring myself to touch her, nor could I bear to keep her confined to a small wing of rooms. I noticed she seemed happier outdoors, with the trees and ocean, so I asked my father for one of the gardens and a contingent of female guards and eunuchs. She flourished there.

"When rumor reached my ears that a pirate band had captured another nymph, I went after them with my elite. Unfortunately, she died shortly after. There was no will left in her." Syre stopped on the path, turning towards Isiilde. "I don't like the way things are, but they are what they are. I do not *collect* nymphs, I rescue them. And I hesitate to say this in the presence of a Knight Captain... I protect them like the druids of old."

"I'll pretend I didn't hear that, Your Majesty."

"Thank you, Captain."

The path ended at a cove. A crescent of white sand curved around a crystal blue lagoon. Isiilde's breath caught in her throat. Syre had brought the ocean to the palace.

Observing her amazement, he explained, "There are tunnels

beneath the city that bring in fresh sea water with the tides. We keep the sharks out."

But his words fell on deaf ears, and her feet pulled her onto the sand. Two nymphs played in the water, and another lounged beneath the sun. Their eyes were joyful, their skin glistened, and their bodies were shapely. When they caught sight of Isiilde, the trio beamed with delight. And all at once, Isiilde was surrounded by a trio of nymphs, moving around her, touching her clothes, her hair, and even her ears with unabashed curiosity.

Their ears were not like hers. Isiilde's swept up and back, ending with a tip, while theirs were far shorter. And their marks, she noted, hung loosely around their necks, a faint twining vine that looked more necklace than collar.

"Hello," she said.

One of them, with blue eyes and rich brown skin, kissed her innocently. The second, with long golden hair and tanned skin, laughed and tugged at her wrap, gesturing towards the water.

"Hello," the third said.

Relief filled Isiilde. She looked at the nymph who had spoken and smiled, politely holding her ground while the other two tried to coax her towards the lagoon. "I'm Isiilde."

"Alara." The nymph smiled in return, tilting her head. She touched Isiilde's arm, trailed fingers through her hair, over the tip of her ear, and finally her cheek. "The sun and moon," Alara breathed in wonder.

"What do you mean?"

Alara did not, or could not explain, but she stepped forward to hug Isiilde. "You will stay?"

Isiilde ignored the question. "Do you like it here?"

"Oh, yes, there are trees and water. And Finn." The nymph's eyes slid sideways, and she abandoned her guest, or forgot about the redhead entirely, running towards Syre. She threw her arms around him with delight, and color rose in his cheeks as the nymph kissed him with abandon. The others rushed to him, and he was surrounded by the sumptuous trio, until they caught sight of Oenghus, standing off to the side. With an attention span of a hummingbird, they flitted over to him.

"Leave me be," Oenghus grumbled.

They erupted with laughter. Hands went to his beard, stroking the braids with curiosity. And finally, the golden-haired nymph simply put her arms around him, snuggling against his warmth.

Syre stared in shock. "They are not usually so... affectionate with strangers."

"Aye," Oenghus sighed, giving the golden-haired nymph a fatherly pat on the back. "Wisps and sprites torment me, too."

When Alara plucked Oenghus' pipe from his belt, Syre reined in his bold nymphs. "Alara, Nimue, Luna, leave him be."

A chorus of laughter answered, and they darted off into the trees. Isiilde stood on the beach, watching their exploration as they gathered fruit, stroking leaves and sniffing flowers as if it were the first time they had ever seen such things.

Despite the sun, the sand, and everything that was beautiful, she shivered, turning her back on the trio of nymphs.

"Not what you expected?" Acacia asked at her shoulder.

Isiilde shook her head. Had she ever been so empty-headed? Isiilde frowned at the question. Surely not?

"They are happy," Acacia pointed out.

Isiilde took a deep breath, steeling herself, and turned back to her kin. Nimue and Luna were attempting to feed Oenghus fruit, and Alara was draping herself around Syre.

"They certainly appear so." She wrinkled her nose. "I am nothing like them now, but I fear I may have been a month ago."

"Perhaps, but no longer. These faerie do not think beyond a moment. I doubt they remember their lives before His Majesty brought them here."

Envy filled Isiilde's heart. To be that innocent. And free. Yet, if given the chance, she would not go back. "I have never felt so alone as I do now."

"That's what my youngest daughter said when we moved to Haven." Acacia slipped an arm around her. "You're not as defenseless as you once were. You can come and go as you please, and perhaps... they will learn from you, and you from them."

"What could I possibly learn from them?"

"That innocence is a beautiful, precious thing." Acacia squeezed her shoulder once, and removed her arm, wading into the sea.

The nymphs abandoned the men, and ran across the beach, diving into the water, and coming up splashing. The stern-faced Knight Captain of the Blessed Order grinned and splashed the nymphs back.

Isiilde closed her eyes with a sigh, and walked back up the beach, to where Oenghus and Syre stood.

"What do you think, Isiilde?"

"I think they have a splendid home."

"It can be yours, too."

"I do not need rescuing."

"Then you can visit whenever you wish."

"Thank you," she said, but did not think she would ever return. "Where is the fourth—Kaia, did you say?"

"This way."

Oenghus tore his gaze from Acacia, and followed in the king's wake. Syre led them into a grove of trees. Kaia was curled in a bed of leaves. Her chestnut hair flowed around her like a blanket, and eyes the color of autumn flickered towards them as they approached. She was smaller and slimmer than her sisters, with ears that were more akin to Isiilde's.

Syre gathered his robes and knelt, placing a hand on her brow, smoothing the hair from her face, whispering her name. She looked at the king, but there was no hate or loathing, only weariness in the nymph's eyes.

Isiilde had seen that look before, so long ago, on the Isle, when she had sung to a woman who was well into the Keening. At the time, she did not understand why someone would want to die. She understood now.

"Kaia, this is a healer—Oenghus and Princess Isiilde Jaal'Yasine."

The nymph barely glanced at the strangers.

"We can barely get her to eat," Syre confided to Oenghus. "The captain said you may be able to help with the Keening?"

"I can try," Oenghus grunted, kneeling on the ground. "Have you ever been healed before, lass?"

Kaia looked at the giant beside her, and nodded her head. She could, it seem, understand the trade tongue.

Isiilde drifted closer. As much as she had wanted to hate Syre, she found she could not deny his kind intentions. "Are you bonded to her?" she asked.

Syre shook his head. "She's never shown interest."

"But she has a mark."

"Yes, bonded to a spoiled nobleman in Nefir. The Knight Captain helped with the acquisition."

"He's dead, then?"

Syre nodded, standing to make room for Isiilde. She bent over the nymph, placing a hand on her forehead. Kaia was cold.

"You want to sit with her a bit, Sprite, and sing to her like you did with that other lass?"

The question blind-sided Isiilde like a slap from his massive hand. She jerked back, standing quickly. "No," she said sharply. "I would like to rest."

Without waiting for an answer, Isiilde hurried away, fleeing the dying nymph and the rest of the empty-headed faeries, silently wishing Kaia a swift and peaceful journey to the ol' River.

CHAPTER 58

MARSAIS SAT beneath a tree in a garden courtyard. A breeze sighed against his cheek, and he closed his eyes, listening to the whisper of leaves. It was a rare moment of peace. But there was still one final step to take before the path was set. The hardest part yet.

His coins chimed, drawing his attention to the present, showing him a vision of beauty wandering through the moonlit garden a minute before she arrived. Those seconds could have been years, and still he would not have had the time to fortify his heart.

To delay the moment, he closed his eyes, and took a breath—one, and then another, until the moment was shattered by her voice.

"You could have asked, Marsais."

"You would have said no." He opened his eyes to a goddess, all fiery-haired to match the fury in her eyes.

"You don't know that."

"Don't I?" He raised an arrogant brow.

"You *should* have asked."

"I could not risk your refusal."

"So you took my blood—you used me as potion fodder!"

"I did."

"You manipulating bastard," she seethed.

"Not manipulation, my dear, but strategy."

"Do not presume to call me 'my dear'. I am not yours."

"As you wish," he said, climbing to his feet.

"As *I* wish? Do not mock me. You never once took my wishes into account. How long have you been scheming? How far back? Did you chart our course after that very first night in the ruins? Using the Lome as our shields, risking Oenghus, and using me as bait to lead you to the scryer? Did you send Luccub to that fiend? Did you help bait her trap so the paladins would have no choice but to play along with your scheme?"

"I could not risk it." Marsais gave a slight shrug of his shoulders. "As with King's Folly, sacrifices must be made. One cannot become attached to a single rune—not even the fire rune."

Isiilde took a step back, the fury in her eyes turning to mist. His resolve nearly shattered.

"Answer me one thing," she whispered.

"Hmm?" Marsais waited, senses swimming as her voice drifted on the warm breeze. The same breeze that stirred the thin silk clinging to her body, the same that brushed a stray tendril of hair curling around her tipped ear.

"Did you enjoy your night with that fiend?"

All he had to do was tell the truth, and she'd be in his arms again—in his heart, with spirits melded. Marsais did not trust himself to speak. His heart warred with his mind, and every passing moment confirmed his betrayal. Soon, it would be too late, but if he spoke now...

Marsais shook the temptation from his mind. He had to stay focused on the journey ahead—on what his failure would mean for Isiilde.

"I'm a man, Isiilde," he answered casually. "Vedra and I have a long history. We were lovers once. Of course, I enjoyed certain aspects of my night with her, or I wouldn't have been able to finish the deed."

Her eyes flashed and her hand came up in response to his stinging words. Marsais would've preferred a dagger in his heart. Isiilde's shoulders trembled, and she gave him another slap for good measure before hurrying from the garden, her head bowed.

Marsais could not bring himself to move, to turn and watch her gliding form. He stood swaying in the night, long after the sound of a single sob died in the courtyard.

Eventually, Oenghus stepped beside him, knocking him out of his stupor. Marsais drew a ragged breath.

"I'm not usually one to eavesdrop, but that conversation was hard to miss from my balcony. You really are a cold-hearted bastard."

Marsais wasn't in the mood. "Isiilde will be safe here. We are no longer bonded. Her spirit will remain intact—no matter what happens to me in the days to come."

"Don't bloody insult me. I know why you did what you did, or I would've killed you by now. You've always been more of a cold-hearted bastard to yourself than to anyone else, Scarecrow."

"It had to be done." His voice cracked.

"Aye." Oenghus rested a hand on his shoulder.

"Blast it, Oen, if you bloody hug me, I'll break down and that would be awkward. More so than our trip through the mountain pass." His voice was hoarse.

"Void," Oenghus swore, removing his hand. "I told you to never—"

Marsais turned abruptly. "Put me out of my misery," he begged.

"What?" Oenghus blinked in confusion—at the desperation in the grey eyes.

"I enjoyed every second of plowing your daughter senseless," Marsais crowed. A scarred fist filled Marsais' vision, relieving him of his suffering.

He fell to the earth.

"Bollocks," Oenghus cursed in realization. Marsais had goaded him into knocking him senseless. "You're a manipulating bastard."

Oenghus nudged Marsais with his boot. His eye would be swollen shut for days. Grumbling, Oenghus knelt, slipping his hands beneath the loose linen, over stomach and forehead. He did not like what he saw. Marsais' spirit was dim—the Keening had a savage hold on him.

There was no point in bolstering what was broken, so he healed the bruises and the eye, and quickly withdrew, shaking the fractured spirit from his senses. He dragged Marsais to softer earth, and stood staring down at his dearest friend.

Marsais' bond with Isiilde had been severed unwillingly. That would, Oenghus knew, be the end of Marsais, no matter the outcome on the Isle.

CHAPTER 59

Isiilde sat on the beach, beneath a silver moon, watching its light dance in the lagoon. Her tears mingled with the sea. She was alone in the moonlight with her thoughts. And in her heart.

The ship would sail with the rising sun, and she would never have to see Marsais again. But his words would never leave her.

One cannot become attached to a single rune—not even the fire rune.

She traced a fire rune in the sand, adding her own touches, until it rippled with heat. Cycles within cycles, schemes within schemes. Marsais had always favored misdirection in his games.

Sacrifices must be made.

A movement off to the side caught her attention. She tensed, fingers splayed, but relaxed, feeling foolish. As quiet as a cat, Kaia emerged from the forest. The slender nymph walked across the sand, and stopped, noticing the redhead on the beach. She hesitated, glancing back at her refuge.

"It's all right," Isiilde reassured. "Are you feeling better?"

Kaia cocked her head.

"Do you want to sit with me?"

Isiilde did not feel like having company, but something in the nymph's eyes tore at her heart. Kaia appeared anxious, but she came. The frightened nymph sat on the sand, trembling.

"Why are you sad?" Isiilde asked, wondering if anyone had bothered to ask.

Kaia's eyes fell, and Isiilde waited, but the nymph did not answer, or so she thought at first. Kaia was tracing something in the sand: a tree.

"You're sad about a tree?"

Kaia nodded, drew a line through the trunk, and erased the top, until it resembled a stump.

"It was cut down?"

Tears shimmered in her wide eyes.

By the gods, Isiilde thought, trying not to think of all the trees she had recently burned and wondering what on earth was she going to do with a crying nymph.

"There are other trees..."

Kaia burst into tears.

Isiilde did not know what to do. She had always been on the crying end of things. She patted the nymph awkwardly, and Kaia curled into a weeping ball, laying her head on Isiilde's lap.

"Maybe you can grow another?"

"Friend." Kaia's voice shook.

"The tree was a *friend*?"

More tears.

Isiilde stroked the nymph's hair, frowning in thought. Did all nymphs share a connection with an element, whether trees, water, or fire? Isiilde thought this likely. After all, she did not like it when people took her fire. It was more alive to her than most humans.

There was nothing to say, no words to comfort. Kaia wanted to follow her friend. At a loss, Isiilde did the only thing she could think of —she began to sing. Though it pained her, though it tore at her heart, she sang for the nymph's sake. The first notes were hoarse with pain, full of sadness and memory, but she willed warmth into her song for the innocent beneath her hands.

She felt like a mother. And in that moment, she finally understood what it meant to protect another.

Isiilde stood on her balcony watching the sun rise over the ocean. She was sure she would never tire of it. Oenghus had already come and gone, warning her not to burn down the palace. He had nearly crushed the life from her before storming out. Her father did not like goodbyes.

Acacia came, too. Helm tucked under her arm, armor polished and restored, looking every bit the part of a Knight Captain of the Blessed Order. She shook Isiilde's hand.

"Keep up your sword training."

"I will."

"Good."

And for a moment, Acacia dropped her stern mask to pull Isiilde into a hug against her armored breast. "You'll be fine, Isiilde."

Isiilde was left speechless.

Marsais did not come.

She leaned against the railing, watching the distant harbor, and the sleek warship that was anchored on the pier. Sailors crawled up its masts, and porters lifted supplies into its holds, while soldiers marched up its gangplank.

When the moor lines were untied and the ship edged towards deeper waters, Isiilde turned from the view, and sat at her writing desk, reaching for quill and parchment. She dipped the nib into the ink well with a flourish, and began to write. Her words flowed across the parchment. After signing her name, she dusted the parchment with sand and rolled it into a tidy scroll, sealing it with a weave.

She placed her scroll on the desk.

Isiilde slipped out of her robe, letting it slither to the ground. An early morning breeze brushed her naked skin. She picked up a small pouch and carried it out onto the balcony, setting it carefully on the railing.

A voice whispered from the past, full of warmth and sincerity: *There is very little in this realm that I would not do for you.*

Isiilde pressed her lips together at the memory. She looked out to sea, to the white sails catching wind, and to the ship that was carrying her friends away.

"You are an utter fool, Marsais," she said to the horizon. The seer's careful plotting had one very significant flaw: Isiilde was free and she could do as she pleased.

Words of power flowed from her lips, tying her to the Gift, and her fingers flashed, weaving careful runes from memory, layers upon layers, until the weave fluttered over her skin like a cloak. And then it crawled, seeping into her flesh. Isiilde gasped with pain. Bones cracked, light flared, and when the transformation was complete, a vibrant red parrot flapped on the balcony.

With a beat of wings, and a musical squawk, the parrot snatched the pouch and took flight, soaring towards the distant ship.

READ THE NEXT IN THE SERIES:
GOD OF ASH
BOOK THREE

If you enjoyed *Flame of Ruin*, and would like to see more of Isiilde and Marsais, please consider leaving a review. Reviews help authors keep writing.

Keep up to date with the latest news, releases, and giveaways.
It's quick and easy and spam free.
Sign up at www.sabrinaflynn.com/news

About the Author

Sabrina Flynn is the author of the **Ravenwood Mysteries** set in Victorian San Francisco. When she's not exploring the seedy alleyways of the Barbary Coast, she dabbles in fantasy and steampunk, and has a habit of throwing herself into wild oceans and gator-infested lakes.

Although she's currently lost in South Carolina, she's lived most of her life in perpetual fog and sunshine with a rock troll and two crazy imps. She spent her youth trailing after insanity, jumping off bridges, climbing towers, and riding down waterfalls in barrels. After spending fifteen years wrestling giant hounds and battling pint-sized tigers, she now travels everywhere via watery portals leading to anywhere.

You can connect with her at any of the social media platforms below or at www.sabrinaflynn.com

APPENDIX

Acacia Mael (ah·kay·shaa may·el) - Knight Captain of the Blessed Order on the Isle of the Wise Ones.

Afarim - Winged race of the Isle of Winds

Ardmoor - Void-worshipping barbarians in Vaylin.

Asmara - A Guardian of Iilenshar, or the Guardian of Love, also known as the Everchild. Asmara was six when the Orb shattered, and has not aged a day since. Daughter of Zahra, sister of Chaim.

Assumer - A race that can assume any shape.

Auroch - A massive bull-type creature found in Nuthaan and the Fell Wastes

Bastardlands - The continent that lies between the west and east. Separated by two chasms on either side, it's believed that the Keeper erected the Gates (chasms) to trap the Guardians of Morchaint.

Berserker's Rite - Some Nuthaanian warriors risk drinking Brim-grog on the eve of the Reddened Month. Most warriors die. The ones who survive have a reputation for being volatile and lethal.

Blessed Order - An Order that worships the Guardians of Iilenshar.

Blood Moon - A day and a night of light. All three moons are visible in the summer sky. The Dark One's moon is closest, playing havoc on coastal areas.

Brimgrog - Nuthaan's sacred brew. Few dare drink the burning brew, and of those few, most die. The rare Nuthaanians who survive the Rite are known (and feared) as Berserkers.

Brinehilde (brin·hillda) - A Nuthaanian Priestess of the Sylph who runs an orphanage in Drivel.

Carpinvale - A small fishing town in the south that exiled Oenghus.

Chaim (high·em) - A Guardian of Iilenshar, also known as the Guardian of Life and the River God. Son of Zahra, older brother to Asmara.

Circle of Nine - The ruling council of the Wise Ones.

Coven - A harbor town that sits directly beneath the stronghold of the Wise Ones.

Da'len - A barbarian tribe in Vaylin.

Dagenir (day·jen·near) - A Guardian of Morchaint, also known as the Dark One. He tried to steal the Orb, and battled with Zahra. The Orb shattered during their struggle.

Drivel - A large city on the Isle of Wise Ones.

Easthaven - The east side of the city of Haven, separated by the Gate and chasm.

Eiji (ee·Gee)- a gnome Wise One.

Ethervenom - An addicting drug made from harvested Plague Viper venom.

Everwar - The endless struggle between light and oblivion.

Fell Wastes - A harsh, mountainous region to the north of Nuthaan, populated by Wedamen.

Fey - Lindale (a race of elves) who rebelled against their nature and were twisted by their dark deeds.

Fomorri (fah·moor·ee) - A race created and twisted by the Fey's foul experiments.

Fyrsta (fears·tah) - The Sylph's favored realm.

Galvier Longstride - A legendary wanderer whose feet never stop moving.

Grawl - The Dark One's Own. Monstrous Voidspawn with void-like eyes.

Guardians of Iilenshar (ill·en·shar) - Six Guardians who survived the Shattering and were blessed with the Orb's power: Zahra, Chaim, Asmara, Zemoch, Oshimi, and Yvesa.

Guardians of Morchaint - Six Guardians who sided with the Void: Dagenir, Shade, Indrazor, Pazia, Mourn, and Silvanthe.

Gwaith - A Merchant kingdom along the Golden Road.

Haimon Goodfellow - Owner of the Glass Goblet.

Harsbane - A poisonous herb. The leaves contain an hallucinogen when smoked.

Hengist Heartfang - First Archlord of the Isle of Wise Ones.

Ielequithe (ill·ay·quith) - Lord General of the Isle of Wise Ones.

Iilenshar- Floating Isle of the Guardians. Coat of arms: the Sacred Sun caught in a maze-like circle.

Isiilde Jaal'Yasine (is·seal·dee jawl·yah·seen) - A combustible nymph with an affinity for fire.

Isek Beirnuckle - Spymaster to Marsais.

Isle of Blight - An island to the south of the Bastardlands that was ravaged when Ramashan, a druid, opened a Portal to the Nine Halls.

Isle of Winds - A grouping of islands off the Spotted Coast.

Isle of Wise Ones - An island off the Fell Coast where the Wise Ones Order is located.

Kambe (cam·bee) - A powerful kingdom ruled by Emperor Soataen Jaal III in the West.

Karbonek (car·bah·neck) - A Greater Fiend from the Nine Halls. A god revered by the Fomorri.

Keeper - A favored servant of the Sylph who was tasked with protecting Fyrsta.

Keening - The inhabitants of Fyrsta do not age like others. They only die of old age when the will to live fades. Someone who has lost the will to live is said to be in the Keening. As a result, many die in their twenties and thirties.

Kiln - A powerful kingdom to the East.

King's Folly - A game of runes that involves two hundred stones, and a cycle of ever-changing power.

Lindale - A race of elves (faerie) who were wiped out during the Shattering.

Lispen's Folly - A whirlpool of chaotic energy churning on the ceiling of the outer sanctum of the main hall, just outside of the Council Chambers of the Nine. Lispen was a Wise One who tried to open a Runic Portal, and disappeared.

Lome (low·meh) - A barbarian tribe in Vaylin.

Lucas Cutter - Paladin of the Blessed Order.

Luccub - An Imp with a tooth fetish.

Marsais (mar·say·es) - A sexy elf immortal.

Medwin - A barbarian tribe in Vaylin.

Miera Malzeen - A Wise One teacher who tried to link with Isiilde and was subsequently burned to a crisp.

Morigan Freyr (more·eh·gen fray·er) - Master Healer on the Isle of Wise Ones. Matriarch of the ruling Nuthaanian tribe. On and off Oathbound to Oenghus. Adopted mother of Isiilde. Savior of Nuthaan.

N'Jalss (nah·jaal·ss) - A Rahuatl Wise One.

Nereus (near·rose) - God of the seas.

Nine Halls - A realm that was overrun by the Void.

Oathbound - Inhabitants of Fyrsta take oaths, vowing to remain together as a couple for a specified amount of time determined by the couple.

Oenghus Saevaldr (oh·won·gus say·val·der) - A formidable Nuthaanian Berserker. Also known as: Wise One of the Isle, Bone Mender, Skull Crusher, the Bloody Berserker of Nuthaan and the Grimstorm of the Fell Wastes.

Oshimi (oh·shim·mee) - Guardian of Wisdom, also known as The Serene One.

Pip - A street urchin from the Dock Districts of Drivel. Brother to Zoshi and Tuck.

Pits o'Mourn - A deep chasm in Kiln. Criminals are lowered into the gorge and none ever emerge.

Pyrderi Har'Feydd (pie·deer·rhee haar·fade) - The first fey.

Rahuatl (raw·tule) - A race of humanoids who live in the Jungles of Rraal. Their culture is steeped in ritual and pain.

Rashk (rash·ka) - A Rahuatl Wise One who has a knack for enchanting.

Reapers - Voidspawn with a taste for fresh blood. Sometimes called Death's children.

Rivan (riv·en) - A young paladin of the Blessed Order.

Shattering - A powerful artifact that the Sylph imbued with her power to fight the Void. When Dagenir, its own guardian, attempted to steal the Orb for himself, Zahra tried to stop him. During their fight, the Orb was shattered, releasing a cataclysmic wave of power that nearly extinguished life on Fyrsta.

Shimei Al'eeth (shim·mee awl·eeth) - A Kilnish Wise One

Sidonie (sid·own·ee) - A Mearcentian Wise One

Soisskeli (soice·kill·ee) - The Chaos Lord who crafted a stave capable of opening Runic Gateways and binding any creature not of Fyrsta. Oshimi, the Serene One, defeated him in battle.

Somnial's Realm (salm·knee·el) - The Realm of Dreams, where all realms touch.

Spine - A tall, naturally formed spire that towers over the Wise Ones' stronghold.

Suevi (sweh·vee) - A barbarian tribe in Vaylin.

Sylph - The Goddess of All.

Tharios - A Wise One from Xaio.

Thedus - A sunburnt man who wanders around the Wise Ones' tower naked.

Thira Olander - Wise One of the Isle, Mistress of Novices, and High Alchemist.

Tuck - Urchin from the dock district in Drivel. Brothers: Pip and Zoshi.

Ulfhidhin (ulf·fid·hin) - The wild god who once abducted the Sylph and fought Karbonek.

Unspoken - or Disciples of Karbonek. A group of devout Bloodmagi who worship the Greater Fiend.

Void - Everything opposite of life.

Weeping Mark - A venomous spider.

Westhaven - The west side of the city of Haven, separated by the Gate and chasm.

Wisps - Tiny faeries who are often captured, put in jars, and used as a light source until they die.

Witchwood - A rare wood that has a natural resistance to enchantments.

Xiao (zow) - A merchant kingdom in the Bastardlands known for their pleasures.

Yvesa (yeh·veh·saa) - A Guardian of Iilenshar. A sprite who is revered by jesters and bards. She has a reputation for being a prankster.

Zahra (zah·rah) - A Guardian of Iilenshar, also known as the Radiant One, Goddess Of All That Was Just, Guardian of Good, and the Divine Savior. She battled with Dagenir when he tried to steal the Orb.

Zander - A Wise One who served Tharios, attacked Isiilde, and was burnt to a crisp.

Zianna (zee·anna) - A gifted Wise One's Apprentice.

Zoshi (zo·shee) - Urchin from Dock districts in Drivel. Brothers: Pip and Tuck.

CALENDAR OF FYRSTA

350 days in a year
10 Months in a year
35 days in a month

MONTHS
Wintertide
Thawing
Greentide
Sowing
Summertide
Faded
Harvest
Reddened
Carvers
Frostmarch

FESTIVALS

The Shadowed Dawn: 35th of Frostmarch to the 1st of Wintertide. Marks the new year with a night and a day of darkness, when all three moons align and the Dark One's own moon smothers the sun.

The Lightened Dusk: 17th-18th of Summertide. A day and a night of silver light when all three moons align and the Sylph's moon shines bright.

The Sylph's Fortnight: 10-24th Summertide. Fourteen days of Festivities dedicated to the Sylph.

Feast of Fools: 1-7th of Greentide. A week of costumed festivities that celebrate the end of winter.